UNSPOKEN

UNSPOKEN

A Novel

GENE NARO

Glidden Publishing
New York

Unspoken

Glidden Publishing Inc.
245 8th Avenue, Suite 368
New York, New York 10011
www.gliddenpublishing.com

Cover Design by George Foster
Interior Design by William Groetzinger

ISBN 978-0-615-18922-2

Library of Congress Control Number: 2006930116

Publishers: Cataloging-in-Publication

Naro, Gene
Unspoken: The story of the O'Brien family and the important truths in their lives that they fail to tell each other/by Gene Naro.

ISBN-13: 978-0-615-18922-2

CONTENTS

Love is ever chosen.

PART I

Taught by suffering, drop by drop,
wisdom is distilled from pain.

Aeschylus

COMPOUND

What mattered to Dan on that afternoon, four days before Christmas, was that Michael was not yet back from a meeting with his economics professor and they were already supposed to be on their way to his family's house on the Cape Fear beach, south of Wilmington. Dan heard him coming up the steps two at a time and saw the sweat on his face as he burst through the door.

"Don't worry, I'll drive, we'll make it in time for your mother's dinner," Michael shouted as he rushed into his room.

"Where have you been?" Dan asked.

Michael was stuffing clothes into a bag. "These people... this is such bullshit."

"What... what are you talking about?"

"He said my analysis wasn't the way it happens in the real world. What the fuck does he know about the real world?" Michael stood up without even closing the bag. "C'mon, let's go."

"I should call my mother and tell her—"

"I said we'll make it. Just give me the keys."

Dan was a few steps behind most of the way down the stairs and out to the car. As they raced down West Main Street, Michael turned the radio up loud.

Dan turned it off. "Look, I have a lot of confidence in seat belts and air bags, but can you just slow down and tell me what's really going on."

"First, he kept me waiting for nearly an hour. Then he basically told me I didn't know what I was talking about. So I told him to fuck off."

Dan was momentarily thrown off his inquiry by the G force as they turned a corner and accelerated toward the freeway onramp.

"Anyway, who cares? In five months, I'm getting the hell out of North Carolina."

"I thought you were going to work for Eastman & Maxwell?"

"No waaaay." Michael looked surprised, as if he'd never even considered it.

◪ ◪ ◪

They had been best friends for as long as either one of them could remember. Everyone who knew them described them as close. In the ways that mattered to most people, they were. They had met when they were two years old. They lived together when they were boys, and they went to the same prep school. In their senior year at Duke University, they were roommates. Like yin and yang, they knew each other and sought each other out. They became like a compound of two different elements, separable only by a cathartic reaction.

Dan moved with the unstudied air of someone who knew all the steps of a privileged life by instinct. He had not been spoiled, nor treated harshly. He sought and received approval by participating in all the customary routines of childhood and adolescence. He knew just when to smile and how to make polite conversation. He had no noticeable eccentricities. Recently, unless you studied him very carefully, you wouldn't see that he was, in fact, uncomfortable.

Michael had been driving for about an hour, speeding southeast along Interstate 40. Dan had been napping for most of that time, but the still bright afternoon sun and the thoughts careening through his head kept him from real sleep. The interior of the 325i afforded plenty of room to stretch out his five-foot eleven-inch frame, but even with the seat moved all the way back and reclined, Dan couldn't relax. Realizing that there was no chance of sleeping for the rest of the drive, he sat up, yawned, stretched his arms and contorted his face. "I'll drive the rest of the way." Michael was lost in his own thoughts and so Dan shouted over the music the second time. "I said I'd drive the rest of the way."

"No, that's all right," Michael answered, as he turned down the radio, "I like to drive anyway. What time is your dad going to be there?"

"Mom says he's supposed to get there about the same time as us. She said they've been in New York most of the week. He'll want to know if you've heard from E&M."

"I know, I know. In Jack O'Brien's world, there are no loose ends."

"You're such a cynic."

"You're such a—oh, fuck. There's a trooper behind us."

"How fast are you going?"

"Seventy something… Fuck! This will be my third citation.." He pulled the car over to the side of the road and looked in the mirror as if to prepare himself for what was next. "Well, pahtner, here comes da law." Michael turned and flashed his "Don't worry, I'll handle this" smile.

The trooper was all business as he examined the registration and license. Then he leaned over with his left hand on the door of the car, close enough for Michael to notice the smell of cigarettes on his breath. "Son, this car is registered to Jack O'Brien in Charlotte. Can you tell me why you're driving it eighty-five miles an hour heading in the wrong direction?"

Before Michael could answer, Dan handed the trooper his license. "Officer, this is actually my car. Jack O'Brien is my father. We're on our way to Wilmington to pick him up. We're kind of late, so ah, my friend must not have noticed that we were, ah… speeding."

The trooper looked at the license. "Stay here," he said. A few minutes later he was back at the driver's window, looking past Michael addressing Dan. Your buddy has two citations for driving over fifty-five. This one's going to be for driving over eighty. I should be taking him with me to the county jail."

He waited and let them sweat. Then he looked past Michael again to Dan. "I'm on the security detail for the Hornets. I know your daddy and I know he wouldn't take kindly to your hotshot friend driving his car eighty-five miles an hour. If you drive the rest of the way to Wilmington, I'll let you go."

The officer turned to Michael. "Son, today's your lucky day, but if I catch you so much as farting on your way through here again, I'm gonna arrest your ass and throw you in jail. Are we clear?"

Dan and Michael were saying "Yes, sir" in stereo as Dan was pulling the handle on the passenger door and heading around the front of the car. Michael had to wait for the trooper to move away from the driver's door before he got out as Dan came around. "Thank you, Officer," Dan said politely as he got in.

Michael made his way to the passenger side without looking at either Dan or the trooper and got in without saying a word.

As they drove away, Dan asked Michael. "Why are you mad?" as he reached for the radio. "Don't tell me you'd rather be spending the afternoon in Nowhere County Courthouse trying to come up with bail. Who cares why he let us go?"

"I do," Michael said under his breath as he stared out the window.

◼ ◼ ◼

Michael Hendricks was the human corollary to the Atlantic hurricane that develops far away from observation and is, at any point before landfall, unpredictable. Its fury can be resolved out at sea or in an epic onshore disaster. His features were a striking combination of his Catalonian and English ancestry. He had dark straight hair, brown eyes, and an aquiline nose. His clear complexion had the glow of a Thanksgiving-in-South-Beach tan. With the same wide mouth and white teeth, he could smile and look like the young David in Bethlehem, tending his father's herds, or he could set his jaw and bare the kind of snarl that made him look more like the wolf than the shepherd.

When Michael and Dan went to Duke together, each was

happy for his own reason to be getting out of Charlotte. It was 1991 and Michael had decided to be a stockbroker. He was enough of an opportunist to accept help getting a job. He had worked hard and got his Series 7 broker's license. There was only one problem. Now that he had what he came for, he had no intention of staying in Charlotte after graduation.

◪ ◪ ◪

Dan was gripping the steering wheel, trying to think of how to ask the question that had been on his mind since they left Durham. Finally, he decided on the direct approach. "Now that I'm awake and driving, would you like to tell me what's really going on?"

"You know how I feel about this place. I've never fit in. I'll do better in New York where, you know, people get ahead by taking on the world and not just by family connections."

"What are you talking about, Mike? You've always been a part of our family. You've got plenty of connections."

"I'm very grateful for everything your family has done for me, but please don't patronize me, man. You and I have shared a lot together. We've even fucked the same girls, but we don't share the same genes and we never will. Now I really don't want to talk about it anymore."

Dan was tapping his finger on the steering wheel and shaking his left foot, trying to figure out how to reopen the conversation. "Look, I see what you mean about not wanting to work at E&M. It's not exactly a happening place. Maybe Dad can get you fixed up somewhere in New York."

"You're assuming that your father would have any interest in what I want to do. You assume that he cares about me. Big mistake, man. Your father's only been keeping an eye on me. That's your mother's obligation to Carla. Sticking me in a backwater brokerage firm in Charlotte is the easiest way to do that. It's not like he offered me a job at the bank or anything. That's where your ass is headed just as soon as you're out of business school."

"Mike, I know he's not your father, but—"

"Do you really think if I said I want to work on Wall Street, he would just dial up Ace Greenberg and tell him to set me up at Bear Sterns?… Keep dreamin', man."

Michael would have kept on in his own pained analysis of the situation, talking to himself, and failing even in that effort to communicate, but for the fact that, in his distraction, he kept changing the radio station and intermittently playing and changing CDs.

Dan was recently empathetic to fidgeting, but this was especially distracting because he was also busy talking to himself and was losing the train of thought in his own private torment. "I like variety too, but can we listen to one song all the way through? You're starting to get on my nerves."

"Sorry," Michael said as he sat up. "Are we really stopping in Wilmington?"

"That was just a line for the trooper. Dad's got a car at the airport. So, what exactly are you going to tell him?"

"That I don't want to die a slow death, stuck in Charlotte, North Carolina, pretending to manage a bond portfolio for the Reynolds Trust."

"I'd try something a little more subtle."

"I just want to GET OUT OF HERE! What's wrong with that? You're going off to business school next year."

"You know where I am on that." Dan shook his head unselfconsciously.

"Then don't go, man. This is totally fucked up! I didn't like the idea of coming all the way out here for Christmas. I don't want to talk to your father about MY life. I don't really want to talk to your mother about Carla. She was your mother's best friend, but she was MY MOTHER! She's dead. She gave up. She checked out a year ago. That's it. You see, I know that, and they do too. They could have convinced her to accept treatment from a real doctor like I tried to, but they didn't. Do they want to hear that from me? I don't think so."

"Mike, they both tried and—"

"Don't feed me that bullshit. Don't look at me like that, and don't tell me how your father only wants what's best for us. And don't give me your bullshit line about accepting things because 'That's the way things are.' Let's talk about the way things really are. You look like shit. You've been stoned practically nonstop for the last three months. Do you think that might have something to do with the fact that you're on your way to a business school you don't want to go to and a career you have no interest in?"

Dan's stare was split—straight ahead, as the lane markers rushed one after another toward the car, and in the rearview mirror as they blurred behind him into the distance. He peered intently, even squinted, to see ahead at the distinct outline of markers as far as he could. He had not yet discovered that God made the world round so he couldn't see too far down the road.

His junior year abroad at the Sorbonne was supposed to be about studying classical design, but he really went to keep from suffocating in North Carolina. He was an A student in architecture, a major as close as he could get to his interest in the arts and still feel like he could say he was studying something acceptably vocational. When he got back, he deflected his family's attempts to talk to him about his time there. All they got out of him was "The food was good" and "I learned a lot."

He arrived back in Durham in the fall of 1994 and sank into depression, which he disguised by telling everyone he was just tired. He coped, as he usually did, by turning his attention away from himself. Now, on their way to the beach there was an obvious target on which to refocus the conversation.

"When we get there, all you have to do is say you don't have an offer from E&M and that you're sort of looking at your options. This week isn't supposed to be about us anyway. We're only going there for my mom. Try to go easy on her, Mike. She wanted Carla to stay with the conventional doctors, but their prognosis was awful.... I know it's been a year, but she's still having a hard time."

Michael was already somewhere else by the time Dan had finished his request.

"Hey," Dan continued, "are you mad at me too?"

"No, I'm not mad at you." Michael looked over at Dan briefly. "You're all I have left of a family…" He turned away again, noticing how gray the sky was, like the day of the funeral. "She didn't need to die for me to know how fucked up life is."

◼ ◼ ◼

They were about twenty minutes from the house, both trying to think of something to say without reigniting an argument.

"Look," said Dan, "I just want to say that… What you said was true about me not being happy. I don't know what to do. When we get back we can talk, but no explosions this week. OK?"

"Sure, no problem. Your parents have done a lot for me. It's the least I can do for them. And besides, I'd do anything for you. You know that."

"Do I really look like shit?"

"Well, yeah, actually you do. But don't worry about it. Most guys would love to look like you even when you look like shit. I'm sorry if I hurt your feelings. We're cool, right?"

"Yeah, we're cool."

They were on the bridge crossing the Cape Fear River when Dan felt a knot in his stomach, which got worse as he drove through town and south to the big stone and glass house at the highest point on the shore road.

"What time is it?" Dan asked.

Before Michael could answer, they heard the ring of the car phone over the music.

"Hi, there," Carolyn's voice carried over the speaker after Michael turned the radio down. "Where are you?"

"Hi, Mom," Dan answered. "Sorry we're late. We'll be there in ten minutes."

"Don't worry, I just heard from your father. They were delayed getting out of their meeting and then there was an ATC hold in Teterboro, so dinner will be late anyway. Your father called when they were over Philadelphia and said they'll be landing in Wilmington at six. Dinner will be at seven. Julie's gone to the Carters'. They're here for Christmas too. Maybe you boys would like to go over to say hi to Elaine before dinner."

"I think I'd like to take a ride over to the cottage before it gets dark."

"Well, it's almost dark now, and you know the generators are off so, stop here first and take a couple of flashlights from the garage."

Dan was more relaxed as they got closer to the ocean. On weekends, between sports seasons and on vacations, he and Michael grew up in a little house on stilts on a road almost at the southern end of Cape Fear. When they were at the beach, camping out in the dunes, or sailing, or any other pursuit that took them out of touch with the rest of the world, they talked to each other. In those early days, they spoke a language of the heart, which they later learned to put aside with the other unself-conscious aspects of childhood. Now, when they felt they had to fill in the silent gaps, their conversations were mostly limited to sports and sex.

"You know," said Michael, "when your mother mentioned Elaine Carter, I couldn't help but think about that operation."

"You mean when she had her breasts reduced?"

"Yeah, what a terrible waste. I think that's why she went to Pomona. I guess she figured she could start over again."

"Mike, I don't think so. She had her breasts reduced because she had some kind of back problem. I don't think they removed her libido."

"God, will you ever forget those tits. They were enough to suffocate you. Remember the time her father almost caught her blowing us on the beach?"

"Yeah, I remember… We should probably stop in and say hi to my mom before we head out."

"We don't have to go there," said Michael.

Dan was staring straight ahead.

"Hey." Michael put his arm on Dan's shoulder. "I missed you when you were in Europe, but I was glad to see you go. I loved being at the cottage when we were kids. It was great. But you've seen what's happening out there: there's no power, its getting run down. If it weren't on stilts, the surge tides would flood it. It'll be gone in the next big hurricane. You need to move on, man." Michael gestured to the large modern house as they were pulling into the driveway, "Now this is more like it. If we're gonna be able to afford a place like this, we gotta make some serious money."

It was 3:50 when they pulled into the driveway, ten minutes before they had first been expected. Michael put on his game face. He turned to Dan, "It's show time."

VELOCITY

It was Jack O'Brien's idea of a sanctuary, a long narrow room —only 350 square feet, 45 feet long, 8 feet wide—but it afforded him a perspective that no other place could offer. In the view from thirty-five thousand feet, the world looked well ordered. Mountains sloped gradually into hills and then plains; rivers flowed neatly to the sea. The electronic equipment in the passenger cabin of the Gulfstream IV was designed for real time access to any information he required. He could be in touch with his top executives located all over the word. What he wanted most, however, in the pause from one distraction to another, was time and space to think.

Fred Bonham, the bank's CFO, was busy at the computer terminals neatly fitted at two workstations, three screens flashing rows of numbers. He was on a call with his staff. Farther up, near the cockpit, Jack could see that his father-in-law, Blake Reynolds, had his seat reclined and the window shade pulled down. Even from the back of the plane, Jack could hear him snoring.

There was something on his mind, something bothering him while he stared out the window at nothing in particular. The meetings in New York had gone well, one after another; now they all blurred together. The lawyers and investment bankers were in favor of the deal; they smelled multimillion dollar fees. He could tell that his two colleagues didn't like it. He wasn't sure why, but he wasn't ready to talk about it yet.

He was traveling at almost the speed of sound, heading south from New York to Charlotte and then on to Wilmington, North Carolina. Sitting very still, he was trying to make the transition from his world as the CEO of a major bank to the head of a family celebrating Christmas. He was thinking about how much easier it was to manage his job than his family. The bank had sixty billion in assets and thousands of employees all over the world.

But the bank was more responsive, more ordered, and more predictable. At forty-four years old, Jack O'Brien had made it to the top by foreseeing and managing outcomes.

His family was another matter. His wife, Carolyn, was the daughter of the man in the front of the plane. When they were married he couldn't have imagined going to work for a hidebound little trust company in a sleepy southern city. But Blake had promised him the chance to run the place. Sometimes by talent, sometimes by luck, but mostly by sheer force of will, he had transformed North Carolina Bank & Trust Company into a well-run money machine.

It occurred to him that Carolyn watched his career uninformed and from a distance. He had reciprocated by knowing very little about, and being even less involved in, her life. All he had to do was put on a tuxedo once in a while and show up at a charity event.

Out of the corner of his eye, Jack saw his father-in-law walking toward the back of the plane.

"You look like you're somewhere else," said Blake.

"Oh, I don't know. Maybe I just wish I were somewhere else." Jack looked up and smiled. "I was hoping that we'd be on time for a change."

"Don't worry about that," said Blake. "Dinner will still be hot when we get there. But after we leave Fred in Charlotte, we won't have a chance to talk about this deal 'til after the holidays, and you know what it's like the first few days back at work. Why don't we get together now?"

They gathered around the conference table in the middle of the plane. Jack decided to wait and listen. Blake and Fred looked at each other, each subtly signaling the other to go first.

Fred started. "You know we're going to do whatever you want to do. But I'm telling you right here. I don't like this deal."

"OK, Fred, I had more than a hunch about that already. Something about the way you sat through all those meetings with your arms crossed said that loud and clear. What I'm waiting to hear is why it doesn't work."

"This ain't got nothin' to do with workin'. The deal works

fine, especially on paper. The numbers look like big tits on a showgirl. But that's not the point. Jack, we ain't in the club. Everything we've built has been from scratch. Not a single acquisition worth mentioning. They've got eighty billion in assets and they're—"

"So you're telling me about the numbers."

"No, I'm just warmin' up." Fred had his right hand slightly raised, but he was squeezing his index finger against his thumb, trying desperately not to point. "Carlton Moore is every bit the son-of-a-gun you are. And he's in the club."

"Fred, what club are you talking about?"

Fred put his hand down flat on the table, hard enough to rattle the spoon out of the saucer of Blake's coffee cup. "You're not payin' attention. You're talkin' about a Charlotte, North Carolina, operation takin' on a money center bank. And don't tell me you're payin' any mind to those investment bankers. If it's a whore you were looking for, we could have saved the jet fuel and fixed you up in Charlotte."

Fred paused, swallowed, and continued, now in a lower voice, and with the index finger back in place, pressed against the thumb. "I'm telling you, I've backed you up on every move, but this is one big mistake. Don't do it."

Jack looked over at Blake, who obviously wasn't going to add anything right now. There was only the indifferent hum of the jet's Rolls-Royce engines. He went to the galley and poured a Diet Pepsi for Fred and a Glenlivet on the rocks for himself and refilled Blake's coffee cup. He came back and slid the drinks across the table.

"I trust your judgment, Fred. The meeting in New York was exploratory." No reaction. "It's my job to look at these situations." He could see he wasn't getting anywhere. "We're the only three people, besides the lawyers and investment bankers, who know we're even thinking about this. We've got a lot more talking to do before we even consider making a move."

"Jack, you've made me a rich man. When Sue and I got married, we couldn't afford a ring or a wedding dress. Now I've got more money than I could ever spend. I may work for you, but I love you like a kid brother. I can see it in your eyes; you're just itching to get in the club. Now that I've said my piece, I'm gonna find out what time we get into Douglas."

Jack took a deep breath and exhaled slowly as he watched Fred walk up to the cockpit and close the door behind him. He took a sip of his drink and looked at his father-in-law. "Well, you're in the club. What do you think?"

Blake was definitely in *a* club, but not in the one Fred was referring to. He was born in 1920, before Black Monday, before the Depression, before World War II. He lived on an estate built near Asheville, North Carolina. Raised to live in a world that had ceased to exist about the time he was born, he grew up disoriented. In 1942, his youth, education, and background were coincident with a sudden need for military officers, though nothing in the former prepared him for the horrors of the latter. He saw castles in flames and towns bombed to rubble and refugees huddled in graveyards where it was difficult to tell the living from the dead. In 1945, a Captain, he led a company of American soldiers into Dachau. It would be another forty years and two more wars before the term "post-traumatic stress syndrome" would come into fashion, but most people just said Blake never got over the war.

Sent home as a major, he was thrust into another war over property, fought by unhappy people who had been spared only the destruction wrought by guns and other more immediately visible damage. His father had died while he was away and left him as the sole trustee of the Reynolds Family Trust, to manage for the benefit of his two married sisters, D'Arcy Commerford and Pamela Briggs, along with a few cousins and all their offspring, twenty-seven in all.

"I don't think really it's about being in any club," Blake started, then paused because he knew there was a grain of truth in what Fred said, but he wanted to come at it from a different angle. "You know the story about Icarus and Daedalus?"

"Yes," said Jack, looking out the port side of the plane to the ocean below. "Daedalus made the wings for Icarus. He warned him not to fly too close to the sun, but Icarus did and he fell into the sea and drowned."

"You know," said Blake, "the Trust Company has been in my family since Reconstruction. When you started, the bank had fifty million in capital, now it has three billion. So you know much better than anyone else how much heat your wings can take."

"I liked Henry Bradford," Blake continued. "I thought Payton Harwood was competent. But remember, like Fred said, they're hired help." He turned and looked toward the cockpit to see if Fred was still out of hearing range. "Now, with that caveat, I will tell you my opinion. A combination of the banks makes sense, but I don't like the idea of a hostile takeover. It's a messy way of doing business anyway, but in banking it's especially messy. And maybe that's my way of warning you not to fly too close to the sun."

"I don't see Carlton Moore letting go of New York Trust without a fight," said Jack. If we stay the way we are, we have maybe three or four years before consolidation makes us irrelevant in the banking industry. This deal will give us a lock on a global franchise."

Blake exhaled and let go his concern. "I've told you, I'm not going to argue with your instincts, and I'm sure as hell not going to argue the numbers with you, especially while we're out at the beach for Christmas. I wish the circumstances of our being there weren't so glum. My daughter's preoccupation with her friend's death has given me the perfect excuse not to have to spend the holidays with my sisters. It's a shame someone had to die to get me off the hook."

"Yeah." Jack sighed and looked out the window. "I guess it is sort of a mixed blessing, but I don't know what to say to Carolyn."

"I'm sorry I can't help you there. You know I was never really close to her. I'd like to think I've been a much better father-in-law than a father."

"Don't be ridiculous. She thinks you're wonderful. I don't know about when she was growing up, but what I hear her say now is that you're a great father."

"Yes, the here and now. I need to keep reminding myself of that. You keep working on the New York Trust deal. I'm going to catch another forty winks. By the way, take some of your own advice and don't be so hard on yourself. I've tried that already. It's a surefire losing formula."

Jack watched Blake retake his seat at the front of the plane. He could fall asleep almost at will, and it seemed he willed it often. He told Jack it was a peace that came with sobriety in his fifties, after his ill prepared youth and the sudden trauma of war.

Unlike his father-in-law or his wife and kids, Jack was born far away from a life of privilege. His father was a master carpenter at the Henderson mill in a place called Cove, North Carolina. He went to Korea in 1952 and returned a year later with a Silver Star and a wounded arm. He went back to the mill and did his job and didn't mention the war or his injury except to say, when people asked him about his arm, that he got it caught in General Ridgway's meat grinder. When Jack was twelve years old, his father slipped off some scaffolding at the mill, broke his neck, and died. He had been carrying his tools under his good arm and when the scaffolding shifted suddenly, he didn't have time to get a grip.

Jack calculated that must have been about thirteen thousand days ago. He was constantly doing calculations in his head. He wondered how many of those days he had spent not thinking of that event. "Not many," he said to himself, but then he was interrupted when he noticed Fred coming from the cockpit toward the back of the plane.

"Hey, buddy," Fred said. He rarely addressed his boss that way, only when they were alone, and only when he wanted to have a personal conversation. "Just promise me one thing. Promise me, you're not gonna ask me to work in New York."

"Fred, why are you assuming we're even going to make the offer?"

"Because I know you." Fred smiled. His big teeth would have looked outsized were it not for his broad face and wide set eyes. He was fifty-four years old, 240 pounds on a six-foot three-inch frame, a big, imposing figure, but his smile was disarming. "First of all, there's nothin' wrong with wantin' to be in the club, and you'll definitely be in after this deal is done. You know I don't care about that. I can see twenty percent earnings growth for the next eight quarters. I know where I'll be fishin' every summer for the rest of my life. But the way I see it, you've probably been thinkin' about this deal for years. So there's no point in my arguin' with you. I'm only tellin' you that Sue and I ain't movin' to New York."

"I'll make you a promise," said Jack. "If we start talking about a headquarters in New York, then you know the deal's gone haywire. I don't know why you keep framing the discussion in terms of my personal interests. This is strictly business."

"Maybe you can fool yourself into believing that, but I don't believe for one second that's what's drivin' you. Now remember, I ain't talkin' to you like your CFO. When we land this plane, that's all I'm gonna be. But right now, I'm tellin' you the truth. I've done that since the day I came to work for you. That was how long ago?"

"How can I forget?" said Jack. "Seventeen years ago. I was twenty-seven years old. I had an MBA and three years of banking experience, and I told you I was going to change the industry."

"That's right," said Fred, "and you did. But I always knew you didn't like the fact that you were captain on somebody else's boat. If this deal gets done, it's not the Reynolds' family bank anymore, not that it really is now."

"Blake has never been anything but supportive," said Jack. "He hung in there while it looked like we might run the place into the ground. You remember how bad it was?"

"Sure I do," said Fred. "You're beholden to him and that grates on you. All Blake has to do for this deal, all he's *gonna* do, is vote yes. You'll finally get the board you want. You'll be runnin' a real money center bank…" Fred was worked up, but not angry. "And I'll make one more prediction. Sure you're gonna have the headquarters in Charlotte. But you'll keep an office in New York, maybe get a bigger apartment instead of the suite at the Pierre. In a few years, we'll all be headin' up there."

"Wow," was all Jack could manage after a very long minute

that passed when Fred was done. When he started again, he sounded like he was trying to convince himself as much as Fred. "Look, I'm sure not planning a move north... not even in the distant future, and I'm sure I don't resent Blake."

"I didn't say you resented him. Those are your words. Don't go volunteerin' the negative, Jack."

"Oh, for Christ's sake, Fred."

Fred raised both his hands in surrender. "I've said my piece. If this is what you want, we'll make it work. After you fire nearly everyone, there won't be much to combine."

"We'll have plenty of time to talk about it back in Charlotte after New Year's. Right now I'm trying to figure out what's going on with my family."

"Yeah, we'll miss you all next week. I hope Carolyn will be feeling better."

"I guess some women just deal with grief differently." Jack rubbed his eyes with the open palms of his hands. "I remember when my father died. My mother didn't have a year to get over it. The day after he was buried, my uncles tried to convince her that she couldn't keep us all together on the money from the death benefits. After they left, she looked right at me and said, 'Now you're the man of the house, and the most important thing is to keep this family together.' She got a job at the mill. Every day she had to walk past the same spot where he died."

He spoke as if he were mucking out a stall, tired of finding the same old shit every time he went into the barn and yet, resigned that this was his life. "You know something, Fred, she never complained... not once."

In seventeen years together, they'd had no more than a few conversations that Fred could remember where Jack had let his guard down and said anything so revealing about his family. All personal inquiries were rebuffed with a polite but unmistakable signal that read, "Go no further." Fred once told his wife that in all the years he'd known Jack O'Brien, he couldn't remember once when Jack wasn't "on."

"Hey, buddy," Fred said, as he put his hand on Jack's shoulder, "it was the same way in West Virginia. We were all miners instead of workin' in the mills.'"

Fred looked over his shoulder to be sure Blake was still asleep and then looked back at Jack. "But you know, you can't explain all that to the Reynolds. They got their own way of seein' things. Sometimes you just gotta ride things out. It's like when Sue had all those problems goin' through 'the change.' You know what I mean? There was no talkin' to her. I just hung in there 'til she was OK again. I don't really know your Carolyn, but she strikes me as a pretty strong lady. I'm sure she'll get over it."

"I guess she will." Jack sighed, then sat forward again. "But for Christ's sake, is that what this is all about?" He was crunching the ice cubes from his drink. "Carolyn wants us all to understand how much she feels, but she doesn't want my help. No one does. Julie's a complete write off. Her only pleasure in our relationship is making me angry. I haven't talked to my son about his life in more than a year. I tried to talk him out of going to France, a total waste of time as far as I was concerned, but he went anyway."

Fred was shaking his head, smiling. "Their circumstances are different. Like I said, you might as well be talkin' about the moon as far as your kids are concerned. You gotta look for things you have in common."

"You're joking, right? I was working to support my family when I was twelve. My kids have never had a job in their lives. They wouldn't survive a day on their own."

There was the sound of a muffled bell and then the captain's voice came over the speaker in the ceiling of the plane. "Mr. O'Brien, we've been cleared to land at Charlotte. We'll be landing in ten minutes."

◪ ◪ ◪

Over the seats, Jack saw Fred's hand, gesturing to make a point to Blake in a conversation at the front of the plane. He heard the motors whirring as the captain extended the wing flaps. He felt a slight decrease in speed. The complexity of motion fascinated him. He liked the expression of actions as mechanical formulae. But just before the cause of things there was a gap. Where did the drive come from?

"They're right," he thought, *"this is a huge deal. Maybe too big. How much stress can we handle? I think we're ready for this one. I was right about the other moves."* Like connecting points in a trajectory, he traced the line of his career all the way back to the early years. He had been alone from the day he arrived. At first, Blake just needled Carl Herrington, the president of the bank, to let him try out the credit card program, then the transaction processing business. The fresh talent looked like kids among ossified dinosaurs. Luckily the entrenched crowd were herbivores rather than carnivores.

The losses started piling up. He had forecast early losses, but from 1978 to 1981, the bank lost a third of its capital, more than twice what he had predicted. Herrington was no fool. The new ventures would work or they would take the bank into insolvency. Either way he would be out of a job. So he lined up the Commerfords and the Briggs and the few institutional shareholders for a proxy fight. When the smoke cleared, Herrington was gone and Blake gave his son-in-law a free hand. Five years later there wasn't anyone other than a handful of clerks who had been working there since before 1975. In 1986, eleven years after Jack joined the bank, Blake made him president.

"I can do this," he said to himself as he sat alone in the back of the plane. He had traced it all backward and forward, and stopped as he always had without answering the question: Why?

ZAZEN

When Carolyn and Jack were designing their new house at the beach, the architect referred to her study, the single room perched above the roof line with floor-to-ceiling windows, as the "widow's watch." In what was left of the late afternoon sun on that Sunday in December, she sat there, cross-legged on a mat, and thought how aptly the room had been named.

She was alone. Dan and Michael had left practically the moment they arrived. Julie had gone out for the afternoon. Carolyn was waiting for them, for her husband and her father, and for some sense of peace in the meditation she was practicing. She had become accustomed to watching and waiting, but now she was searching to understand why her best friend had died.

There were photographs on the walls, more on the shelves, and hundreds in the albums she kept. She was a collector of pictures, which never spoke out of turn or told sad stories. Still photos, older black and white images of her life, early color Polaroids, and more recent 35mm snapshots. To someone unfamiliar with her story, they all looked like reflections of a happy life. No one ever put pictures of people crying up on the wall.

There were the pictures of the little girl in front of the big house, with her chauffeur and her nanny, out for a ride in the country. There was the one of her in jodhpurs and boots and helmet being led on a pony by the stable master, and the picture of her smiling face covered in flour as she "helped" the cook. She had many companions growing up, but none to take the place of a mother who had run away to a twenty-five-room apartment in the Faubourg St. Honoré or a father slowly drowning himself in a bottle.

If you looked very closely at the picture of her reading in bed, you could just make out the titles on the nightstand—The

Complete Works of Emily Dickinson, Pride and Prejudice, To the Lighthouse. There was a drawer full of photos from her days at the Country Day School—class photos, first- graders in their uniforms, and high school seniors in skirts with pullover sweaters.

On what little wall space there was that wasn't glass, there were photographs of her family—her two children, her husband, and her father. They seemed to change effortlessly over the years, to grow, to mature, to age—Christmas skiing vacations, fires on the beach, so many happy moments captured, others left unrecorded on film, but no less vivid in her memory.

She had taken down the pictures of Carla; all except the few left on her desk. There was the one of the two young women pushing carriages. You couldn't tell from the picture that one of them was an heiress and lady of the house, and the other one was her son's nanny. They looked like two best friends showing off their little boys.

Carla had grown up in Charlotte, and won a scholarship to UNC at Chapel Hill. Her dream was to be a designer, to live in New York, and to travel the world. In 1967, with her degree and $1,200, she moved to New York and a job at the Halston fashion house. Six years later she was pregnant, unmarried, and back in Charlotte looking for anything to support herself. She finally resorted to taking a job that Carolyn had advertised two years after Dan was born. She stayed through the summer after Julie was born, but after three years at the O'Briens', she was anxious to get on with a job doing anything other than being a nanny and a housekeeper.

Carolyn and Carla's relationship made a seamless transition to a close friendship. If Carolyn ever "let her hair down," it was with Carla. In the gardens at the Reynolds' family estate, Chatsworth, Carla taught Carolyn how to paint with watercolors. She introduced Carolyn to Buddhism and the practice of Zazen, sitting cross-legged in the lotus position, in a quiet room. At the beach, they went for long walks and collected shells, which they arranged with driftwood and beach glass on the windowsills. They drank wine sitting in front of the fire, noticing the patterns in their lives, talking for hours at a time.

There was another picture of the two of them on the beach in 1993, a copy of the one she had on the mantel in the Charlotte house. It was a spring weekend, just before Carla went for a routine examination. There were no pictures of that summer, of the Fentanyl ampoules or the wigs. No pictures of the fall in Charlotte and the all night vigils, and no pictures of the Thanksgiving funeral. No one ever takes pictures at funerals unless the deceased is famous or died in some public way.

◣ ◣ ◣

Now, a year later, from her widow's watch, she saw Julie's car heading back along the road from town to the house. It occurred to her that though they fought over many things, her sixteen-year-old daughter had become practically her only companion.

"What can I say to her?" Carolyn wondered.

There was no single event in Julie's adolescence that could be blamed for transforming her from a quiet but happy child into a cynic. Julie had always been different. Carolyn knew it would be up to her to bridge the gap. "But how?" she asked herself. She left the comfortable confines of her study and found Julie downstairs, rubbing her hands in front of the fire in the great room.

"Hi, Mom."

"Hi, there."

"Where's Dan and Mike?"

"They went out to the cottage."

"Any word from Dad?"

"He'll be here about five-thirty with your grandfather. What's new at the Carters'?"

"Nothing. There's never anything new there. There's nothing new here either. I should have at least brought Carlos with me."

"Julie, you already spend so much time with him, and besides, can't you be with us for a few days?"

"I am here. I just drove three hours with you and you hardly said a word to me."

"Well, it's hard to get a word in while you've got that thing plugged into your ears."

"Mom, that's just an excuse. We never talk. We either sit and say nothing or we fight. Do you really want to know what's going on in my life? I don't think so."

"What is going on, Julie?"

"How can I talk to you about my life? Right now my life is the band and Carlos. All I've ever heard from you about my music is when you ask me to turn it down. Carlos doesn't like to wear a condom when we have sex. He say's he's negative and he's not with anyone else, but I don't want to get HIV. That's the kind of stuff I deal with, Mom. It's a long way from the perfect life you think you lead."

"We, ah… we talked about your… your situation with Carlos." Carolyn inhaled deeply, "Be calm," and exhaled slowly. "I thought we agreed that you were going to use birth control and, sweetheart, you know, didn't we also talk about… well…"

"Unsafe sex?" Julie was aggravated.

"Yes…" Carolyn couldn't talk. She was trying to think of something reasonable to say. "Just be calm," she said to herself less convincingly. When she finally started again, all she could manage was, "I wish things were different between us."

"Mom, I'd like things to be different. But seriously, we just don't connect. The minute I really open up and tell you what's going on with me, you get that horrified look on your face like I'm some kind of freak. You have no idea what I'm going through. What if I leave the band? What if I get pregnant with Carlos? Sure, I'd have an abortion, but when I think of who I'd want to talk to about it, you know, Mom, it wouldn't be you."

There was a strained pause as Julie didn't see this particular conversation going any better than so many others like it. "We're here," she said. It's Christmas. I know you're having a hard time. I don't want to make it any worse. I've got to go check my messages. We can talk later if you want to." She went over to the couch where her mother was sitting, kissed her, and went up the stairs.

Carolyn sat for a while, motionless. As she watched her daughter walk away, she thought, "She's right. I never have talked to her. There's so much I could tell her and I haven't. I don't really try to get close anymore because it's like touching a hot stove."

Julie retrieved her messages on the answering machine back in Charlotte. Before she went downstairs, she thought, "There must be something I can say to her." She found Carolyn downstairs in the kitchen, wondering the same thing.

"Mom, I'm sorry if I came down on you. It's just that—"

Carolyn held up her hand. She didn't want the apology. "Some of what you said was obnoxious, but most of it was true. We really hardly know each other. A lot of that is my fault. There's something I'd like to tell you. Would you come upstairs with me?"

Carolyn poured herself a glass of Chardonnay. Everything in her study was designed to be comfortable. The lines, the fabrics, the arrangement of the furniture, all had Carla's touch, and when they finally settled on the couch near the fire, Carolyn thought, "Well… here goes."

Julie spoke first. "You know, this is really the only room in the house that I like. Dan and I always liked the cottage better."

"Speaking of the cottage," Carolyn hadn't even started and she was already off the subject, "there's a story about my pregnancy with you that goes with that place. When we moved back to Charlotte, your father and I started trying to get pregnant again. He used to say that all we had to do was sneeze and it would happen. But after a year with no results, he insisted on consulting a specialist, who told us that we were both working too hard and that we had to get away."

"Get away from what?"

"The phones, I guess. Don't you remember, when they asked you in first grade what your father did, you said, 'He talks on the phone.'"

They both laughed.

"So, we started the 'baby campaign.' Your father bought what he told me was a 'weather-worn' place here at the beach where we could go on weekends to get away and relax. It was what we could afford on his salary, because he wouldn't take any money from your grandfather. I wasn't expecting Chatsworth, but the house was literally falling down."

Carolyn smiled, looking out the window toward the ocean at the last shades of dusk, as if she could see it all in the telling of the story.

"We went to the beach nearly every weekend. We had time for walks, time with Dan, and time for each other. The cottage was what Carla used to call pure potential. I told her that I got pregnant with you because Jack started saying that maybe it wasn't the sea air I needed but a place in the mountains instead. I couldn't bear the thought of another little fixer-upper!"

"So that's how I was born. Wow, what a great story! How come you never told me before?"

"Oh, I don't know, Julie. There are so many stories like that. I don't know why I never told you. I guess for a long time, you seemed too young. And then more recently, you seemed disinterested. Actually, the story of my pregnancy with you wasn't the one I intended to tell you. It was my pregnancy with Dan that I thought of when you mentioned having sex with Carlos."

"I don't get the connection," Julie said.

"Well, you know I met your father in college, but I never told you how. When I got to Duke, there was a boy there from Charlotte Catholic whom I had been dating for several years. I was in love with him. His name was Steven Baldwin. Anyway, we went out on lots of dates when we were in high school and, no, we never did it, but by the time we were in college, I thought I would die if he didn't ask me to marry him someday."

"What did he look like?"

"He was what you'd call a hunk. He reminded me of Montgomery Clift."

"Mom, first, I've never used the word 'hunk,' and second, who's Montgomery Cliff?"

"Clift, not Cliff. He was an actor. Anyway, Steven was on the track team and one day he brought one of his teammates over."

"Let me guess. That was Dad, right?"

"Right. I think your father fell for me that night. He was at least as handsome as Steven, but in a different way."

"Was he a stiff then?"

"Oh, Julie, for God's sake, your father is not a stiff. You've just never given him a chance. He was what I'd call beguiling. The first thing I noticed about him was his eyes. I watched him talking to other people at the party and I caught him looking over toward me a few times that night. I knew he liked what he saw."

It was getting dark outside. Carolyn began to see her reflection in the glass. She was tracing the lines of the story in the eccentric pattern of shadows cast by the fire.

"You know, it's amazing how the years can pass. It all seems like a blur to me now. I went out with your father all through college. He and Steven ran on the track team for four years. We often dated with Steven and what I called his 'flavor of the month.' Sometimes it was just the 'flavor du jour.'"

Julie was listening to Carolyn, noticing that the fire was going out, but not wanting to interrupt. She was letting her mother wander at her own pace on forgotten paths in her memory. These were places where she had not been in a long while. It seemed like she was getting lost. "Mom, didn't you say this was a story about Dan?"

"Oh, yes. I guess I did get a little off track. I couldn't decide if I should even tell your father that I was pregnant. We hadn't talked much about the future. He had his draft deferment and since I had no invitation to join him at the business school, I planned to go to London, to work at Christie's. I was going to the NCAAs in Atlanta, so I decided I would stay for a few days after the event to visit a cousin and have an abortion. And I was not going to tell him. I was at the finals to see him and Steven win the 4 x 100. They looked like gods on the winners' platform. So, after the celebration, your father drove me to my cousin's house. I wasn't actually looking at him when I blurted out the truth that I was pregnant and that I had decided to have an abortion. But when I turned to face him, there was no doubt in his eyes and no doubt in my heart when he asked me to marry him."

"What an incredible story," said Julie. "I guess I never thought about you having sex before you were married. Does Dan know any of this?"

"Of course not. Carla was the only person I ever told."

"Do you ever wish you'd held out for the other guy?"

"Oh, Julie, that's such a silly question. I don't look back like that. I mean, you know, when I was in college, I wished that Steven would do more than stop by occasionally, but there were so many other things to keep me distracted. My relationship with your father had…, um…, progressed—"

"Yeah," Julie blurted out, "progressed enough to get pregnant."

Carolyn smiled and looked down. "I loved Steven, but… well, I realized it was all in my head and… it's hard to love a thought for very long. It occurred to me to pursue him, but that sort of thing didn't come naturally to me, and besides, your father was so interested in me… I don't regret the choices I made."

"Whatever happened to him?"

"Steven didn't come back to Durham after the race. Your father told me that he had to go up to New York on family business. He hadn't called or even sent me a card or flowers after we announced our engagement. I wondered if he didn't regret letting me get away. I thought about how I would tease him at graduation."

"He just left?"

"Well, he didn't attend graduation. We heard the news of him enlisting in the marines. It was like getting a report of a death in the family. I pressed your father for an explanation. You know how he can be when he doesn't want to talk about something. Finally, he told me that he didn't know why Steven suddenly left without a word, but that he and Steven had had an argument in Atlanta after the NCAAs. It was over something that had been building up for a while and it just exploded. He refused to discuss it any further. He hoped that Steven would have the good form to come to our wedding, but if he didn't, your father wasn't about to let it spoil our happiness."

"Did he show up at the wedding?"

"No" Carolyn sighed. "We were married at Chatsworth. It was an absurd affair. Anyone who knew, which by the time of the wedding was nearly everyone, was supposed to act like they didn't know I was pregnant. I wasn't showing so that made the dress one of the easier aspects of the occasion. I was mostly worried about your grandfather making it down the aisle sober. Dan was born about seven months later. By then we were living up north in Cambridge, so there was no one around to do the nine-month calculation."

"So," said Julie, "you never saw Steven again? That was it?"

"You know, I have learned that the power of denial is as strong a coping mechanism as any belief. I survived by assuring myself that there was nothing wrong, that he was only going away for a while, that he would get over whatever it was that made him go, and that he would return safely to Charlotte and eventually look us up... But he never did."

"Mom, I hear what you're saying about no regrets, but, I mean, if you really want to know the truth, you don't sound very convincing."

"Oh, I don't suppose I make any sense these days... What I do regret is that we couldn't have done more for Carla. I miss her so much. She seemed to have such an intuition for things. She was really my only friend."

"Mom, you know, while we're in the mood for telling true stories and all, I've been wondering how you deal with the fact that Carla slept with Dad?"

As the words were leaving Julie's mouth, it was as if an air-raid siren had gone off somewhere in Carolyn. Her face reflected the barriers that went up inside her. She stared at her daughter, who stared back at her with a matter-of-fact look. All Carolyn could manage was a hoarse "What?"

"Well," said Julie, "I never would have said anything, but I guess I was kind of inspired by your story about Dad and the other guy and getting pregnant with Dan and all. I've been wondering about it for a while. And I guess I just figured, what the hell? I might as well ask... Mom, are you OK?"

"What... ah... how did you..."

"Know?"

"Yes."

"Michael told me this summer when Dan was in France. One night, we had been talking about you and Dad and Carla, and then later on, after we had sex, Michael told me about the affair between Carla and Dad."

"My God, Julie, you slept with Michael?"

"Mom, you just told me about your sex life before you got married and now you're flipping out because I was with a guy you'd be thrilled for me to marry? C'mon."

"I'm sorry, Julie. I just don't know what to say. I guess I'm shocked."

"Why are you shocked? When Michael and I were camping out in the dunes last summer, you knew what was going on. But you didn't want to talk about it. Didn't you just say something about denial helping you to cope? The only difference between then and now is that before we hadn't talked about it. And as far as the Carla affair is concerned, you've known about that for fifteen years. You're only upset because now you know it's not your secret anymore."

"What did Michael tell you?"

"You know... Carla worked for us, and she and Michael lived in the apartment over the garage."

"Yes."

"He said that when he was three, he found Dad and Carla in their apartment in bed. It was one of those things that happened so fast and he was so young. When he got older, he sort of put it out of his mind. Then in the summer before Carla died, he asked her about it and she told him. She said it happened right after they moved in. You were pregnant, she was lonely, there was some shit going on at the bank, Dad was under a lot of pressure and depressed. She said that they both realized they were out of control pretty quickly and that they stopped a few weeks after it started."

"That's about it," Julie continued. I mean, it's not like I was shocked or anything. I could see why Dad and Carla were attracted to each other. What blows me away is, you've known about the affair all this time and you never spoke to Dad about it? That's what's incredible." When Julie was finished, she stared at Carolyn, waiting for her to say something spontaneous, to blurt out whatever truth it was that had been held for so long.

Carolyn was sitting upright. She was trying desperately not to think about it, so she turned her attention to something else. "Julie, would you do me a favor and check the pot on the stove. Just stir it a few times. And would you get me another glass of wine? In fact, why don't you bring the bottle up here."

"Mom, are you sure you're OK?"

"Yes, I am… I… um… I'd like another glass of wine and a minute to collect my thoughts."

After Julie had gone, Carolyn could hear the faint sound of rain against the glass. She sank a little deeper in the chair. Then she covered her face with her hands and began to cry. She cried politely, as if it was something she had learned to do, rather than an uncontrolled act of grief. As she heard Julie coming back up the stairs, she dabbed her eyes with a tissue. She went over to the fireplace to add more wood and turned on the light on her desk.

"The soup is fine," Julie said, " and no sign of Dan and Mike. They should be back soon. It looks like it's started to rain."

Carolyn poured herself more wine and took a sip before putting the glass on the table in front of her.

"I don't know why I never told your father that I knew," said Carolyn. "I suppose there was no single reason. When Carla told me, it had been years since she and Michael moved out. But I didn't know the part about Michael finding them."

"Did Carla say why she told you?"

"Oh, yes. She said that we had become friends and that she had to say something about what had happened. To her, it was simple: tell the truth and move on. I never knew Carla to be anything but direct. At the time, I was horrified…" Carolyn's voice trailed off.

Julie reached over to touch her, to bring her back to a reassuring connection with the present.

When Carolyn spoke, she didn't look at Julie. She was somewhere else. "I couldn't imagine that sort of thing happening to me. Later, I thought, 'What an incredible risk she's taking.' I was on the board of St. Alban's. I got her the job there. She knew the Reynolds Trust paid Michael's 'anonymous' scholarship. Your father..." Carolyn took a deep breath and exhaled, trying to expel the memory from her lungs. "Your father arranged the mortgage for her house. It's strange, as I look back on it now. I'm in awe of how well she sized up the situation. I think she knew I wouldn't tell your father and that life would go on."

"Didn't you want to shoot them when you found out?"

Carolyn sighed. "Sweetheart, rational people don't shoot other people."

"Mom, we're not talking about what you thought, we're talking about how you felt when you found out that your best friend had been sleeping with your husband."

"She wasn't my friend at all when it happened, but we had certainly become best friends when she decided to tell me. We were sitting in the kitchen in Charlotte. I think she told me there because she knew that's where I was the most relaxed." Carolyn picked up her glass of wine. With her other hand, she ran the tip of her index finger over her bottom lip. She closed her eyes, as if to look inside herself and remember the scene.

"One minute we were talking about a recipe and the next thing I knew, she said there was something she had to tell me. I was so stunned at first, I don't think I actually showed any reaction. Then, after she left, I was angry. She had told me about something that had happened years earlier, but it was as if it had happened that week. I felt betrayed. I felt like someone had broken into our house and ransacked all my private possessions."

Carolyn took another sip to calm herself. "It was hardest in the first year after I found out. Your father had been under enormous pressure. He hadn't wanted to take the job at the bank, but I helped convince him to do it. Then when he got there, he ran into some major problems. By the time Carla told me, things had become unbearable for him, and we were what you'd call...

estranged, I guess."

"You mean you weren't having sex?"

Carolyn looked away. "Yes."

"So then what happened?"

"Things got much better at the bank. Your father and Blake were spending a lot of time together. He seemed so much happier. It's incredible how men wrap their lives up in their careers. I can't remember exactly when, but I think it was about a year after Carla told me, that your father and I started sleeping together again. It's strange, we never talked about why we had stopped or why we started again."

"Mom, I understand everything except the part about how you slept with Dad without resolving the affair with Carla."

"I don't know that I understand it either, Julie. I'd like to tell you I've resolved it, that I've forgiven him. But really what I've done is manage not to think about it for long periods of time. At first it was weeks, then months. I guess it's been a form of denial. But you're right, I haven't resolved it."

"How do you know he hasn't done it with anyone else?"

"I don't know. I don't believe he has, but I don't know."

"And you don't think you could ask him?"

"Not without bringing up the entire issue. And I really do wonder, after all this time, what's the point?"

"The point is that it still bothers you, and it won't stop until you talk to him about it."

"I suppose you're right. I wish I had brought it up, the way Carla did. I mean, it's not that we reconciled overnight, but we sorted things out pretty quickly. I can't decide if it was because I wanted to forgive her, or if I was just so lonely and she was the only person I could talk to. We took you and the boys out to the cottage and talked the whole weekend. We cried. Well, actually I did most of the crying. After she said she was sorry, she said she intended to get on with life. She didn't believe in remorse. She used to say, whenever I would start dwelling on the past and something I regretted, 'Oh, Caraleen, fuck remorse! It never deed anyone any good.'"

Julie laughed at her mother's imitation of Carla's latin

accent. "You really loved her, didn't you?"

"Oh yes, I loved her. She was the most extraordinary person I've ever known. She was my sister, my mother, and my friend. I loved her very much."

"Were you and Carla ever lovers?"

"Julie, please!"

"Mom, why should you be offended by that question?"

Carolyn looked down and rested her head in her hand. "Oh, I don't know, I'm not offended... But we weren't." As she looked up, she ran her fingers through her hair. "We were... we were gentle with each other. Sometimes when we would be relaxing after working in the garden or going for a walk on the beach, we would give each other hand massages or foot massages. We colored each other's hair. When she was very sick, I bathed her..."

Carolyn stared at the fire. The freshly cut wood hissed as it lay on the hot embers. It was as if she suddenly remembered how she used to cry when she was a girl, alone in the big house at Chatsworth. A memory she had put away. Then she cried so loudly, her body shook.

Julie was frightened. All she could do was wrap herself around her mother and hold on. When she got up to get the box of tissues, she saw the headlights of a car coming out to the house from town and another set of headlights coming north from Fort Fisher.

"That must be Dad and Dan," she said.

"Oh, and I'm a mess," Carolyn said. "Go downstairs. Just tell them we've been talking about Carla and that I need a few minutes to freshen up."

Carolyn got up and hugged her daughter. "Oh, Julie, I'm so sorry I let all this time pass without us talking. I promise that we'll do better. I'll do better. We'll talk more. Will you forgive me?"

"Hey, Mom, what was it Carla said? 'Fuck remorse.'"

MOMENTUM

Jack walked through the lobby of the Reynolds Tower and into the bank's headquarters, as he had every day since he started working there, in a hurry. He had been at a loss to understand the point of spending Christmas week at the beach when his wife proposed it. On his return to Charlotte, he realized that he still didn't "get it," but now he had more urgent distractions on his mind. On this first Monday in 1995, he knew he had to win over his father-in-law and his CFO to his plan for a hostile bid for New York Trust.

At 7:30 a.m., the lobby was deserted. On the fifty-eighth floor, Catherine McDonald was already at her post. The major domo of the chairman's office, she headed a staff of four women who looked after Jack, Blake, and Fred. She had already been with the bank for twenty-two years by the time he got there in 1975. Now in her early sixties and unmarried, with no apparent interests outside the bank, he wondered what she would do when she retired. As he had for the first day of every year for at least a decade, he addressed her by her first name.

"Good morning, Catherine."

"Good morning, Mr. O'Brien."

"I don't suppose there's any chance this will be the year we start on a first-name basis?"

"Oh, Mr. O'Brien, I guess I'm just from the old school. You know what they say about old dogs and new tricks." She handed him his coffee.

"How was your Christmas?" he asked, not expecting more than a perfunctory reply.

"Oh, fine. I went to my sister's in Greenville… I'm just revising your schedule. Joyce left me a note that you called while I was away. You want to meet with Mr. Reynolds and Mr. Bonham at three p.m. and clear your calendar for the rest of the day?"

"Yes, that's right."

"Bill Hunter will be here with the Consumer Credit Group at nine. There's a briefing on the Annual Report at eleven. The fund manager's lunch is at noon at the Downtown Club with Mr. Reynolds and Mr. Bonham. Everyone you're expecting is confirmed. Their stock positions and trading-activity reports are in the folder there on your desk."

"Thank you, Miss McDonald, and ah… Happy New Year."

"Happy New Year, Mr. O'Brien."

◼ ◼ ◼

Jack's office was a large open space, even by the standards of most CEOs. The area where he worked included his desk with a couple of high-back chairs in front of it. There was a more informal sitting area with a couch and two armchairs around a coffee table, and a conference area with a table that sat twelve. The furniture, the artwork, even the flooring were all distinctly contemporary. Within the four walls of a company operating in the most conservative of industries, Jack had created an atmosphere where everything and everyone was expected to be at the leading edge.

And yet, NCBT, like many other corporations where employees subsume their sense of self, had its own dialect. Vernacular and particular turns of phrase were adopted by senior executives and used by aspiring subordinates like a coded language that identified them to each other as being in the same loop with the CEO. Monkey see, monkey do. Monkey hear, monkey speak. Jack's troop of banking simians were set apart from all the other business primates in Charlotte. They conformed by being icon breakers. The hours they kept, the risks they took, their appetite for risk were all decidedly not traditionally southern. Their bonuses were rumored to be bigger than their salaries. They drove expensive foreign cars. Even the way the cadre of hard charging young officers dressed distinguished them from other executives in the city. Their suits were made-to-measure by the leading Italian designers, rather than off-the-rack from Brooks Brothers.

Promptly at 9:00, Bill Hunter arrived with his team. Jackets off, everyone was sitting at the conference table, drinking coffee.

"Looks like another piss-poor year for Consumer Credit," said Jack, smiling. "I'd really like to know if you all have any intention of ever producing decent results?"

Everyone laughed.

They were all trying to be relaxed. Considering that the news was so good, it should have been easy. Bill was responsible for a ten-billion-dollar loan portfolio that had become a license to print money for the bank. They reviewed the prior year's results and an updated 1995 forecast. Jack listened attentively and interrupted with the kind of questions that would have seemed innocuous to anyone uninitiated in this ritual. Even if they didn't know the reason behind the reason for every question, they all knew the CEO and his style. This was like open-heart surgery without anesthesia and the patient expected not to show any signs of being in pain.

When they were done, Jack addressed his questions directly to Bill. "I don't see any fluff in these numbers. But you know, I can't help but get the impression that they're a little too conservative. I think your people here have admitted that you're over-reserved against defaults. You didn't capitalize any of last year's expansion costs. Back both those factors out and your earnings would have been a lot higher. But I see that your proposed budget for '95 shows only another thirty percent growth year."

"Christ, Jack," said Bill, "Not many people in this industry would use the word 'only' when you're talking about these kinds of projections."

Jack was undeterred. "Let's just say I'm looking for a real stretch this year. Can you hit a target of around thirty-eight percent growth?"

All the number crunching, polite banter, and smiles of the last two hours had come down to a very direct and very unpleasant two-way conversation. Everyone on Bill Hunter's team was staring into their coffee cups and holding their breath.

"I'm telling you right now," said Bill, "there's no way we could maintain that kind of trajectory into '96."

Jack was staring. "Just answer my question, Bill."

Bill bit down on his lower lip, baring his incisors, inhaling through his nose. "Yeah, if that's what you need this year, we'll hit that target."

"Good," said Jack, as the rest of the table exhaled. "I've got another meeting. Thank you all very much." As they all got up to leave, Jack put his arm on Bill's shoulder. "Hang on for just a minute. There's something I want to discuss with you privately."

When Bill Hunter got back to his office, Mary Rogers was waiting for him. She was his second-in-command and had been sitting next to him during the meeting. "Well, what did he want?"

"I gotta tell ya, the guy's a piece of work. First he pins me to the wall for an hour. Then we go over and sit on the couch and he starts asking me about Marsha and the kids. Then Catherine comes in and reminds him he's gotta go. So as I sit forward to get up, he sits forward, puts his hand on my shoulder, and says, 'Bill, I want you to know that I'm very proud of what you've done. I want you to know how much it means to me.' He said it just like that. I mean, we're talking about the Ice Man here."

"Incredible!"

"But wait, that's not all. Then we both stand up, and I put my hand out, you know, to shake his hand. He takes my hand, and then, I can't believe this... he hugged me."

"He did what?"

"You heard it right, he hugged me. I mean, it was the stiffest hug I ever got, like he just started taking hugging lessons and he wanted to practice on me or something."

"Unbelievable. Do you think he's working on becoming human?"

"I don't know, but for Christ's sake, don't discuss this with anyone else. Clear?"

"Absolutely."

■ ■ ■

Jack was in a good mood as he crossed the North Tryon Street plaza in front of the Reynolds Tower on his way to the Downtown Club. He smiled as he passed a few people he knew, but didn't stop. He was perfectly capable of making small talk; in fact, under the right circumstances, he was good at it. But he didn't have time for that. He was in motion. Jack was a runner and he understood the importance of momentum.

The luncheon was the perfect arena for him, with Jack, Blake, Fred, and five institutional money managers, a small clique of investment professionals who had started accumulating NCBT stock for their funds in the late eighties and the early nineties. Gary Glaser, who had been running the Pilgrim Fund since its inception, held fifty million shares at an average cost, adjusted for splits, of just over eight dollars. He was sitting on a paper profit of two hundred million and he was getting itchy. He had to be convinced that there was still plenty of S&P-beating gain in his investment.

In the private dining room, Jack saw Glaser and Emeric McDonelly, who was in charge of the Harbor Fund, which, after the Reynolds Trust, was the bank's largest shareholder.

"Gentlemen," said Jack as he shook their hands, "it's good to see you. I guess we're the first arrivals."

"Emeric and I were just getting ready to bet on how much you'll beat the consensus earnings estimates," said Glaser. "It's only a hundred-dollar bet, Jack. I don't suppose you'd like to place your own wager?

"C'mon, fellas," said Jack, "you know we haven't announced the fourth quarter yet, but we haven't disappointed the Street in ten years and we sure are not about to start."

"OK, Jack," said McDonelly, "let's say fourth quarter '94 is a great quarter, like everyone's expecting. I think what we'd all like to hear is how much growth there is left in the bank's business lines."

"Well," said Jack, "that really is the question, isn't it?"

◣ ◣ ◣

It was three o'clock in the afternoon, after the fund managers had been sent back to New York and San Francisco. Blake and Fred were relaxing in the armchairs of the sitting area in Jack's office. Blake had his feet up on the coffee table. Fred was signing some papers that Catherine McDonald had brought in. She was standing, as much over as in front of him.

"Did you say that Jack was on his way back from Walter Weckstein's office?"

"Yes, Mr. Bonham. He stopped there after lunch. I expected him back by now. There's another signature line on the second page of that one."

"OK, Miss McDonald. Take these down to Treasury and ask Alan Schwartz to let me know how our position looks at the end of the week. That's all. And could you pull that door shut? Thanks."

Blake looked across the table at Fred. "Mr. Bonham, what did you think of lunch?"

"Well, Mr. Reynolds, I think Jack O'Brien could sell ice cubes to Eskimos."

"I guess I'd be inclined to agree." Blake chuckled. "Jack was right at home. He can be so wooden at times, but when he's really comfortable, especially when he gets going on the vision thing, he's a different person." Blake leaned forward. "Tell me, while we're waiting on Jack, what do you make of this New York Trust idea?"

"It's like I said on the plane, I don't like the idea of expanding by acquisition in such a big way. All the business we have now we got by starting something and growing it. This deal is gonna change everything."

"I've looked at his memo," said Blake, "and it's a pretty convincing argument. Where's the fatal flaw?"

"That's just it, Blake. Maybe there isn't one. Jack's convinced that we can't keep on the way we've been. He's sure we have to do something major."

Blake rubbed the palm of his hand against his chin. He put his feet on the floor. "Do you think we have to do something, Fred?"

"That depends on what you mean by 'have to.' When we were losing money faster than I could count it, we had to do something. There's nothing like that forcing our hand here. But you know, there's other realities we have to consider now. Like the fact that we're managing this place for the benefit of guys we had lunch with today. And you heard their questions about earnings growth. So now, if you're asking me, 'Do we have to do something to keep a three-times book valuation?' then the answer is, yeah, we probably gotta do something."

"But not this something, right?"

"Oh, heck, I don't know, Blake. Here's what I think we ought to do. I'll put together a team of our own analysts. I'll have 'em work up in New York with the guys from Morell Finch so no one asks any questions around here. Let's say by the end of January, early February, we ought to bring in the division heads for their opinions on what we can cut from the combined companies. Then... well... I guess we put our heads down and go for it." Fred looked across the table. "Don't worry, Blake. The way I see it, the worst that can happen is that we stick our tails between our legs and come on back home."

The air pressure in the room changed when the door swung open and Jack strode in, taking his jacket off as he walked over to the sitting area. "Sorry I'm late, guys. I got held up at Walter Weckstein's office." Jack sat between them, put his feet on the table and his arms over the edge of the couch. He looked to his left and his right. "Hey, why the glum faces? You all look like you just lost your best friend."

■ ■ ■

It was cold and raining. There wasn't much to see from where Dan sat at his desk in the apartment, staring out the window. He looked forward to April, as if another week and a change in the weather would somehow make a difference to him.

Michael was in a hurry to get to the airport for his flight to New York. He had a second interview with a brokerage firm and he wanted to nail down an offer. He was desperately searching for clean clothes to stuff in an overnight bag and a way to end a frustrating conversation.

"Dan, see the space where it says 'accept?' You check that box, fill in the rest of the information, and sign your name at the bottom. Put the form in the envelope and mail it. It's that simple."

Dan was motionless, avoiding even looking at the acceptance letter in front of him.

"You know," said Michael, "it's so fucking incredible to me. You got into Tuck, Sloan, and Wharton, and now you get this personalized invitation from the fucking dean of Harvard," Michael looked up and raised his hands for dramatic effect, "and, why am I not surprised, the dean just happens to be your father's former classmate and good friend. Think of how many guys would kill to be in your shoes, and all you can do is sit there and look like you've been sentenced to death."

"A slow death," said Dan.

"Dan, here's the last thing I'm going to say about this." Michael took the letter and waved it in Dan's face. "Why is this different from anything else you've done in the last twenty years? It's just one more brick in the fucking wall." Michael slammed the letter down on the desk. "You're so twisted because you don't know what to tell your father you're gonna do if you don't go. Why don't you try cutting loose for a change?"

Dan kept his head in his hands as he answered. "What are you talking about, Mike? Listen to yourself. Aren't you the one who hasn't called E&M yet because you're waiting to hear from the firm in New York? You're not going to blow off a sure thing until you've got an alternative. I don't have an alternative. I don't have any idea what I want to do. I don't have any other place to go."

Michael took the arms of the swivel chair and turned Dan around to face him. "Then come with me. Let's both get the fuck out of here. You can find a job in New York, some job, any job, until you figure out what you want to do. Man, you'll never have no place to go to as long as we're brothers." Michael looked at Dan. "Come with me."

It was as if the words that Michael spoke set off an avalanche of emotions, and Dan was buried under the weight of joy and guilt, hope and sadness, love and fear. Had he been able to answer Michael, the voice would have come from so far inside him that no ordinary ear would have heard it.

Suddenly, Michael realized the time. "Oh, shit, I have to run. Listen, if I get the job, we'll go out Friday night and celebrate. Jen wants to set you up with a friend of hers." Michael was shouting as he was running down the stairs. "I'll call you as soon as I hear anything!"

"*I should tell him*," Dan thought to himself. "*I have to tell him.*"

That night, Dan ate alone. When he couldn't stand to listen to the rain against the window anymore, he watched TV. When he went to bed, he lay awake for a long time. When he finally fell asleep, he had the same dream he'd been having, off and on, for years. The settings varied, but it was always the same condition: he couldn't breathe. It was a strange thing about breathing: when he could, he didn't think about it, but when he couldn't, he couldn't think about anything else. He struggled, under an ocean of water, or an avalanche of snow, or sometimes out in the open, but always without air to breathe. He woke up with a start, realized it was only four o'clock in the morning, found his bearings in the bedroom, and lay down again.

When he got back to the apartment later that afternoon, Dan listened to the messages on the answering machine. There were two calls from friends, congratulating him on getting into business school. Then there was a message from Michael. "Dan, I got the job. I got the job! I'm gonna hang out here today and tomorrow morning to look for an apartment. I've already called

Jen. We're on for dinner at the Giraffe with her and her friend, Tali, tomorrow night at eight. I'm buying. We'll go to Avalon afterward. Hey, man, I hope you thought about my idea of coming up here. You'd love it. I gotta go. I'll see you tomorrow."

███

The Giraffe was the best French restaurant in Durham. If undergraduates were seen there, it was usually with their parents, wealthy parents. As far as Michael was concerned, he was celebrating his manumission and he didn't need anyone to pay his way anymore. Dan picked up Michael at the airport. They met the girls at the restaurant.

Jennifer was the perfect match for Michael. She was tall, beautiful, and ambitious, and smart enough to acknowledge the basis of their relationship. She knew where she was headed, which was not to New York with Michael, but "for the time being," she told her friends, "he's a fantastic fuck." Tali was a dancer, just finishing at the North Carolina School of the Arts in Winston-Salem. She was five-foot six, with long blond hair. When Dan saw her, he thought she looked like Kim Basinger in *9 1/2 Weeks.*

"We'll start with a magnum of Dom Pérignon," Michael said to the waiter. While they were waiting for the champagne, Michael regaled them with stories of New York and his new job. "There's one huge room, the size of a city block. There must be a couple of hundred brokers there, all in cubicles, screaming into the phones. They put out ten IPOs in one month. Some of the guys are making more than a half a million a year. It's incredible!"

Their waiter, Raymond, delivered the menus, elaborate and written in French. "Listen," said Michael, "you girls have any questions on the menu, Dan here speaks perfect French. He was in Paris all last year. Right, Dan?"

"Yeah, I was in Paris, but my French isn't perfect." He smiled as he looked down. "It's good enough to read the menu, though."

Raymond spoke English with a thick accent, but to add to the ambiance of the evening, Dan was the interpreter for their table. He spoke French fluently with Raymond, whose gaze was unmistakable.

For the rest of the evening, Dan drifted in and out of the conversation. When Raymond wasn't at their table, taking an order or delivering food, Dan's eyes followed him around the room. He tried with mixed success to show polite interest in Tali and her career.

"I'm going up to dance at Martha Graham's school in the fall," she said. "I've got a scholarship. I'm hoping to get into the company for a few years at least. Then I guess I'll figure out what I want to do next."

"That sounds exciting," said Dan. "I'm jealous."

"Jen told me you just got into business school."

"Yeah, that's not so exciting. To tell the truth, I'd rather be doing what you're doing."

"You're a dancer?"

"No." Dan smiled. "I've always been interested in dance, but I'm not much of a dancer myself."

"Oh, great," thought Tali, *"And now I get to spend the rest of the evening with him in a club. I'm gonna kill Jen. What a shame. He's so cute."* Tali watched Dan telling Jen a story about Michael. He appeared reticent at one moment and then in another totally animated. There was an subterranean trace of the erotic in the way he moved, even in the way he sat or unself-consciously gestured with his hands.

Jennifer was all apologies when Dan and Michael left them to get the car. "Tali, I'm so sorry. He's always been a little shy, but I've never seen him like this before. Michael told me he's been sort of depressed, but I swear I had no idea it was this bad."

The next time Jennifer was alone with Tali was in the line for the ladies' room at the club. "So, how's it going?" Jennifer asked.

"I can't believe it," said Tali. "He's really cute, and he seems a lot nicer than at the restaurant. Hey, Jen, is he gay?"

"What?" Jennifer looked shocked.

"Well, you know," said Tali, "a lot of the guys at my school are gay, so, you know, I usually know when someone is."

"Tali, you're such a total fag hag. No, he's not gay. Michael would have told me."

"It's not that I care or anything," said Tali as the door to the ladies' room swung open and a woman came out. "Jen, can I go first? I don't think I can wait 'til you get out."

◼ ◼ ◼

They went back to the apartment when the club closed. Michael and Jennifer wasted no time in disappearing into Michael's room, the subsequent sound effects leaving nothing for Tali and Dan to wonder about.

Dan looked sheepishly at Tali. "I had a great time tonight. You know, you don't have to stay here if you don't want to. I could drive you back to Jen's apartment if you don't want to stay."

"No, I'd like to stay, if that's all right with you."

Dan looked up as if to see if she was still there, and then he looked down again. "Sure, I'd like you to stay."

They were, in bed as they had been on the dance floor, connected to each other's rhythms, two bodies in motion until the music was over, and then they lay still. Dan was as much relieved as he was excited to have sex with Tali. When he rolled over on his back, she turned on her side and pressed herself next to him.

She propped up her head with a pillow and her elbow, and with her free hand, she stroked his smooth chest. "You know," she said, "I'm afraid Jen will say something to Michael, so I want you to know that earlier tonight I asked her if you were gay."

Dan was staring up at the ceiling, thinking of Raymond and the phone number on the piece of paper that he had slipped in Dan's coat pocket as they were leaving the restaurant. "Why did you ask her that?"

"Oh, I don't know. I guess at first I thought of it when I noticed you looking at the waiter. I don't know. Anyway, it's no big deal to me, even if you are, but I didn't want you to get upset if you heard from Michael that I asked. You're not upset, are you?"

Dan wasn't paying attention to her.

"Anyway," said Tali, "I think you're really nice and I hope we can see each other if you come up to visit Michael in New York… Hey, are you there?"

"Huh? Oh, sure," said Dan, "that would be great. I'd like that… Let's get some rest, OK?"

Tali fell asleep lying next to him, with her arm draped over his chest. Dan couldn't sleep. He was remembering the time in the summer before he left for France. Julie had noticed the way he was looking at Michael on the beach and she casually asked him if he had "the hots" for Michael. Jack heard the comment and before Dan could attempt an answer, he angrily rebuked his daughter for challenging what he called Dan's "manhood."

"What am I gonna do?" he thought. *"What the fuck am I gonna do?"*

HAIKU

On the day of the meeting, Jack was keyed up but confident of the outcome. Taking the advice from Blake and Fred, he had a series of private briefings with each of the directors. Blake's sisters got courtesy phone calls. That was all Jack could stomach and besides, they were lost causes as far as he was concerned. The others got lunch appointments. Even with a couple of the old guard who had never really trusted him since the near-disaster losses of the early eighties, he put on his most patient and sincere demeanor. Six of the eleven directors were his appointments. They liked and respected him. None would have said they were close to him.

The day was choreographed like a Wagnerian opera with a well-directed cast. All ready to take their cues were Blake and Fred, the accountants from Coopers & Lyttle, the investment bankers from Morell Finch, and the lawyers from Carter, Squire & Monroe. If Jack had a name for this opera, it would have been *Flight of the Prostitutes.*

As chairman of the board, Blake opened the meeting with comments on the 1994 results. It was the twelfth consecutive year in which earnings had grown more than 20 percent, an extraordinary feat, for which Blake gladly gave his son-in-law all the credit.

Fred Bonham was on stage next. He walked the directors through the pages in the thick spiral binders in front of them. The details and the cheese danish were all intended to lower heart rates and, if possible, induce sleep apnea. For those directors who were still sentient, Fred introduced the auditors from Coopers & Lyttle. The engagement partner had been on the account for ten years. It was his gravy train, and he was salivating over the thought of the fees that the NYT deal would generate. Not to be outdone by the cast members who would follow him, he kept on until lunch, with long fawning answers to the few perfunctory questions from members of the audit committee.

After lunch, Jack introduced the investment bankers, led by the managing director, Payton Harwood. When Jack met him for the first time in New York, he couldn't help but think of the hapless millionaire character, Thurston Howell III, from the TV series *Gilligan's Island*. It was a lasting and fairly accurate impression. Harwood talked about the limits to the bank's growth in its current market niches and pointed out that, had the bank engaged Morell Finch earlier, they would have focused on this issue. But now, they simply had to do something. This was the "make 'em feel bad, then make 'em feel good" approach.

What they were all supposed to feel good about was that New York Trust was a wounded adversary and the timing for the tender offer was perfect. The combination of the two banks would wipe away every cloud from the horizon. Harwood even had the obligatory easel with the whiteboard graph of earnings that grew on and on, far into the next millennium. It sounded too good to be true, but this was theater, where suspension of disbelief was an intended result.

Then it was Henry Bradford's turn. He was a senior partner at Carter, Squire & Monroe. He approached the deal the way a hyena checks out the remains of a wildebeest after a lion has finished with it. He recognized a meal. He knew he had no risk in getting involved, but he was instinctively cautious, as if he believed that the dead could rise and in some reincarnation, take their revenge on carrion eaters.

Bradford first made the necessary oblations to the experience and sophistication of the board (even though he knew none of them had been involved in anything like this before). He was only *reminding* them of their fiduciary duties. They had to plan on an initial negative reaction from the *target* and there was a probability of a protracted battle, which, he added, they might lose. When Bradford was finished, all eyes were on Jack O'Brien.

Jack figured he needed about an hour to wrap things up. He folded his hands and rested them on the table as if he was about to lead the directors in prayer. "I've had the opportunity to visit with all of you prior to this meeting. You all know how I feel. Put simply, I think the acquisition of New York Trust will establish NCBT as one of the world's premiere financial institutions. It will add prestige to Charlotte and tremendous value to our shareholders. But I want to be sure we have a full and complete airing of any concerns about the transaction before we vote."

Ron Duby was the first to respond. He spoke slowly and carefully as if he had thought out and even practiced what he was going to say. "In the ten years that I've been on the board, whenever we reviewed our strategic plan, acquiring New York Trust wasn't even on the wish list. And I think it's fair to say that if someone had brought up the idea, we all would have dismissed it as simply not feasible. Let's say the auguries have changed, but we all know they can turn against us just as they have recently turned in our favor."

No one knew for sure which way Duby was leaning. He operated under the mistaken impression that this was supposed to be a true deliberation of the proposal before them. His comment about the uncertainty that would follow a hostile bid was thoughtful and obviously sincere, but it made a discordant sound in a meeting that was staged for a single purpose.

Duby interrupted himself, looking around the room, fearing that his preamble was being misunderstood. "I probably should have said before I started that I am in favor of going ahead, and my position is primarily based on the confidence I have in management. Jack, I'm going to vote 'yes', but I am uncomfortable with the degree of uncertainty about the events that will follow once the first shot has been fired—"

"Now hold on," grumbled Elliot Packard, who was one of Blake's college classmates. "With all due respect to my fellow director, I think we can't be saying we're in favor while we're goin' on about the dangers of uncertainty. I've been on this board since Blake and I got back from the war. And, yes, I know all about the bad patch we got in, but let's face it, that's ancient history. Being a director of this bank has been the easiest job in Charlotte for a long while. We just come on in here, about this time every year, and listen to how our boys won the World

Series again. Nobody in this room could figure we'd have it so easy forever. Tell me something, Jack, what's the absolute worst thing that could happen if we lose this thing?"

"Well, Elliot," said Jack, relieved at being served up such a soft-pitch question, "I think we need to realize that a tremendous amount of senior management time will be put into this, so, if we lose, there is certainly a lot of lost opportunity cost. We will have spent somewhere between two and five million on fees, depending on how long the offer is outstanding and what kind of reaction we get from NYT. If we lose, our stock price will go down, no question about it, and our reputation will be damaged for a period of time."

"Is that it?" asked Elliot.

Jack looked at Henry Bradford.

"There is the possibility," said Bradford, obviously walking on eggshells, "that this offer, if it fails, could put NCBT in play, for basically the same reasons that NYT is in play now, wounded reputation and lowered stock price. Under those circumstances, there are any number of domestic or foreign financial institutions that might make an offer for a franchise as valuable as this one."

It would have been inaccurate to say that the directors didn't understand Bradford's answer, or for that matter, any of the answers the professionals gave them in the next half hour or so. There were other risks that they talked about, but without any real connection to the "downside" possibilities of making a hostile tender offer for a New York money center bank. Elliot Packard had summed up their mood well, without understanding Ron Duby's earlier expression of caution. True, they were accustomed to winning, but no less true, they were totally unprepared for war in its corporate form.

Blake's sisters had been quiet for nearly the entire presentation. Finally, D'Arcy Commerford spoke up. Of the two sisters, she was the designated "wet rag" on all of Jack's pep-rally bonfires. "We've spent too much time, as far as I'm concerned, talking about what happens if we lose. What I'm concerned about is what happens if we win. Merging two very large, very different banks will take time and it won't go smoothly. I want to know what happens to the dividend if we start running up big losses again."

"D'Arcy," said Blake, obviously cutting his sister off, "there's no one in this room who doesn't understand that there are risks in combining the operations of two banks. And I know you're entitled to be concerned about the dividend, but after twelve years of record earnings, I think Jack's ability to run a bank speaks for itself… I think at this point, I would entertain a motion…"

◼ ◼ ◼

Back in his office, Jack put his feet up on the credenza behind his desk and called Carolyn.

"Hey, sweetheart, you ready to leave?"

"Hi, there. Yes, I'm all packed. How did it go?"

"As expected. Ten to two in favor. Your aunts were the 'no' votes. Blake is meeting with them now."

"Honey, I called Sally Weckstein and told her we'd be a little late. Dan and Michael are here. They want to talk to you before they drive back to Durham."

"Did they say what it's about? Is anything wrong?"

"Well, they look fine. Actually, they seem kind of excited. I didn't think I should try to pry it out of them."

When Jack turned around to hang up, Catherine McDonald was at his desk. "Mr. Reynolds called while you were on the phone. He'd like to see you before you leave."

Jack was distracted, wondering what Dan and Michael wanted, when he went into Blake's office. "What's up?"

"I just had a visit with my sisters. As we expected, they're not happy. They're worried about the impact this deal could have on earnings. We spent a half an hour going over what they called your 'history of losses from the eighties.' Basically, they want to know what happens to their dividend payouts if the deal goes through."

"Other than carp about it," asked Jack, "what can they do? The board voted ten to two in favor."

"Well," said Blake, "they can exercise their right to nominate another board member."

"Fine," said Jack, as if they had asked for Coke instead of Pepsi at the board lunches. "I don't care."

"Jack," said Blake, looking like the bearer of a bad omen, "they've nominated Carl Herrington."

Jack was focused on his goal. He had a habit of dismissing what he thought were minor annoyances. He paused, but only briefly, to think about what it would be like to have Carl Herrington as a director. "Put him in the proxy statement. I don't give a damn. After the merger, they won't have a right to be on the board. They won't have a right to go to the toilet as far as I'm concerned… Look, I've got to run. Carolyn just called. She said Dan is at the house and he wants to talk to me."

"Is anything wrong?"

""She said she doesn't think so. We're meeting the Weksteins for dinner in Wilmington, so I need to get home. Blake don't worry about Herrington. We'll all be civil to each other. I'll see you on Monday."

In his car, on the way home, Jack thought a little about having to deal with his old nemesis, but mostly he wondered about what his son wanted. He hated not knowing what was going on. He pulled into the driveway and noticed the lawn had just been cut. He noticed a few weeds as he was coming up the walk and made a mental note to talk to the gardener.

After the pleasantries were exchanged, Carolyn went upstairs to get her bags. Jack sat with Dan and Mike in the library. "OK, fellas, what's up?"

"Mr. O'Brien, I've decided not to go to work for Eastman & Maxwell. I got an offer from a firm in New York and I'm going to take it."

The news was a surprise to Jack, but he wasn't sure if it was good or bad, so he bought some time to think about it by asking the obvious question: "What firm in New York?"

"D. L. Baird. They're a small firm, but they're involved with a lot of exciting new companies and I think I can do well there."

"Michael, D. L. Baird is a bucket shop. They sell penny stocks. For Christ's sake, you've got three years training at one of the best regional firms. Why the hell would you hook up with a bunch of hustlers?"

"Mr. O'Brien, I know they don't have the best reputation, but you know, they're cleaning things up, bringing in more qualified people. I really think I'll stand out there. I'm sure I would have done well at E&M too, but I want to work in New York."

When Michael finished speaking, he could hear the ticking of the clock on the mantel. Jack didn't have any more questions. He was sizing up the situation, evaluating his options, predicting outcomes. In one way, it wouldn't have been accurate to say Jack "decided" he was happy with Michael's announcement, because decisions usually involve deliberation. Jack didn't have time for that. His reaction was much more spontaneous and intuitive. But in another way, decision was the perfect word, because "decide" literally means, "to cut off." In the span of time it took to lift a glass of sherry off the table, take a sip, and put it back down again, Jack had cut Michael off.

"Have you told Tom Weathers about this?"

"No, sir. I wanted to tell you first. I'll call Mr. Weathers on Monday. I also wanted to thank you and him for giving me the chance to work at E&M for the last three years and for the job offer."

"You know, Michael, I've got lots of friends in the brokerage business. If you'd like, I could still get you an interview with any firm in New York." Jack would have made the introductions, but he knew Michael wouldn't take him up on it.

"That's very generous of you, but no, no thank you, Mr. O'Brien. I've already accepted the offer from Baird and I want to keep my word."

"Of course," said Jack. "I understand. I'll be one of your first clients. When do you start?"

"May first, sir."

"Before graduation?"

"Yeah. I really don't feel like hanging around for the cere-mony thing. I mean, you know, with everyone telling me how proud my mother would have been to see me graduate. I'm actually packing up this weekend and driving my stuff up to New York."

"Well, we'll miss you, but I understand." Jack turned to Dan, who was sitting in an armchair, looking out the window, detached from the conversation. "Hey, sport. Your mother said you have news too. Let me guess, you're engaged, right?"

Before Dan could answer, Michael was on his feet and extending his hand to Jack. "I'll leave you two to talk. I need to go. My grandfather is picking me up. I'm going to spend some time with him before Dan and I drive back to Durham this afternoon." He turned to Dan, still staring out the window. "I'll see you later, man."

Dan looked at Michael. "Yeah, sure. I'll pick you up at five-thirty." Dan's eyes followed Michael to the door of the library. His mouth was dry. His heart was racing. His palms were sweating.

Jack was relieved at the thought of having Michael out of Charlotte. He figured that maybe they would see him at Christ-mas and once or twice in the summer. Case closed. He was in a mood to kid with his son. "OK, sport," he said, "what's up? Who's the lucky girl, eh?"

Dan managed a halfhearted smile. "I'm not engaged, Dad, but there is something I want to tell you. I've decided to defer admission to business school for a year. I'll get an internship at one of the AE firms in New York. Mike and I are gonna get an apartment there. I wanted to tell you about it before I call the dean's office."

"Son, what's wrong?"

"Nothing's wrong. I just feel like I would be better off if I got some work experience."

"Dan, trust me, you'll have the rest of your life to get expe-rience. Look, I know Michael going off to New York sounds exciting, a lot better than sticking your nose in the books for another two years, but time will fly by and then you'll be done."

"I know it will go fast, but if I go, I want to get the most out of it. Right now, I don't think I would."

"Son, I know you haven't been yourself lately. We haven't really talked since you got back from France, but look, I'm your father. I know about these things. Don't you think there were times when I was your age that I felt burned out? What you have to do now is put your head down, keep running, and get over the finish line. I'm sure you'll feel differently after graduation. We'll spend some time at the beach. You'll get your batteries recharged."

"I don't think this is really about my energy level."

"Sure it is. You're run down. Be honest with yourself and admit it. And, on top of that, you see Michael going off on his adventure. Who wouldn't want to put off school for another year?"

"I don't think you're hearing what I'm saying."

Jack raised his voice. "I'm hearing exactly what you're saying and that's why I'm telling you, stay the course." Jack was sitting forward on the edge of an armchair. He put his sherry glass down on the table so hard it almost broke. "Look, Dan, your mother is finally getting back on her feet. She's really looking forward to your graduation. For Christ's sake, don't let some passing anxiety screw that up."

Dan was drawing a breath, about to make one last attempt to get his father to understand that this was no brief moment of anguish, but a lifetime of torment that had to be resolved.

Then Carolyn appeared at the door. "Hi, guys. I'm sorry to interrupt, but if we don't get out to the airport we'll miss our dinner in Wilmington." Carolyn looked at Dan, again staring out the window. "So what's the news?"

"Well," said Jack, "Michael is going to take a job at a brokerage firm in New York, and Dan and I were just agreeing on why a year's deferment doesn't make any sense for him."

"A deferment?" asked Carolyn. "Why would you want a deferment, Dan?"

"It's a long story, Mom," answered Dan, "and you have to go."

Carolyn looked at her husband and waited for a signal that she should join them, but this was a conversation Jack wanted to end. "Honey, I'll be right out."

After Carolyn was gone, Dan could hardly contain his frustration. "Dad, you just heard Mike, whom you got a job and a lot of high-profile exposure at Eastman & Maxwell, tell you that at the eleventh hour, he had decided not to work there, but at another firm, which you called a 'bucket shop.' And, if that wasn't enough, he told you that he had accepted the offer before he even consulted with you. You wished him good luck and told him that if he wanted to reconsider, you would get him a job at a more prestigious firm in New York."

Dan looked down. His voice was more pleading than accusing. "You even told him you'd be his first client…why can't you be that supportive of me?"

Jack sensed that his son was caving in so he switched to a less strident tone. "Michael is making a huge mistake, a terrible mistake, the kind of mistake that will affect the rest of his life. But I'm not his father. He's never shown me the respect of someone whose advice he trusted or even wanted. What am I going to say, 'Don't go; let me tell you why it's stupid to take a job at that firm?' Dan, I'd be wasting my breath. What you're calling support is just indifference at this point. You, my son, are a different matter. I love you."

Jack sighed. He could see he wasn't getting through. "I've got to go. Trust me, you'll be fine when you've had a breather this summer. In the meantime, let's not upset your mother with all this, OK?"

Dan and Jack were looking at each other. They had heard each other's arguments, but neither one had changed his mind. Neither one trusted the other to say what was really on his mind.

"I'll think about what you've said, but I have to tell you, right now, I feel the same as when we started this conversation. I won't say anything to Mom before graduation. I'll have decided by then what I'm going to do."

"Sure, pal. We'll talk when you get to the beach. I know

you'll see things differently."

They both stood up. Jack put his arm around his son. "I love you, Dan. I only want what's best for you."

◧ ◧ ◧

Michael was driving, racing along Interstate 85 toward Durham. He was genuinely interested in what had happened after he had left Dan with his father in the library, but mostly he wanted to get back to the apartment and finish packing. "It sounds to me like he talked you out of it."

"No," said Dan, staring straight ahead. "It was more like a stalemate. They were on their way to some dinner. It just wasn't a good time to talk about it."

"Hey, whatever," was all Michael said as he turned up the radio.

It was 7:30 when they arrived at the apartment building with the U-Haul trailer, 9:30 by the time they had the last of the boxes crammed in with the furniture. "C'mon. Let's get something quick to eat. I'm starved," said Michael as he secured the padlock on the back door.

They sat in a booth at Spiro's and had pizza and beer, a college staple, a ritual to mark the end of an era.

"I guess this is the last time we'll eat this grease." Dan was suddenly struck by the sense of "last" things: their last drive to Durham; their last night in college together; maybe their last night together. "*Maybe I should tell him,*" Dan thought. "*How would I say it? What would he say? Would he still want me to come to New York? What if he didn't? Then what would I do?*"

"Are you all right?" Michael asked.

"Yeah, I'm just thinking."

"You think too much." Michael smiled, but Dan didn't smile back. "Hey, Dan, I want you to come to New York, but it's OK if you don't. We've been brothers for twenty years. We'll always be brothers." Michael saw that Dan was staring off somewhere and he saw what looked like tears beginning to well in Dan's eyes. "Christ, you're not all right. Buddy, what's wrong?"

"Nothing," Dan said as he wiped some tomato sauce off his face and blew his nose. "I want to go with you, you know, now. I want to get out of here. I feel desperate."

"It's up to you," Michael said. "I'm leaving at five tomorrow morning. You don't have much stuff, but there's no way we're gonna fit another thing in that trailer. Graduation is in two weeks. You said you would hang around for that so your mother would be happy. I'll have an apartment in New York by then. If I get a one bedroom, I'll make sure it's big enough for two beds. But for Christ's sake, don't let your father railroad you. After graduation, just tell him you're leaving and leave."

"Yeah, sure. That's what I'll do."

"Hey, Dan, it'll be great. We'll be stars up there." Michael could see Dan was still staring out the window. "There's a party at Jen's. Let's go hang out there for a while."

"No, I'd rather go back to the apartment. I feel like smoking a joint."

"Dan, in case you didn't notice, there's no furniture in the apartment except for your desk, the stereo rack, and your bed."

"That's OK," said Dan. "We can sit on the floor. I don't care. I don't feel like going out." Dan looked across the table at Michael. "*Why don't I tell him?*" he thought. "*No, no, I can't. Then I would have no one.*"

"Fine with me," said Michael. "Let's go."

They sat on the floor in the nearly empty living room of the apartment and got high. They talked about their lives, reminisced about being boys at St. Alban's. They laughed. Finally, when it was after midnight, Michael said he had to get some sleep. "I've got a twelve-hour drive ahead of me. Let's pick this conversation up in three weeks. OK?"

They had slept together many times in the twenty years since they met as boys and there was nothing unusual about their sleeping together that night. Michael could tell that Dan was still restless. "Don't worry, Dan, everything'll work out. I'm telling you we're gonna kick ass."

"Yeah, sure, Mike. Mike…"

"Yeah."

"I love you."

"I love you too, Dan. You're the only person who under-stands me. I'm glad you're coming to New York. I hoped you would. Good night, man."

In a little while, Dan could hear Michael snoring. Dan lay there, awake, staring up at the ceiling. He was stoned. He could-n't sleep. He sat up and looked over at Michael, the most beau-tiful human being he had ever seen. He thought about reaching over and touching him. But he couldn't. And when he couldn't take the torment any longer, he got up, closed the bedroom door, and went out to his desk. He sat there. In the light from the streetlamp that came through the window, he could see pic-tures of himself and Michael. And there, pinned up with the pic-tures, was a poem his mother had sent him.

> sitting silently
> doing nothing
> spring comes
> and the grass grows by itself

He put his elbows on the desk and his hands on his forehead and cried. He kept on crying until some extraordinary capacity to deny the obvious brought him back to the notion that in time, when they were in New York, things might work out for him and his dreams might come true. Dan went to the bathroom and splashed some cold water on his face. Then he went and lay down next to Michael and fell asleep.

◼ ◼ ◼

Carolyn woke early on Saturday morning. She sat up in bed, lis-tening to the familiar sound of her husband's breathing and watched the sun come up over the ocean. She knew Jack was exhausted because he was usually awake before her. On the way to the airport, on the plane to Wilmington, before and after dinner, she accumulated the details of Jack's conversation with Dan and Michael the way an anthropologist collects small fragments from an ancient dig site. It frustrated her that she had to drag information out of her husband when it related to a subject he didn't feel like discussing.

"Look, honey, it's simple," he said. "Michael is leaving the nest. That's not a bad thing. Dan got cold feet about going to business school and thought about going to New York with Michael. I talked him out of it. Case closed."

She wondered what he thought as he was lying there. Did he dream sweet dreams, or were there problems to fix and things to build in that place called sleep where most people go to rest? The sunlight filled their room. He opened his eyes and smiled at her. He drew himself close to her, put his head on her lap and his arm around her. She ran her fingers through his hair.

"How long have you been awake?" he asked. Even from his first moment of consciousness, he measured things.

"Oh, I don't know. I didn't notice the time. I watched the sun come up. I've been thinking about Dan. He looked so unhappy yesterday."

"Sweetheart, don't worry. By the time he left, I had him back on track."

"Jack, he's not a train."

"I know that. But you know what I mean. I just think he's run down and he needed to get pointed back in the right direction."

"Yes, he seems tired, but I'm talking about something else. It really hit me yesterday when I saw him in the library. He's unhappy. He's been unhappy for a long time. I should have canceled dinner last night. We should have stayed and talked to him."

"Carolyn, I can see what's happening. He's led a sheltered life. He's been a boy with his best boyhood friend, and now his best friend is leaving. Dan's facing the reality of becoming a man. Trust me, it's normal to be anxious about this stuff. Neither of us would be doing him a favor if we start treating him like he's a kid with a runny nose."

He saw the pain in her face and he knew that his answer

hadn't satisfied her. "Look, I promise I'll talk to him. We can both spend some time with him when he comes here after graduation... OK?... Now, speaking of needing some tender loving care, kiss me and tell me how crazy you are about me."

In their conversation, they had come to the edges of what separated them; each strained, one harder than the other, to reach across the distance. Their words failed, as words ultimately do. But when they kissed, their passion filled the gap.

His drive, his potency, were aligned with his physical strength and his professional success. After so many millennia, men still go out from their homes to stalk the woolly mammoth. Jack had returned, from the hunt, ready to complete the demonstration of his virility.

It is ironic that the word "consummate," which describes the sexual fulfillment of a marriage, has the same root as the word "consume." When they made love, in ways that went beyond the mechanics, he took her in. He lay on top of her, wrapped his arms around her, he opened his mouth and kissed her, he consumed her.

There was no part of her husband's body that Carolyn did not know intimately. His lips, his skin: the softness of it in places, the contrast with the strength of his body. She touched it all, tasted it all, and loved it all. Of the two of them, she was more inclined to want to shrink the distance between them, to be sad when she would try and fail. But she was mostly sad to think that Jack accepted the limitations of their relationship and that perhaps he was even content to live with them.

Carolyn was not as likely to initiate sex as Jack was and, when she did, it would usually be some oblique reference, a coded message before bed, like: "I'm going to take a shower. Do you think I should shave my legs?" Jack was more likely to say something like, "Hey, sweetheart, wanna fuck?"

She tried to interest him in books she read about improving relationships. One book was about sex and karma. "Or was it," he would ask, "sex and chakra or sex and tantra? Honey, the last thing I need is advice on sex from a short guy named Rajeev who thinks that drinking his own piss is healthy."

The closest he ever came to getting third-party information on sex was when he started reading *Men's Health* magazine. He had been fully operational since he was a teenager and there are some things that some men just have a knack for. He couldn't understand why men worried at all about how big they are. He kidded with her that if he thought at all about changing his sexual dimensions, he'd go looking for a plastic surgeon who could make his tongue a few inches longer.

They stayed in bed until it was time for lunch. In the afternoon, they went for a walk on the beach. That's how she knew for sure he was in an exceptional mood. If he made it to the beach at all in the last few years, it was usually to sleep. In bed, on the couch, in a deck chair, or on the beach, it didn't matter, the preferred activity was sleep. He walked with her, but only after a lot of prodding, sometimes bribery, and occasionally playful blackmail.

It was a glorious, warm, sunny day, still several months before the season started. They had the beach to themselves. She collected shells and stones as they walked, gifts from the sea to decorate the windowsills. There was something on her mind and she was trying to think of how to bring it up. She knew Jack didn't give straight answers to direct inquiries. So she had to plan how she was going to dig for information. In rare moments of honesty with herself, she would admit to having grown tired of what often passed for communication between them—a lot of work for small fragments of the truth.

"I gathered from your conversation with Walter Weckstein at dinner last night that your takeover may be a bigger risk than you first thought."

"Oh, I don't know, sweetheart. Walter's a lawyer. His firm has been our local counsel for years. I think he's a little sore that we got New York counsel for this deal."

"Jack, you've heard me say this before, but I swear it's true. I learn more about what's going on from what you say to other people than from what you tell me. I only knew this deal was in the works from what I heard you tell Fred Bonham over the phone."

"Well, it's been a very fluid situation. I guess I haven't tried to give you the Headline News, up-to-the minute details."

"I haven't asked for that, Jack. It's just that Walter sounded very worried last night. You used to pay careful attention to what he had to say. When he asked you if you were biting off more than you could chew, it sounded like he thought you were."

"Oh, I know. I know what he thinks. And I'm sorry if you feel left out. Let me put it this way. The bank can't stay the way it is."

"But Walter was saying you had other options besides taking on New York Trust."

"I know. I know. I have lots of options, especially in the eyes of the people who don't have to live with any decisions, but I want to tell you something else." Jack stopped and put his hands on her shoulders as if to brace her while he delivered the news. "I want to get out, Carolyn. When this deal is done, we'll spend a few years consolidating things. I know who the next CEO of the bank is going to be. I'll let him run the place. Blake and I can sit back and wait for the next move, which is to sell the whole thing."

"Jack, what are you saying?"

"Don't you think I know what kind of life I have? We fly around in a private jet to places most people only dream about. But don't you realize I can see what's going on? My children are growing up like strangers to me. My daughter can't stand to be in the same room I'm in. My son won't talk to me. Do you think that's my idea of being a parent? When was the last time you and I spent a day together like today?"

"Jack, I don't see what that has to do with your taking such a big risk on this deal. I hear what you're saying about why you need to make the deal in the best interest of the bank. And of course I'm happy to hear that you want to get out of the rat race you've been in, but you're talking about a plan that will take four or five years to complete. Jack, Dan is twenty-two. Julie is seventeen. Your kids won't keep fresh in the refrigerator until you're ready. They're not growing up. They've *grown* up. Dan tried to talk to you yesterday. You brushed him off."

"I didn't brush him off."

"OK, fine. You go ahead and tell yourself that you had a two-way conversation with him. Listen to yourself, Jack. You just said it would take years to straighten out the consolidation of the banks. You have this grand plan to get out of it all, but first you have to get in deeper. Have you ever heard the expression, 'The operation was a success, but the patient died?' Jack, I love you. I know that you are really trying, but please don't ask me to pretend not to see what is happening."

"I'm not asking you to pretend anything, Carolyn. I'm asking for your help. I'm dealing with this the only way I know how. I need a few months to get this deal squared away… In the meantime, I don't want Dan to do anything stupid. When the merger is done, I'm going to take some time off. We should plan a trip somewhere."

He realized that he still had his hands on Carolyn's shoulders, holding her at arms' length. There was nothing left for either of them to say. He drew her close. They held on to each other. They were both afraid. She had been the one to push the conversation to the brink, but now they were both equally willing, perhaps even eager, to back down to a place more familiar, if not more comfortable.

"C'mon," said Jack, 'let's go back to the house. I want you to lie down next to me. I need you."

FRICTION

After graduation, Dan was alone in the apartment. His family had driven up for the commencement events, the pictures, the luncheon, the pomp and ceremony, and then they went back to their own distractions. He had planned to tell them he was leaving straight from Durham to New York. But everyone, except Dan, was so busy being happy about his accomplishments and bright future that there just wasn't the right opportunity to break the news. So now the plan was to drive to the beach, get it over with, and then get a connecting flight from Wilmington.

There were still a few of Michael's things in the closet, a few more in the laundry. Through sixteen years of school, they had worn each other's clothes, but he always knew which socks or underwear or shirts or whatever belonged to him and which to Michael. It was this sense of separateness that he had struggled for so long to overcome. To his emotional despair and psychological isolation was added the undeniable reality of now being physically alone.

It was ironic that when everything else had fallen away and Dan came to face himself, he saw his life so clearly. Now he couldn't believe that he had stayed for so long on the path his father had chosen, almost talked into another two years of someone else's life. He had been trying to get to a breaking point gradually, to work his way into a change, waiting until the conditions were more favorable. Then, in an instant, none of that mattered at all.

As he was packing, he played a recording of Handel's *Messiah*. It was a family tradition to attend the annual performance by the Charlotte Symphony. He still knew most of the words by heart, an unusual choice of music for the time of year, but perfect for his state of mind—Christmas in June. It was hot.

Wearing just his briefs, taking things off the shelves, wrapping them in newspaper, he was sweating. His hair was wet. The stereo was blaring and he sang as loudly as he could, packing away the things of his life: pictures, trophies, mugs, books, banners. He sat down on the floor, breathing heavily from stacking boxes, and listened to the music as he took in his apartment, an empty shell except for the boxes, the stereo, and the dust.

Behold I show you a mystery
We shall not all sleep
But we shall be changed
In a moment, in the twinkling of an eye
For the trumpet shall sound
And the dead shall be raised, incorruptible
And we shall be changed

By the late afternoon, everything was in the car. He dropped the apartment keys at the management office and, walking out, bumped into a fraternity acquaintance.

"Hey, Dan, you all packed up?"

"Yeah, I'm on my way to the beach."

"Good luck at B-school."

"I'm not going. I've decided to go to New York and get a job."

"Gee, that's sudden. What happened?"

"I guess I changed. I mean, I changed my mind... I'll see ya!"

"Yeah, good luck, whatever!"

He took one last unsentimental look speeding along Erwin Road to the Freeway. The top of the car was down. His shirt was off and the late afternoon sun felt good on his shoulders. He could barely hear the engine over the blare of the car's stereo system.

Hallelujah, hallelujah!
Hallelujah, hallelujah!

It was late on Friday night. He saw Julie's car in the driveway, but not Carolyn's, no sign of either of them or his father in the house. He went straight to the refrigerator:

Dan,

I left this note where I was sure you would find it! Welcome home. I'm in Wilmington at a club where Julie's band is playing tomorrow night. I tried to call you in Durham but your phone's been shut off since last week. We'll be back very late so don't wait up for us.
Love, Mom

He sat down with his second dinner and called the number in New York. He got an answering machine.

"Mike, this is Dan. Listen, I've decided to go for it. I'm going to tell my dad over the weekend. My flight gets in around two on Monday. I hope your place is big enough for both of us."

It was about eight-thirty on Saturday morning when Dan went downstairs and found Julie showing off what she would be wearing at the club later that evening.

"My God, Julie," said Carolyn, "that dress looks almost feminine. What happened to the combat fatigues?"

"I think she looks great," Dan said, as he walked into the kitchen.

"Hey, Dan, how are you?" Julie asked, giving him a kiss.

"I'm so glad you're here," said Carolyn. "I was trying to call you last week because I wanted to be sure you'd get here in time."

"In time for what?" Dan asked as he went to the refrigerator.

"To hear your father's big secret. I was trying to get him to tell you at graduation, but he said he couldn't talk about it yet, not even with you."

"Talk about what?" Dan sat down at the table and emptied a half a box of cereal into a mixing bowl and poured a quart of milk over it.

"He's making a big announcement at the annual meeting, something about buying another bank. We're all flying back early Monday morning to be there."

Dan didn't look up from his cereal. "Well, I have an announcement too. I'm leaving on Monday morning. I'm not going to B-school, at least not next year, maybe not ever."

"Uh-oh," Julie sighed.

"Honey, isn't it a little late in the process to be changing your mind?"

"It is late to be pulling out, Mom. I'm not happy about the timing, you know, handling it this way, but I'm just coming back to where my mind was before Dad talked me out of it. I'm going to take at least a year off."

"You know your father won't be happy to hear that… I guess we'll just deal with it when he gets here."

"No, Mom. *I'll* deal with it when he gets here."

"OK," said Carolyn. "Let me put it a different way. You get to tell him, but we all have to deal with the consequences."

"So, what are you going to do instead?" asked Julie.

"I'm going to New York."

Julie smirked at Carolyn while Dan was looking down, eating his cereal. Carolyn frowned back at her and then Julie asked the next obvious question.

"So, where are you going to live?"

"I'm going to stay with Mike. He's got an apartment already."

Julie rolled her eyes. Carolyn frowned even harder.

"Mom, Dan and I are going for a walk. What time did you say Dad is coming?"

"He's flying with the Wecksteins on the ten o'clock from Charlotte and they're going to drop him here, so I'm expecting him for lunch. You know, Dan, it's probably not the best time to break this news to him."

"There's never a good time to tell Dad anything he doesn't want to hear. C'mon, Julie, you said you wanted to go for a walk."

They made their way onto the beach and out toward the surf. *"They're so beautiful,"* Carolyn thought as she watched Dan and Julie. *"Why can't we just let them be?"*

They headed north along the beach for a while without saying anything. Julie was so much younger and yet light-years ahead of Dan in self-confidence. She'd poked fun at her older brother's stiffness ever since they were children. Now she sensed that this was not the time for teasing.

"You know it won't be so bad, Dan. I mean, at least you don't have to live with him like I do. After you deliver the news, you won't have to even see him."

"I don't dislike him like you do, Julie. Actually there have been lots of times when we got along fine."

"Come on, Dan, be real. You get along with Dad when you're doing as you're told. It was easier when you were a kid and Dad said it was time to get a haircut. Big dif' when you're talking about what to do with your life."

"I'm not going to argue with you, Julie. He's given me a lot of good advice and just because I take some of it, doesn't mean he's wrong or I can't make up my own mind."

"Dream on, dream on." Julie sighed, then took his hand in hers and gently swung it forward and back again like they did when they were children. It was low tide and the water was only a few inches deep for a long way out. The waves didn't come in breakers, but in sheets, led by shallow ripples making irregular patterns as they flowed to the shore.

They sat down on the sand, Dan with his legs stretched out and crossed and his arms like two tent poles behind him. He stared out at the ocean. Julie lay on her stomach, her head resting in Dan's shadow. They didn't talk for a while.

"What's going on with your band?" he asked.

"We're doing OK. I think we're getting a little stale in Charlotte, or I don't know, maybe it's just that Carlos and I are getting stale... Are you going to New York because you and Michael are an item?"

"Julie, for Christ's sake." Dan sat forward and brushed the sand off the palms of his hands. "Where do you come up with this shit?"

"So," she said, undeterred by Dan's attempted deflection, "you're going to New York and you haven't even told him?"

"Told him what?"

"That you're in love with him."

Dan pulled his legs up and put his elbows on his knees. He leaned forward and rested his head in his hands. He took a deep breath. "No… No, I haven't told him."

Julie rolled over on her back. She rested her head in his lap and looked up. "Do you think maybe you haven't told him because you know he doesn't feel the same way about you?"

Dan frowned. "Maybe. I don't know. I don't know anything. I don't know what the fuck is going on in my life anymore."

"Well, if you want my opinion, he's straight, but there's only one way to find out. Just tell him how you feel. Dan, you're twenty-two years old. You're a really smart and good-looking guy. You worry about Michael like you worry about Dad. You're always waiting for the right moment. Blurt it out and then live with it. Be yourself."

"I might do that if only I could figure out who I am."

"Getting out of here is a start. I'm not sure moving in with Michael is such a great idea, but hey, if that's what you're feeling, go for it."

"How is it that at seventeen you're so sure of everything and I'm still flailing around?"

"You made it easy for me," said Julie. "You've always been the science experiment Mom and Dad obsessed about. You've been trapped in one of those sterile glass dishes. They gave up on me pretty early. I smashed every container they tried to put me in. So I got more fresh air."

"Come on," said Dan as he got up. "Let's go. It's my turn for fresh air."

They were not in a hurry as they walked back to the house. Dan put his arm over Julie's shoulder and drew her close to him, as much for luck as for comfort.

◣ ◣ ◣

Jack O'Brien had his jacket off as he paced back and forth in the kitchen, the portable phone to his ear, his white shirt unbuttoned at the collar, and his tie at half mast. He looked strangely out of place in his own house.

"Fred, what do you mean we haven't got the filing right? For Christ's sake, we've been screwing with that document for a month. I'm supposed to be calling Carlton Moore at home tomorrow night to tell him he's lunchmeat, and you're telling me some pencil-necked geek lawyer can't get the fucking form into the SEC. No good, Fred. No good. You call Henry Bradford and tell him I'm gonna burn his goddamned house down if I have to go in front of a shareholders' meeting on Monday with nothing but my dick in my hand... Fine. I'll expect to be on the phone with you and Henry at eleven."

"Gee, Dad," said Julie as she and Dan walked in on the end of Jack's call, "I'd hate to see you with nothing but your dick in your hand."

"Julie, I haven't got time for your crap." Jack stormed across the kitchen and hung up the phone. "Your brother and I have something important to talk about."

Julie and Dan glared at Carolyn, who stared back, but said nothing.

"C'mon, son, let's go outside." Jack went out to the deck. Dan followed and closed the glass doors behind him.

From the kitchen, Julie and Carolyn could see them sit down at a table on the deck. They sat across from each other, the way the Russians and Americans did in the Cold War. Jack didn't wait for Dan to give him the news, he didn't have to, so he started to speak in slow, measured tones, the way he always did when he talked Dan into or out of something.

"Why did you tell him?" Julie asked.

"I don't know," said Carolyn. "I was just trying to help."

"You didn't. You should have let him tell Dad himself."

Through the glass they could see Jack pacing back and forth. Dan was still seated at the table, his hands folded in front of him.

"Maybe I should go out there," Carolyn said.

"Don't be ridiculous, Mom," Julie said, as she went over to the stove. "Do you want some tea?"

Julie and Carolyn tried to pretend they were not looking out the window as Jack and Dan talked. Actually, Jack did most of the talking. Then Dan got up from the table and, even from inside the storm-proof house, they could tell he was angry and shouting. The muscles in his forearm were tense as he pointed his index finger at his father. Saliva sprayed in the air with every invective, the way mist rises from waves when they crash against rocky cliffs.

Carolyn was heading for the door. Julie cried, "Mom, don't!" Then the phone rang. Carolyn stopped and picked it up.

"Hello... oh, Fred, yes it's me... No, he can't come to the phone right now... I understand Fred. I'm sure it's urgent, but he really can't come to the phone... What?... Uh-huh... uh-huh... You're sure this can't wait ten minutes?... OK. No. No. It's OK, I'll get him." She turned smugly to Julie. "I have to go out there."

When Carolyn opened the door, she smelled the sea air and heard the sound of the wind and the waves because there was a momentary pause in the verbal shelling. Before she could interrupt, Jack let go a barrage.

"This is the stupidest fucking thing I've ever heard in my life. Forget about the humiliation you'll subject me to. Just forget about that. Can't you see it's you I'm worried about?"

"Jack... Jack!" Carolyn shouted. "It's Fred Bonham on the phone. He says it's urgent. He says it can't wait five minutes. He needs to speak to you right now."

Jack didn't even acknowledge Carolyn as he walked past her into the kitchen. Dan was standing at the rail of the deck. He flinched when she came up behind him and put her hand on his shoulder.

"What did you say to him?" she asked.

"What difference does it make? He's incapable of hearing anything I have to say."

Julie joined them out on the deck. "Hey, Dan, do you want

to go for a ride or something?"

"No, I'd like to be left alone for a while. Maybe I'll go for a swim. I might get lucky and drown."

Carolyn was shocked. "Honey, don't even think things like that."

"Well, in case you don't drown," Julie said, "come to my show tonight. I have to leave at five to go set up. Or you can drive out later with Mom."

"Oh, Julie, I won't be able to make it tonight, not with your father worked up like he is," Carolyn said. "Dan, why don't you go with Julie? You haven't heard her sing in a while."

"OK," said Dan, "I'll be ready to go any time you are." He walked down the stairs and out to the beach.

When Julie went looking for Dan, he was lying on his bed, staring up at the ceiling, changed and ready to go. They were walking through the great room when Jack emerged from his study, still dressed in the same shirt, his tie in the same position, as when he had arrived.

"Where are you going?" Jack said as he wiped the sweat from his forehead. "We're not through."

"I'm through, Dad. There's really nothing left to say. I asked you to help me with the deferment. I realize now that was a huge mistake. I should have just told you then that I didn't want to go at all. I never should have applied. I'm leaving for New York on Monday."

"And you think that's it? You think you're going to go to New York and get a job and support yourself? And I do hope you mean support yourself, because if you think I'm underwriting this plan, you really have lost a screw."

"Dad, lots of guys with no family connections find jobs. And as for money, I never asked you for money in April and I don't want any now. I only wanted you to understand."

"Understand WHAT? Understand that you're behaving like a fool. That I understand. Everything else I just don't get."

"Dan, I have to go." said Julie. "If you want to stay here and talk, that's OK with me."

"No," Dan answered, staring at his father. "We're done talking. Let's go."

For another instant the three of them stood there, frozen in a triangle.

"Son," said Jack. He sounded hoarse. He swallowed before he continued. "I haven't had any sleep in almost a week. On Monday, I'm announcing one of the most important transactions in U.S. banking history. I have to go back to Charlotte tonight. Let's pick this up on Monday, right after the annual meeting."

Dan was shaking his head, an involuntary reaction. "There's no way I'm showing up at any meeting in Charlotte on Monday."

"OK. OK." Jack sighed. He was exhausted, but his mind was racing. "I understand, this is important to you... I can fly back here Monday. We can talk about this, work things out..."

"No. I'm leaving Monday morning." Even as the words were leaving his mouth, Dan couldn't believe that he was actually saying them.

There was only so far that Jack would let himself be pushed. "I know you're upset, but if you leave before I get back, you're on your own... You have to understand that."

"I'm sorry. I wish you understood that being on my own is what I really want.... Good luck with... whatever it is you're doing. Come on, Julie, let's go."

Julie followed Dan through the kitchen and out to the garage. They didn't say another word. They got in Julie's car and drove away.

When Carolyn came down from the widow's watch she found Jack changing his clothes in their bedroom.

"I have to go back to Charlotte tonight. The SEC filing on the New York Trust deal is all screwed up. The *New York Times* is reporting the deal in tomorrow's paper. The directors, the

lawyers, the investment bankers, all of us, are getting bombard-
ed with calls. Carlton Moore has called the house in Charlotte.
I can't manage the situation from here."

"Did you talk to Dan?"

"Not really. I've been on the phone with Fred and the
lawyers. So, while all hell's breaking lose, I asked my son to wait
'til Monday night when I can get back here to talk... You wanna
know what he did? He went off with Julie. He said he's leaving
Monday. I told him he was on his own."

"Jack, don't you think that's extreme? He's not joining a cult.
He's going to New York to get a job."

"He's doing this to spite me. He's screwing up everything
I've done for him. I won't accept that. I can't accept that." Jack
sat down on the bed and put his head in his hands.

She went over to him and touched his shoulder. "I'm sure he's
not doing this to spite you. I'll spend some time with him tomorrow. I think I can work out something with him. We'll all be there
on Monday morning and you two can patch things up. OK?...
Are you on the commuter or is Fred sending a plane for you?"

"He said the Citation would be in Wilmington at six."

"I'll make something for you to eat and we can talk on the
way to the airport. You must be starved."

He stood up and hugged her. "I love you."

"I love you, too," answered Carolyn.

She left him to finish dressing and went downstairs.

◤ ◤ ◤

Julie was five years younger, three inches shorter, and at least
fifty pounds lighter than her big brother. She fit easily in the
Miata convertible her parents had given her for her seventeenth
birthday. Dan sat cramped and uncomfortably sideways in the
passenger seat, leaning against the door, watching the way the
wind rearranged Julie's hair. They were driving north toward
Wilmington at sunset. The sunglasses kept the hair out of Julie's

eyes. A few times she casually pulled it back behind her ears, but then the wind sent it all flying again. Dan thought she looked like Audrey Hepburn.

They didn't talk. He wondered what she was thinking. He used to think of her as a rebel, who would, if she could, change the world, or at least change her family. But it suddenly occurred to him that she was not like that at all. She had no interest in establishing a new order for anyone else.

◣ ◣ ◣

Julie had been a big baby, weighing just over nine pounds in 1978 when she was born. Carolyn swore that Julie started the delivery process on her own. According to the doctors, she wasn't due for three weeks. Even from the beginning, Julie lived by her own schedule, coming into the world when she was ready.

She started dance classes at six years old. By seven she refused to go on stage at the annual recital. Julie told her mother that she was not into looking "cute and dumb," flung her tap shoes against the wall and said, "If you want taps, then do it yourself!" At nine years old it was piano; at ten, painting. Carolyn tired of trying to get Julie involved in extracurricular activities. Sports were out of the question. She had no interest in anything cultural or involving participation with "boring" people.

By the time she was in the seventh grade, Julie knew what she wanted more than anything: to live in Seattle and join a grunge band. She was five foot eight, with sandy brown shoulder-length hair, one of the most beautiful girls in her class. But she deliberately camouflaged her beauty with her posture—knees forward, slightly bent—and the clothes she wore—the baggiest rags she could find at the secondhand stores.

It was in the tenth grade, when she was fifteen, that she met Sofia Buchanan. Sofia claimed she was a "channel" for Isis and her entire family was psychic. "Julie, you can sing, right?" Sofia asked her.

"Yeah, I can sing."

"I knew it. This vibe I'm getting from you is in overload."

Julie's first reaction was to tell this crazy girl to fuck off, but something about her voice, and the look in her eyes, captured Julie's attention.

"Look, I'm getting a larger picture here. I manage a band called Internal. We're rehearsing in my aunt's house on Friday night. Come and sing with us."

A few days later, Julie knocked on the door of Sofia's aunt's house. She didn't know what to make of the woman who opened the door. Her face had fine porcelain doll-like features, which were offset by her salt and pepper hair, pushed back in a short-cropped style and a broad frame of a body. "Hi," she said, "You must be Julie. I'm Ellen. Sofia told me you'd be coming. She's out picking up a microphone cord or something. The band is in the basement. Let me introduce you."

Julie followed Ellen to the back of the house and downstairs to the basement. There, setting up, were Jamal on keyboards, Mack on drums, and Carlos on guitar. "Hi, guys," said Ellen, "this is Sofia's friend, Julie." Julie knew she had finally found a place to belong.

Jamal was silent. He looked mulatto, with slicked-back dark hair and big features. Mack had long dreadlocks, beautiful skin, a mixture of Asian and African American. He stood all of five feet tall.

But it was Carlos who got Julie's attention; shaved head, Dominican bodybuilder type, with tattoos from head to toe. "Sofia says you can sing."

"Yeah, I can sing. Can you play that guitar?" Julie asked.

Carlos wasn't going to be shut up that easily. "Who have you been singing with?"

Julie took off her coat and went up to the mic. "Do you want to start, or not?" She looked at Carlos. "Well?"

"Whoa," said Mack, as he took his seat at the drums.

Carlos kept his icy cool. "We need to know what type of a voice you have. We'll play a round. You sing when you're feeling it."

The band started playing an intense house beat, adding rhythm as if they could feel the music already playing in her mind.

She took the mic and started singing.

Too many voices—too many choices
   living in my head
   living in my head.
Too many voices—too many choices
   living in my head
   living in my head.
Need a place to run to
   need a place to hide
Just to find a place
   to Survive
Just blank faces
   running out of places
Think I'm going to die.

Sofia and Ellen were standing at the top of the stairwell, in shock at what they had heard.

"Stop! Stop!" said Ellen. "Julie, my God, where did you get that song? And your voice, you sound like a wild animal, trapped by something, trying to be free. It's incredible!"

Everyone loved Julie and her sullen hollow voice. Everyone except Jack and Carolyn, who didn't like it...at all. They weren't about to let their teenage daughter perform in clubs, but it was the first time she had been emotionally attached to anything, and the consequences of saying "no" were completely unthinkable. So they negotiated an arrangement that made none of them happy, but it was something that they could all live with. Julie would sing only on Friday and Saturday nights and only in Charlotte, where Carolyn could pick her up. Occasionally, Carolyn went in to hear the last set. She looked out of place, but Julie appreciated, if grudgingly, her mother's effort to be connected to what she was doing.

Dan, of course, missed all of the early performances. He was in France for most of 1994 and by the time he got back in September, he went straight to Durham. He received guardedly enthusiastic reports from his mother. "Dan, I'm not sure what to make of it, but what's come over Julie is incredible. She's so happy with the band." And biting sarcasm from his father. "Your sister's finally gone completely over the edge. She's running with a bunch of lowlifes."

■ ■ ■

The place was called NoNo's. Underneath the name on the sign was an inscription that read, "A bar for real people." It looked like an oversized one-story ranch house in the middle of a dirt parking lot. The front of the building was painted black with a door in the middle. As he got closer, Dan noticed that there were hundreds of what looked like sperm painted in bright colors on the plywood siding, all swimming toward the door.

Inside, Carlos, Mack, and Jamal were finished connecting instruments, amplifiers and power. Dan had already met the guys. He watched them go through the motions of completing the setup, running through a few songs, and then there was a break. To Julie this was already routine, another club, just another gig. She had her sights set much higher.

"We're on from nine 'til eleven, and eleven-thirty 'til one," said Julie. "We'll have time to change and put on makeup after we eat."

They sat in the back room and ate greasy cheeseburgers and fries and smoked a little weed, since no one in the band was old enough to be served from the bar. They talked about getting a CD together, trying to play at bigger places, maybe in D.C. Carlos said he had a cousin with connections in New York.

Dan asked a few questions, but he was mostly listening to the conversation. It seemed to him that Julie's life had the trajectory of an arrow that had escaped gravity. She had, early on, understood the consuming power of resistance. Even the air can be a source of friction, changing kinetic energy into heat.

Objects man-made or otherworldly, trapped in the pull of heavy atmosphere, all eventually fall, leaving brief fiery trails of their descent. So she sought out a life untrammeled by even the least weighty restrictions. *"Julie's already free,"* he thought, *"and she's only seventeen."*

The rest of the evening went by in a blur. He did a few lines with two girls he met while he was waiting for a drink. They sat in the back seat of a car in the parking lot and used a hand mirror and a straw from a juice box. Dan was kissing one of the two and he figured there wasn't any point in putting up an argument when the other one decided to help herself to the bulge in his pants. Neither one of the girls had any interest in letting their catch out of the car, but he explained that it was his sister who was singing and he had to go on back inside.

He spent the rest of the evening sitting at the bar, watching Julie, and trying not to notice the girls pointing him out to their friends. Despite the buzz of the coke, mixed with the beer and the distraction of thinking about going to New York, he was still captivated by the sight of his sister working the crowd.

The last number opened with the stage dark, the music a mysterious blend of instrumentals and animal sounds, as if it were the opening of a movie. The band members were painted in body makeup like reptiles. Julie entered, wood pieces as horns in her hair, hooves for shoes, looking like a centaur.

> I'm a Hybrid—yes I'm a Hybrid
> You can judge me—but I don't care
> I don't live though your fears
> I'm more than woman, I'm part beast
> I'm not pretentious or a freak.
> > I'm more than woman, I'm part beast.
> > That's why I'll never be your bitch!

By the end of the number, the crowd on the dance floor was screaming. A few of the men had their T-shirts off, waving them over heads, as they sang the refrain with Julie, "I'm more than woman, I'm part beast. That's why I'll never be your bitch!"

◨ ◨ ◨

"You were incredible!" he said as Julie was driving back to the house.

"It was OK," was all the reply she cared to make on the subject of her performance. "I saw you leave with those two girls. What was that all about?"

He smiled. He looked out the window, then back at Julie. "It was nothing…. Well, I mean…."

"You don't owe me an explanation. I was just curious… So, your flight is on Monday morning?"

"Yeah."

He looked back out the window just in time to see the flash of a shooting star, burning up as it fell to earth. He felt her reach over to touch his shoulder.

"I'm really happy for you," she said. "Don't worry about Dad. He'll survive."

"Yeah, I guess he'll have to." He reflected on the way he'd apparently glided through life. And now, suddenly, there was this seemingly unavoidable jarring conflict. He had been wondering if he hadn't shielded himself or pretended not to notice the heat. But now he was thinking that there was something more. He couldn't put his finger on it. But it had the feeling of something that was building, an accumulation of pressure that he thought was likely to explode.

CRITICAL MASS

The sun came up indifferent to the cares that darkened the moods of the family in the big house below. Dan and Julie were still asleep. Carolyn was up early, expecting the phone to ring when it did. After knowing her husband for twenty-five years, she figured he would be calling to tell her that he had solved the problem.

"I've been thinking," said Jack.

"Why am I not surprised?" she replied, as she sipped her coffee.

"Let's say it's a lost cause, you know, getting Dan to start business school this fall."

"Instead of just saying it, let's honestly admit it."

"OK. OK," said Jack. He already had a plan worked out. "Even though it's ridiculously late, I can get him a deferment. And let's say if I get him a deferment, he'll agree to go next year."

"Yes," said Carolyn, "I think he might agree to go in a year."

"Do you think there's any chance we can get him to work in Charlotte for a year?"

"Jack, I thought we agreed to keep this conversation in the real world."

The irony of Carolyn's response was lost on both of them.

"OK. Here's the deal. He's got a stock account at Schwab and a checking account at Citibank. The stock account is restricted, but he'll need that for tuition anyway. I checked the account at Citibank. He's got about $6,000 in it. I've been putting in $1,000 a month for spending money. If he agrees to take the deferment and to go next year, I'll up that to $3,000. I'll get him a decent apartment in New York and a one-year job at an AE firm in the city."

"That sounds pretty good, except I don't think he'll need the apartment. He's planning on living with Michael."

"Honey, I know you loved Carla and I don't want to upset you, but I'm telling you, Michael is bad news for Dan right now."

"Jack, I know you love Dan and I don't want to upset *you*, but if there are too many strings on this deal, your son is going to tell you where to get off."

Carolyn waited during the pause, waited for her husband to calculate his next move. "OK," said Jack. "Let's just go for the deferment, and I'll make sure he has a job and enough money to live on."

"What exactly do you mean by 'let's'?" asked Carolyn. "Are you asking me to carry this water for you?"

"Honey, I have a directors' dinner in twelve hours and an annual meeting in twenty-four hours."

"My God, Jack, Dan is your son. Doesn't he come ahead of a business deal?"

"Carolyn, I'm under a lot of pressure. I only want what's best for him and I don't want to see him get hurt. Please… I love him. I just can't be there right now."

"I know you love him. When he gets up, I'll encourage him to do as you suggest, but that probably won't be for another few hours. He and Julie didn't come in until early this morning. Where will you be today?"

"I'll get to the bank about ten and be there until the directors' dinner at seven. I love you, Carolyn."

"I love you too," said Carolyn. She hung up the phone and sat for a while and watched the clouds on the horizon. *"Red sky at morning,"* she thought, *"sailor take warning."*

The house was designed to withstand a hurricane, but open to the flood of light that came with the sunrise over the Atlantic. So it was hard to stay in bed for very long, even for Julie and Dan who had been out late. When they came down for breakfast around 10:00, they were both more relaxed than they had been the day before. They were sitting in the kitchen when Carolyn poured herself another cup of coffee and joined them.

"So how did it go last night?" she asked.

"Julie was great," said Dan. "The place was packed and the audience loved her."

Julie had her face in a book, but Carolyn was accustomed to asking questions more than once. "Julie?"

"It was OK. I liked playing in a new club. The people were more like on vacation, you know. I thought we did OK. Maybe Dad will let us do a gig in New York when Dan is up there."

"Well, I talked to your father about that this morning. I have some good news, Dan."

He listened as Carolyn laid out Jack's proposal. Julie went back to her book. In addition to the deferment, the job, and the money, Carolyn decided to tell him about the apartment that Jack had offered, but only if Dan wanted a place of his own. When she was done, he got up and put his breakfast dishes in the sink. There wasn't anything especially unreasonable about the proposal, but Dan knew his father all too well. "What happens next summer if I'm still sure I don't want to go?"

"Well," said Carolyn, deciding to wing it, "then I suppose we'll just have to deal with that."

"No," said Dan. As he turned around to face her, he leaned back against the counter, his feet sticking to the smooth tile floor. "No, I'll get this agreement thrown back in my face. I'll be reminded that I made a deal. No. No more deals. I don't know what I'm going to do eventually, but I'm absolutely sure I'm going to make my own decisions. No." Dan was shaking his head. "Tell him I said 'Thanks, but no thanks.'"

Dan put his hands in his pockets and looked down at his feet as if he'd been transformed by the conversation into the young boy who once waited in a long line at the state fair and then refused to get on the Ferris wheel.

It wasn't until Julie turned a page that she noticed Carolyn was staring at her. "Don't look at me. Dad is on the Olympic team of manipulation. If I were Dan, I'd be suspicious too."

"You're both missing the point," insisted Carolyn. "Your father loves you both very much. He really is trying to help. Dan, don't just stand there like you're completely blameless in all of this. Maybe he did talk you out of a deferment in April, but the fact is that you went along with it and now your father will be tremendously embarrassed if you announce at the last minute that you're not going. Maybe you think that by offering you an apartment and money he's trying to control you, but look at it from his perspective. He loves you. He's showing it in the way he knows how."

Dan sat down at the table. "If it will help him save face, I'll ask to put off admission for a year. But I won't make any promises about what I might decide to do when I get to New York. I don't want him to get me a job. I don't want him to get me an apartment. I want to get by with the money I have. You can also tell him that I love him too, although I'm sure he won't believe it."

He slid his chair back and the sound of the wood against the tile floor echoed off the walls of the kitchen. The only other sounds were his footsteps and the sliding-glass door closing behind him.

Carolyn sat with Julie for a few minutes. She sipped her coffee and watched her daughter read and turn the pages of her book.

"It just occurred to me," said Julie, "that they're so much alike."

"Whatever do you mean?" Carolyn asked.

"Why are men always trying to prove something? I can see Dan not wanting to agree to take any job that Dad throws at him, but I'd at least let him make some introductions. It's stupid for him not to take the apartment. It's totally moronic for him not to take any money."

"Julie, why in God's name didn't you say that when he was sitting here?"

"Because it wouldn't have mattered. At this point Dan would sleep on the street before he would take any help from Dad. I'm not saying it's smart. In fact, I think it's stupid. But it's a fact, Mom."

"Julie, I asked you a question. Why didn't you tell him that you thought he should take the apartment?"

"Because, Mom," Julie put the book down on the table. She began by slowly annunciating each word in a low voice, "because then I would get involved in a conversation about the reason, the *real* reason, why Dad's offering the help in the first place and why Dan doesn't want it. Dan is going to New York because he wants to be with Michael. He's in LOVE with Michael. Trust me, Mom, Dad has that all figured out."

Julie stood up and started shouting because she could see, reflected in Carolyn's face, gates slamming shut in her consciousness. "Dad wants to give him a job and an apartment and money because he figures if he can't keep him out of New York, he can at least keep him distracted from Michael. Dan knows that and Dad knows. But of course, they're not going to talk about that, because we don't talk about shit like that in this family. That's why you're getting up, and that's why you're walking away from me, because you don't want to talk about it either." The rest of Julie's spleen was vented to an empty kitchen. "That's why I'm staying the fuck out of this pathetic soap opera of an argument!" When she was finished and all she could hear was the sound of her own breathing, Julie sat down and went back to reading her book.

◪ ◪ ◪

It was early in the evening. Julie and Dan had already left for Wilmington. There wasn't anything to set up for the band, but leaving at least relieved them of any obligation to talk. The sun had made its way to the horizon behind the house. Carolyn called it the "pink hour," her favorite time, when the bright blues of midday gave way to softer tones. She knew Jack would be getting dressed at home. She thought about his routine of working out in the afternoon, laying out a suit, shirt, and tie, showering, reading a magazine while he sat for a few minutes with just a towel wrapped around him, then getting dressed. Her husband was a man of regular habits. So she waited until she was pretty sure he'd be downstairs in the library before she called.

"Hi, sweetheart," he said, "how'd it go today?"

"Well, it's funny, I started out talking with Dan, but I wound up arguing with Julie."

"Oh, for Christ's sake, Carolyn, why do you let her get under your skin?"

"I know you've got a dinner to go to and a hectic schedule tomorrow—"

"Don't worry about that, I've got time. Tell me what happened."

"Jack, I think we should just let him go. He's so determined. It's like he has blinders on. He's willing to ask for a deferment, but he won't make any promises that he'll go next year."

"Let me talk to him."

"He's gone to Wilmington with Julie. Jack, he's leaving in the morning. Let's try to make this as civil as possible. He's not joining the Foreign Legion. He's getting a job in New York."

"Goddamnit. I can't believe it. Carolyn, he doesn't have the remotest idea what it's like to be out on his own. I'll fly there tonight. I've got to talk to him."

"Jack, that's ridiculous. He won't even get in until after midnight and don't you have a very important meeting in the morning?" Carolyn waited through the silence, but she could hear him thinking.

"OK. OK. Here's what we'll do. I'll talk to him in the morning, before the shareholders' meeting. I'll say, 'Look, I can be there at three this afternoon.' There's no way he won't wait eight hours for me… I can turn this around."

"I think you're getting overwrought."

"He's my son. What am I supposed to do?"

She sighed and looked out at the surf. She noticed the waves were coming in to wash away the footprints and the sandcastles, all the evidence of anyone who had been there that day. "Maybe nothing," she said, "maybe we're not supposed to do anything."

"I don't believe that," said Jack. "Look, sweetheart, I have to call Carlton Moore, and then I've got the dinner. Just get Dan on the phone in the morning. OK? Everything will be all right. I can handle this. I love you. You're doing great. OK?"

"I love you too, Jack.."

When he hung up the phone, Jack could feel his headache,

not the ordinary kind that pulsated in his temples and went away with four aspirin. He felt the pain at the back of his head, at the base of his brain, where all the involuntary functions are located, and the spot where evolution placed the control center for survival. The pain radiated out from there to his neck muscles. He noticed because he had a hard time holding the phone against his shoulder while he fumbled with his address book.

"Hello, Carlton, this is Jack O'Brien calling... Yes, I'm sorry to be calling you at home on a Sunday evening... I'm fine, Carolyn's fine, we're all fine... Yes... Yes... Well, actually, that's why I'm calling. The rumors are true, Carlton... Uh-huh... Uh-huh... Well, we concluded that the kind of talks we were having were not going to bear fruit, so we're making a formal proposal to you and your shareholders. The papers are being filed with the SEC tomorrow morning. The offer is at a premium to where your stock has been trading, even with... uh... even with the run up over the last week or so... Uh-huh... Uh-huh...Carlton, the offering document is available now, actually. Our lawyers are contacting your people after you and I speak. I'm calling you as a courtesy so you can have some time to look at it before the market opens tomorrow... Uh-huh... I know that's fourteen hours from now. Carlton, it's not a long document... I've got to go... Carlton, I'm sorry you're upset. I think you ought to read what we've presented and then I'm sure we'll work something out that will be beneficial to all of us. Good night."

◣ ◣ ◣

The condition, critical mass, describes the minimum amount of material required to sustain a chain reaction. Anything less and there is a slow, predictable decline in energy. Although the term is usually used in nuclear physics, it really makes little difference whether the subject is atomic or human. When there is an accumulation of the right materials under the right conditions, a chain reaction occurs. All that is left to discover is whether it is the type that powers reactors or explodes bombs.

It was 7:00 a.m. on Monday morning when Carolyn went to wake Dan. The shades were drawn, but there were no drapes in the room so it was already well lit. She stood in the doorway and called his name until the form under the covers began to move.

"Hi, Mom, what is it?"

"Dan, I need to talk to you. Can I come in?"

"Yeah, sure, what time is it?" He sat up, yawned and rubbed his face with the open palms of his hands. "Is something wrong?"

"No, no… I…" She sat down on the edge of the bed. "I talked to your father last night. I explained to him that you wanted to go to New York on your own and that, for now, you want to see how things go without any help from us."

"From him… I said 'from him'" The hair on the back of Dan's neck stood up.

"Dan, he wants to talk to you."

"Mom, there's nothing to talk about."

"There's a very important meeting this morning and he's already upset that we're not all going to be there. He wants to fly here this afternoon. I checked the airline schedule. You could still get a flight early this evening, or even first thing in the morning. He's only asking you to wait a few hours."

"No way, Mom. No way. I know you're trying to help, but you don't get it. If I wait for him, he's not coming here to hear what I have to say. He's just going to try to talk me out of leaving. That's what happened in April. If I stay, we're going to get in a worse argument. If I talk to him on the phone, he's going to lay some big guilt trip on me."

"I don't see the harm in waiting eight hours."

"I'm sorry you don't, Mom. I'm not going to wait and I'm not going to talk about it."

◼ ◼ ◼

"Jesus Christ, I can't believe it!" Jack was practically screaming into the phone. Carolyn had to hold the receiver away from her ear. "My own goddamned son won't even talk to me!"

"Jack, this is getting out of hand. I don't think either of you is thinking straight.'

"Carolyn, I'm so mad, I can't *see* straight. I've never asked that boy for anything and now he won't even get on the phone with me!"

"He's not a boy."

"He's an asshole!"

"Jack, stop! I'm not going to stay on the phone if you keep screaming at me like this. You two need a cooling off period... Let me make a suggestion... You were going to introduce him to a few people in New York. Why don't you let me give him their names and phone numbers? That way you'll know there's at least someone for him to call if he decides he wants some help."

"Carolyn, now I think you need your head examined! Do you really expect I'm going to allow someone else to stand in for me as a father when he wakes up and realizes that he needs some help? The kid needs to find out just how cruel the real world is. But, trust me, he'll never starve. He knows how to get to a phone booth and make a collect call... Sweetheart, I can't believe this is happening. He's never done anything like this before."

"He's never said 'No' to you."

"Eight hours. That's all I asked for."

"Jack, you've got your meeting to go to. I know you both love each other, but this argument has gotten out of control. In a few months, he'll have a job and he'll have settled down and we can all talk to each other calmly... I'm sorry we won't be at the meeting. Are you still coming here tonight or am I not worth rushing back for?"

"Are you kidding, of course I'm flying back tonight. You're all I have."

"Well, that's not true and you know it, but I'm glad you're coming. Call me when you take off from Charlotte. I'll pick you up in Wilmington. We'll go for a walk on the beach. Now it's my turn to tell you everything will be fine."

Carolyn decided to wait for breakfast until Dan and Julie came down. She sat at her desk for a while and looked at framed pictures of Jack and Dan on the beach when Dan was a boy. She noticed an old photo album on the shelf and started to turn the pages. There were pictures of Jack when he was in college and in a few of the photos she saw Steve Baldwin, the man she once loved and who had disappeared from her life. In the spring, she had seen a more recent picture of him in the *Duke Magazine* for alumni and an article about him heading a big law firm in New York. She hadn't seen him in twenty-three years, but she recognized him immediately, before she read the caption.

Breakfast was quiet. By the time Carolyn got downstairs, Julie already knew that Jack had called and Dan had refused to talk to him. Julie never had any interest in attending the annual meeting with her mother, so she was relieved to be let off the hook. It wasn't a long or emotional good-bye between her and Dan. To Julie, life was matter-of-fact.

Dan was starting on his second bowl of cereal when Carolyn came back from walking Julie to her car. She sat and waited for him to say something, but all she heard was the crunching sound of flakes and nuts.

"I hope you don't eat Michael out of house and home."

"Don't worry, Mom. I'll contribute my share for food expenses."

It was Carolyn's turn to talk. As soon as she finished telling Dan about her last conversation with his father, she regretted telling him, especially the part about the world being cruel. She had told Jack that she didn't want to put any "spin" on his proposals, but for most of the last twenty-four hours, she had. She tried to make the best presentation and she urged Dan to see things from his father's point of view. She realized she had been more upset than she realized by the fleeting glimpse of Jack's raw anger, hearing him call Dan an "asshole."

None of what she reported came as a surprise to Dan. His reply was short and simple. "I don't need him to tell me anything about how cruel the world is, and I sure as hell don't want to meet any of his friends." He got up and started to leave.

"Dan, wait, I was thinking that when you get to New York it would be a good idea if you could call someone in case you need some help." She showed him the *Duke Magazine* article and the picture of Steve Baldwin. She told him the story about growing up with him, about what a wonderful man he was, about his friendship and falling out with Jack.

"Are you serious? You can't be serious. I'm not going to call anyone who knows Dad, even a guy he had a fight with before I was born. I mean, the fact that you like the guy, that you were even in love with him, the fact that he maybe doesn't like Dad, that's all in the plus column, but Mom, I don't want a favor from anybody."

It ought to have been simple. She only had to wait for him to come down with his bags and then drive him to the airport. But she went to the phone and dialed New York directory inquiries and got the number and address for Stockton Alpert, the firm where Steve Baldwin worked.

When Dan appeared at the door, she stayed seated at the table with an index card in front of her. "I know you're angry at your father and you don't want any of his help, but I assume you're not mad at me. I'm sure you won't need to call Steven, and maybe you'll never call him. I'd still be a little reassured if I knew you had the number, just in case."

"In case of what, Mom?" He was obviously aggravated.

"Oh, Dan, please. I don't want to argue with you. It's such a small thing to ask you to take one index card with you."

"Mom, I don't want to take the number because I don't want you to be thinking that I might call him…. I have to check one of these bags. If we don't leave now, it won't get on the plane."

The ride to the airport was quiet. They talked a little about Julie and the band. Carolyn had a way of not letting some seemingly small things lie and, almost as a strange corollary, of not talking about major issues that she knew needed resolution. She wanted to talk to Dan about what Julie had said. As they got closer to the airport, she knew she was running out of time.

"Is Michael meeting you?"

Dan was staring out the window. "No, he'll be at work. I'm going straight to his apartment."

"I'm glad you'll have him to show you around. What kind of place does he have?"

"I don't know much about it. He returned my call from a car phone on the way to the Hamptons. He said it's a small one bedroom. I left the address and phone number on your desk... Mom, don't you think it's time you got a new car? I mean, I know Volvos are supposed to last a long time and this station wagon has lots of great memories, but this thing must be twenty years old."

"Your father has been threatening to buy me a new one, but this car gets me where I want to go." Carolyn was only momentarily distracted from her inquiry. "Won't that be kind of cramped?"

"Apartments are expensive in New York. We'll manage."

"You two have always been close. Like brothers."

"Mom, you need to get in the right lane or you're going to miss the exit."

Dan checked his bag while Carolyn parked the car. They went through security and to the gate. The flight was already boarding. He couldn't wait to get on the plane. She was clutching the index card in her hand.

"You have the AT&T card so you can call home anytime. I know you've never used the American Express card, but promise me if there's anything you need, you'll use it. I'll just pay the bill when it comes. No one will have to know." She turned down the collar of his shirt. "Please tell me you'll call as soon as you get settled."

"Mom, don't cry. I'll be fine."

Carolyn was fumbling with her purse, looking for her sunglasses. When she dropped the index card, Dan picked it up as she put the glasses on.

"Now you look like a movie star," he said. He couldn't see her eyes, but he noticed tears were still running down her cheeks. "I'll keep this card if you promise you'll stop crying."

She hugged him. "I love you so much." Maybe it was all the

tension of the last few days, or the sense of having failed at her shuttle diplomacy, or maybe it was just an overwhelming sadness that comes with separation. Whatever the reason, she stood there, holding on, crying. Dan hugged her until the gate agent came around to where Dan could see him.

"Sir, we're closing the flight. If you're going to Charlotte, you need to board the plane now."

Carolyn let go. She took off her glasses and wiped her eyes. "Good-bye, Dan."

"Bye, Mom. Please don't worry. I'll be fine. I'll see you soon. I love you."

◥ ◥ ◥

At ten o'clock on Monday morning, the Joshua Reynolds Auditorium was packed, the standing-room-only crowd anxiously awaiting the start of the annual meeting. The announcement of the NCBT offer for New York Trust had crossed the news wires at 8:00 a.m. The price was $65 for each share of New York Trust common, a 40 percent premium over where the stock was six months earlier, almost 20 percent higher than where it had jumped to when the speculators got wind of the pending offer. In the first hour of trading, the stock rose from $54 to $59, but seemed to stall around $60. This was not a good sign.

Conventional wisdom had it that New York Trust was by no means a dead duck. So when the stock leveled at $60 a share, it was a clear signal that there were still some doubts among smart investors. The mood in Charlotte, however, was positively ebullient. This was the new South, and Jack O'Brien was its rising star. The annual meeting had the feel of a tent revival rather than a sedate corporate gathering. The applause was raucous when the directors came onto the dais and took their seats at a long table.

Blake went to the lectern and tapped the microphone. "Good morning, everyone. I'm Blake Reynolds, the chairman of the board of North Carolina Bank and Trust. I'm glad to see there's so much enthusiasm for the new CD rates we announced in this morning's papers."

Everyone laughed, even the accountants from Coopers & Lyttle, seated in the front row.

"By now you all have heard the news about the branch we're planning on opening up in New York."

Blake worked the audience. He was every inch the perfect southern gentleman banker, with a wit as dry as the martinis he once enjoyed so much. "We do have some other business to conduct this morning and then there's a press conference in the room just across the way, so I'm going to get right to the introduction of our chief executive officer, Jack O'Brien. Jack has been the driving force behind the transformation of our trust company into a major financial institution. So without further ado, ladies and gentlemen, please welcome Mr. Jack O'Brien."

The standing ovation went on for several minutes. It was hard to imagine that in the early eighties the bank had been practically insolvent. Jack O'Brien had long been well known in Charlotte. For years, resentment seemed to stick inextricably with the name recognition. Now, he was being welcomed into the pantheon of the city's business gods.

"Ladies and gentlemen," Jack opened with his trademark smile. "This is a great day for NCBT and a great day for Charlotte." He paused. There was complete silence as everyone waited for him to start speaking again. He looked out across the auditorium and then down again at the words of the speech in front of him. He realized that he was alone, on this day, perhaps the biggest day of his career, of his life. Somehow, things had gotten out of whack. Despite his efforts, his family was not there. "*There was the bombshell from Dan. Maybe I overreacted. I had to fly back early. Then I got caught up in all the meetings, but I held the deal together. The deal! For Christ's sake, they have no idea how important this is.*"

But, of course, there wasn't anything he could do about that now. He swallowed, looked up, and smiled again. "It's an honor to be here. And it's been a privilege to be part of such a great company, a great family… In the last twenty years we have been growing. We have been building a base of capital, of expertise, of strength. Now we are ready to take the next step forward in our development as a world class financial institution."

As he went on, the atmosphere of approval charged him. It flowed from the air into him. He had received the authority to wage corporate war and he was being given the kind of sendoff that Rome once reserved for its most revered generals.

"I'm looking forward to telling you more about the announcement we made this morning. But, before we turn to the business of the bank's future, we do need to spend some time on what happened in 1994. There are several matters to be voted on by the shareholders, including the election of directors and the appointment of our auditors. So I'm going to turn the podium over to our corporate secretary, Mr. Walter Weckstein, of Cummings, Howard & Weckstein."

The rest of the meeting went as expected. There wasn't anything to excite the interest of the crowd like the pending takeover, which was the subject of all the questions from the floor.

When the meeting was over, Jack thanked all the directors, even Blake's sisters and the bank's new director, Carl Herrington, for their support. Then he went across the hall to the press conference, which was packed. The national media didn't seem sanguine that the takeover was a forgone conclusion. John Lawton, chief banking correspondent for *Barron's*, pointed out that the offer was well below the $80 price that New York Trust common stock fetched before its much-publicized derivatives scandal.

Jack handled the questions like he'd been born for the job. He was smooth and confident. It was obvious that he had mastered the numbers. There was no doubt that if anyone could pull off the takeover of a New York money center bank from an out-of-town base, it was Jack O'Brien.

In the back of the room, out of the glare of the TV lights, Blake saw a familiar face.

"Well, Doctor," said Blake, greeting his fellow director, Ron Duby, as if he were asking for a clinical opinion, "what do you make of all of this?"

Ron put his coffee cup down on the table and folded his arms in front of him. He wanted a few seconds to think of something polite to say. "I admire Jack. I believe in his vision. And of course, I respect his capabilities.... "

"But?" asked Blake.

"You and I have been through all this before. This is a running leap into uncertainty. It will either prove to be a stroke of genius or incredible folly. I'm in no position to predict the outcome and I haven't been able to get a clear sense that our CEO is any more certain of this than I am. You know I've never been close to Jack..."

Blake decided not to follow up on the pause. The two men stood there, watching Jack field questions from reporters.

"I guess I think he can do it," Ron continued. "We've never really talked, except at meetings. Ever since I took my father's seat on the board, I've just watched him tackle one challenge after another. Any of us could fault him for being too businesslike, maybe even a little distant, but you know, my family trust is a hundred million dollars richer for having the benefit of his leadership."

"Yes," said Blake. "We're all the beneficiaries of his ambition. But you know what they say about living and dying by the sword..."

As Blake was finishing his sentence, Jack concluded the press conference.

"Well, Doctor," Blake continued, "I believe at this point our instructions are to mingle with the assembled members of the media and exude confidence." Blake gestured. "Shall we?"

PART II

I teach one thing and one thing only:
that is, suffering and the end of suffering.

The Buddha

UNCERTAINTY

As the plane approached LaGuardia, Dan thought about the New World he was entering. On a map, New York looked about six hundred miles from Charlotte. But from his perspective, it was uncharted territory. He remembered the medieval maps in history books, the ones made before circumnavigation proved that the earth was round. At the edges of known habitation, the cartographers printed the warning *Ne plus ultra*, or "Go no further." Beyond the realm of everyday experience, there were dragons and monsters. This was a new beginning and he had adopted the motto of the explorers, *Plus ultra*, or "Go further." Even as he was about to reach his destination, he had no idea where his exploration would take him.

The flight arrived at around 2:00 p.m. and he took a cab to the address in Tribeca, an old brick building with five apartments on each of six floors. It was hot, in the nineties, and humid. It would be another hour until the stock market closed, so he sat on the front stoop and took in the street scene, watching a team of workers emptying the contents of a moving van across the street. His attention was lost watching one of them, muscular physique and skin glistening with sweat. Once when the man was coming out of the building and taking a breather before the next load, he saw Dan staring at him. Their eyes met for only an instant, but Dan was so distracted that he didn't notice the girl coming up the steps.

"Hi, you must be Dan. I'm Angela."

It took Dan a few seconds to come out of his daydream, but he managed to say "Hi."

"I recognized you from the pictures Michael has of you guys. He talks about you all the time. He'll be home in about an hour."

Dan followed her up the six flights of stairs to the rear apartment. It was a small one-bedroom with a galley kitchen.

"You can put your bags down anywhere. The sofa pulls out to a bed. Michael said he'd talk to you about the living arrangements. I'd love to sit and talk for a while, but I need to get ready for class."

She disappeared into the bedroom and shut the door behind her. A few minutes later she came out to apply some makeup in the bathroom mirror. From where he was sitting on the couch, Dan could see her backside, and thick wavy black hair that came down to where her legs met her hips. She was all lines, smooth and shapely ones. He thought she was beautiful. She was too busy to notice that he was staring and too self-absorbed to see that he was in shock. He had just stepped from his world of tormented desperation into his dream, where he would be "living" with Michael, only to find this interloper who would ultimately be nothing but in his way.

When Angela left, he turned on the television and lay with his head and feet over the ends of the couch. He practiced what he would say. It would have been more than understatement to have said, "This isn't what I was expecting. I thought you and I were going to share an apartment." He kept on like this until he heard the familiar footsteps coming up the last few stairs. He was standing when Michael came through the door.

"Hey, man. You're here. Great! You finally got the fuck out of Charlotte." He threw his arms around Dan and squeezed. "I'm so happy for you. You're gonna love it here."

In the moment that Dan had to deliver his prepared remarks, the look of the man in front of him erased everything like a magnet wipes out a recording on a tape. All he could manage was, "Hi, Mike, you look great."

◣ ◣ ◣

In the first week or so, the three roommates tried to get along and settle into a domestic urban routine. On the Fourth of July weekend, they went to clubs, hung out until early morning and then came home; Michael and Angela to the bedroom, Dan to the sleeper sofa.

Dan learned that Angela was an aspiring actress and model who worked the breakfast and lunch shift, three days a week, at a restaurant in SoHo. As far as Dan could tell, that was enough to pay for her makeup and acting lessons. Michael paid for everything else. She had come to New York from Buenos Aires in 1990, when she was eighteen, with an Argentinean delegate to the U.N. She got a green card under circumstances that she only vaguely described as "working connections."

Dan figured out that Angela's survival instincts were as sharply filed as her nails. He thought that she had attached herself to Michael like a tick on a well-fed carnivore. To be fair to Angela, Dan acknowledged that the relationship wasn't entirely parasitic. Angela worked hard at taking good care of her host. At night, Dan could hear her working.

Angela was as observant of Dan as he was of her. She got it, like Julie did, merely by noticing the way Dan looked at Michael. So in no time at all, Angela and Dan recognized each other as competitors. Each wanted the other gone. Michael was oblivious to it all. He was much too wrapped up in his new job, his new life, to notice the subtle tension between his main squeeze and his best friend.

During the day, Dan worked on résumés and cover letters at the Kinko's on Duane Street. He researched job openings at the business library at NYU. After the market closed, Michael and Dan trained at the gym near the apartment. If Angela had an acting class, they just hung out in the neighborhood, but usually they all met back at the apartment for dinner. Frustration was a dish Dan ate cold. Michael talked about getting a bigger place as if it was even a possibility that they would all stay together. Angela and Dan knew something had to give, but neither knew how long things might go on as they were.

It is a common human trait: to want to know when and how something will happen. When Dan followed Michael to New York, he knew that he would tell his friend the truth, but he thought it would be at a time and place of his choosing. He was still trying to come to things in a carefully planned way. But Dan was like a particle, as described by the physicist Heisenberg, whose exact position and momentum cannot be precisely determined simultaneously; only the probability of its location at a particular time can be predicted.

On the weekend after the Fourth of July, there was a break in the heat that had been laying over the city since Dan arrived from Charlotte. Angela left on Saturday morning to spend the night on Fire Island, a chance to meet someone who could help her land a job; at least that's what she told Michael. He didn't care. Dan and Michael hung out for the day. They went to the neighborhood shops for food and supplies; they did the laundry; they talked. They didn't get to the gym until about seven o'clock. They were eating a couple of burritos on a bench in the park near City Hall when a man approached them. Dan wasn't paying attention until he heard the man say something to Michael.

"Hey, are you a porn star?"

Dan looked up. He was sure he must have misheard the man. Michael sounded only a little annoyed when he answered. "What do you want, pal?"

"Would you boys be interested in making some money?"

Michael looked right at him. "What do you have in mind?"

Dan looked over at his friend. He couldn't spit out the food in his mouth, but he couldn't swallow it either. So he just sat there with his mouth full.

The man was dressed in jeans and a banded-collar shirt. He wasn't bad looking, maybe late thirties, early forties. "I have a place around the corner. What would you boys charge to come back and spend some time with me?"

Michael finished taking a sip of his drink and wiped his mouth with a napkin. He answered the question as if the man had asked him for the time. "It's a $1,000 for the both of us for an hour."

Dan held the same bite of food in his mouth without chewing. The saliva was building up. Finally, swallowing became involuntary. He gulped.

The man smiled and looked at them. "That's too much money, even for a couple of good-looking studs like you."

"Then get the fuck away from me, creep!" Michael looked like he was getting ready to hit the guy. His body was coiled.

The man turned and walked away, quickly crossing the street. They were heading back to the apartment when Dan finally spoke. "I can't believe you said that to him."

"Why? It made him go away, didn't it?"

"No," said Dan, "I mean about the money. What if the guy had $1,000?"

"He didn't have $1,000."

"Mike! What if he did?"

"Then we would have gone with him. For $1,000 you could close your eyes for an hour, couldn't you?"

◥ ◥ ◥

After they had showered and changed, around eleven they went out to the Limelight, a club on West Twentieth Street that had been converted from a church. Standing in line, Dan noticed the cornerstone and the brass plaque—the Church of the Holy Communion. The limestone structure had been transformed for worship in a style unimaginable in 1846 when it was built. It looked familiar, like the English Gothic-style chapel at St. Alban's, but nothing could have prepared him for the scene inside.

There were groups of guys and their girlfriends, drinking, laughing, straining to hear each other, standing around the perimeter where once the faithful made the Stations of the Cross. The main dance floor was in the center of the church where the pews had been cleared out. The stained glass windows were back-lit, images of the saints, St. George, frozen in time, slaying the dragon. The apostles and martyrs looked on undisturbed from their vantage points as hundreds of the devoted danced to the blaring music. On what had been the altar, go-

go boys writhed and flexed and added to the effect of flesh worship under the red houselights.

Michael had only been in New York for about two months,
but already he knew where to go, whom to be seen with. Dan
recognized some of the people at the club from the gym, a few
from the neighborhood. It was pretty much a straight club, but
on the dance floor, people mixed, and a few times, Dan and
Michael were dancing with a group. They drank a lot; they had
a good time. Dan got to tell the story about the man in the park.
No one seemed surprised. When they left the club, it was a perfect summer night, warm enough to walk around in a T-shirt. It
was much hotter upstairs when they got home about three
o'clock on Sunday morning; maybe ten degrees warmer than
outside, and the air was very still. There was only one window
fan in the apartment, the one in the bedroom.

"You can sleep in here if you want to," said Michael, as he
turned the fan up high. "I've been meaning to get an air conditioner, but I put it off because I figure we'll be getting a bigger
place soon."

They got undressed and lay on top of the sheets. Dan had
his arms folded behind his head, staring up at the ceiling. He
looked over. Michael was on his stomach. His eyes were closed.

Dan whispered. "Mike, I need to talk to you." Then he
raised his voice, but only a little. "Mike? Hey, Mike." Michael
was asleep. And then, as he had so many times before, Dan
thought, "*Later*," and he turned over and went to sleep.

Dan would ask himself, whenever he remembered that
night, what it was that woke him up. At first, he noticed the
heavy left arm lying over his shoulder. In his half-dreaming,
half-waking, he felt hard pulsing flesh against his lower back,
then teeth and a tongue on the skin of his shoulder. He'd had a
lot to drink, so as he woke up, slowly, he was disoriented. "*Oh
my God*," he thought, "*is this really happening? I can't believe
this is happening.*"

It was as if every nerve ending in his body was sensing something and trying all at once to send a signal to his brain, which,
in the rush of sensation and the fog of semiconsciousness, dared

not send any instructions to move, lest the dream be jarred. Michael's leg was partly over Dan's. He could feel Michael's feet. His ankles were pressed together from the weight. He couldn't move. He felt Michael's hand reach up and take his hair, pulling his head back. He felt an open mouth on his neck and a tongue that darted serpent-like and then caressed softly in places where teeth had left small imprints.

He leaned against Michael, who rolled away and onto his back. He turned and then pressed his body against Michael's. Dan kept saying to himself, "*I can't believe this is happening.*" There was no part of Michael's body that Dan didn't want to touch, but most of all, he wanted to kiss and when he did, he had to stop, to catch his breath and to look at Michael's face. His mouth was partly open, his lips wet where Dan's mouth had just been. His eyes were closed.

Apart from the rapture of being in the moment, Dan increasingly felt two other more ordinary but undeniable sensations. One was an awful headache that was obviously the beginning of a hangover. The other, as he pressed against Michael, was an immediate need to empty what felt like a gallon of beer from his bladder. He whispered, "I'll be right back."

When he returned, Michael was on his side, with the sheet pulled over him, facing the wall. He knew Michael was asleep because he could hear the familiar snoring. He got under the sheet and curled his own body against the outline of Michael's. He tried to wake Michael, first by whispering to him, then kissing the back of his neck, but there was no exciting such an inert mass. So he fell asleep too, wrapped around Michael, touching every square inch of skin possible, as if some chemical reaction had just created a new and inseparable compound.

The ibuprofen that he took when he got up during the night was partially effective. His hangover wasn't as bad as it would have been when he finally woke up. The bedroom was well lit. Michael was gone. He got up and went to the bathroom, put on a pair of sweatpants, and sat on the couch. He was still waking up when he heard the key in the door.

Michael had a look on his face as if this were a Sunday

morning not unlike any other. "Hey, man. I got you the paper and some bagels to go with that coffee." He dropped the bags with a thud on the table in front of Dan and went into the bedroom without another word.

Dan followed him and sat on the bed, as Michael rooted through his closet for something a little more formal to wear to the firm's client brunch later in the morning. "Mike… ah, about last night. We need to talk."

"Talk about what?"

"About what happened." Dan was sitting against the headboard. He pulled his knees up to his chest. He was feeling sick.

Michael held up a pair of chinos and a polo shirt. "Do you think this looks OK?" He was obviously in a hurry and not paying attention to Dan.

"Mike, I'm talking about what we did in bed last night."

Michael stopped for a moment as he was getting undressed and stood up, facing Dan. "You know, it's funny, I had a dream that something happened. I guess I must have been fucking drunk. I'm sorry, man. I hope I didn't freak you out or anything."

Dan was taking shallow breaths. He felt as if he couldn't inhale all the way. "Mike, I wanted you to do it… I liked it… I wanted to have sex… I love you."

Michael stopped again after he zipped up his trousers. "Oh, c'mon. I love you too, but for Christ's sake, it's not like we're gay or anything."

Dan was staring down at the dark reflection in his mug of coffee. "I don't know if I'm gay, but I know I wanted to have sex with you. Yesterday, you told me you would have gone with that guy for a thousand dollars. I wouldn't have, not for a million, not even if I could close my eyes. I thought when you woke me up and… you were hard… you were kissing me…"

Michael recoiled, "Dan, forget about that creep in the park, man. I was only bullshitting you when I said I would have gone with him. Well, I don't know, maybe for $10,000… but anyway, about last night, we were drunk. I might have rolled over or something. I'm sorry. I'm really sorry…" He noticed the tears in Dan's eyes, which even he couldn't ignore. He put on his shirt and a pair of loafers and sat on the bed. "I know you're under a lot of pressure, but I've known you my whole life. I know you're not gay."

Dan looked up. "You don't know me at all." Then he turned away. "You've got someplace to go right now. Just go. I'll be fine. I'd really like to be alone for a while."

"Are you sure?"

"Yeah, just go."

It was about eleven that evening when Dan got back to the apartment. He wouldn't have come back at all, but he had nowhere else to go. He sensed a momentary break in Angela's self-absorption. She knew something was up but Michael hadn't said anything. Michael and Angela both had to be at work early on Monday. That was their excuse when they went into the bedroom and closed the door behind them.

Dan was tired. He hadn't slept on Saturday night and he had been walking nearly all day. He pulled out the couch and lay his sleeping bag across the mattress. At first, all he could hear was the squeaking of the metal bed frame in the next room. That was the way it usually started. Then came the low muffled sighs. Tonight it seemed that Michael was determined that he should hear it all. He'd seen the marks Angela's nails made on Michael's back. Tonight, she was digging in, and Michael wasn't telling her to stop. He cried out when he came.

◰ ◰ ◰

At dawn, Dan was huddled on the fire escape platform outside the apartment. He'd fallen asleep there, finally, to the sounds of the city. He caught a glimpse of Michael and Angela, still in bed, as he looked back over his shoulder into the apartment. He went inside and started making coffee.

The noise woke Angela. She lifted her head and saw him through the open door of the bedroom. "Make enough for us too."

Michael got up, scrambling over Angela, naked. "Hey, I saw you out on the fire escape last night. I promise I'm going to order an air conditioner this week. How'd you sleep?" he asked as he disappeared into the bathroom without waiting for an answer.

"Like an owl," Dan said as he poured three cups of coffee.

"Owl?" Angela looked puzzled. She was standing at the bathroom door waiting for Michael.

"Never mind," Dan replied.

"That's a bird." Angela seemed proud to have made the identification.

"Yes," Dan said, as he handed her a cup of coffee. "Hunts by night."

"What hunts by night?" Michael asked as his body brushed by Dan on his way back to the bed. Angela returned from the bathroom and got under the covers with Michael.

"I know a bird that hunts by night," Angela said as she reached toward Michael's groin.

Dan walked out of the bedroom, pulling the door shut as he left. He got dressed listening to Angela and Michael, at it again, as if he had just been room service, delivering coffee.

He decided to move out that day. He put the clothes he needed for a few days in a backpack. Everything else went in a couple of duffel bags, which he carried to a self-storage warehouse and put in a locker. He came back to the apartment for lunch and called Michael at his office. Dan could hear the sound of what seemed like hundreds of phones ringing and people shouting while he waited for Michael to come to the phone.

"Hey, man. What's up?"

"Mike, I'm moving out. I wanted to let you know and I didn't feel like leaving a note."

"Hey, buddy. I hope you're not still upset about Saturday night."

"I am, but it's not just that. This isn't a good situation for me, Mike. I meant what I said Sunday morning. I love you. I wanted to have sex with you. It wasn't just because I was drunk. I—"

"What... five-eighths?... No fucking way! Hold on, Dan... I already confirmed the order at a half... Then go back to their trader and tell him I'm gonna burn his house down. You hear me? Nobody fucks with me like that! Right... Hey, Dan, man, I'm really sorry about Saturday night. Why don't you hang out for a while? We can talk when I get back this afternoon."

"I'm already packed and gone, Mike. I just wanted to say good-bye."

"OK, motherfucker... twenty thousand shares at ten and nine-sixteenths. I'll take it out of your ass next time... Dan... ah, I gotta go. I love you, man. Please hang out for a while."

"I love you too, Mike. I'll call you when I get settled in a place."

After he left Michael's apartment, Dan went to a newsstand and bought copies of the local papers. Later he was in front of a bulletin board at NYU. He jotted down several numbers from the notices. Armed with classified pages and bulletin board postings, Dan once again was leaving a familiar but painful relationship and set out on his own.

He knew the layout of New York, but except for his brief stay with Michael, his experience of the City was centered on the suite at the Pierre Hotel where his family stayed on occasional visits. He had dined at the best restaurants, shopped on Fifth Avenue, and enjoyed the plays on Broadway. None of that had prepared him for his current expedition. He was alone and disoriented, with no idea of the hovels that sometimes pass for living quarters in New York. "*Plus ultra*," he kept repeating to himself. "*Go further.*"

◪ ◪ ◪

He was dressed very neatly, his marked-up newspaper showing the apartments to let and to share section. He entered the first building on his list as someone else was leaving so he didn't ring the buzzer downstairs. He approached the apartment door cautiously and knocked, leaning in to catch the unfamiliar sounds: a man's voice in what seemed like genuine anguish, the smart crack of leather on something soft, flesh perhaps, a heavier, domineering, husky voice saying something about "sins," and "payment," and "pain" promised, more to come. Dan hesitated, then knocked, a second time, louder, but still trying to be polite.

Inside the apartment, a large, balding, middle aged man done up in S and M gear—leather G-string, motorcycle boots—was strapped to a bed. Over him, also fully dressed in leather, topped with a blond wig, stood Mary Magdalene.

"Oh! Ah! Oh! Mary."

"You pay for your sins! You pay for your sins!"

"Ah! No more! Yes! No more. Don't stop! Oh, Mary! Yes! Oh, Mary!

Dan was trying to be brave, but he was also curious. He knocked again. The response, this time, was immediate. He heard footsteps coming toward the door. "Who is it?"

"I... ah... the room."

"Oh, shit!"

"I... I could come back if it's not... ah—"

"Hold on! Just a minute! I'll be right there."

Mary whipped her client once more with the leather strap and taped his mouth closed. "Be a good boy!" she said, as she ran through the living room, snatching up an elaborate dressing gown trimmed with ostrich feathers. After much behind-doors hustling, the door was flung open and the spectacle of a six-foot tall, blond-wigged, flamboyantly gowned, African-American woman greeted Dan. But it was not Dan's eyes that were the most shocked, since they had several seconds to adjust to the scene. It was his ears that couldn't match the voice with the vision.

"Hi. I'm Mary," said the vision in a full tenor voice.

"I could come back—"

"No! Come in," she insisted, or was it he who insisted? Dan decided to trust his eyes for now. She grabbed him and pulled him into the room. "I'm working, but I can show you the apartment now."

She showed him the living room first, which was as dark as

the hallway with the heavy velvet drapes drawn, but with one pull on a cord, Mary drew them back and the room was flooded with light.

While she was adjusting the drapes, her belt loosened and her gown fell open. Mary clutched the gown to her chest, but Dan got a view of a very large leather, nail-studded jockstrap. Mary wrapped the gown around her quickly. Now Dan's mind was in complete overload.

"Wow! Nice view," Dan said hoarsely, as he struggled to get grounded. He noticed that the place was neat and clean, and even the old tired furniture looked like it had been arranged with care. "Large place."

"Wait 'til you see your room." Mary took his arm and led him toward the back bedroom. The room looked great, but Dan was really paying attention to the muffled cries coming from down the hall. To distract him from the noise, she told him about all the closet space. "Lots of room for your lacrosse sticks and roller blades."

Mary opened a closet door and a variety of leather and metal things rained down on Dan. He picked them up one by one: chains, belts, whips, studded implements and accoutrements of, on reflection, obvious purpose. Dan stared back at what was still left hanging there: rows of leather outfits.

Mary shut the door quickly. "I'll have all that cleaned out before you come," Mary said.

Sounds of the man's anguish drifted from the other bedroom.

"I have some other places to see. Can I call you later?" Dan said.

"You won't find a better deal than this. Five hundred, and your own view."

Another louder cry came from the other room.

"Thank you," Dan said, edging his way out of the room, then almost running to the door and out.

Mary grabbed up a handful of the more lethal-looking implements and headed for the closed bedroom door. Glaring at the man on the bed, she warned him, "If you fucked up this deal,

I'm really going to beat the shit out of you. Bad boy, my ass!"
She laid a heavy one on him and pulled off the tape, just to get
the satisfaction of hearing him scream out loud.

The sound of cries and thuds, shouts and whip snaps echoed
down the corridor as Dan made his getaway.

◤ ◤ ◤

He made his way down a side street in the Village, checked the
newspaper, then the numbers of the once-elegant but now run-
down brownstones as he moved along. Then he noticed a small
group of young people clustered around a set of steps leading to
a basement, each one carrying the same collection of classifieds.
He brushed past them. *"There must be some place for me to
live other than in a hole."*

Dan was walking in circles. He literally had no place to go.
He found himself in Midtown at Fifth Avenue, looking forlorn-
ly at the spires of St. Patrick's Cathedral. He walked around
Rockefeller Center and by the NBC studio and peered in to see
the CNBC show, which he could hear being broadcast from
speakers on the building. Dan Dorfman was starting to give his
report.

"The Wall Street press is abuzz over the audacious hostile
bid by NCBT for New York Trust. At first the Street dismissed
Jack O'Brien's attempt at admission into the elite club of banking powerhouses, but the betting is now going his way and the
arbs are buying NCBT calls at a frantic pace. Carlton Moore is
no pushover and don't expect him to give up without a fight, but
I'd be buying New York Trust common all the way up to $80 a
share."

Dan was tired and very hungry. He couldn't believe that it
had come to this, but there was no way he would call his father.
He walked another ten blocks up Fifth Avenue, past the most
expensive window displays in America and into Central Park.
From the southeast corner of the park, he could see the top

floors of the Pierre and the windows of the suite where he had stayed with his family. He imagined himself laying in the over-sized tub and ordering room service. It was warm. He liked the cut grass and fresh air smell of the park. He sat on a bench for a while. Then he walked a little further and found a thick hedge of low-lying bushes that looked like it was well enough out of the way and laid down.

At about 3:00 a.m., he was awakened by a flashlight and the sound of a policeman's voice and told to move on or he would be arrested. More than a little disoriented, he started walking back downtown where there was another share advertised in the papers he was carrying. He stopped at an all-night diner to eat. At 9:00 a.m., he found the place, an apartment building in the West Village, off Greenwich Street.

◤ ◤ ◤

He walked down the long, narrow, dark corridor that was the hallway on the third floor. The sound of his steps echoed off the walls. As he made his way past the first few numbered doors, he had the feeling that he was being watched. He stopped, froze, then turned his head and only heard the sound of a door closing. At the end of the corridor, he found the door he was looking for, 3R. He knocked and was relieved as an elderly but harmless-looking man opened the door.

"Are you… is this the apartment?" Dan asked.

"Yes, please come in." The man gestured with his arm and stepped aside for Dan to enter.

As he walked into a large but dimly lit living room, some-thing brushed against his ankle. He looked down and at first he thought it must be a cat, but then as it got a little farther away from him, he could see it was a mechanical doll. His eyes were drawn to the walls where there were literally hundreds of dolls and an uncountable number of parts of dolls: arms, legs, torsos, heads, and other pieces unidentifiable.

"I make them," the man said. "The dolls. They're my children."

"Oh," Dan said. He suddenly realized that his mouth was very dry and he was looking over the man's shoulder toward the door and wondering if he could run out without knocking the man down.

"You can play with any of them if you want," the man said. "You don't have to walk or water them." He picked up the walking doll and talked to it. "Do you think you can live with this nice young man? Say "Hello.""

"Hello," said Dan.

"Not you! Him! He can say 'Hello.' Say 'Hello!'"

"Can you... Can you show me the room you're renting?" Dan asked.

"Room? What's this? This is the room."

Dan showed the man the newspaper with the ad he had circled. "But it says 'two-bedroom apartment to share.'"

"Yes," the man replied, as if it should have been obvious. "I sleep in the other bedroom and this is the room to share. You don't mind sharing it with the children. Do you? Where are they going to go? I can't put them out on the street!" He stepped past Dan and began to touch some of the dolls on the shelves. "There, there. Quiet, children. Be nice to the young boy."

Dan was beginning to back out of the room. "I don't think..."

The man turned around. "There's enough room for both of us here. They do need a father. Single parents are never good enough."

"Well... Yes... I agree... Well, thanks..." Dan finally gave up worrying about being polite and ran, leaving the door open behind him. The walking doll followed him out into the hallway, saying in a recorded voice, "Hello... Hello... Hello."

◣ ◣ ◣

It was still morning when Dan walked to the warehouse district, not far from the apartment with the dolls, to a large commercial building in sight of the docks and the river. A brisk warm summer breeze, full of the smells of decay, rustled the newspaper in his hand. He checked the ad and then searched for the address on the building, finally stepping into the street. As he looked at the front of the building, a window on a high floor opened and a man, his head done up elaborately in dreadlocks, waved cheerfully at him, flashing both open hands at him, indicating "Ten."

Dan entered the building. He found the elevator, and seeing the sign "Out of order," he began to climb. As he reached close to the tenth floor, he recognized a familiar smell in the smoke-laden air. The door to the apartment was open. No one came out to greet him, but he heard a rich Jamaican voice.

"Ya', mon. Com' in."

Dan entered tentatively. He was already keenly aware of the need to keep the exit in sight. Then he looked around. In the room were three men, looking very much like the one who hailed him from the window. Each man was stretched out on a cot, leaning back against the wall. Every inch of space was filled with personal belongings, except for one remaining cot, neatly done up.

The man who beckoned him in offered Dan a joint. "Toke, mon?"

"Is this the share?" Dan asked as he exhaled.

"Right 'chere, mon," said the man, pointing to the empty cot.

"All that space, huh? How much, you say?"

"One hundred dollars a week," said all three in unison.

Dan started to leave, but noticing the neatly made cot, he went toward it and stretched out. "Give me a minute to think about it." He was stoned. He told himself he only wanted to rest, but soon he fell into a deep sleep. The others ignored him, continuing to pass the joint.

◨ ◨ ◨

It was still early in the afternoon when Dan emerged from the warehouse. He felt a little better, with four hours sleep, but he was hungry. He inhaled three cheeseburgers at a fast-food restaurant on Tenth Avenue and thought about his options. He still had lots of circles around notices in the papers, but his enthusiasm for confronting the eccentrics of the world was waning.

He wondered why he had knocked a second time at Mary's apartment, even after he had heard the sounds of the man in distress; why he went in, even after Mary opened the door and he saw what, he was pretty sure, was a man dressed impossibly like a woman.

"*What the hell*," Dan thought. "*I'm not going to sleep in a park again. This would be an incredible story to tell Julie. I wonder if she would believe me?*" But it wasn't just a sense of desperation that made him call Mary. He had enough money to stay in a cheap hotel and he wasn't feeling the need to prove his newfound bravery. There was something about the chemistry of the situation that urged him on. Dan was, at last, learning to go with his instincts.

He left the restaurant and went looking for a phone booth. "Hello, Mary? It's Dan. You know, Dan O'Brien. You know... I had an appointment yesterday to see... You know... the room... Yeah! Yeah! Me. You were right. Still want a roommate? ... Great! ... Yeah, I'll come over now."

There was no mistaking the person who greeted him at the door.

"Hi, I'm Marty. C'mon in." Marty greeted him with a firm handshake, dressed in jeans and a cut away T-shirt that showed off a very masculine, well-sculpted body. "Is that all your stuff?"

"No," said Dan, "the rest of my things are in a storage locker. I'll get them later. Right now, I'd like to take a shower."

"C'mon in the kitchen. We'll talk about the living arrangements."

Marty talked as he sliced a ginger root and put it in a cauldron of boiling water along with a few other ingredients that

Dan only recognized as things that looked like they came out of the ground.

"Like I said," Marty continued, "the room is $500, cash, on the first of the month, no excuses. This is the eighth, so you owe me $375… now. You can use the phone number here if you need to reach me, but don't give the number to anyone else. If you have to take calls here or if you need to call out long distance, get a line put in your room."

"That won't be necessary," said Dan, as he slid $375 across the counter to Marty. "I have phone mail hooked up to a pager."

"My room is off limits," said Marty. "That's where I work. You saw yesterday what I do. When I'm taking a call, you need to be either in your room with the door shut or not here. I don't see clients here a lot. Most of my work is out calls, but I can usually give you some notice when someone is coming in. I'm pretty much gone most of the day, either with voice lessons, or the recording studio, or rehearsing at a club."

Marty went over to the stove and scooped out a mug of the boiling liquid from the cauldron. "You want some tea?"

"Yeah, sure," said Dan. "What kind of stuff do you record?"

"It's my own stuff. I don't really put a label on it. Did you say you want to take a shower?"

ENTROPY

D an and Marty settled into a domestic routine that, in its own way, became ordinary. The quiet of their apartment was interrupted only by one of Mary's clients. Nothing was ever said about these episodes. Dan simply listened to his music with earphones when the racket became too much to ignore.

It took a while for Marty to open up. He didn't trust anybody, and for good reason, Dan would learn. Marty was the youngest of three brothers. He was born in 1962 at the base hospital at Fort Dix in New Jersey. In 1968, his father told him that he had to go away, to a place on the other side of the world, but that he would be back soon. No one told him that his father wasn't coming back, but Marty knew. It was a kind of knowing, an ability to sense, if not see, the future that Marty would much later recognize as a connection to the flow of life's energy and events. He knew, but being only six years old, he cried. A few months later, his father was transformed. There was nothing left of a body to send home, so Marty's father became a picture on his dresser and a name, along with forty thousand other names, carved in stone on a memorial that was built in a low glade twenty tears later. His father's death was a punctuation in Marty's life; not a period, but one of a series of commas that strung together phrases of abandonment and survival, disappointment and struggle.

Dan was as interested in learning about Marty's life as Marty was in holding the rest of the world at bay. "I don't do Oprah interviews" was a frequent response to Dan's inquiries. "I'm not the 'tell all' type. I'd prefer that people know as little about me as possible." But Dan's persistence was more than a match for Marty's reticence and, little by little, he began to get a picture of his roommate. Dan was more willing, in fact eager, to talk to Marty about himself. Over dinners, or at other times when they were together, Marty heard his story: growing up in Charlotte and struggling to meet his family's expectations. But these seemed like no big deal to Dan, in comparison to his love for Michael.

"Bwana, I can cure you of that problem in a hurry."

"What's a 'bwana' and what do you mean 'cure'?"

"'Bwana' means 'buddy' in Swahili. You're in love with some pretty Latino boy. He ain't in love with you. 'Cure' means, go get yourself another boy. There ain't no end of 'em in this town. We'll go out. I'll show you."

"I don't think it's that easy, Marty. Michael is special. I don't think I'll ever feel the same way about anyone else."

"OK," said Marty, "you're on. I have to meet some friends in Chelsea later. Let's go eat right now. I'm so sure you'll get cured tonight, I'll pay for us both. We can eat at Eighteenth and Eighth, and then we'll go hang out. If you come home alone tonight, our dinner's on me, otherwise you pay."

They sat at a small table by the front window. Marty faced inside the restaurant and Dan was seated so he could see the parade of people walking by. He started in again with his "How did you get here?" questions. Maybe it was a sense of comfort or maybe Marty just figured that if he gave up and answered the questions, Dan would at least move on to another topic. Whatever the reason, as they were sitting over dinner, Marty finally opened up.

"One day, a few months after my father died, my mother came home and said, 'We're goin' to Grandma Rosie's house.' She packed up my two brothers and me; we rode the train and then the subway, to Lincoln Place. Grandma was a retired nurse. She lived in a two-bedroom apartment on the second floor of a building right on the square. It was the most godforsaken place in the universe, burned out buildings, addicts sleeping on the streets, and what was incredible, as I look back on it now, is that there were gangs actually fighting over it. Even as a kid, I couldn't understand why anyone would want to stay there one second longer than they had to."

"Anyway, right after we got there, my mother looked me

straight in the face and said, 'I'll be back as soon as I can. Grandma will take care of you and your brothers until then.' Not a tear in her eyes, she just turned and walked away. I knew she'd never come back and she never did. I haven't seen her since."

"Wow," said Dan, "so I guess you were like an orphan."

"I don't know. It depends on what you mean by orphan, but you know, my grandmother found me one day, wailing in my room. She gave me the best advice I ever got from anyone. 'Crying won't bring that selfish woman back, so wipe your tears and be strong. You only got yourself in this world.' From then on, I told myself that I would never depend on anyone or ask another living soul for a thing."

"Didn't you have your brothers, I mean, didn't you guys help each other out?"

"My brothers are fuckups. The oldest one's a dealer. I hear he's back in Brooklyn. Last time I saw him was ten years ago, just before he got sent up to Attica. My middle brother is an addict, at least he was five years ago when I found him sleeping in the stairwell of my grandmother's building."

"Your grandmother must have done something right. You seem pretty together."

"She did the best she could. I guess my brothers were too old to pay attention to her, but man, I worshipped that woman. When I was a kid, no one dared to go out at night, so she and I would be holed up in her place. She told me stories of growing up in Baltimore. She was a singer."

"So that's how you got into singing."

"Sort of. I guess you could say she inspired me. She sure as hell didn't encourage me, but once… She was a jazz singer. During the Depression, she made it big, singing in clubs in Baltimore and Washington. Her name was Rosie B. She met this older guy who became her manager. He told her he was going to marry her and make her a star. Anyway, she gets booked at the Cotton Club, you know, the whole thing, thirty-two-piece orchestra, red roses on all the tables. She was in her dressing room, getting ready for the show, and there's a knock at the door. She's thinking it's gonna be her man with a ring. But it wasn't. It was his wife with a gun. She sticks the gun in my grandmother's face and says she's gonna kill her. The guy comes in. His wife shoots him straight through the heart and then she blows her brains out, all over my grandmother's evening gown."

"Jesus Christ, Marty. That's incredible. How did your grandmother get over that?"

"She didn't. She never sang another note. They put her in Bellevue for a while. Then, on account of her being pregnant with the guy's daughter, who happened to be my mother, they let her out to go live with her sister in Brooklyn. She didn't ever sing again, but she had all those old jazz records, a few she recorded and lots of others, you know, Billie Holiday, Ella. I used to sing along with them about as soon as I learned how to work the record player." Marty was chewing his food and humming as if he had just put on one of her records.

"Anyway," Marty continued, "when I was at the School for the Performing Arts, I was rummaging around in her closet, looking for a fan, and I found a trunk with some of her old evening gowns from when she used to sing. I put one on and turned up one of her records real loud. I was singin' my head off. I never heard her come in. Boy was she mad. She didn't speak to me for I don't know how long. But that's when I knew I was going to be a singer."

"Whatever happened to her?"

"'Bout five years ago, I went out to visit her. That's when I saw my middle brother lyin' in the stairwell. Grandma was eighty years old. She knew I was trying to get my own act together. Anyway, she told me to go in the trunk and get out her red gown. She had one of those full-length three-way mirrors. She told me which one of her records to put on and where to sit. Then she went over in front of the mirror. And she said, 'If you're gonna be a singer, you oughta know what it's supposed to sound like... Man, it was incredible! It was like, I don't know, like she took sixty years off her life. She was *beamin'*. She sang the whole record, both sides. Then she said she was gonna lay down for a while. I helped her get in bed. She asked me to wake her in an hour. I remember she kissed me."

Marty stopped. He took a sip of water. "When I came back she was dead. I buried her next to her sister in the plot at Wood-lawn." He put his glass down. "So you see, bwana, you ain't the only one alone. And even after you get yourself a boy, you're still gonna be alone. He'll just be keeping you company for a while. Speaking of which," Marty said, as he wiped his mouth and put his napkin down on the table, "we gotta get going. I'm countin' on you to pay for dinner."

"Gee, Marty. Why don't we just split the bill? I don't think I feel like betting on something like this."

"We can split the bill for now, but I'm countin' on you handin' over my half in the morning."

"I'd really rather not. I mean, you know, it's not like I'm going to meet someone on the street. I'm more likely, you know, to want to get to know someone."

"I know you're talking like you want a relationship. That's because you're in some bullshit morality in your head. But, bwana, I've been watching your eyes. I know what you really want. You're like a little kid in a candy store. Go ahead. Take some. Ain't nobody gonna tell you to stop but you. You'll figure out what kind you like and how much you can handle." Marty could see that Dan was trying not to get it.

"Dan, go out that door and walk north. They call it the Runway. Trust me, if you just loosen up a little, you'll connect. You know how you look at someone when you're really interest-ed? Well, just notice if you're getting that look back. C'mon, let's go."

They walked a few blocks up Eighth Avenue. It was a hot summer night and the Runway looked like JFK at 7:00 p.m. There were large and small bodies in motion, some on the taxi-ways, some landing, and some getting ready to take off. There were planes coming and going from what seemed like all over the world. Dan kept his eye out for one of the newer models from Air Iberia or Air Chile or Aerolineas Argentina, something dark and lean with sleek lines. They stopped at an outdoor cafe in Chelsea and sat at a table that made a perfect observation deck. Marty got up to talk to some friends who were out for the evening.

While he sipped on a drink, Dan thought about the conversation he had with Marty. He noticed that he was beginning to feel comfortable. Though it was new to him, it felt like what he always wanted home to be like, a place from which he could venture out and taste the world. He thought about the way a baby explores his environment by trying to put everything within reach in his mouth. *"It was a fitting reference,"* he thought, *"Marty's comment about a kid in a candy store."*

"Why not?" he thought. There was no doubt that he was hungry and there was, in fact, no one but himself to determine what he should or shouldn't do. *"Plus ultra,"* he thought, *"go further."*

When Marty came back to the table, he had his four friends with him. They were introduced quickly and Dan had already had a few beers. He could only remember Reyes' name. It didn't matter. Reyes was the only one of them he was interested in. Reyes was Spanish. Of course, in some ways, Reyes reminded Dan of Michael. He had dark brown eyes and straight black hair, but he was Andalusian from Seville, not Catalonian like Michael. He was shorter, stockier. If Michael cut the figure of the tall slender matador, Reyes was more like De Niro in *Raging Bull.* But the difference that mattered the most to Dan was that Reyes was looking for it. And he was looking right at Dan.

At about eleven, they all decided to head for the club. Another friend of Marty's had a show that was starting at midnight. They were walking back down Eighth Avenue. Dan and Reyes weren't keeping up.

"My apartment is on Seventeenth and Seventh," Reyes said. "Let's stop and get something to smoke before the show."

Dan hesitated. He thought about Marty's advice and his own new motto. He didn't need to call the tower for clearance. He simply announced that he was taking off. "Hey, Marty! We'll see you guys at the club."

"Yeah, sure!" Marty shouted back, smiling, "I'll see you later, man."

Dan and Reyes walked a block east and up to the third-floor apartment, which was cluttered with tripods, lighting, and the photography equipment that Reyes worked with. The bed, a mattress on the floor, was like an afterthought in a photographer's studio.

Reyes rolled a joint while Dan looked around at the prints on the walls and shelves. Paper was scattered on every square inch of flat space in the apartment, with two exceptions: there was a narrow corridor of clear walkway that led from the kitchen, through the bedroom, and into the den where they were sitting, and there was nothing on the bed except wrinkled green sheets, two pillows, and a blanket.

Reyes took his time. They got high first. They talked a little about Reyes' work. Then they didn't talk at all, not a word. They got undressed and into bed and didn't go to sleep until Reyes realized he had only a few hours until it was time to be at work.

In the morning, Dan passed Marty on the staircase as he got back to the apartment. Smiling, he handed Marty $40.

"See, wasn't I right?" asked Marty as he stuffed the money in his pocket. "In no time, you won't even be able to remember… what was his name?

◪ ◪ ◪

"Pull the corset tighter, I have a show in an hour and a half. I'm going to kill that little fucker Tony. He calls himself a costume maker. I gave him $100 for some secondhand corset that he didn't fix right and now the damned thing's too tight."

"Maybe you gained a little weight around your stomach."

Marty was looking at himself in the mirror. "Don't start no shit. I haven't got time for it. Anyway, go downstairs and get a cab. We gotta get there with a little time to walk around before the show. Everyone's going to want to know who my boyfriend is tonight."

Dan was puzzled. "Who is your boyfriend tonight?"

"You," Marty said, "at least for the grand entrance."

Marty was in a foul mood. Even as they were turning on to

Eighth Street, he started screaming at the driver. "Move it!" The cab pulled up to the entrance door of the Sound Factory Bar a few minutes before Marty's deadline. Dan couldn't believe his eyes. Standing in line was a collection of the strangest, the best-looking, and the most bizarre people he had ever seen in his life.

Marty looked at Dan. "It's time for Mary," he said. And then she stepped out of the cab, bald, muscle body, black corset and G-string, with knee-high black and white boots.

"Hi, Mary, what's up?" asked the doorman.

"My cock, and you?" Mary replied as she adjusted the G-string.

"Well, some girls have all the luck. Who's your new boy?"

"Tito, this is Dan. He's with me."

Tito shook Dan's hand with a firm grip. "Be careful inside. There are barracudas all over the place. They will eat you up when Mary has her back turned."

Dan's eyes got big and he blushed and followed Mary through the door. "Why is it that everyone seems to think I'm such a novice?"

"You stare too much. Besides, Tito has been the doorman here for years. He's seen it all. And if I were you, I'd be especially careful of Tito. His dick is bigger than your leg."

"How do you know?"

"Because we had a bet one time and he pulled it out and showed it to me. OK, I've got to go backstage. See that bartender over there with his shirt off?"

"Marty, they all have their shirts off."

"I mean the one on the left, the pretty blond one in the army pants."

"Yeah, I see him."

"His name is Glyn. Tell him Mary said to give you the papers for the entries in the show. Then bring them backstage to me."

It was twelve-thirty and the place was packed, body-to-body, men, women, some were hard to make out. They were all in motion—go-go boys with bodies as if they had fallen out of exercise magazines.

Dan was standing still, taking it all in, and didn't notice the guy with the baseball cap standing in front of him.

"Ecstasy? Crystal? K?"

Before he could answer, he felt a familiar hand on his shoulder. "Dan, the bar's that way."

"Hi, Mary, I was just asking your friend if he needed anything."

"Joel, this is my boy tonight and I will fuck his mind up in my own time. Dan, I need those papers. I'll walk you over there. It's probably safer that way."

When they got to the bar, Glyn waved to Mary, but Mary didn't have time for small talk. "Give me the entry papers. Glyn, this is Dan, my new roommate. Take care of him."

"Hi, Dan. What are you drinking?"

"Beer's fine. Whatever you have on tap."

Dan sipped his beer compulsively, with his back to the room, and followed Glyn with his eyes. He was about Dan's height, longer blond hair, and a lean physique, with an attitude of pure sex. Every so often, he'd casually notice Dan noticing him, but without seeming to pay much attention. He had customers to tend to and this was not the first time he'd been stared at.

In the span of half an hour Dan had downed three more beers. A few minutes after one o'clock, the crowd started moving toward the stage and the bar slowed down a little. Glyn came back over to where Dan was sitting. "So where are you from, Dan?"

"North Carolina."

"Oh, a southern boy. I knew there was something I liked about you. My lover is from South Carolina. We met when he was stationed at Fort Jackson."

The music stopped and Mary came on stage. "I'm a ho' but I'm a little bit better than all of you bitches out there tonight. Are you ready for the show?"

The crowd cheered as Mary strutted across the stage. Dan had his back to the bar and was watching the stage when he felt a tap on his shoulder. He turned around and saw Glyn leaning over the bar. "You seem like a nice guy. Don't worry about being new here. You've been staring at me for the last half hour. I have something for you, something I know you want."

He motioned toward the wall at the end of the bar where Dan went without a word. "Crouch down under here," Glyn said as he pointed to the space under the service bar. When Dan got down on his knees under the bar, Glyn unzipped his fly, dropped his pants a little, let his dick and balls flop over his belt, and started pulling. Dan was excited, ashamed, hungry, embarrassed, but mostly frozen as he was kneeling there, knowing what to do, knowing what he wanted to do, but frozen in place.

It only took Glyn's hand on Dan's head, pulling it toward his crotch, and then Dan had Glyn's dick in his mouth as Glyn jerked off harder and harder. As he got more worked up, Glyn shoved his dick against the roof of Dan's mouth and he gagged. Glyn couldn't see him or hear him. He just kept going until he was ready to come. He pulled out and shot his load on Dan's shirt. Then he stood there with his elbows on the bar and smiled as the last drop of cum hung in the air. Dan reached for the bar towel in Glyn's back pocket and tried to wipe the stain off his shirt.

He watched Glyn's hands reach down and put his pants back in order and then he saw two legs walk away. Dan turned with his back to the wall and slid down until he was sitting. His feelings of exhilaration and shame mixed with the beer on the floor. He got out from under the service bar and started to walk away, hoping no one had seen what happened.

"Hey, Dan, where you goin', man?" Dan heard Glyn's voice over the stage music, behind him. Glyn was grinning, laughing. Dan didn't answer. He turned again and walked toward the stage.

There was a skinny-looking androgynous type wailing a song by Guns N' Roses in an operatic style. He had on big man's shoes, a woman's hoop skirt, no shirt, and one big braid of hair sticking on top of his head. While he was singing, out stepped another one, a twin or a clone. They started singing together and throwing each other around like rag dolls.

The next contestant started out in a trash bag, singing a

blues song, a poor imitation of Billie Holiday. Then off with the trash bag; underneath was a lacy leotard and body paint, and into a punk rock song by the Go-Go's. There were several more contestants, but Dan was more interested in the atmosphere and attitude of the people on the dance floor to pay any attention to the rest of the show.

Mary popped back on stage. "All right, let's give these bitches some applause. It's art in the making. Hell, I'm launching more careers than Ed McMahon ever did. Now it's time for my number. You white-bread, low-class Chelsea boys better pull those Andrew Jacksons out of your pockets, 'cause Mamma ain't working for free."

Dan wanted another beer, something to drink compulsively, something to get the taste out of his mouth. He was too embarrassed to go back to Glyn, but he saw another bar across the room. Before he got there, he made eye contact with the bartender. He looked about eighteen at the most. Dan said, "Hello." The boy said, "No English," but he looked at Dan and that was enough.

"Me llamo Dan."

"Me, Pedro."

Dan's Spanish was rusty, but he managed to get beyond the introduction and into a simple conversation. Pedro was on vacation from Venezuela and said he liked American blond boys with blue eyes.

Mary started with a song by Grace Jones, "I'm Not Perfect (But I'm Perfect for You)." The photo slides that Marty put together and projected on himself made him look like he was pieced together, constructed like a robot. Eyeballs, arms, legs were projected onto Mary's body. The strangest effect was the changing projection of genitals from cock to pussy and back, over and over again.

Marty was a hit, but he wasn't carried away in the moment. He had bigger dreams than to be a popular MC at a talent show in a gay club. He wanted a record deal and who the hell was going to give him one? That's all he cared about.

Dan took Pedro backstage. Marty was changing into overalls and a fisherman's hat. "Who's your little friend?"

"His name is Pedro. You were great."

"The night's just begun. Come on. We have some damage to do."

Marty led them back out onto the floor and spotted the drug dealer, Joel. "Spot me some K." Marty took the vial and headed straight for the restroom with Dan and Pedro. The restroom was a scene in itself. There was a line waiting to get to the stalls. Boys were going in two or three at a time. There was another big guy, almost as big as Tito, who knocked on the door about every three minutes. He didn't seem to care what was going on inside, sex, drugs, whatever. His job was to keep the line moving. There were boys standing around the urinals, sort of cruising, watching guys pissing, hoping to see some huge cock, maybe get lucky.

Inside the stall, Dan, Marty, and Pedro barely had room to move. "Dan, just snort it."

"Damn, Marty, this stuff is disgusting. It's burning the shit out of my nose."

Pedro snorted it as if he were inhaling confectionery sugar. Then came a big bang at the door. "Come on, boys, move it. Out. Out." Dan jumped and nearly knocked the powder out of Marty's hand. Marty managed to snort what was left on the key and put the vial back in his pocket.

When they got back on the dance floor, the music was blaring. The DJ, Junior Vasquez, was at the turntable. It was about four in the morning and the club was pumping. Go-go boys were dancing on platforms in every corner. Body to body, men on the dance floor, most of them with their shirts off, rubbing, dancing, pulling. Dan started to feel hot. He took off his shirt. He thought he was watching a movie in slow motion. The music was blending with the flow of his blood. The lights were flashing.

They kept on dancing until about six-thirty. Dan and Pedro had been doing bumps of K in the crowd. "Vamos, vamos," Pedro shouted to Dan over the music. Marty had it figured out so Dan didn't need to tell him where he was going. They sat anxiously in the cab on the way home.

It was seven-thirty and they were taking a shower together. Dan couldn't believe how beefy Pedro was. They were standing under the shower, sucking and pulling each other's nipples. Pedro got on his knees, the water pouring into his eyes. He took Dan's cock in his mouth. Then he turned Dan around and started licking the crack of his ass, his tongue going deeper, until Dan couldn't take it anymore.

When they fell on the bed, they were both still wet. Dan licked Pedro, head to toe. He started to take Pedro's cock in his mouth, but then he remembered being on his knees earlier that night. He turned Pedro on his stomach and started biting on his neck, down to the small of his back to his ass, perfectly round, arched up, waiting.

They woke up at about two-thirty in the afternoon. They heard some moaning in Marty's room. Dan knew it was one of Marty's clients, so he rushed Pedro to get dressed and leave without making any noise.

◼ ◼ ◼

By the end of the summer, Dan was going out every night, usually without Marty. He had mailed his résumés and he was waiting to get called for interviews. Why not relax? He had, as far as he could tell, made a spontaneous transformation from an uptight, Type A, worry-about-everything kind of guy to this free and easy lifestyle. He loved it.

He was a new face in the clubs, which prized fresh meat above all. He was tall, lean, and blond. He put together an unconventional, exotic, look. There was always a place where Dan could go for sex and he wanted it almost all the time. He had been in New York only a few months. He already had lots of fuck buddies. But he still liked the thrill of someone new, the excitement of the hunt, a primal, sometimes overwhelming, urge. He enjoyed the rush of the drugs he took, but his body was ill prepared for the abuse. He had led a sheltered life. Now, he was throwing off years of frustration and, without realizing it, much of his vitality. He slept later and later. It took progressively longer to recover from weekend binges.

Marty had seen it all before. It was a familiar and repeating pattern of new arrivals in the city, a law of nature that spontaneous processes are irreversible, that all elements in the universe tend to entropy, the process by which energy degrades into heat. As more and more energy is lost, it is unavailable for conversion to mechanical work. Because of this, it is said that the universe is inexorably running down.

The human experience is a unique anomaly to the law of entropy. In the power of the mind, something can be made out of nothing. Marty knew that Dan had to find his own way, that he had to realize there was no next thrill to go to after the thrill of "going out" was gone. So he tried, when he could, to talk to Dan about what he was spiraling down into. In a resigned way that comes from having seen life at the brink of chaos, Marty knew there was only so much he could say.

◼ ◼ ◼

"So, how's the new star of the firm holding up?" Chris Alexander was standing in the door of Michael's office, surveying the stacks of files, and taking a measure of how much stress Michael could handle.

"I'm OK," said Michael. He didn't sound convincing. "I can't believe this stuff wasn't more automated before I got here. I mean, how the hell did you guys keep track of everything?"

Chris laughed. "I guess we didn't. That's why we pulled you out of sales. You've got more experience in back office systems than any of the kids out there." Chris gestured to the brokers that Michael could see through the glass wall that separated his office from the trading floor. "Mike, a year ago we had fifty brokers, now we have five times that many. There's bound to be growing pains. Hang in there, kid. You're gonna make a lot of money here."

"Hey, Chris," said Michael, "while you're here, I've got a question for you."

"Yeah, what is it?"

"You know the Paramount Medical IPO we did last week?"

"Yeah."

"Well, one of the insiders who registered his shares for sale, Harvey Kahn, had us wire the proceeds of his sale to an account in the Caymans. Here, look." Michael held out a wire transfer confirmation slip.

"So, what about it?" Chris asked.

"You see the account name at Barclays, it's Lexicon Holdings. Well, last week I settled a purchase for Carmine. He bought about $400,000 of Two-Year Treasuries from Solomon. Anyway, I got a call from Kevin Pollard over there confirming payment, and he says they got the money from a Barclays branch in the Caymans, an account called Lexicon Holdings…" Michael paused. He was waiting for Chris to explain, but all that came back was a blank stare. "Chris, are you trying to tell me that it's a coincidence that one week, we do an IPO and wire an inside seller $800,000 from the proceeds of the sale of his stock, and the next week, the owner of our fucking firm buys $400,000 in T-bills, paid for from the same account? Is that what I'm supposed to think, Chris, that it's a *coincidence*?" Michael lowered his voice before he finished. "Chris, I know we cut a few corners around here, but… I gotta ask you… what the fuck is going on?"

Chris Alexander looked at Michael. He took a few seconds to think. He turned to the desk outside Michael's office where his secretary was sitting. "Cathy, hold Michael's calls, OK?" Then he came in and shut the door behind him. He pulled up a chair and sat close enough to Michael so their knees were touching. He leaned forward and spoke in a low voice as if, even with the door closed, he was worried about being overheard. "Mike, let's you and I have a little talk, OK?"

◪ ◪ ◪

It was a Friday in the middle of October. It had been unseason-
ably warm for most of the last six weeks, but the city had shak-
en off its summer slow pace. Dan had his "I'm going out" look
when he came upstairs about ten.

"Marty, I'm going to Esqualita's. It's Cafe con Leche
tonight. I'll meet you after your show."

"Dan, I thought you were going to help me. How do you
expect me to get this stuff to the club?" Marty gestured to a
large metal cage with props in it.

"You didn't have trouble taking it to the club before I started living here. I don't mind helping you, but we need to leave
now. I promised Reyes and Luis I would meet them for the best
buns contest."

"My God, Dan, haven't you seen enough ass up close and
personal so you don't have to go running like some high school
boy in heat to see it on a stage?"

"Just because you're old and jaded doesn't mean that I have
to live that way."

"Fuck you! You don't know shit. You think your pretty
boyfriends give a fuck about you? You're just another piece of
meat, nothing more. You better wise up quick and realize who
your true friends are."

"Marty, I don't need you to tell me who my friends are. I left
that shit back home. I said I'd help you with the goddamned
props if you can leave now."

"Get your white-trash ass out of my sight before I beat that
ungrateful attitude out of you. I'd do it now, but I'm afraid you'd
like it. Who knows what you'd like these days, and besides you
can't afford it."

Dan couldn't believe the way Marty turned on him. He
always got edgy right before a show, but tonight he was especially wound up. At least they wouldn't have to see each other for a
few days. Marty was leaving from the show that night to stay

with some friends on the Jersey shore.

When he got to the club, there were B-Boys, Spanish Boys-from-the-Hood, and Rough Trade, all lined up outside. Dan walked up to the doorman, gave him a kiss, and went straight inside. Dan spotted Reyes and Luis talking with one of the dancers.

"Hello, hello, Baby Buddha," Dan said as he kissed Reyes' shaved head.

"Hey, what's up?" Reyes replied.

"The rent. Who's the dancer boy with Jose?" Dan was still interested in anyone who looked at all like Michael. The music started and the dancer got up on the bar.

"That's Rex. He's Cuban and he's straight," Reyes said.

"Yeah," said Dan, sipping on a beer and staring. "Straight on my dick."

"Only if you pay for it, Dan."

Rex was about five foot nine, beautiful full lips, nice big chest, small waistline, bubble butt, and huge thighs.

"Reyes," Dan said, "I've got to have that boy."

"Well, you better get some cash."

"How much cash?"

"At least a hundred bucks."

"Fuck that," said Dan, "at least while I'm broke. Buy me another beer, would you?"

There was another dancer, tall, black, with a cut up body. Dan looked up and he had danced over on the bar to where Dan was standing, with his dick practically in Dan's face.

"How much to touch?" Dan asked.

"For you, free," the dancer replied.

Dan smiled and shyly rubbed the head of the dancer's cock.

Reyes came back with the beer. "Yo, Dan, do you want this or are your hands too full?"

Dan took the beer and smiled. He motioned to the dancer to lean down and whispered in his ear. "I want to talk to you later."

Reyes and Dan moved over to the front of the bar with Luis and his friend Jose. "Look, look up on the stage," they said. They pointed to a Cuban boy and a blond in a shower stage prop with water pouring down on them. The blond boy dropped his towel and started soaping himself up. The Cuban boy just stood there while his partner teased him. Then the black dancer who had been on the bar in front of Dan stepped in and started washing the blond guy in the shower. They started making out while the Cuban guy jerked off. As they looked like they were about to come, the lights blacked out and the curtain came down.

His friends standing around the bar loved it, but there was a layer of ordinariness to their reaction, as if they'd seen a great pass play on the wide-screen at a sports bar. Dan was shocked, not at the idea of sex as public entertainment, but by his continuing realization of how much of the world he had never seen before. A few minutes later, he turned around and there was the black dancer who had been on the bar and then in the shower show. "Hi, I'm Brooke," he said.

"Hi, I'm Dan. You looked great up there."

"Oh, please," said Brooke. "That's just to pay the rent. It gets boring fast. It's all just an act."

"Well," said Dan, "you're a good actor."

Brooke smiled at Dan. "Are you hungry? Let's go get something to eat."

"OK, let me go tell my friends I'm leaving." Dan found Reyes hitting on the blond boy who had been part of the shower act. "Hey, Reyes, I'm gonna go get something to eat. Spot me twenty bucks."

"Who you gonna eat for twenty bucks? You cheap bitch, you better pay me back."

Dan and Brooke went to the Yaffe Cafe on Seventh Street and Avenue A in the East Village. Brooke said he had a wife and kid and that he was putting himself through engineering school at NYU.

"So are you gay or what?" Dan asked.

"'Or what,' I guess. I like both."

"So where is your family?"

"My wife and daughter are in St. Thomas."

"You look so sad."

"I just have a lot of decisions to make. I have two more years of school and I don't think I can keep this up for that long."

They ate the tuna sandwiches, and in between bites, told each other what there was that they found worth telling. The waitress with the tattoos running down her arms, fish people or something, and Chinese symbols tattooed on each finger asked them if they wanted coffee. "Just the check, please," said Dan. He paid her and turned back to see Brooke looking out the window, at nothing in particular. "Hey, it's an hour back to Brooklyn. I just live around the corner on Ninth Street. Would you like to come back with me?"

"Did you think I came with you just for a snack and conversation?" Brooke asked.

Dan smiled and started to get up. Brooke reached in his pocket and handed Dan a couple of pills. "Here, take these."

"What are they?" Dan was cautious, but not afraid.

Brooke smiled. "They'll make the sex better. You can tell me later how many more you want."

Dan swallowed the pills with the glass of water on the table.

He took Brooke back to his apartment. He already knew what Brooke had to offer. Brooke wanted him to take off his clothes slowly and leave his boots on. He got undressed to the beat of the Maxwell CD. Brooke was jerking his big dick, getting aroused watching Dan. Then Dan got closer and closer. Brooke started feeling Dan's cock and ass.

Dan was nervous. He didn't understand why, because he'd been back to his room with plenty of boys before. He was sweating, short of breath, but he figured that was just from having walked so fast from the diner. He couldn't tell what Brooke wanted. Then Brooke grabbed him, started kissing his nipples, sucking his cock. He turned Dan around and kissed his ass, slowly whispering how he was going to fuck him, but first he wanted Dan to ache for it, beg for it.

Dan froze. He could actually feel his heart beating in his chest, racing. He was starting to feel sick, but he wouldn't let himself focus on that. He had never actually been fucked. He had tried it a few times, but it never worked for him. Some of his friends told him, "It's great. You just gotta relax." But this was-n't anything he was doing on purpose. He realized that when he opened his eyes and tried to focus on something in the room, that his vision was blurred. He was sweating profusely.

"There was no way," he thought, *"that he was going to be able to take Brooke's cock."* But he was so caught up in the moment that he just lay there when Brooke started pushing the head of his cock into Dan's ass. He could feel himself starting to lose consciousness.

It was the pain, or maybe just a momentary lapse back into the real world, that made Dan flinch. "Wait. Wait." he said. "Put on a condom. There's lube in the drawer." When he spoke, he noticed that his speech was slurred. He felt like he was mov-ing in slow motion when he reached for the condoms from the drawer in the nightstand and turned around to put one on Brooke's cock. He started kissing Brooke and sucking his cock. It had the taste of powder on latex. He looked up. The room was spinning.

That was all he remembered, but then he tried not to remember or even think about that night and the few days after. The fact that Marty was away for the weekend was both fortu-nate and unfortunate for him at the same time. Marty could have helped, but he was relieved that no one found him in the condition he woke up in.

He remembered having the sensation of being dry and wet at the same time. His mouth was dry, bone dry. His skin was wet. The sheets were wet. When he lifted his head slightly, he noticed a dry crust in his hair and on his face and then when he put it down again, a gel like liquid, but more sticky than smooth. It took what seemed like forever to roll over on his back and as he moved his legs, he had the feeling of lying in something like paste that made the sheets stick to his legs.

The afternoon sun was in his left eye. The right one was covered with a film. He reached for a pillowcase, the edge of the sheet, anything to wipe his face, but everything was either dry and crusted or wet and slimy. His sinuses were plugged, but he was becoming increasingly aware of the overpowering cloud of smells, organic smells, the kind that come from a garbage pail or a portable toilet left out in the sun.

He began to notice the passage of time because he could tell the sun had moved by his window, just checking in on the scene in the room and then moving on, in its routine course.

When he finally organized a quorum of muscles to move his entire body, he rolled off the side of the bed and put his feet on the floor. There was a T-shirt on a chair to wipe his face and clear his nose. When he realized that he had been lying in his own vomit and shit, he nearly passed out on the way to the bathroom.

Everything was an effort. He had to focus on discrete instructions to each muscle in his body to balance on the edge of the tub, grasp the hot and cold water taps, and turn the shower spigot. He sat in the tub and let the water run over him.

He watched globs and pieces of shit go down the drain. When the water ran clear, he summoned his will again and stood up, to rinse out his hair and wash the rest of his body. In the mirror, through the mist, he could see that his skin was pale, but at least clean. He started to dry himself off, but then he felt like he had to lie down again.

He woke up on the couch on Sunday morning. He knew he was feeling a little better because he was incredibly hungry. The door to his room was closed, but the whole apartment smelled foul. When he finally got up and opened the door, it was the fear of Marty coming home and finding the scene in front of him that motivated him to clean it all up.

Sunday was a gray autumn day. The sheets, the towels, the clothes, everything went in a big trash bag and out to the Laundromat. Every window in the apartment was open and the fans labored noisily to blow away the evidence. When, in the late afternoon, the skies opened up in a downpour, even the air was rinsed clean of the lingering smell of Lysol.

As he set about cleaning, he didn't have much time to think about Brooke. He was worried about how he was going to get a new mattress without having to explain anything to Marty. He found a place in the Yellow Pages that would deliver on Monday morning.

It was about the same time that he went looking for his money and his credit cards that his beeper went off. It was a 911 call from his mother. Someone had spent the last forty-eight hours buying about $12,000 worth of electronics equipment with his AMEX card and there was almost as much charged on the Visa and MasterCard. She said she just wanted to be sure he was OK.

He was relieved to get the cash he needed, wired to him on Monday, but it was excruciatingly painful to try to carry on a conversation with his mother. By the time Marty came home on Monday afternoon, the new mattress had been delivered. Dan had to pay the deliverymen $50 each to take the old one away. "You look like shit" was all Marty said before he went out to the recording studio.

It took the rest of the week before the police reports were filled out and he had replaced his license and his credit cards. He had to make up a story about losing his wallet at the diner. There was no sign of Brooke, anywhere. Marty figured something was wrong, the way Dan was moving so slowly, but he didn't know how wrong until Friday when Dan said he wasn't going out. "What happened last weekend, bwana?" he asked. Dan just made an excuse and stayed home. He had been in New York for four months and felt literally run down, wrung out, and run over. He wondered what the hell he was going to do now.

CHAOS

Life in the apartment on Ninth Street kept pace with Marty's frenetic schedule: his fitness regime (six days a week at the gym) and reserved times at the recording studio and dance hall; all a blur of activity, purposeful, pursued not so much with enthusiasm but with high energy and hungry ambition. Occasionally, the day would be punctuated by one of his "appointments." It took over an hour for Marty to be transformed into Mary. Sometimes Dan would watch the process in utter amazement, but he never met any of the clients up close. If he was home when they came, he stayed in the back bedroom and turned up the music on his earphones.

In contrast to Marty, Dan was a study in slow-motion anxiety. He had come to New York partly running away from his family, partly running after Michael. Now he had come to a place where he had to stop and face himself, and he did not like what he saw. In the last two weeks in July, he had started his job search in earnest. He printed cover letters and résumés at the Kinko's on Astor Place and he hand delivered them to dozens of design and construction firms in Manhattan. He was a Phi Beta Kappa graduate from a respected university with a B.S. in architecture, and he was only looking for an entry-level position. In a city with so many opportunities, how difficult could it be to find a job? By Labor Day, he wasn't especially disappointed that he hadn't heard from anyone yet, but in October, when the form rejection letters started coming in, he was more than merely worried.

October was still warm. There was hardly a sign that the leaves were about to fall, except for the lack of children in the park during the day. There was no air-conditioning in the apartment and Dan didn't like to spend much time indoors, staring at the four walls of his room and at himself in the mirror, wondering about the wisdom of striking out on his own, sometimes listening to the seemingly sympathetic sounds of anguish in the next room.

He often found himself sitting on "his" bench in Tompkins Square Park, waiting for the all clear signal, the raised window shade in the front room. One afternoon, he watched a man in a suit emerge from the front door and look nervously down Avenue B. He hailed a cab and got in. Dan was struck by the irony of how ordinary he looked, not unlike one of the teachers at St. Alban's or one of his former neighbors in Charlotte.

Upstairs, Mary was in the transition back to Marty. The wig was off and the girdle was loose, but the makeup was still on and Marty looked a little tired. Dan went to the refrigerator, poured himself a glass of milk, and sat at the kitchen table as Marty nursed a mug of ginger tea.

"Any luck at Bechtel?" Marty asked.

"No, they said they'd keep my résumé on file, but they don't have any entry-level openings."

"How many letters have you sent out?"

"So far, about a hundred. I don't get it. The job market can't be that tight."

"What exactly don't you get, Dan? You're sending form cover letters with a form résumé. Trust me, all the firms you're talking to are hiring people like you, but your letter just winds up in the dump out on Staten Island. I told you, you've got to learn to network."

"But Marty, I don't have any connections. Besides, I'm trying to get hired on what I know, not who I know."

"Dan, nobody gets a job because of what they know. Now we've been through all this before. You can keep banging your head against that wall or you can stop and pay attention. It's almost Halloween, you've been here four months, and you ain't even had an interview. You say you came from money, but as far as I can see, you didn't bring much of it with you. You tell me that you've got November and December rent, but not January. I'd like to help you out, but I've got my own shit to deal with. You know what I mean. I make five hundred bucks a call, but my work is what you'd call… ah… well… specialized, so I don't do but one or two calls a week. By the time I pay for my own living and lessons and studio time, that's all gone. Now look, are you tellin' me there isn't anybody you know in this city besides me and that asshole you left down in Tribeca? No classmates, nobody?"

"I don't know anyone," said Dan. "My mother gave me the name of a guy who she and my dad went to school with. He's a lawyer. She said he might be able to help me if I needed it."

"Well, shit, if that's all you got, then start there. All you got to worry about is paying for that milk you're drinking and the room down the hall. If you got a number of someone who might help you get a job, let me tell you, I'd be calling that number today, 'cause otherwise, your ass is gonna wind up back on the street or back home in Charlotte."

"I wonder," said Dan, "if I could just tell him I'm a Duke graduate and I'm looking for an introduction to a firm. But how could I meet him without telling him my name? I really don't want my father involved in this."

"Dan, you still don't get it. It doesn't matter what you tell him. You're young. You're good looking. Make something up. Be exotic. Tell him you're an actor, or a model, or a psychic, or a fucking belly dancer. It doesn't matter. Everybody in this town has got a line of shit. You're so naive, but that can get you some-where too. Just use it to your advantage. Work the tools God gave you."

"OK, I'll think of something. I'll be the Peter Sellers char-acter in that movie *Being There*. Did you see it?"

"Yeah, I did. Chance, the gardener. He was naive too. He liked to watch. I have a couple of clients like that. Weird shit, man. Well, don't be sittin' around watchin' for too long. Your ass is broke and you better be thinking of something to do about that in a hurry."

The number was in the inside pocket of Dan's Filofax, on a neatly folded index card, written in Carolyn's small careful script. The next morning, after Marty headed out for the day, Dan called.

"Stockton, Alpert, Slade, Meacher and Angel."

"Steve Baldwin, please."

"Please hold. That extension is 8703. I'll transfer you."

"Mr. Baldwin's office."

"Mr. Baldwin, please."

"Who's calling?"

"This is Chance Gardner."

"And what is this in reference to?"

"It's a personal matter."

"I see. Does Mr. Baldwin know you, Mr. Gardner?"

"Well, no. Not exactly."

"I see. If you'll leave me your number, Mr. Gardner, I'll tell him you called."

"Thank you. It's 695-0260."

"Here in New York?"

"Yes."

"And that's G-A-R-D-N-E-R."

"Yes, that's right."

"I'll be sure he gets the message."

"Thank you. Good-bye."

"Good-bye."

Dan hung up the phone and sat for a while in the kitchen. Marty kept everything in his place well arranged. He knew what he wanted and where he was going and had set about ordering his life to get there. Marty was thirty-two. He had been trying to get a recording contract since even before he graduated from the High School of the Performing Arts, fourteen years ago. He wrote and produced his own act, a kind of androgynous cyber-metal combination of music, lyrics, and hypershock staging.

Marty told Dan that he was sure that when his act finally clicked, it would hit big. His message was important. He had to stage it in such a way that was just as provocative as truth ulti-mately is, but not so weird that people wouldn't stop to pay attention. Turning tricks for a thousand dollars a week had become for Marty not just a means to an end, but a window into the dark side of society. He came to think of himself as a kind of therapist. He told Dan that he kept more marriages together than any uptight psychiatrist working out of an office on Central Park South.

Everything was in order in the apartment except Dan. So he went for a walk. He thought about what Marty had told him, about working the tools God gave him. He was good at architecture, the challenge of designing something was interesting to him, but he couldn't imagine pursuing it for fourteen years, with or without success, the way Marty had pursued his music career, and still be as excited as Marty was.

Dan knew that what drew him to Marty was his own affinity for performing. He was shy, but in one way or another, he had been performing for most of his life, and doing a rather good job of it. He learned to play the piano when he was very young, but he was not encouraged, so he gave up playing in high school. He could still read music well, and he loved to sing when he was sure no one else was listening. He took dance classes, which he enjoyed, but he understood that, for boys, such activity ended early. Each year, he had a part in the school play, but never a major role, nothing that would lead anyone to conclude he had a serious interest in drama.

By the time he had walked from the East Village to Hudson Street and back it was already late afternoon. He went straight to the refrigerator. Marty came in just as he was sitting down to inhale a sandwich and some milk.

"Do you do anything while I'm gone besides eat?" Marty asked.

"Listen," Dan said between bites, "I've figured it out."

"I can hardly wait to hear about it. Should I be sitting down?"

"Seriously," said Dan. "I know what I'm going to do. I'm going to be an actor."

"Great. This morning you were an architect, this afternoon you're an actor. They both start with *a*. Now, let's see, what else could you be? Well, asshole starts with *a*. Absolutely fucking crazy starts with *a*. Dan, do you have any fucking idea how many actors there are in this city? What do you know about acting?"

"School plays."

"Oh, great! Why didn't it occur to me sooner? Of course! School plays! Why don't you just rush down to Forty-second Street now. I'm sure the Schuberts are putting on something just perfect for you to star in. C' mon, man. You need a fucking job. Did you call that lawyer?"

"Yeah."

"So?"

"I told his secretary my name is Chance Gardner. She asked me if I knew him. When I said no, she couldn't get off the phone fast enough. What's wrong with me being an actor?"

"There's nothing wrong with it, Dan. It's just that it takes years to make it, and in the meantime you gotta eat and live somewhere and you need money for that."

"Fine, so I'll get another job in the meantime. I could be a model. You've said so yourself."

"I said you're good looking for a white boy. That doesn't mean you're gonna make a living at it right away."

"Look, you're always talking about how miserable most of your clients are because they're trying to pretend they're something that they're not. So why should I want to wind up like them?"

"Maybe you've got a point," said Marty, "but I'm talking about reality here. You need a job. There's no fucking way that anybody's going to pay you to be an actor. I can at least see you getting a gig as a model, but you need a portfolio. I'll make a deal with you. You remember Pierre, that guy around the corner on Ninth Street? You know, the French guy."

"Yeah, I think so. He's a photographer, isn't he?"

"Right. He owes me a favor. I put him together with one of my clients who does a catalog for men's underwear and gym stuff, kinda like International Male. Anyway, Pierre had to fuck him, but my client used him for a bunch of photo shoots and he was smart and he networked, so now he's legitimate and he owes me for it. I'll talk to him. You gotta come up with the money for the film and the paper, but he'll put a portfolio together for you. You might get lucky and get hired. In the meantime, you call that fucking lawyer every day. Maybe he knows someone in advertising."

"Deal."

After dinner, Marty went around the corner and down the street and made the arrangements for Dan's photo shoot.

Pierre was used to working with all types of models and he did portfolios for first-timers like Dan. He had lights in his apartment and a backdrop that rolled down from the ceiling. He wasn't much older than Dan, maybe twenty-eight, dark hair, fine facial features, lean. He'd come from a small town in Provence when he was eighteen, but he really grew up in New York, the hard way. He noticed but didn't really care about Dan's obvious attraction to him. He showed Dan a few sample portfolios, men and women, all beautiful.

"Marty told me you have plenty of clothes. We'll do some shots outside in the park, you know, fashion stuff. We can use some underwear and gym clothes I've got from the catalog and we'll do some nudes in here."

"Nudes?"

"Sure, you never know what the agencies will ask for and… ah… don't be surprised if Calvin Klein doesn't call you right away. In the meantime, if you don't mind hanging out with older guys, you could probably get something pretty regular with one of the escort services. Basically, they're looking for young, good-looking guys. The pay is good and the clients are usually harmless. Once in a while you get a weirdo, but that's really rare."

"Have you ever done it?"

"Yeah, that's actually how I met Marty. We went on a call together. I got tired of it pretty quick. I don't know how Marty keeps it up. Now I make decent money doing photography and computer graphics. I haven't worked for a service in years, but they advertise in the *New York Press*. Here, they're all in the classifieds." Pierre ripped out a section of the paper on the table, circled several ads, and handed it to Dan. "Listen, we gotta get started. I'm doing a video shoot in a club tonight and I need a few hours to set up."

◪ ◪ ◪

It was the end of October and Dan received the last form letter from a design firm he'd applied to back in August. He hadn't thought about his aborted attempt to find a job as an architect much in the last six weeks. He wondered about his sudden shift to this new course. Perhaps he had jumped to something different too soon. The letter went in the trash and with it his momentary angst about his decision. He embarked on the campaign to find work with fresh optimism. Every day he headed out to some new modeling agency or visited one where he had already been.

His expenses were relatively small compared to what he was used to spending in Durham. The phone card bills went to Charlotte and were paid by Carolyn. It was the one concession he made to her before he left for New York. He checked the voice mail once every few days, because he promised to, even though the message system was tied to a pager, which he carried with him. He was sitting in the park one afternoon, talking to himself, when he felt the familiar vibration of the pager. He went to a nearby pay phone.

"O'Brien residence."

"Hi, Juanita, it's Dan. Is my mother there?"

"She's in out in the garden. I'll get her."

Dan thought of the scene in Charlotte. It was probably still warm there. The entire house lot could have fit in just one of the many and varied garden plots at Chatsworth, where a dozen full-time groundskeepers were employed, but Carolyn tended to the shrubs and flower beds with as little help as possible. In the quiet of the phone booth in the market on Eighth Street, Dan heard the familiar footsteps coming to the phone.

"Hi, there."

"Hi, Mom."

"I was just putting in some bulbs for next spring. How are you, dear?"

"I'm fine, Mom. You paged me?"

"Oh, yes… well, I was going to page you anyway, but I got the AMEX bill and I saw a charge for $1,500 at a photo store and… well… I don't want to pry, but I just wanted to make sure the charge was yours. You know I've been worried ever since we had that trouble when you lost your wallet."

"Yeah, Mom. It's mine." He waited another few seconds and hoped his mother would go on to another subject. He knew she was concerned and that she loved him, and he thought in that instant that he wanted her to know about his new direction.

"Mom, the charge is for portfolios I had made up. I haven't had much luck so far with the design firms, and I'm going to do some modeling to help pay the bills here."

"Modeling? Well… ah… that sounds… like it would be interesting. You're a very handsome young man. You look just like your father did when he was your age."

"Mom, please don't say anything to him. He wouldn't understand and I'm only going to do this for a little while to earn some money."

"Dan, why won't you let him help you? You don't have to be a model. He's not angry anymore. He loves you. We all do. And we miss you. Why won't you let him at least make an introduction for you at one of the firms up there?"

"I want to do this on my own. We've been through all this before. I miss you all too, but I want to make something work here without having to feel like I had it handed to me. I don't even know if I want to be an architect anymore. I don't know what I want, but I know I want to figure it out by myself."

"Have you called Steve Baldwin?"

"Mom, please try to understand. I want to do this on my OWN!"

There was another long pause and he was trying to think of something to say to relieve the tension, but he couldn't, and he just didn't want to talk anymore about himself.

When Carolyn started again he could hear all the worry and anxiety in her voice. "Have you seen Michael lately? How is he?"

"No, I haven't seen him since July. He's really into his new job and his girlfriend. I should give him a call."

"Well, you'll at least see him at Thanksgiving."

"Mom, I have no idea if he's going to Charlotte for Thanksgiving. I don't know if I'm going to Charlotte for Thanksgiving."

"Dan, what's wrong?"

"Nothing. I'm just trying to get myself established here. Mom, I'm all right, really."

"Well, I suppose the mountain could always go to Mohammed. Your father has even been to New York a few times in the last several months. Maybe I could hitch a ride with him sometime and we could take you out to dinner."

"I don't want to do that right now... Mom, please don't cry... I'm fine. I really am. I just need a little time to be by myself."

"I love you, Dan."

"I love you too, Mom. Please don't worry. I'm fine. I'll call you soon. OK?"

"OK, dear. Bye."

"Bye, Mom." He hung up the phone and noticed the knot in his stomach, an awful tension, which he relieved when he reached in his pocket for his credit card. He left it in small pieces in several trash barrels as he walked back to the apartment.

When Carolyn hung up the phone, she sat at the kitchen table for a while until Julie came in.

"Who was that?"

"Huh?... Oh, it was your brother. He says he's trying to do some modeling to pay his expenses while he's looking for a job."

"Cool. Maybe he'll meet a nice guy and settle down."

"Julie, why do you insist on talking like that? You know how it annoys people."

"The truth is annoying, Mom. What's for dinner?"

"Juanita will fix you something. Your father and I are going to the museum benefit tonight. That reminds me, I guess I should start getting ready."

Upstairs, Carolyn sat in front of a mirror with a liner pencil and thought of what she would tell her husband. Unlike most of her contemporaries, she wore a minimal amount of makeup. It was only a coincidence that not much was needed. She mostly couldn't be bothered with all the putting on and taking off. What little she used was as much a ritual habit as it was a deliberate cover of a face on which the lines of age were drawn softly.

By seven o'clock when the driver came, there was still a trace of twilight and the air was cool enough for the wrap that draped over her evening gown. When the car arrived at the Reynolds Tower, she saw Jack crossing the plaza in his tuxedo. "*How handsome he still looks.*" She wondered what was on his mind. She only knew for sure that whatever it was, he wasn't likely to say.

He kissed her when he got in the car. "You look beautiful, honey. By the way, the press may be asking about what's going on with the takeover. Blake and I have been giving them the 'No comment' response until we have the clearance from the Fed. So don't be surprised if we get pressured to say something tonight."

"I talked to Dan today."

"Great. How's he doing?"

"It sounds like he's having a hard time. I tried to get him to talk to you and get some help, but he seems determined to get by on his own."

"Well, that's good, isn't it? Let's face it, he's led a sheltered life. You thought it was a good idea for him to try to be out on his own for while, and I agree."

"You didn't at first."

"I do now."

"Maybe you should call him."

"Didn't I just hear you say that he doesn't want to talk to me? Remember. He's got something to prove. I'll check in with him at Thanksgiving. I promise not to say 'I told you so.' In the meantime, he's smart enough not to get in too much trouble. Don't worry, he won't starve."

"Is that what it would take for you to call him first?"

"Sweetheart, don't be silly. Of course not. We're here. Smile for the cameras."

◪ ◪ ◪

There were a few portfolios left on his desk and Dan took to absentmindedly going through them, wondering how he might have looked better or if the choice of pictures was right or if the layout was as good as it could have been. He had been, he was sure, to every modeling agency in New York. There wasn't much else to do in the apartment, his few possessions having been repeatedly rearranged in his small room. It was raining on a late October morning. Marty had left for the day. Dan kept the folded page of the *New York Press* in his Filofax with the same index card on which his mother had written Steve Baldwin's number. By now he knew Steve's secretary, Beverly Rosmore, and she was obviously irritated when he called again.

"Hi, Beverly, this is Chance Gardner."

"Good morning, Mr. Gardner."

"I'm just wondering if Mr. Baldwin is in."

"He is, but he's in a meeting. Mr. Gardner, I should tell you that Mr. Baldwin is a very busy man, and unless you can tell me why you're calling, I don't know when he's likely to have the time to call you back."

"Well, actually, you see, I'm a Duke graduate too, like Mr. Baldwin, and I've just moved to New York and I was hoping that maybe Mr. Baldwin might have a few minutes to talk to me and that maybe he would have some suggestions for me about employment."

"Mr. Gardner, there are hundreds, maybe thousands of Duke graduates in this city. Mr. Baldwin is a lawyer, not an employment agency. I really think it would be more appropriate for you to call the employment office at the university or the alumni club here in New York. I need to go now. Good-bye, Mr. Gardner."

Just as she was hanging up, Steve Baldwin was reaching across Beverly's desk for a document. "Who was that, another stockbroker?" he asked.

"Some guy named Chance Gardner who's called here a half-dozen times and finally told me he's just graduated from Duke and wants to meet you so you can help him find a job."

"What'd you tell him?"

"I told him to get a life. It's ten-thirty and you're supposed to be at Morgan Stanley in twenty minutes. There's a car waiting for you downstairs."

"Thanks, Mom."

"Go!"

◼ ◼ ◼

"Elite Escorts."

"Ah, hi. I saw your ad in the *New York Press*. I'm interested in working for you."

"Let's start with your name."

"Ah... Chance... Chance Gardner."

"Hi, Chance, this is Phil. You need to come in for an interview. Our offices are in Chelsea. Can you come by today?"

"How about now?"

"I can't see you right now, but can you be here at twelve?"

"Fine."

"We're at 225 West Twenty-eighth on the second floor. I'll see you at noon."

It took half an hour to walk to Chelsea, and it was 11:00 a.m. He put on a pair of jeans, a T-shirt, and a denim jacket and headed out the door. As he got closer to Eighth Avenue, his pace slowed considerably. He stopped more often, looking at window displays in which he would normally have no interest. He looked at his own reflection in the glass and wondered what the hell he was doing. He stopped in a fast-food restaurant and a scraggly-faced man, drunk and smelling foul, sat down on the chair opposite him in the two-seated booth.

"Spare some change?"

"No, actually, I'm sort of broke too."

"What makes you think I'm broke? Donald Trump is lookin' for money all the time and he ain't broke. You don't look broke."

"Oh, but I am, and destitute too. I'm on my way to hell. Would you like to join me? You could be Virgil, a friend of mine, and not by chance, sent by my lady Beatrice to lead me through the paths of the Inferno." Dan waved his hand, gesturing to the other patrons in the crowded, noisy restaurant. "Here we are at the chasm of pain, which holds the din of infinite grief."

The man peered back at Dan through the film of cataracts. He wiped the snot from under his nose and his sleeve caught a few pieces of egg sandwich from an earlier meal.

"Kid, you're fucking crazy."

"I am," Dan said earnestly. Noticing that it was just twelve, he started to get up. "We're all crazy here. But don't worry, it's medication time and soon I'll feel no more pain. Are you sure you won't join me?"

The man got up, shaking his head, and shuffled away, leaving a trail of fumes that momentarily changed Dan's complexion, a mix of smells, urine drying in the man's pants and the gaseous remains of partially digested garbage.

Just a few minutes after twelve, Dan rang the buzzer in the foyer of the brownstone. When he got to the second floor, a thin man answered the door at the end of the hallway and beckoned him in.

"You must be Chance."

"Yes."

"That's a good name. We have a few boys named Chance, but no other Chance Gardner. I assume that's not your real name."

"That's right."

Phil led him into a small office, sat behind a desk, and motioned to a chair for Dan to sit in. "You can take your jacket off," he said, as he took up a clipboard and a pencil. "I've got another appointment at twelve-thirty so we'll have to cover some things quickly. I assume you've never worked like this before."

"What makes you say that?"

"Because your hands are shaking. But that's OK, some people have to work hard at being inexperienced. Obviously, for you that's not a problem. I've been doing this for a while. I have a good client list. No weirdos. If you tell me what you can and can't do, I won't get you in over your head. OK?"

"Fine."

"Tell me little about yourself, really, just a little."

"I was born and raised in Charlotte. I have a Bachelor of Science degree from—"

"No, no, no. I don't care about that. What do you like to do?"

"What do you mean?"

Phil put down the clipboard and sighed. "Let's start like this. What do you like, sexually? Are you a top or a bottom?"

"Huh?" Dan was wondering to himself, *"What should I say?"*

"Oh, boy," said Phil. "Are you sure you want to do this? Have you ever been fucked?"

"Well, yeah, sort of, but I don't want to do that."

"So, you like to fuck?"

"Yeah."

"OK," said Phil. "We'll say you're a top. How old are you?"

"Twenty-two."

"You're about five eleven?"

"Right."

"We'll say six feet. How big are you?"

"About one-seventy."

""Oh, God," moaned Phil. "Not your weight. Your dick, how big is your dick? No. Don't tell me. Just stand up."

Dan looked around to see if anyone was watching.

"Are you sure you can do this?" Phil looked impatiently while Dan stood up. "Take off your T-shirt." He looked across the desk and then started writing and talking out loud, clinically, reciting statistics. "Blond hair, blue eyes, college boy. Six feet, one hundred and seventy pounds, forty-four chest, thirty-one waist… hmmm." Phil lowered his eyes looking across at Dan's groin… "eight inches, cut." Then he continued writing silently at the bottom of the form as Dan stood there.

"Can I get dressed?"

"Oh, yeah, sure… Here's the deal. My clients are executives, lawyers, doctors, etc. They're all professionals, very discreet. Some of them are easy. They just like to hang out with good-looking young men. Generally speaking they don't want some-one who's jaded. They want someone just like you. For an easy call, the rate is $150. You make a hundred bucks. That's basical-ly no sex. They may want to jerk themselves off or they may want you to help." He peered over his glasses at Dan. "Don't looked shocked if they ask for help, OK?"

Phil got up and kept talking as he opened the drawer in the filing cabinet behind him. "If you change your mind about get-ting fucked, by the way, that's a bottom, the rate is $300. No matter how professional and safe the client looks, you gotta make him put on a condom. If you're a top, do I need to explain that?" Dan shook his head. "OK, if you're a top," Phil contin-ued, "the rate is $200." He closed the filing cabinet drawer and sat down. "Obviously there's a supply-and-demand thing going on here, but I don't have time to talk about that now. Let's just start with an easy one."

"Umm… OK."

"They pay you $150, cash up front. Fifty bucks of that comes back to me. You deliver my cut the same day for an after-noon appointment, next morning if you work in the evening."

"I need to do this during the day when my roommate is out," said Dan. "I can't take a client at home after four and you shouldn't call me. I have a pager. I'll call you back right away."

"That's not a problem," said Phil. "Never, absolutely never give your phone number to a client. All calls come through me. If I find out you're working around me, you're finished. You got it?"

"Right. I got it."

"Now listen," said Phil. "This is really simple. Just do what I tell you and you'll be fine. This job isn't as bad as you've probably heard. You'll make good money working a few hours a week, a lot more money than you'd make working forty hours, folding T-shirts at the Gap."

"This is the only personal advice I'll give you. Just keep working your portfolio. You say you want to be a model. That's the job you really want. Well, understand this, at some level of any job, you're selling yourself for money. Some of the clients you'll meet are really powerful and well connected. They've got a father thing going on. Some can actually help you and a few will want to. They like it better if they think you're dependent. You know what I mean? You'll do fine. I gotta go."

Dan was hungry again when he left, so he stopped for another cheeseburger, this time taking it to go and eating it in the park. He was so distracted that he didn't notice the sound of his pager when it first went off. He rushed upstairs to return Phil's call.

"Elite Escorts."

"Hi, it's Dan."

"Dan who?"

"I mean Chance. Chance Gardner. I'm returning your page."

"Oh, hi. I have a client for you. He's perfect. He's from the South. He's a banker. He's charming. He even looks like you. All you have to do is play with yourself and look interested."

"Ah… so… ah… fine, when do you want to send him?"

"This afternoon."

"This afternoon! It's two o'clock. My roommate gets home at five-thirty!"

"He'll be there at four. Don't worry. He's got to catch a plane at Teterboro with some other guys at six. He'll be in and out in a half-hour. I gotta go. Do you want the call or not?"

"Ah… yeah, sure. I'll take it. You're sure he'll be out by four-thirty."

"Chance, just bring my fifty bucks in the morning. Bye."

Dan went to his room and put away the pictures of his family in the top drawer of his desk. He drew the blind and turned on the lamp on the nightstand. *"The brim of hell,"* he thought, as he closed the door to Marty's room and walked down the hall to the kitchen. His mouth was dry and he was sweating. He thought about taking a shower, but then decided to help himself to one of Marty's joints instead. "*Just a half of one,*" he thought, "*just to calm down a little.*" He sat in the living room with the window open and the fan on and he wasn't paying attention to what he was doing until he realized he needed a clip to hold the roach, which he drew on until all that was left was ash.

In the fog of his free-floating anxiety, he didn't notice what time it was until almost four fifteen. He waited another few minutes before he panicked and called Phil. "Where is he?"

"So he's a few minutes late. Relax. He'll be there and, trust me, he's not going to stay for tea. He'll be in and out in a few minutes."

"Phil, it's four-thirty. You told me he'd be here at four."

Before Phil could answer, Dan heard the buzzer. He ran to the living room window and looked out to the stoop and there was the shape of a man in a suit, so he ran back to the phone and hung it up without talking to Phil and ran to the intercom in the kitchen.

When he heard the knock at the door, Dan could feel each beat of his heart in the veins that were throbbing in his head. He didn't bother to check in the spyglass. He fumbled with the deadbolt and pulled on the handle and opened the door, half-thinking he would run past his visitor and out into the street.

"Hi, you must be Chance. I'm Wes. Can I come in?"

"Oh, yeah, sure." Dan said as he stood aside and motioned for the man to come inside. The simple exchange of ordinary greetings helped to orient Dan. Suddenly he realized that the fan was still on high speed and making a terrible racket. As Dan went to the window and unplugged the fan, the man came in and closed the door behind him.

"Sorry I'm late. I had a hard time getting a cab. Phil told me this is your first time. I figured he was lying, but I guess he wasn't. Where are you from?"

"No, he wasn't lying." Dan stopped and looked at his client. It was hard to tell his age, early forties, Dan thought. His hair was graying, but his skin was clear and smooth. He was about Dan's height and weight, someone who took good care of himself, attractive; he could have been a model for the Ralph Lauren suit he was wearing. "I'm from Charlotte."

"I'm from Atlanta," the man said. "Maybe we should go to your room."

Dan pointed down the hall and he followed, noticing how apparently at ease his client seemed, even in a strange apartment.

"Let me help you with that," he said, when Dan started to take off his T-shirt. "You really are nervous," he said, as he pulled it up over Dan's head. "Don't worry. I'm sure not going to hurt you. I have a son your age." He reached down and unbuttoned the fly on Dan's jeans and reached behind him to slide them off. Dan stepped out of them and stood there sweating.

As the man started to take off his jacket, Dan interrupted him. "I need to go to the bathroom. I'll be right back"

"Sure. Take your time. Are you sure you're all right?"

"Yeah, I just need to get some water."

Dan went down the hall and into the bathroom and locked the door behind him. He sat there, naked, on the toilet, bent over with his head on his knees, his face in his hands, thinking, but not really thinking at all, just a thousand million synapses firing at once. This wasn't at all like meeting another boy or even an older man at a club. It was the crash of things falling to the floor in Marty's room that shocked him upright and he ran out of the bathroom to find his client standing in Marty's room with some strips of satin cloth in his hands.

"What are you doing in here? This is my roommate's stuff. You've got to get out of here."

"Your roommate has quite a collection."

"I can't do this," Dan said. "You need to leave."

"Relax, son, I'm not going to hurt you, really. Come here. Sit down."

Dan sat on the edge of Marty's bed and the man sat next to him, so close their bodies were touching. He put his hand on Dan's leg.

"You seem like a nice kid. I know you need the money. Why

don't you just lay down here? I can take care of myself. I'll give you $250. I'll be out of here in a few minutes."

He put his arm around Dan and drew Dan's face to his shoulder. Dan smelled familiar cologne. When he was a boy, sometimes his father would put a little dab of it on his cheek. It made him feel grown up. Now it made him sick.

"Just relax," the man said, as he gently laid Dan down on his back. "I'm not going to hurt you. All you have to do is lie still."

The feel of the satin on his wrists and ankles was soft and not at all restricting and in the haze that settled over the bed, Dan watched as the man stepped back and viewed him.

He got undressed and put his clothes neatly over a chair. He walked around to the foot of the bed, stroking a hard on. Then he knelt on the bed between Dan's outstretched legs. "You're beautiful," he said softly, as he touched Dan.

Dan flinched and felt the tug of the restraints.

"Oh, oh, that's it. You can pull on them a little."

"I don't want to do this. I want you to go."

"Relax. I won't hurt you. Relax, I just want to touch you a little."

"Untie me. Let me go. I want you to leave."

"Ah, that's it. That's it. Oh. I like it like that. Oh. You've got a great body."

"Get out. Get out of here now. Get the fuck out of here!"

"Hey, don't yell. Somebody's going to hear you."

"Untie me and get OUT OF HERE!"

Dan was screaming and looking up and behind him at his left hand, trying to untie the knot, and he didn't notice that the man was off the bed until the pillow covered his face and he couldn't breath. He kept writhing and he thought he heard something like, "OK, I'll go, just stop screaming," but the pillow was covering his head and he didn't see Marty come in and land the force of his weight with his elbow between the man's shoulder blades.

"Motherfucker! What the fuck are you doin'?"

As the man fell away and the pillow with him, Dan could see the look of horror on Marty's face. Their eyes met for a fiery instant and then Marty turned his attention to the body in front of him getting slowly up off the floor. Marty's knee and lower leg connected just below the man's shoulder, in a kick to the side of his chest that sent him against the wall in a daze.

"Get the fuck out of my house! You motherfucker!"

Marty hoisted him up by his arm and dragged him out the door. Then Marty came back for his clothes, lifted the wallet, and threw the pile out the door on the man as he was struggling to get to his feet again.

"You come back here again and I'll kill you!" was all Marty said as he slammed the door.

Dan was completely disoriented, sobbing, and when Marty untied him, he contracted spontaneously into the fetal position, his hands covering his face.

"You stupid fucking idiot!" Marty shouted. "You could have been killed! Are you fucking crazy?"

Marty went on screaming for a while, but every time he paused to take a breath, all he could hear was Dan crying, and when he finally sat down on the bed, Dan recoiled and only cried louder.

"All right, all right," Marty said. "It's all right. He's gone, Dan. No one's going to hurt you."

Marty got on the bed and curled himself around Dan and they lay there for a while. He stroked Dan's hair.

"You're soaking wet. I'm going to go fill up the tub and I want you to stay in it for a while. Will you be all right for a minute?"

"Yeah."

"Do you want a blanket?"

"Yeah, thanks… Marty—"

"Don't talk. Just rest here. I'll be right back."

A few minutes later, Dan was in the cast iron tub with the claw feet, sweat running down his face, steam running down the walls and the mirror. Marty came in with a joint. He took a drag and passed it to Dan. "Here, have some of this. It will help settle you down."

"I'm all right."

"I know. Just have some anyway. Are you sure you didn't sprain anything?"

"Yeah."

"Did he hit you?"

"No."

"Where the fuck did you get that bright idea?"

"Pierre gave me the number. He said that's how he met you."

"Remind me to kill Pierre."

"It wasn't his fault. I did it on my own. The manager at the service told me the guy was harmless. I shouldn't have let the guy tie me up."

"Did that idea just come to you?"

"Don't worry, it won't happen again."

"You're damned fucking straight it won't happen again."

"Now, let's see," said Marty, as he opened the wallet in front of him. "Who was our psycho visitor?"

"His name was Wes," said Dan. "He's a banker."

"Wrong, scrotum head. Here's his card. Let's see… his name is Alfred Grant. Hmm… he's an LLP." Marty looked up, "What's an LLP. Is that like a nurse?"

"Marty, Alfred Grant is a law firm. Lemme see the card."

"No, I got it. Here it is. His name is Wes O'Connor. Here's his license. He's forty-nine. Not in bad shape for forty-nine. He's married. Aren't the kids cute? Take a look."

"Marty, I don't want to look at his pictures."

"Suit yourself. Oooohh weeee! Mr. Wes was flush. Oooohh, baby. There's… ah… let's see." Marty counted the cash. "There's eleven hundred and forty dollars Mr. Wes left behind."

"We can't keep that."

"Oh, you're right, I'm sure Mr. Wes went straight from here to the Twenty-second Precinct to report a missing wallet. Get a clue, Dan. I checked the door five minutes after I threw him out. His ass was dressed and long gone. You ain't never gonna hear from that dude again. Ha, ha, we's rich."

"How can you laugh about it?"

Marty turned to Dan and his countenance was transformed.

"You feelin' better now, bwana? You ready to have a serious conversation?… Man, you could have been killed. For all I know, if I hadn't come home early, you *would* have been killed. And if it wasn't this time, it would be next time. Do you want to talk about something not to laugh about? You ain't in Charlotte no more, Dan. This is New York. People here eat their young. I've been doin' this for six years. I lost track of how many times I've had a knife pulled on me. A real psycho stalked me for almost a year. See these marks on the back of my arm? Client bit me so hard I had to get treated for a puncture wound at St. Francis. Nowadays, I screen my clients myself. I take a particular kind because I know they're weak and they're desperate, and believe it or not I actually feel sorry for them. You're too good, man. It takes guile to survive in this business and you haven't got one fucking ounce of it."

"I have no money."

"Well… that's not exactly true. You got at least eleven hundred and forty dollars. I ain't gonna throw you out. You're like family to me, man. You're gonna come work on my show with me. It's OK, Dan. We'll think of something."

Dan reached his long arm out over the tub toward Marty, who took his hand and held it.

"You just hang here for a little while longer. I'll go make us some dinner. I know eatin' always makes you feel better."

ADAPTATION

The lights in Michael's office were wired to a motion detector. He had been sitting still long enough for the automatic switch to turn off everything but his Quotron. So he sat there in the dark, noticing the neatly tabulated rows of stock trades, in reds and greens against the blue background of the computer screen. In six months, he'd landed his own office, and several assistants, helping to manage what he had come to realize was an enormous penny stock scam operation.

It had all happened so fast, but as he told Angela, repeatedly, he had the "need for speed." He was at the office six days a week. Worthless stocks were peddled to thousands of retail clients like small, but not lethal, doses of arsenic. Some clients got sick right away; others seemed to have an incredible capacity and strange willingness to ingest poison. They all lost money and eventually closed their accounts, but as Michael and the principals of the firm reminded the brokers, "There are twelve million people in New York, and more coming every day. Stay on the phone. You'll get new clients."

Many times he thought of Dan and his sudden departure. There was a picture of the two of them on his desk. He wanted to call, but the firm was turning over hundreds of clients a day and Michael's job was to keep track of the living, the sick, and the dead. All those years in the back office at Eastman & Maxwell were paying off. But it was getting harder and harder to keep up. He would finish each day, each week, each month, exhausted, burned out, telling himself, *"I gotta call him."*

Through the wall of glass in front of him, he could see the lights of the skyscrapers in Midtown. This was what and where he'd always wanted to be: a player in the center of the universe. But not like this. He'd been sitting there, trying to figure out how he was going to move $3 million from the firm's clearing bank to an offshore shell company and then into the vapor world of numbered accounts, several of which were his own. He was breaking so many laws, he'd long ago stopped trying to keep track of anything but the task at hand. Maybe it was the darkness of his office, maybe it was the fact that he had been sitting so still, but he couldn't help thinking to himself, *"What the fuck am I doing?"* He sat forward and the motion turned on the lights in his office. He reached for the phone and dialed a number in Charlotte that he knew by heart.

◼ ◼ ◼

Marty knew Dan could sing and move well, but now he needed to know if Dan had the stage presence, the attitude to pull the attention of an audience. He wanted to bring Dan into the group as an equal, not just someone playing an instrument, or as a vocalist to showcase his own talent. He had worked with lots of backup before, but never with a partner, and he was nervous, waiting for Dan at the recording studio. It was already 8:00 p.m. and they only had the studio booked for two hours.

Dan was out of breath when he got there. "Sorry I'm late." He took his backpack and coat off in the control room and went into the studio. "I'm ready."

Marty's voice came through over the intercom. "OK, remember, be careful with the P's and S's. They make the microphone pop." Marty queued up the music. "Start with the first verse, man."

"Forgive me, Father, for I have sinned." Dan sounded like he couldn't decide if he should be talking or singing.

"Remember, Dan, you're supposed to be an altar boy. It works if you're nervous, but you need to sing. OK, start again with the first verse."

"Forgive me, Father, for I have sinned," Dan sang like he was in pain. It came to him naturally.

"That's excellent, excellent!" Marty said. "Now we'll take

that piece and put it in just before the section where I'm singing. Marty started pushing buttons on the equalizer and control panel. Then he mixed the rhythms and beats with each of their voices.

Marty's singing began in a whisper. "Your secret's safe. Your secret's safe. They know you're straight." Marty laid the track of Dan's voice mixed with his voice next.

"Wow, Marty, that sounds great," said Dan. "How did you do that?"

"Years of training, bwana, years of training," said Marty. "Dan, this is going to work. Believe me. You know, I've always worked alone, but together we have something powerful… Let's take a medicine break. It makes me think clearer."

"OK, where's the restroom?"

"In the back on the left."

Marty rolled the joint. "So how do you feel?"

"Great, I really feel good."

"So what will we called ourselves?"

Dan laughed. "How about the Two Tops?"

"That's stupid. It needs to be something like Gender Benders or Bending Genders."

"What is it with you and this gender thing? It's always gender this and gender that."

"Because that's what performing is all about, being whatever you want to be, freedom to cross lines, blurring things that people think are so fucking clear, but aren't."

Dan exhaled and squinted. "I think this marijuana is making everything blurred for me."

"That's it!" said Marty. "That's it. Blurred Genders."

Dan and Marty were laughing together. They were stoned. Marty settled down and then looked like he was trying to figure out the logistics. "In between you looking for a job, and me doing calls, we'll need to stick to a schedule to make the song work. Then we need a few more songs and we have an act."

❖ ❖ ❖

When they got back to the apartment, Marty saw the pained look on Dan's face as he played the message on his machine.

"Hey, Dan, it's Mike. I got this number from your mother. Listen, man, I'm really sorry it's been so long since we've talked. I miss you. I really do. I've got tickets to the Duke – St. John's game this Thursday at the Garden. Let's get a drink at the alumni reception and then go to the game. Call me tonight."

"Don't look at me," Marty said, "you're the one who's in love with him. You decide if you're gonna call him. I'm goin' to bed… Of course," Marty's voice trailed off as he walked down the hall, "he sounds like an asshole to me."

Dan sat alone in the living room for a while, listening to the radiator's noisy, clanging advice. "Call him. Don't call him. Call him."

"It's 11:30," Dan thought. *"He's probably in bed by now, probably fucking Angela. I wonder if she screams as loud now that I'm not there to hear it."*

The switch, from rational to irrational thought, from voluntary to involuntary motion, was evident when Dan picked up the phone and dialed the number in Tribeca. The voice that answered helped to complete the transition.

"Hey, Dan, what's up, man?"

Dan exhaled. "I'm returning your call, Mike."

"Yeah, well, like I said, I got tickets for Thursday. Should be a great game."

"I guess it will be, Mike, but I think we need to talk first."

"Yeah, we can meet at the alumni reception before the game."

"No, I mean really talk, Mike, not just some cocktail conversation."

There was a pause in the conversation. Michael said, "Yeah." Then another pause as if he had stopped himself and realized there was something in Dan's voice that marked a change in the way things had been since they were boys. Michael started again, this time not so sure of himself or his friend. "Whatever, Dan, you know, we don't have to go to the game. We can just get together and talk. Like I said, I miss you."

"I've missed you too." Dan ran the tip of the index finger of his left hand over his bottom lip as he cradled the phone with his other hand and his shoulder. "Let's meet for coffee. I'll see you at the Tic Tock Diner at five on Thursday. It's on Thirty-fourth and Eighth. We can go to the reception and the game from there."

Dan sat still in the living room, staring at the cracks in the ceiling. He heard the sound of Marty coming out of his room and going into the bathroom, the toilet flushing, the footsteps coming into the living room and the air going out of the cushions in the couch as Marty finally sat down.

"How'd it go?"

Dan finally stopped trying to make sense of the pattern of lines and cracks and looked at Marty. "We're going to a basketball game on Thursday. We're going to meet for coffee first."

"You look like you're hurtin' real bad."

Dan sighed. "I was just thinking about how everything is connected, you know, like there are no accidents. The *S* in my initials stands for Saul. It was my grandfather's name."

"Yeah… and…"

Dan sighed. "Did you ever read the Old Testament, Marty?"

"Yeah, sure. Grandma took me to church just to hear the gospel singers."

"Remember the story about David? When he was a boy, he was found by King Saul, and he went to live in Saul's palace."

"I know," said Marty, "and Saul raised him as his own son."

"Right. And Saul's son, Jonathan, was David's friend." Dan looked back up at the ceiling. "I got interested in the story because of my name. You know, even before I knew what it meant, I knew that David and Jonathan were lovers. I used to have this fantasy that Michael and I were like them. There's no one in my family I'm closer to than him. When I went to the Academy in Florence and I saw Michelangelo's *David*, I thought, my God, he really does look like Michael."

"Hey, man, the way I remember it, that story doesn't have a happy ending."

"No, it doesn't. Saul turned against David. He was jealous. Of course the Sunday school teachers didn't say why, but I knew. So Saul plotted to kill David. But Jonathan chose David over his father. He saved David's life and then he died in the battle between his father and David."

Marty saw the tears on the rims of Dan's eyes. He was about to say something when Dan cleared his throat and sat up. It was as if posture could bring him back to the world of hard facts. He sniffled and wiped his face and when he looked at Marty, his eyes were clear.

"You know, Marty, I realize that I was angry at Michael because he wouldn't fit into my neat little dream world. Maybe I got so fucked up this summer trying to pretend I didn't feel the way I really do. I don't know if he can accept me for who I am, but I've got to accept the facts about us."

Marty was opening his mouth to speak, but Dan interrupted him.

"He's not an asshole, Marty. He just doesn't love me the way I love him. I don't know if he knows how to love anyone… You know, it's strange, he sounded so sad over the phone, sort of lonely. He said he missed me."

"It's your thing, bwana… Hey, you want me to fix us something to eat?" Marty smiled.

Dan smiled back and then laughed. "No, that's OK. I'm fine. Thanks Marty. I need to get some sleep."

� ◪ ◪

On Thursday night, Marty was expecting Dan at Il Panino, their favorite "red sauce place" in the East Village. He had worked at the studio until ten and he was just sitting down to a late dinner when Dan came in, breathless, looking like he had run all the way from Madison Square Garden.

"You're not going to believe what happened tonight. It's incredible!"

"Let me guess. He realizes he's gay. He loves you. And you two are moving in together."

"No! Nothing like that."

"Well, start at the beginning, but remember, the restaurant closes at midnight."

"It's incredible," Dan said as he tore into the bread on the table.

"You said that already."

"OK. I was early at the Tic Tock. You know, we were supposed to meet there for coffee."

"Right."

"So, I was sitting in the booth and I saw Michael get out of the cab."

Marty listened as Dan re-lived his meeting. He was puzzled by the fact that Dan was so animated, excited actually, retelling such a sad story, as if there was some happy outcome, which he could not imagine.

"He looked awful," Dan said, "even when I saw him through the window of the diner, I could tell. I was in a booth toward the back, but I was facing the door, and he saw me when he came in. He looked like he'd been holed up in a cave for the last four months."

As Michael walked toward the back of the diner, Dan stood up to greet him.

"Hey, man," Michael said, "it's great to see you." He hugged Dan, like he needed to hold on to him. "Sorry I'm late. We had trouble settling a few trades. You want some coffee?" Michael gestured to the waitress. "Two coffees, please."

They looked at each other from across the table for a while. Twenty years together, "Like two peas in a pod," their mothers used to say. As close as two people could be. Dan couldn't tell if he was looking at a complete stranger or the ghost of his old friend. Michael's skin was gray. There were bags under his eyes. He was constantly sniffling and pressing his nostrils together, the kind of habit that so many of Dan's club buddies had from inhaling too much white powder.

Finally, it was Michael who spoke. "I've missed you, Dan. I

really have. I'm sorry about us getting all fucked up in July. I didn't know what to say. I still don't know what to say. I mean—"

"Mike," Dan interrupted with his prepared speech, "I was mad when I left you in the summer. When I told you I loved you, I was mad that you didn't love me the way—"

Michael started to say something, but Dan cut him off. "Listen to me. Listen. My not talking to you earlier about how I felt was my fault, not yours. We'll always be brothers, but I realize now we won't be lovers."

Michael was looking down at his coffee.

"I want you to look at me," Dan said, "and tell me you still love me and that you accept me for who I am. Can you do that?"

Michael looked up. There were tears welling in his eyes, but he was struggling not to cry. He looked down again. "Sure, Dan, you're all I have left of a family."

Marty had been listening to Dan's narrative while eating and drinking, digesting it all slowly. He noticed Dan had stopped and was looking at him. "I'm still waiting," Marty said as he put his wineglass down, "for the incredible part."

"Don't you get it, Marty? I looked at him and I thought, now that he knows, he can't say it! He can't say he loves me."

"What's so incredible about that? The guy's an asshole, Dan. There's *nothing* there for you."

"You're wrong Marty. He's just fucked up right now."

"So, you *like* fucked up? C'mon, Dan, tell me the rest of the story. I'm dying to hear something incredible."

Dan stared at Marty. *"You're just like him,"* he thought. *"Take no prisoners; shoot the wounded; only the strong survive. What's the point of trying to tell you anything?"* So he decided to pick up the story again at the reception. He didn't tell Marty what happened when they were leaving the diner. As he and Michael both got up from the booth, Michael hugged him, and he said it so quietly, as if to be sure no one else in the world would hear him. "I love you, Dan." Then he looked down again and said, "C'mon, let's go."

They got to the reception and put on their nametags.

Michael was drawn immediately to a wide-eyed and well-endowed high school senior who was applying to Duke. Dan joined in their conversation for a little while, watching Michael reconstruct his facade of confidence. Suddenly, he heard a man shout from across the room, "Steve Baldwin!" Dan turned and watched him shake hands vigorously with the man Carolyn had described as her high school sweetheart.

"Oh my God," Dan thought, *"this is my chance."* Then he realized he was wearing a nametag with "Dan O'Brien" written on it. He excused himself from the conversation with Michael and his fawning admirer, and headed in Steve Baldwin's direction, removing the nametag as he made his way through the crowd.

When he reached the hors d'oeuvres table, he saw that Steve Baldwin was engaged in a conversation with the man who had called his name. *"I'll wait until they're finished,"* Dan thought, *"then I'll introduce myself."*

Across the room, Richard Wein was regaling his friend with the story of his day. "It's so sad, Steve. You know, we've been their investment bankers for years. I used to think Carlton Moore had a brain, but the way this one's going, we'll be out of a client by early next year."

"C'mon, Richard," said Steve, "I rather doubt Goldman Sachs will hang black crepe on the doors if NCBT gets New York Trust. Say, on another subject, do you think you could manage to turn around without making it obvious? Get a look at the blond kid over by the hors d'oeuvres table."

Richard glanced over his shoulder and then turned sharply back to his friend. "Steven, listen to me. There are laws against sex with minors."

"Oh, Richard, you're such a killjoy. There's no harm in looking and besides, he's no minor."

"You know, Steven, I don't mean to bring this up, but it's been a year since Chad died and I haven't seen you with anyone since then who looked like they were old enough to have a learner's permit."

Steve's eyes were fixed across the room as he spoke to Richard. "Whenever someone says they don't mean something, they always do. I'm tired of hearing that drivel from you, whether you say you mean it or not."

Richard was about to defend himself when a man standing at a microphone at the end of the room began to address the crowd. "Ladies and gentlemen, on behalf of the Duke University Alumni Association of New York, I'd like to thank you all for joining us tonight for what I'm sure will be a fantastic game, which I should add, is about to begin. So you all want to start heading for your seats."

As the announcement was being broadcast, Dan had his back to Steve. "*Oh, fuck,*" he thought, "*how am I going to go up to him now? He must be with that guy. How am I going to introduce myself?*" Dan turned around to check on the position of his target and there, now standing in front of him, was Steve Baldwin.

"That's some plate of food," Steve said. "Don't they feed you at home?"

"*What a cool-looking guy,*" Dan thought. Steve was Dan's height, about six feet, dark hair, brown eyes. He was dressed in a suit, but it was tailored to show off a very well kept physique.

"I'm Steve Baldwin," he said, extending his hand.

Dan put his plate down on the table. "Hi. I'm Chance Gardner. I've been trying to meet you for the last few months."

"Well," said Steve, "I'm glad you've succeeded, but I assure you I can't imagine why I would have kept you from that."

Dan looked down. "I've actually been calling your secretary. She wouldn't put me through."

"Oh, that's Beverly all right, the palace guard."

Richard Wein came up behind them and put one hand on Steve's shoulder, the other on his arm, and gently pulled Steve in the direction of the exit. "Excuse me, fellas, but we have clients to meet. Right, Steve?"

Richard looked at Dan, who was obviously uncomfortable. "Hi," he said, "if you haven't been to Durham yet, I'm sure you'll love it. There are thousands of kids there, your age."

Dan stiffened and shot a glare back. "Actually, I graduated last spring."

Steve was letting himself be pulled away and then he stopped. "What did you say your name is?"

Their eyes met.

"Chance." Dan swallowed. "Chance Gardner."

"Call my office tomorrow. I'll tell Beverly to put you through. OK?" Steve smiled.

"Sure," said Dan. He was embarrassed about the lie, annoyed at being treated like a kid, but completely charged with a sense of excitement he didn't understand.

Marty listened as Dan finished the story about the game and saying good-bye to Michael. Dan carried on about how "cool" Steve looked and how he couldn't believe his fantastic luck.

"You're right, bwana," Marty said as he paid the check, "that is incredible. You've got to get in there to see him. Now, remember, you told me that you had your back to him. All he could see from across the room was your ass, so he wasn't coming over to talk to you about your IQ. And, like you said, when he introduced himself, he was definitely giving you the look. So now we've got to make sure you look hot the next time you see him."

"Marty, for Christ's sake, do you have to reduce everything to sex?"

"C'mon," said Marty, "they want to clean up here. We can talk on the way home."

Walking down Second Avenue, Marty didn't hold anything back. "How many times do I have to tell you? It's the common denominator. Just because people don't talk about it more doesn't mean it isn't true."

Dan didn't say anything. There was no arguing with Marty. "*Besides,*" Dan thought to himself, "*what if he's right?... Maybe he is right.*"

Steve took Dan's call the next day as arranged. He invited Dan to his office for sandwiches at the end of the week. When Dan arrived, Beverly showed him in. It was a large corner office, with glass walls and a view up Park Avenue toward the Pan Am Building. Steve was on the phone. He gestured for Dan to sit down on the couch. Dan looked at the arrangement of photographs, degrees, and awards on the wall as Steve talked. There were lots of pictures of Steve with celebrities.

Steve finished his call. "Hi," he said as walked over to Dan and extended his hand, "Beverly admits that you have been calling. I'm sorry I didn't recognize your name when we were at the game. I get so many calls from brokers."

Steve sat down in the chair in front of the coffee table. "Beverly ordered us some sandwiches. From the way I saw you eating at the game, I told her to order a large platter." They both laughed. Steve realized he was staring. "I know I don't know you, but I'd swear we've met before."

"I don't think we have met," Dan said, "but I know what you mean."

Dan told Steve about his photo portfolio and attempts to find work as a model. It was a conversation that proceeded in fits and starts. They ate and talked between interruptions.

"Do you always get this many calls?" Dan asked.

"I'm afraid so, and I'm going to have to get back to work soon." Steve was scrambling because he had a two o'clock appointment and he needed at least an hour to prepare.

Then Beverly came in. "It's Marc Jackson and he says he has to talk to you."

"Excuse me," said Steve. He took the call at his desk. Dan wandered over to the far end of the office, trying not to overhear the call. This was not the meeting he had hoped for or expected: a few bites of a sandwich, a few lines of conversation. *But there's something here for me,*" he thought. Looking out the window, he could see the faint reflection of the man at the desk. *"I know him."*

Steve was talking on the phone and thinking of how he was going to salvage something of this meeting. *"I shouldn't have done this over lunch."* He was listening to his client, but his eyes were fixed on the silhouette of the young man at the window. *"I know him."* He looked down at his scribbled notes, legible only to him and Beverly. He wanted to be sure he had it all down before he hung up. Then he looked up again and it hit him; he made the rather obvious connection.

"Hey, Marc, there's a young man in my office and I've been

talking to him about his modeling career. I want to send him over to see you."

Dan was trying not to pay attention. It was his polite upbringing. But he heard the comment as he stared out the window harder. To distract himself, he tried reading the license plates of the cars on Park Avenue.

"I know I'm just a lawyer, but you know I have good taste… uh-huh… uh-huh…"

"Say yes. Say yes," Dan thought, *"Oh, please, say yes."* He thought of the time he was at bat in little league and his father had come to watch and he promised all kinds of things to God if he would only let him get a hit.

"Marc, he's got a great ass."

It was a reflex reaction: Dan turned around and looked at Steve, who suddenly realized he'd been lost in his own thoughts and had been caught off guard. He looked down at his legal pad. Dan looked back out the window.

"OK…. OK…. I appreciate it…. On this other matter, I'll have Tom Hogan get back to Bob. I think the Master License Agreement covers you, but I just want to be sure. OK… OK… Sure, next week sometime. I'll have Beverly check your calendar with Gina and make a reservation for us. OK. Bye."

Dan knew the call was over, but he waited until Steve came over to the window, waited for Steve to say something first.

"Chance, I have to go." He held out a piece of paper. "Sometime this afternoon, call this guy and arrange to get your portfolio over to him. He works for Marc Jackson. There's an audition next week. He'll fill you in on all the details. If this doesn't work, I know lots of people in the business so I'm sure I can get you fixed up with something."

Dan took the piece of paper and made sure he could read the writing. He looked up. He wasn't sure of what to say.

"Listen," said Steve, "I'm sorry this was such a rush job. We should have met outside of the office. I'd like to help you. Whatever happens with this, call me. I'll make sure Beverly knows to put you through. OK?"

Dan was putting on his coat. "Don't worry about the lunch.

I really appreciate your seeing me. I'll call you as soon as I hear about the audition." Dan extended his hand. "Thanks again."

"You're welcome," said Steve as he shook Dan's hand. "Beverly can show you how to get back to the elevators. It's a bit of a maze out there."

◨ ◨ ◨

The house faced east on Queens Road. Even on a cold Sunday after Thanksgiving, the sun flooded through the oversized windows in the library. It was warm. She kept playing the same music over and over again: Mozart's Clarinet Concerto in A Major. To Carolyn, it was a haunting melody, the solo clarinet, and then the orchestra's refrain, as if in harmony with the plaintive cry of the spirits she heard, "We know, we know, we miss her too."

There was a picture on the mantel of the two of them, Carolyn and Carla on the beach on a glorious summer day. She could almost hear the sounds of waves over the sweet sad music. She sipped a glass of wine and sat alone. She heard the front door open and Julie's footsteps in the hall.

"Hi, there!" said Carolyn, "I thought you weren't coming back until tomorrow. How'd it go?"

"We finished early. It went fine." Julie took off her coat. "Where's Dad?"

"He's in New York. They had to leave yesterday because…" Carolyn put her hand to her forehead. "I can't remember exactly why. It was something to do with the bank."

"Mom, are you OK?"

"Yes, why?"

"Did you drink that whole bottle of wine?"

"Oh, Julie, don't be such a snoop. I've been listening to music."

"Mom, I thought Dad wasn't leaving until tomorrow. I didn't think you'd be here alone."

Carolyn was struck by the irony. *"Out of the mouths of babes,"* she thought. *"I've been alone most of my life."*

"Mom, I know you were upset about Dan not coming home for Thanksgiving, but I really think we just have to give him some time to get himself together."

"I asked you to call him." Carolyn couldn't help herself. She had to bring it up again. She had practically begged Julie.

"And I told you why I wouldn't. I told him I would let him be alone for a while."

"I don't understand," Carolyn thought. *"Who would ever want to be alone?"*

Julie sat down on the couch and took her mother's hand. "Did you go to Carla's memorial mass this morning?"

"Yes."

"I should have stayed. I'm worried about you."

"Why," asked Carolyn, "because I'm having a glass of wine?"

"No, because it's two o'clock in the afternoon and you're having a *bottle* of wine. Mom, I really am sorry. I should have told them I couldn't do the recording this weekend."

Carolyn sat forward and took Julie's hand in both of hers. "You know, Julie, I used to think that happiness was a relative thing. I looked at everything I had: a handsome and successful husband, wonderful children, and a caring friend. I had everything. Sometimes I would think of Carla and all her struggles, trying to raise Michael on her own with only a teacher's salary, then getting cancer, and yet she was happy. Even if I wasn't, I at least thought I should be." Carolyn sighed. "Now, I don't know what to think."

"I can't believe it." Julie's anger was building. "I can't believe Dad left you here alone."

"Oh, Julie. You say it as if you're surprised." Carolyn thought, *What can I say to her?* She got up and turned off the music and then came back to sit on the couch. "I don't think I ever told you why your father and I didn't have any more children after you and Dan." Carolyn was looking out the window and talking as if she were telling the story to herself. "We didn't use any birth control after you were born. I figured I wouldn't worry about having any more children. If it happened, it happened. You had just turned three when I realized I was pregnant again. There was so much going on. Everything was finally turning around for your father at the bank. I was just recovering from Carla's... from her disclosure to me. After about two months, I had gained a little weight, but I wasn't showing."

"Then, one Sunday night, after we had gone to bed, I started to get these terrible cramps, you know, sort of like when you have your period, but much worse. I went into the bathroom... When I saw the blood in the toilet, I realized that I'd had a miscarriage... Your father slept through the whole thing."

"You mean you didn't wake him up?"

"Well, I told him when I got back to bed. By then, it was almost time for him to get up. He had to catch a plane somewhere. He asked me if I was all right, but you know, it was one of those questions with the subtle message: 'I hope you're all right, because I have to leave.' I told Carla about it that morning when she came to get Dan. We kept the boys out of camp. She stayed with me for the week until your father came back. I made a doctor's appointment the next week and started on the pill."

"Mom, I have to ask you this question. Why do you stay with him?"

Carolyn leaned forward and hugged Julie. "Oh, sweetheart, I know it's hard for you to understand, but... I love him. We're different. You've heard the saying, 'men are from Mars, women are from Venus.'"

"Yeah, but Mom, he's from Pluto, you know, far away and very cold."

"But in his own way, Julie, I know he loves me. He's trying to be strong for all of us. He has this idea in his head that he needs to protect us."

"We don't need to be protected, and besides, how is that supposed to be enough?"

Carolyn extended her arms, with her hands on Julie's shoulders. "That hasn't been enough, but it also hasn't been all there is. I accepted the fact that your father had to leave yesterday the same way I accepted the fact of his leaving after I miscarried. You know, if all the defining events of our marriage involved him leaving, then, of course, we would have been separated long ago."

"Mom, it's not me you have to convince. You're the one who's married to him."

"Oh, I know, Julie. I wish you could see that there is another side of him that is not only capable of loving, but also wants to be loved. I do love him. We have shared some wonderful intimate moments together." Carolyn paused. "I wish there were more… Anyway, some days are better than others, and today has been a not so good day."

Julie was looking down. For a change, she decided not to say what she was thinking.

"Look at me," said Carolyn. "I'm glad you're home. I love you, Julie."

"*Saying it back isn't enough,*" Julie thought. "*I want to do something.*" There was the obvious salve. "Mom, I promised Dan I'd give him some time to get himself together in New York… I'll get him to come home for Christmas, OK? We'll all be together."

ACCELERATION

"What are you wearing?" Marty was busy packing for an out call in the West Village after his voice lesson, but he knew that today was Dan's big day.

"What do you mean, 'What am I wearing?' Marty, it's a job modeling their underwear and they're supplying that. I don't think it matters what I wear before I get undressed. I'm going to the gym at ten. I'll try to get as pumped as I can and then I'm supposed to be at the audition at one."

"You don't get it, Dan. They want a look, and how you look before you get undressed is important." Marty went to Dan's closet and rifled through a pile of mixed clean and dirty things on the floor, picking out Dan's outfit for the day. "Here, wear these. I gotta go. I'll see you there at one. I'm not going to let you fuck this up. We can't afford it."

"Marty, I'll be fine."

"I know," Marty replied. "I'll see you at one."

Dan took his time finishing the bowl of Frosted Flakes and walked up and down the hall in his underwear, trying to move the way Marty had shown him over and over again. He looked in the mirror. He would be turning twenty-three in a couple of months. He had no job and, except for Steve Baldwin's introduction, no reason for high expectations of getting this job. But he was not worried.

Ever since Marty had taken him in to work in his group, things had been happening for him. The talk he had with Mike before the Duke basketball game had been their first honest conversation since childhood. He finally met Steve Baldwin and managed to get some help, ironically enough, without having to use his family connections. It was Steve who sought him out from across the room at the reception. Suddenly he was aware of himself and he liked what he saw when he looked in the mirror.

Dan arrived at the address on the West Side on time, freshly pumped from the gym, dressed in the clothes Marty had selected. He watched a parade of young men, each one more perfect than the one before, check in at the desk and disappear into the elevators. At a little after one, he started to get nervous; at one fifteen, he was worried; at twenty after, he decided to go in without Marty, which is what he wanted to do in the first place. Just then, Marty appeared through the revolving door. The wig was off, but the makeup was still on. He was breathless and sweating. He looked like he'd run all the way up Eighth Avenue.

"Where the hell have you been? I hope you don't think you're coming in with me looking like that."

"Just be cool, man. I had a client get a little out of control on me. There was a fire on Thirty-eighth Street and I got stuck in a cab. Let's go, I'll get cleaned up when we're upstairs."

Marty took Dan's arm and started him toward the elevators, past the security guard whose jaw was on the desk and who couldn't help but ask, who's… ah… she?"

They answered simultaneously. "His agent." "My bodyguard."

When they got upstairs, the auditorium was filled with a variety of competing noises and visions: men with headsets shouting commands; gaffers setting lighting and staging equipment in place; and bodies in motion, in various stages of undress. It was a cattle call, a much bigger group than Dan had expected. If he was going to get picked out of this crowd, it would take a miracle.

Marty sized up the situation instantly. "Go sign in, get two numbers."

"What are you talking about? How am I supposed to do that?"

"Look at me." Marty stared straight at Dan. "Just do it. I'm going to get this shit off my face. I'll meet you over there by the runway. Go."

Before Dan could answer, Marty was gone. Dan checked in, got a pair of bikini white briefs with a numbered tag and a safety pin. Inspired by the "I'll kill you if you don't" look that Marty flashed at him, he managed to walk away with a second pair of briefs and a number for a name he read upside down on the list, Gary Stewart.

"Here."

"Good boy. We're gonna get hired. I'll walk right behind you. Just walk like you're trying to get my attention with that tight little ass. Understand what I'm saying?"

There was a table at the end of the runway, where Marc Jackson and a few his designers and executives sat. It was a culling process not much different than the stockyards in Kansas City, and this beef was just as pumped with artificial fillers, flavors, and growth hormones.

"So what do you think?" asked Bob Pirraglia, the man in charge of the new ad campaign.

"Nothing so far," said Marc. "They all look the same. Wait, who's the blond kid coming down now? What do you think of him?"

"Let's see, number 176. His name is Chance Gardner. He's apparently not with an agency. How did he get in here?"

"Oh my God. That's the boy Steve Baldwin sent over. Oh, Steve, you do have good taste. I like the black guy behind him too. Nice bodies. They look good together. Who's he with?"

"There's got to be a screw-up because the number says he's Gary Stewart. But Gary Stewart is a white guy from the Ford Agency."

"Wherever he's from," said Marc, "let's see what they look like in print."

They spent the rest of the day in front of lights and cameras. There was more the next day. On Thursday there were video shoots, and on Friday, Marty and Dan were back at the apartment, joking about how they had performed, when the phone rang.

"Hi, this is Bob Pirraglia. I'm calling for Marty Cunningham."

"Hey Bob. This is Marty. What's up?"

"Marty, you may remember we met for a few minutes yesterday at the Marc Jackson offices."

"Yeah, Bob, sure."

"We'd like to use you with another guy we think you'd work well with to be the signature models for Marc's new line of men's underwear."

"Hey, Bob, yeah, well that's great. Sure, sure I like the underwear. And I'm sure I'll look great on a billboard in Times Square."

"We'd like you to come in Monday morning at ten. I'm sending you a contract by courier this afternoon. You should look at it over the weekend and if you have any questions, we can discuss them when you get here. OK?"

"Sure, I'll see you on Monday morning."

When Marty hung up the phone and turned to his friend, Dan's face belied the double disappointment of knowing not only that he hadn't been hired, but that his friend would go on without him.

Marty was pacing. "Hey, it's like, incredible. I can't believe it. I don't know what to say. I thought for sure that we'd both get picked, the way that they were talking and all. I mean, well, at least we'll be able to keep working on the show with the money… Are you all right?"

"Sure, I'm fine. Just disappointed, I guess. I mean, for me, I'm disappointed. I'm happy for you, Marty."

"Look, I'm disappointed for you too, but at least we got one of us earning some serious money to use for the show. I'm gonna go get changed. Let's go out to dinner and celebrate. Can you get the phone?"

"I don't know if I feel like going out," said Dan as he answered the phone. "Hello."

"Hi, this is Bob Pirraglia from Marc Jackson's office. I'm looking for Chance Gardner, but I think I may have the wrong number written down here."

"You have the right number. This is Chance Gardner. Marty and I share an apartment."

"Oh, I didn't know that. Well, I guess we won't have to worry about you guys getting along. Chance, I have some good news for you."

◼ ◼ ◼

"Mr. Baldwin's office."

"Hi, Beverly, it's Chance."

"Oh, hi, Chance, he's on another line right now. Can I have him call you back? Oh, wait, he's waving at me. He says, 'One minute.' Can you hold?"

"Sure."

"Hi, Chance. How are you?"

"Did you hear? I got hired. Can you believe it?"

"Hey, Marc's got great taste, why should I be surprised. What'd you get hired for?"

"You mean, you don't know?"

"I just opened the door. I figured you'd do the rest."

"Me and this guy I live with are going to be the models for an ad campaign for a new line of underwear. It's incredible. I mean they're gonna pay us a lot of money and we're gonna have our pictures on buses, billboards, and in magazines, all over the place."

"Buses, billboards, and magazines. Sounds great."

"Yeah, they're sending me this contract, and I really don't have any experience with contracts."

"I have to interrupt you, Chance. My firm represents Marc's company, so I can't talk to you about that. Besides, even at your new salary, you couldn't afford my rates. But let me give you a name of someone who does this kind of work. He's very good and you can afford him."

"I can afford to take you out to dinner and I'd like to do that, but I'm not too familiar with nice restaurants."

"OK, I'll suggest something. I'll have Beverly make us a reservation and call you with the details. It won't be too expensive."

"Sure. Steve, thanks again. I'll do a great job."

"From what you've told me, Chance, all you have to do is look great, and I know you won't have any problems with that."

Beverly Rosmore was standing at his desk when Steve hung up the phone.

"OK," said Steve. "Why are you looking at me like that?"

"You know perfectly well why I'm looking at you like this. That boy is young enough to be your son, or more precisely, you're old enough to be his father."

"Beverly, he just invited me to dinner."

"Dinner, schminner. I've known you since you came here. Even then you were older than him. I know when you get that look in your eyes."

"Beverly, I'm certain he's not like the others."

"Steven, they're all gold diggers."

"Not this one. He actually reminds me of someone I knew when I was about his age. Yes, that was a long time ago, even before you… a long time ago… Anyway, call Sheila and tell her we want a booth for next Tuesday at seven. And ask David Marshall to come up here with the Exchange National Bank file. Am I still on for dinner with Felix?"

"Eight-thirty at Harry's and don't say I didn't warn you about taking a Chance, if you get my true meaning."

"Bye, Beverly."

Dan was early for dinner at the Time Cafe on Lafayette Street. He'd spent the afternoon with the lawyer Steve recommended, a nice enough man named Arthur Gould in a medium-sized firm on Third Avenue. Arthur went over all the commercial terms in the contract and reminded him that he shouldn't talk about it with Steve because Stockton Alpert represented Marc Jackson in other matters. He settled into a booth and distracted himself, noticing the clock above the bar with the spinning minute hand, the detail on the three Corinthian columns, the dreadlocks on the man at the table in front of him.

At eight o'clock, an hour after they had arranged to meet,

the hostess came by with a message from Beverly Rosmore: Steve sent his apologies. He had been unexpectedly delayed and asked if Dan would please order an appetizer and wait for him for dinner. He would probably be there in a half-hour.

By nine o'clock, the restaurant was full with the noise and distraction of beautiful people in meaningful conversations. He passed the time by eating bread and butter and looking around. He asked about the photographic mural that covered the back wall, a desert scene that could have been the American Southwest or the African Sahara. "Oh, yeah," the waitress replied as she refilled his water glass, "that's one of those questions that everyone asks, but no one knows the answer."

He was looking toward the door when Steve arrived. He waved and was about to get up when Steve stopped at a table on the way and exchanged greetings with a small party, the kind where you're not sure you recognize anyone, but you think you ought to because they have a look that ordinary people don't have.

Steve made his way over to the booth with the window looking out on Great Jones Street and noticed the remains of several baskets of bread in the form of crumbs.

"I'm awfully sorry about being so late. We're working on a very tough deal. But that's no excuse, you should let me buy you dinner, at least."

"Oh no, you're my guest. I insist."

"Marc tells me you brought a friend with you and that you're both going to be the feature models for his new underwear line. That's great. I had no idea when I sent you over there that it could have worked out so well. Frankly, I was just hoping you might get a runway job."

"So was I, but it just seemed to click for us, literally. I can't thank you enough. This is a cool opportunity for me and I wouldn't have gotten near it if it weren't for you."

"I was glad to make the introduction and besides, now Beverly can stop telling you to get lost. I'm sorry about that. She's actually a very nice lady. By the way, I don't normally send people to see my friends without at least doing some background check. I've been incredibly busy so I didn't get around to calling the registrar's office until yesterday, after you got hired. They have no record of a Chance Gardner graduating this year or the year before. Marc doesn't care if you went to Duke or for that matter where you came from, as long as you look good in his underwear, but I don't like being lied to."

"I'm sorry, I'm really not a liar and I really did graduate from Duke this year. I've been using the name Chance Gardner because I've wanted to get away from everything to do with my family. I followed a friend of mine here because I thought we would be lovers, but things went really badly for us. Actually we were sort of trying to make amends when I met you at the Duke alumni party."

"So what happened?" Steve asked.

"Well, I guess he's straight," Dan answered. "That kind of put a damper on things for us. I think we'll stay friends, but I was pretty screwed up for a while. In fact I was really desperate when I called you."

"That's not exactly a ringing endorsement."

"I didn't mean it like that. What I meant was, I don't know what I would have done if you hadn't helped me."

"I assume you've told the folks at Marc Jackson your real name. Did you call Arthur Gould about your contract?"

"Yes, I told their lawyer and Arthur Gould my real name."

"And now you're going to tell me?"

"I really don't want to. I want to forget my name. I want to start over again. I like being Chance Gardner."

"OK, Chance, we'll leave it like that, at least for now. You must be starving. I eat here all the time so we'll order whenever you're ready."

Just as Dan started looking at the menu Steve got up and greeted a tall beautiful woman who Dan thought he recognized but wasn't sure from where. They talked while Dan pretended to be focusing on the menu. He couldn't help but notice how at ease Steve seemed as he had been in each of the different settings of their prior meetings. Dan wondered if there was any situation where Steve wasn't in control of things.

"That was Lauren Hutton. She has a place upstairs," said Steve as his friend walked away and he sat down. "We both eat here often. Do you know what you want?"

"Is that a trick question?" Dan smiled.

"I mean from the menu," Steve replied. Their eyes met. It was a small thing. No words were exchanged in the instant it took, but Steve knew for certain that this was no ordinary young man who had hit on him for a job and maybe whatever else might come with it. Steve had been around, seen, and sampled the best of each year's fresh arrivals in the city. He couldn't get over his utter fascination with Dan. When the waiter or some other distraction drew his attention away for a minute, he had to turn back and be reassured that this young man was actually as attractive to him as when they met only a few weeks ago.

Dan was at first drawn to Steve the way a drowning man is drawn to a lifeboat. It wouldn't have mattered the size or shape, only that it floated. Now his life had been transformed and his enthusiasm was untrammeled by the cynicism that comes with finding out in time that it almost never just so happens that the person you're trying to meet is at a reception you're attending and that he really does want to help you.

For now, Dan was captivated by the mere notion that a powerful man would point him in the direction of an opportunity and then stand back, not seeking to control every aspect of the final outcome, but simply wait to hear the results of his protégé's efforts.

They talked until a little after midnight. Dan asked most of the questions. It seemed to Steve that there wasn't anything about Dan that wasn't enthusiastic. It seemed to Dan that Steve knew it all, had been everywhere, tried everything, and yet he was patient with Dan's questions, not pedantic. And Dan, rather than being uncomfortable in the role of the ingénue, enjoyed all the attention with no strings.

"I'm still sorry about keeping you waiting for so long. Are you sure you won't let me buy dinner?"

"Not this one, but how about the next time. I guess I'm hoping that there will be a next time."

"Sure, let's make it soon. I'm leaving at the end of this week for Switzerland. I'll be back right after the first of the year. I'll call you when I get back. OK?"

"Yeah, that would be great."

They walked out to Lafayette Street to get a cab.

"So I'll see you in a couple of weeks." Steve extended his hand.

"Merry Christmas," Dan said. But he didn't let go of Steve's hand or his eyes, and in the time that Steve had to react, the fraction of a second that seemed to last until his heart simply had to take another beat, Steve leaned forward and kissed him, not a polite New York air kiss, but a kiss on the lips with his eyes closed for an instant. He was not in the least bit in control of himself or the situation but simply letting go and being in the moment. Then he recovered and said, "Good-bye," got in the cab, and headed back uptown to his apartment.

Dan said "Good-bye" barely audibly and really not until Steve was most of the way in the cab and pulling the door shut behind him. This was like nothing else he'd ever felt before. He knew it felt good and he wanted to feel it again.

◪ ◪ ◪

Carlton Moore arrived at Douglas International in a chartered Gulfstream IV with a small entourage of NYT executives and staff, but no lawyers. Jack had reluctantly agreed to the meeting, three days before Christmas, on the condition that they would just talk business. He had no interest in listening to a high-priced debate over who had the winning motion or cross-motion filed in the Delaware Chancery Court, or who had the better argument with the bank regulators.

When Moore called Jack, he said that he wanted to fly down to Charlotte, a not unnoticed gesture, and talk candidly about the terms under which there could be a mutually acceptable merger of the banks. Moore came with Wilfort Carrol, his president and chief operating officer; Charles deMornay, head of NYT's consumer banking; and Jim Gordon, the bank's chief financial officer. There were a few other staffers who were there to carry bags and hand out papers and run the slide projector.

Jack, Blake, and Fred had met all the senior NYT team many times at the banking conferences and at other places where private jets flew them on vacation. Before they all sat down in the board dining room in the Reynolds Tower, they got politely reacquainted while they stood and sipped coffee from china cups that the Reynolds family had brought from England in the eighteenth century.

Jack had the uncanny knack of being able to appear to be completely focused on a conversation with one person and simultaneously absorb the essence of several conversations going on around him. While he was discussing the opportunities for global custody business with deMornay, he watched and listened to Moore working his father-in-law.

Carlton Moore was sixty-two years old, six feet tall, perfectly preserved and dressed, and every bit the scion of a New York banking family. His great-great-great-grandfather had been one of the merchants who traded the first stocks on Wall Street in the 1800s. His grandfather was a pal of J. P. Morgan. Carlton went to Choate and Yale. He served in Korea. He lived with his wife in their Upper East Side townhouse during the week and on the family horse farm near Reading on weekends.

It was natural that Moore would be drawn to a conversation with Blake. They had much more in common than their bloodlines and besides, Moore understood that although Jack was the CEO, Blake controlled the largest block of NCBT stock. When breakfast was announced, Jack joined them, and since he had already exchanged pleasantries with Moore, he laid out the schedule for the day.

"Carlton, we have a dining room set up for your staff people just down the hall. They'll join us after breakfast with Fred's staff in the boardroom. We should be finished eating by ten-thirty. We've allowed until lunch for your presentation. Then Blake and I and our team will spend some time going over your proposal. We'll meet back in the boardroom at two with our questions, and we should have you back out to Douglas by six o'clock at the latest."

"Jack, that's fine. I was just telling Blake how much we appreciate your taking the time to hear what we have to say, and I'm sure you'll be favorably impressed."

At breakfast, the seven men sat at a round table. They ate poached eggs on toast and sipped their coffee and talked around the edges of their problem. They all knew that when the dust settled, half of them would be out of jobs. But none of them needed jobs.

There was already a Moore Wing at the Metropolitan Museum. DeMornay came from a wealthy French family, and Carrol had married almost as well as Jack. Only Fred Bonham among them might have been concerned about his $850,000 salary, but he was a multimillionaire based on the value of his NCBT stock and options. There was only so much money he could put into a motor home and only so many places where he and his wife wanted to drive it.

The enormity of the proposed payout for NYT shareholders meant there was only one reason there could be opposition from the inside officers and directors. The bank was their stage. It was the *sine qua non* for meaning, rather than mere existence. So really, while everyone talked about shareholder value, what drove Carlton Moore and his colleagues was that Jack O'Brien was proposing to take away their very lives.

It became clear to the NCBT contingent that Wilfort Carrol's job during breakfast was to talk about the consolidation of the banking industry and the advantages the combined bank would have. "*I wish he'd tell me something I don't already know,*" Jack thought to himself. "*If this doesn't get any better, we've really wasted a day.*"

When they assembled in the boardroom they were joined by the staff from NYT and three of Fred Bonham's top people who were there to pick apart any of Carlton Moore's numbers. "That is if we get any numbers," Fred whispered to Jack as they left breakfast.

A briefing book marked "Confidential" was in front of everyone and Moore's presentation was pretty much from the book. Two hours later, when only Jack, Blake, Fred, and his analysts were in the room, Jack was the first to speak.

"I can't believe they flew all this way to deliver such a bullshit proposal."

"I'm not sure, Jack," said Fred. "The numbers are different the way they're proposing it. It's more of a stretch to believe they can keep so much of the structures of both banks in place and still produce the earnings. But I like the idea of getting my arms around that before the merger."

"But what about the lockout provision?" said Jack. "If we don't agree on the numbers under their proposed deal, we would have to agree not to pursue a hostile deal under our structure for three years. And let me just say this right now: you know damned well as I do, that we won't agree on the numbers and that they'll wind up locking us out."

"Jack. First, I believe they think we can agree on the numbers, otherwise they wouldn't be throwing a two hundred million dollar breakup fee on the table. That's an enormous sum of money. We could add four billion of new earning assets to our books with that kind of money or pay a two-dollar-a-share dividend, which I'm sure would get Commerford and Briggs off Blake's back for a while."

"OK," said Jack. "I admit they impressed me with the breakup fee. But let's say we work together and agree on the numbers on paper and that the merger goes through. You know as well as I do that's only the beginning. Realizing those savings will take a ruthless approach to executing the plan. I don't think Carlton Moore has the guts to do that as CEO, in which case we have massive dilution of our earnings. I'm not willing to take the risk that a year from now, our shareholders are going to be holding stock that is worth maybe half of what it's worth today."

Blake had been sitting at the end of the table, almost absentmindedly taking notes. He hadn't said anything since Moore and his team were sent off to another conference room. "Jack, why don't we let Fred's boys see if they can get a better handle on some of the numbers in this book, and you and I and Fred will visit in your office for a little while."

The three men gathered on the couch and two armchairs arranged around a coffee table. Blake started with what had been on his mind since Moore finished his proposal. "The real problem here is that Carlton is proposing to be the CEO of the combined banks. Isn't it?"

Jack waited for a minute, which is not the same as thinking for a minute, before he answered because he didn't want to appear to be fixated on what he really was fixated on and which everyone knew he was fixated on. "Blake, that is a problem, but not *the* problem. It's the whole approach they're taking that bothers me. Keeping the executive offices in New York and the administrative offices here, trying to cut a little here and there rather than just lopping off huge chunks of costs, which is what is really needed."

"But Jack," said Fred, "they've completed four acquisitions in the last six years and they have gotten the cuts they promised."

"You're right, Fred, but those were regional banks in the Northeast with tremendous overlap and no competing cultures arguing over whose ox is going to get gored. The acquired banks were wiped out. When Carlton brings up their experience with rationalizing acquired banks, if anything, he makes my point. It's not about ego. That's not why I'm opposed to the proposal we heard today. I'm sure that it won't work."

"OK," said Blake. "It's two-thirty. Do we have anything to propose before we put them back on their plane to New York?"

Jack relaxed a little because it was clear to him that while he had not convinced Blake and Fred that the NYT proposal would not work, they were still prepared, as they had been from the beginning, to back him. But all he could think of to say is what he had told Carlton Moore when the tender for NYT was made back in July. "Don't fight the acquisition. Work with us. And you'll have a chance to affect the way the combined banks look after the merger." Blake recommended that he and Jack visit alone with Moore to tell him their decision. They would meet in Jack's office and he would do the talking.

When he was done, Jack noticed the trace of a surprised look on Moore's face when he heard the decision. He had been watching Blake and Fred during the day, and could see that he was getting through to them.

"Jack," said Moore, "I've never failed to take an opportunity to tell you how much I admire what you've done here. But I must also tell you, you're making a terrible mistake. It's true the hostile tender that Bank of New York made for Irving Trust was eventually successful, but you know that was a terribly nasty fight and, I promise you, that one will look tame compared to this battle."

Moore got up. His face was flush. He was pointing at Jack. "I personally spoke to Governor Whitman yesterday about attending the opening of our new processing center in Newark. If you think she's going to let two thousand white-collar jobs get wiped out in her state without a battle, you're horribly mistaken. Your problems with Cuomo and the legislature in New York will be just as big if not bigger."

"Carlton," Jack interrupted, "we've said we'd would work with you in preserving as many jobs as possible."

"Jack, that's pabulum and you know it. Save that stuff for the ads in the papers. This is going to be a very protracted fight, and I assure you that before it's over, you will regret the decision you've made today. We're in the process of hiring Stockton Alpert and we'll be exploring all our options including an offer for your bank. The managing partner there, Steve Baldwin, has never lost a takeover and we're not about to change that record now."

Moore lowered his voice to a quiet, measured tone. "I have one more thing to say. The next few months will be unpleasant for all of us. But we're all gentlemen and I want you to know that the door is always open to discuss a mutually acceptable resolution at any time. Gentlemen, thank you for you hospitality, and Merry Christmas."

While the NYT plane was receiving clearance for its flight back to New York, Blake and Fred were seated in the boardroom with Jack, discussing their options.

"Steve Baldwin," said Blake, "isn't that Harrison Baldwin's son? Wasn't he a classmate of yours, Jack? Jack?"

Jack didn't respond until Blake nearly shouted his name and he didn't realize his hands were shaking until he spilled the drink he was holding. "Huh? Oh, yeah, he was… I haven't seen him in twenty-three years… Guys, I gotta go. My son is home for Christmas and I promised Carolyn I'd be home by five."

◼ ◼ ◼

Julie saw Dan get out of the cab and walk toward the front door. His full-length Armani coat and suit unbuttoned and flowing behind him. He wore them like medals. Though he walked with confidence, his face belied the apprehension he felt. But his countenance beamed when Julie opened the door and ran down the steps to meet him.

"Hey, you look like a movie star!"

"Hi, Julie."

"I can't believe it. You look incredible! You've got to tell me all about it."

"Can we get inside first?"

"Yeah, Dad's not home yet so we have time to talk."

"Where is he?"

"Where else? The bank. Mom just talked to him. He said he'd be home by five. Mom's in the kitchen. I can't wait to hear about Marc Jackson."

Dan put his arm around Julie's shoulder and they walked into the house where they found Carolyn in the kitchen with Juanita, preparing dinner.

"Hi, there! Merry Christmas!" Carolyn raised her hands, covered with the juice of the eggplant she was cutting, as Dan walked toward her. Then she hugged him with her forearms. "You look so handsome in those clothes. I don't want to get ratatouille all over you. You look wonderful. I was so worried when you told me about modeling. I thought, My God, he can't lose another pound."

"I've been lifting weights, Mom," Dan said shyly. "They actually want me to gain a little muscle before they start shooting for the ads."

"Are you taking steroids?" Julie asked.

"Julie!" Dan shouted.

"Steroids?" Carolyn asked.

"Well, I am," said Dan, "but they're part of a training program. Julie, when are you going to lose that big mouth of yours?"

"Be careful," Julie said, as she picked at the food on the counter, "Carlos says they give you zits."

"Carlos is on steroids?" Carolyn asked. "What's going on here?"

"Mom, you're so out of it." Julie repeated her familiar refrain.

"Oh, sweetheart," Carolyn rinsed and dried her hands and hugged Dan again. "Whatever you're doing up there, be careful of any drugs. It's such a fast-paced life. I've been worried about you, but you're home now, and you look great." She looked at Julie. "And let's not be talking about steroids when your father gets home."

"Yeah, let's not have a real conversation. Let's talk about the weather instead."

"Julie, so help me, if you get your father wound up tonight, I don't know what I'll do, but you'll regret it. Now Dan, you go freshen up. You have time to take a quick shower if you want to. Your father won't be home for another half-hour. We'll sit down to dinner when he gets home."

Julie followed Dan up to his room and couldn't wait to ask him about his new life, but Dan was clearly aggravated.

"Julie, why did you ask me about the steroids? How is it that you always seem able to find the most aggravating thing to say in even the most pleasant situations?"

"Oh, Dan, why didn't you say you weren't?"

"Because I don't like to lie."

"It's no big deal. Mom needs to get with reality anyway. Are you doing any other drugs?"

Dan remembered how much he really liked Julie's candor, even with the aggravation that came with it. "Once in a while," he said, "you know, recreational stuff. Nothing major. How about you?"

"I'm a mess, but not from the drugs. I just want to get out of here. I'm still with Carlos. He's a little too clingy for me, but he's doing a lot to promote our band. He wants to take us to New York. But of course, Mom and Dad won't let me go. I'll be eighteen in April. Then they can't make me stay. I think I'll go in the summer. Maybe you can help us find a place."

"Julie, don't be ridiculous. You should go to college."

"OK, Jack. Whatever you say, Jack."

"That's a low blow."

"Truth hurts."

"Well, the truth is you should go to college. Just because Dad thinks so too doesn't make it wrong."

Dan slipped off his tie and unbuttoned his shirt and sat down on the edge of the bed next to her and started to take off his shoes.

"Mom tells me you've got a roommate," said Julie. "What's he like?"

"He's a huge black guy. He's a singer and an entertainer. He's incredible. He actually saved my life. He's modeling with me in the ads for Marc Jackson. You'll meet him when you come to New York, before your freshman year."

"A singer. That's cool, I'll send you one of our CDs for him to listen to," said Julie. "Whatever happened to Mike?"

"He's still in New York. He's working for the same broker-age firm. We had a pretty bad argument after I got there in July and we didn't speak for a few months. Then he called out of the blue in November and we went to a basketball game together. I guess you could say we're on speaking terms, but we hardly ever speak. I've been too busy."

"Too busy to see anyone?"

Dan had his back to Julie, putting the few things from his bag into the bureau. "What do you mean?"

"You know, romantically."

"I've been too busy. Hey, I've got to take a shower."

Julie noticed when Dan stood up and took off his shirt and reached for the towel that he had bulked up, that he looked great, but that he was uneasy, as he had always been, whenever she asked him about his personal life. That was never a reason for Julie to give up on a question, especially one she thought was important.

"You mean you're not seeing anyone?"

"Oh, Julie, you're such a voyeur. Get out. I've got to take a shower."

He closed the door behind her, put his trousers on the bed, and noticed himself in the mirror. He did look different, better, maybe even "great," as Marty kept reminding him. He also felt a familiar knot in his stomach when he thought about the dinner he was about to have.

The hot water on his back felt good as he tried to think of exactly what he was going to tell his father. Then he heard a knock on the bathroom door and a familiar voice.

"Hey, sport! How are you doing in there?"

"Hi, Dad. I'm almost through. I'll be right down."

◼ ◼ ◼

When at last they were all gathered around the dining room table, they clung to the rituals of polite eating. Though they had so much to say to each other they filled the intermittent silence with talk of anything but what they were feeling.

Dan had agreed to come home after he landed the modeling job partly because he now had something to say about what he was doing besides feeding on the flesh of other wanderers in New York. He did it because Julie asked him to, because Carolyn begged him, assured him that his father wanted to see him, that Jack couldn't wait to hear all about his new life. After six months of being away from his father, Dan looked across the table and saw a vision of what he might have been, as if the ghost of Christmas future had transported him to see the specter of a middle-aged man in an unhappy life.

"I wish Michael had come," Carolyn said to Dan. "It seems so strange to have Christmas without him here."

"You asked him and I did too," said Dan. "He's in his own world now."

"Mom," Julie said, "Michael has always been in his own world. It's just that before, he had to be here for holidays. Now he doesn't."

Dan noticed that things were different between Julie and Carolyn. Julie still said things that upset her mother, but Dan sensed, as Carolyn did, that Julie was only pointing out things that everyone knew, but chose to ignore.

Dan still found her candor unsettling. "*But maybe,*" he thought, "*getting a little shaken up is worth the price of living in the real world.*" She was right about Michael, as she had been about so many other things. In the past, he didn't always get it so, she only seemed annoying to him. He thought about how many years he had tuned her out and knew that he wouldn't do that any more.

"So, Dan," Julie said, "you still haven't told us about Marc Jackson. What's he like?" Julie talked to her brother with a genuine curiosity about his life because it seemed to her for the first time that he finally had a life.

"I haven't spent much time with him. I really haven't started the job. And there's not much to it, actually. I'm not contracted for anything but the underwear line."

"Don't they turn over models pretty regularly, Dan?" Jack couldn't stop himself. He had to help Dan see that this was a dead-end job. That was Jack's job: to help his son see and understand the world. "*Why?*" he thought to himself. "*Why won't he let me help him? For Christ's sake, he's my son.*"

"Yeah, Dad, they do," said Dan. "Even Mark Walberg. ran out of gas as the Calvin Klein model. I don't expect to be doing this for too long. I don't really know what I want to do. I guess I'm just taking it one day at a time right now."

"Your mother told me you applied for some jobs at architectural firms. You know, I've been thinking, maybe I could come up there and we could have lunch with a few people I know. I'm sure we could get you fixed up with something."

Dan was chewing, which bought him a few seconds to think about how to tell Jack he didn't want his help. *"Doesn't he get it?"* Dan thought. What he wanted to say was, "Maybe I don't know what I want, but I'm sure I don't want the life you have."

"Oh, sweetheart," Carolyn said, "that would be great. Julie and I could come to New York too."

"I think it would be great to see you all," said Dan, "but I'd rather you just came for a visit."

Jack put his knife and fork down slowly and inhaled, then he looked down at his plate and slowly exhaled. "You know, son, I probably said a few things back in July that I wish I hadn't. Maybe it seemed like I was pressuring you but I really only want the best for you. There's nothing wrong with that."

"Dad, you're right. There is nothing wrong with wanting the best for me. But what I really wanted in July, what I want now, is to try things on my own. I understand you think I should be following the same path as you did. Grandpa got you a job at the bank and you've been successful—"

"So now you're accusing me of relying on someone else for my success. Well—"

"Dad, I'm not accusing you of anything. If you're happy at the bank, I'm happy for you. Right now, I'm happy doing what I'm doing."

"Son, you can't spend the rest of your life walking up and down a runway in your underwear!"

It was nine o'clock and Carolyn was sitting in the kitchen, alone. There were tears running down her cheeks, but she made no sound and Jack didn't see her until he opened the refrigerator door.

"Hi," he said. He sat down next to her and put his hand on her hand. "I'm sorry. I really screwed up. I shouldn't have said what I said. I shouldn't have yelled at him. I don't know what came over me. He's so naive. I don't want to see him get hurt."

"Jack." Carolyn was whispering. "He's gone. You two were screaming at each other when he left. How much more hurt can he get in New York?"

"I don't know. I'm sorry. I'm sorry."

Carolyn sat up in the chair and wiped her eyes. "I was thinking about something Carla told me a long time ago. She said that what comes out of someone isn't a response to something outside. It's a reflection of what is inside. Why do you get angry around Dan? What is it about him that brings out the anger in you?"

"I don't know, Carolyn. I don't know. I'm sorry. I'll go to New York. I'll apologize to him. I love him."

"I can't take this anymore, Jack. Julie and I had to beg him to come home for Christmas. Tonight he told me that you have to deal with him on his terms or he'll never come back. It's your anger, that's the problem."

"Maybe you're right. Sometimes when I look at him, I think, 'What can I possibly say to him?' I didn't have the choices he has. I was working to support my family when I was half his age."

"What is that supposed to mean to him?" Carolyn pleaded. "He doesn't see the world through your eyes. He's trying to live his own life. Can't you see that?"

"I'll go to see him. I promise I'll make things right."

GRAVITY

Stockton Alpert Slade Meacher & Angel occupied twenty-two floors in the Cutler Building on Park Avenue at Forty-ninth Street. There were five hundred lawyers working there, another three hundred in far-flung outposts, Beijing, Buenos Aires, Budapest, and the world's financial centers, Tokyo, London, Frankfurt. It was the first day of January 1996. The offices were closed, but two partners were huddled at the end of a table that would have accommodated forty. Steve Baldwin, fresh from the slopes at Gstaad, had a stack of files in front of him. He was dressed in a pair of Levi's and a sweatshirt. He was shaking his foot under the table.

Josh Angel, the old man of the firm, the former managing partner, and now the senior member of the seven-member executive committee, sat on Steve's right at the head of the table. He had on a blue suit, starched white shirt, and a red tie. He always wore red ties. And he had nothing in front of him but a pad of paper and a pen. He was doodling as he spoke. "Deadlines have a way of focusing the mind, Stevie. I told Carlton Moore he'd have our answer by tomorrow. In half an hour, our colleagues will be in here, and if we're not going to accept this assignment, they'll want to know why we've turned down the chance to be involved in the highest-profile takeover battle on Wall Street."

"We have plenty of reason to say no," said Steve, "even if you don't take into account the potential conflict. I've read the public filings and the press stuff. These guys look like goners to me."

Josh didn't look up from the circles and lines he was drawing on the page. "The executive committee is not going to buy that argument. Baker & McKenna has already lost this one, and besides, maybe nobody lost this one. It's an enormous benefit to everyone except the executives at NYT. Even for them, it won't be so bad. Sure they'll be out of jobs, but most of them will make millions from the deal."

"C'mon, Josh, Carlton Moore didn't call you because he wants us to negotiate their severance packages. He called you because we have a perfect record, and I'm telling you there's going to be a lot of bad fallout when we lose."

Josh finally looked up. "Spare me the Chicken Little arguments. Here's what counts. You're the best in the business and three million dollars in fees." Josh drew a big "3" on the page. "That's a conservative estimate of what this assignment will bring in. We both know that's what's on the committee's mind right now. So why don't we get to the real reason why you don't want to take this assignment, because if we're going to discuss it in an open meeting, we had better decide what to say in the next twenty-nine minutes."

They were an unlikely match. *"You're a rich kid,"* Josh had told him, *"but I won't hold that against you."* When Steve joined the firm seventeen years earlier, Josh was forty-seven, and already one of the most influential lawyers in New York. With a small group of extraordinarily talented and ruthless workaholics, Josh Angel built Stockton Alpert into one of the world's premier law firms. He was one of the few people Steve knew who thought in complete paragraphs. He could annihilate any poorly argued position. But Steve knew he wasn't being attacked. Josh had the luxury of an unassailable record that could afford his fierce loyalty to a protégé, but he also had his own agenda.

"Steve, let me summarize our earlier conversation and you tell me if I've got it right. You and Jack O'Brien graduated from Duke about twenty-three years ago. While you were at Duke, you were, you were… ah…"

Steve, looking down, finished the sentence. "Lovers."

"Right," Josh continued, "lovers. In fact, you planned to live together after graduation, as a couple. Jack made a sudden decision to marry Carolyn Reynolds, who was pregnant with their child. You and he argued over his decision."

"Bitterly."

"You haven't seen or talked to him since. You're concerned

that a relationship that ended twenty-three years ago…" Josh drew a big "23" on the page. "You're concerned that this might be a potential conflict that might be grounds for you to decline the assignment of heading the New York Trust defense."

"Those aren't my words, but, yes, I'm concerned about the conflict."

Josh looked at his watch, got up, and sat on the credenza at the end of the room. "I don't need to explain the conflict of interest rules to you. This isn't about a legal conflict. The truth is you'd just as soon dodge this one and I'm telling you it ain't gonna happen unless you want to dig up some very old garbage and throw it on this table for your partners to examine."

Steve didn't answer.

"C'mon, Stevie. Let me tell you how we're all going to feel better about this. You say that your relationship with O'Brien was a secret. I'm probably the only other person besides the two of you who's even aware of it."

Steve looked up and exhaled slowly. "As far as I know, yes."

Josh was obviously pleading as much as he was arguing. "It just seems to me that the connection is *so* tenuous and it was *so* long ago and…" He made a big "X" on the page. "*So* unlikely to be a problem. Bringing this up in front of the executive committee is only going to embarrass you unnecessarily. After all, you're a level-headed guy and by all accounts, Jack O'Brien is a happily married man."

Married. To Steve, that was the operative word. All the other members of the executive committee were happily, unhappily, or formerly married. How could he possibly explain his situation to them? Even Josh Angel, who wanted very much to help him, couldn't understand. And as for the rest, they had made him managing partner because he brought in the big-money, high-profile clients. They were all rainmakers. He was *the* rainmaker. But in the apparently close-knit circle of the firm's executive committee, there was still uneasiness with any issue relating to Steve being gay.

"So," said Josh, "subject to the committee's approval, I will accept the assignment on behalf of the firm. For purposes of disclosure, I will tell Carlton that you and O'Brien were best friends at Duke, but that you haven't seen or talked to him in twenty-three years. That's it. Right?"

"Right."

◩ ◩ ◩

Jack O'Brien was pacing the length of the large sitting room at the Pierre. There were three large double windows, framed by heavy drapes. The riders in the English country hunt paintings on the walls paid no attention to the room's two occupants, the only objects out of place in an otherwise perfectly decorated suite. There was a commanding view of Central Park South. But from thirty floors up, Jack was removed from the sounds of traffic and the sight of pedestrians hurrying in the mid-January cold along Fifth Avenue. The skaters at Wollman Rink looked like little stick figures in the background of a Currier & Ives print.

The disembodied voices came out of the speakerphone and hung on the air. Jack and Fred were impatiently listening to their lawyer and investment banker, both skilled in the tactics of corporate war, trying to convince them that they were in the end stages of a winning campaign.

"Jack, it doesn't look good that we won't meet with them." Henry Bradford was deferential but firm. "It's just going to be you, Fred, me, and Payton, with our counterparts at New York Trust. I know Steve Baldwin well and I know what advice he's giving Carlton Moore right now: Get the best deal you can."

"Jack, Payton Harwood here." In person, Harwood was never charismatic, but over the speakerphone, he was positively wooden. "I couldn't agree more strongly with Henry. I've known their fellow at Goldman ever since he got a place on Dune Road next to ours in Bridgehampton. He knows they've got a losing hand. This is really the best time to put closure on our terms." Harwood cleared his throat, searching for something, anything, to say that didn't sound like a cliché.

"Like I said, Jack," Bradford interjected, "Steve Baldwin is a pro at this. I mean, present company excepted, he's one of the best in the business. Now remember, he called me and at first, he proposed that Payton and I meet with him and Richard Wein, which I know is not Carlton Moore's style at all. I'm telling you, Jack, there was an edge in his voice when he asked about having a meeting. We've been trying to figure what's going on with those guys... You knew Baldwin at Duke, didn't you? ... Jack? ... Jack?"

Jack walked over to the couch and sat down. He sat forward to get close to the mic built into the phone on the coffee table. "Yeah, I knew him, but that was more than twenty years ago. Henry, I'm not interested in another meeting until they've agreed to the offer on our terms. Period."

There was a long silence and then Bradford continued. "Jack, I'm only pressing this because you're paying for my best advice... Would you authorize Payton and me to meet with our counterparts? You know, Jack, that was actually Baldwin's preference when he called to suggest the meeting."

Fred could see Jack's face getting red. Then the second phone line rang and while Fred was walking across the room to get it, Jack took a deep breath and picked up the receiver from the speakerphone. "Look, guys, that's an even worse idea. You know as well as I do that Carlton Moore is calling the shots in this deal."

Fred picked up the other phone, said "Hello," listened, and started gesturing to Jack.

Jack mouthed the letters "OK" to Fred and then continued. "Guys, I've got to take a call from my wife. Let the situation ride for a while. I know you're both experts at this, but, I have to tell you, I have no interest in another meeting until they say they're ready to accept our offer. As for the details, you know I don't give a crap if Carlton is Nonexecutive Vice Chairman, but that's not what they want to meet about."

"Jack—"

"Henry, listen to me, the momentum is all in our favor. Give it a little more time and they'll throw in the towel. I'll call you tomorrow and let you know how the dinner goes. OK, bye."

Jack hung up the phone, pressed the Line 2 button, and picked up the receiver again without a pause. "Hi, sweetheart. I'm running out the door to catch a flight to Washington... Yeah, I told you I called... Uh-huh... Carolyn, he's not picking up the phone. I've left several messages and he's not returning my calls... Honey, what's the point of going by his apartment if he's not there? I've got to get to a dinner that Jeff O'Neil set up for me with Lloyd Bentsen... I know that... Of course, but..." Jack looked up and noticed that Fred was standing by the window, trying not to overhear the conversation. He put his hand over the receiver. "Fred, go ahead downstairs. I'll be right there." Jack took a deep breath and went back to the phone call. "Uh-huh... Carolyn, I'm trying..."

◨ ◨ ◨

When he finally got off the elevator on the ground floor, Jack bounded through the lobby toward the Fifth Avenue entrance. He found Fred at a table against the wall in the trompe l'oeil–muraled Rotunda, sipping a cup of coffee. Fred's glum look and rumpled suit seemed an extension of the artist's eclectic collection of classical and modern scenes. Neptune was frowning as Venus poured water from a shell over Fred's head. On the adjoining panel, Nehru watched philosophically, while from across the room, Jacqueline Kennedy looked at Venus with a wry sense of humor painted in her slightly upturned lips and eyes.

"Fred, I gotta make a stop on the way out of town. Do me a favor and take a cab out to LaGuardia. If we don't make the four o'clock shuttle, we'll get the five. Call Jeff O'Neil's office and warn him that we might be a few minutes late. OK? I'll see you out there."

When Jack came out of the hotel, the scene at street level was not as picturesque as it had been from his suite. The three inches of snow that had fallen during the day were turning to slush in the late afternoon heavy rain. The traffic at three o'clock was practically at a standstill.

Ron Davis was standing at the car by the rear passenger door. He was an earnest young man from Bayside, Queens, about Dan's age and build.

"LaGuardia, Mr. O'Brien?"

"No, Ron, we're going to make a stop first." Jack opened up his address book. "295 East Eighth Street."

"Isn't that in the East Village, Mr. O'Brien? That's gonna take us a long way out of the way."

"Yeah, I know." Jack sighed as he slipped off his coat. "A long way."

There were times that Jack felt things that he wished he did-n't, but no matter how hard he tried to be rid of them, they remained. At times he wished he could feel a certain way, and struggle though he did, there was emptiness where he wanted something to be. He managed, he coped, by putting himself away in discrete reservoirs with a complex system of dams and channels. Some of what was stored up had been there for so long that it was like a fetid sunless lake of memory. He thought of what had seemed like unrelated decisions, one laid upon the other, serving to hold back a flood, not by design of some well crafted bulwark, but more like a pile of pick-up-sticks, made tenuously stable merely by their angle of repose.

It had taken them almost fifteen minutes to get to Rocke-feller Center and they had another forty blocks to go. Jack looked absentmindedly at the windows of the shops—Harry Winston, Christian Dior, Gucci—as if peering into the fulfill-ment of someone else's dreams might distract him from the pain of his own memories.

In an effort to make every traffic light, to dart between bus-es and cars when there was an opportunity, and to avoid pedes-trians seeking refuge from the rain, Ron applied the brakes and the accelerator in generous and nearly equal measures. Conse-quently, the Town Car began to feel like some diabolical inven-tion designed to shake the senses out of its passenger. But Jack was beginning to feel more than just physically uneasy. One or two pick-up-sticks at a time were falling out of place and memories were spilling over the dam.

"Jack, it doesn't look good that we won't meet with them… You knew Baldwin at Duke, didn't you?"

Jack sat up and looked forward at the traffic ahead of them. *"For Christ's sake,"* he thought, *"it was a long time ago. Could he still be angry? Does it even matter to him now? Maybe he doesn't even think about it anymore. I can hardly remember what the big deal was."*

"I'm telling you, Jack, there was a real edge in Baldwin's voice when he asked about having a meeting."

"We were just kids. He must have found someone else. And besides, it's not such a big deal now, being gay. It was so long ago."

Suddenly a cab cut them off, trying to make a left turn at Fiftieth, and Ron jammed on the brakes. "Goddamnit! Ron, your driving's gonna make me throw my fucking guts up! There's gotta be another way to get to the East Village."

"I'm sorry, Mr. O'Brien. Maybe we'll do better going down Park. I'll turn at Forty-eighth Street."

Jack breathed a little easier as the car picked up speed on the elevated road through the Helmsley Building and Grand Central Station and then through the tunnel to Thirty-third Street. He checked his watch: fifteen blocks in five minutes. He hated traffic.

He put his head back against the seat and closed his eyes for a minute. It came back to him in waves, the kind that wash over you when your head is turned or your hands are wiping the salt from your eyes. It blocked out everything else. Of course he remembered. He remembered the touch, the strain, the fire of muscles, tense and pressing one against the other, the mixture of sweat and saliva, the taste of salt, the struggle and then the moment of being swallowed up in the void, the near loss of consciousness, and then lying, completely still, silent, except for the sound of breathing.

◪ ◪ ◪

Dan was soaking wet when he finally got back to the apartment. He played the message on the machine. "Hi, sport. It's Dad. Listen, I'm sorry we haven't been able to connect. I'm gonna stop at your place on my way to the airport. I just want to talk to you, Dan. I'm sorry for what happened at Christmas. I'm really trying, sport. Please give me a chance."

It was an irony completely lost on both of them that for most of his life, Dan had wanted his father to discover him, to get to know the real Dan O'Brien, not the one Jack was trying to mold. And now, as Jack was practically beating a path to his door, Dan could think of nothing else but trying to escape. There was no nearby subway station. He had no idea when his father's car might arrive. Dan unplugged the answering machine and bolted the door.

◪ ◪ ◪

When they got to Union Square they headed down Broadway. "I'll have you there in the next few minutes, Mr. O'Brien. I'm sorry it's been such an awful ride."

"That's OK, Ron. Do me a favor and put the divider up." Jack heard the whir of the glass panel dividing the passenger compartment of the car from the driver as he opened his cell phone and dialed Dan's number. He let it ring. Somewhere around ten rings he started counting. He lost track of how many times it rang, waiting even for the answering machine, which now wasn't picking up. Jack hung up the phone. *"He's there."*

They turned left on Eighth Street. At Cooper Square, there was a ten-story building with a side façade of uninterrupted brick that had become a giant billboard. Jack noticed the ad for

Samsung—an outstretched arm over a microwave oven that was balanced on the hip of a shirtless model.

He remembered the day they said good-bye, the awful ache in his stomach, the pained look on Steve's face. *"I did the right thing. I know I did the right thing for both of us. I've had a good life... Maybe he's gotten over it. What am I worried about? I mean, for Christ's sake, I don't know anything about him now. He's got his own life."* Jack dialed Dan's number again, still no answer. *"Who cares about Baldwin anyway? I've got a son to worry about. I wonder what the hell he's thinking."*

"Doesn't he see I'm trying to help him?"

"What is that supposed to mean to him?" Carolyn pleaded. *"He doesn't see the world through your eyes."*

Jack saw the students hurrying across Lafayette Street as the car drove into the East Village. *"What am I going to say to him? He's just a kid. He has no idea how much I love him. I never even knew my father. Now my son won't even talk to me."*

"Jack, there's something I want to talk to you about... Do you think Dan might be gay?"

"Oh, Carolyn, don't be ridiculous."

The car slowed as it went around Tompkins Square Park to the corner of Avenue B and Eighth. At 295 East Eighth Street they found a five-story squat-looking brick building with a mansard roof and an inscription in the stone over the door— "Talmud Torah Darchei Noam 1916–1926." "Oh, shit!" said Jack. "I hope that's old. I hope he hasn't joined a goddamned cult!" He dialed the number one more time.

Inside, sunk into the armchair with a seat cushion that was practically on the floor, Dan listened to the phone as he ran the tip of his index finger over his bottom lip and kept praying. "Go away. Please go away." He wanted to run out to the limo on the street below and shout through the window at its passenger, "Get out of here! Get the fuck out of my life!"

"This is ridiculous," Jack thought. *"What am I doing here? I've missed my flight. He's not answering the phone. I know he's there. What am I going to do, stand there banging on the door?"* As he looked out at the rain falling across the deserted

street, Jack was aware of an increasingly sharp ache in his stomach and the feeling like there was no air in the car. He saw a woman crossing Avenue B, coming toward the car. "*I love him. If he only knew... Who knows what he is... What if he is gay?... He doesn't have to be.*"

Jack felt an overwhelming urge to get out of the car. He pulled on the door handle. Forgetting to put his coat on over his suit, not even realizing where he was walking until the water from all the slush in the street began to soak through his shoes, he practically bumped into a woman.

"Meester! Please help me. My children are hungry." She clutched at Jack's suit coat, which, even in the fraction of a minute he stood there, began to get soaked.

"Lady, I can't help you." Jack was trying to get past her without knocking her down. He turned to back away and as he pulled harder, her grip loosened and he fell backward. "Oh, fuck!" he screamed as he tripped and fell onto the slush-covered pavement.

Ron Davis leapt out of the car to rescue Jack, pulling him out of the puddle and back into the car. Getting back into the driver's seat, he was so rattled by the encounter that he gunned the accelerator and sped down Avenue B. The low-lying buildings seemed to close in on them until they got to Houston Street. When he lowered the glass partition, he could see Jack through the rearview mirror, loosening his tie, gasping for breath.

From behind the heavy curtains in the living room window, Dan saw his father being helped in the car and watched it speed away.

"Jesus Christ, Mr. O'Brien, are you all right? You want me to drive you to Beth Israel?" He ran the red light at Delancey Street and nearly plowed into the side of a van.

Jack was rolled to the other side of the car, as it swerved to avoid a crash. When he got up again, he was straining to regain his composure. "I'm OK, Ron. Really. Just get me to LaGuardia. OK? Get me there in one piece. I'm all right."

As they crossed the Williamsburg Bridge and sped along

the BQE, Jack looked back at the Manhattan skyline. His aggravation gave way to a brief consciousness of his over-whelming anxiety. The shock of his son's rejection made him shudder. He sat up in the seat. His shoes, socks, and his pants from below the knee were soaked through. His jacket was wet. The water running from his hair mixed with his tears. Then he leaned forward and put his head in his hands. "*Oh my God. What am I going to do?*"

◪ ◪ ◪

"I can't sing these lyrics." Dan had the sheet music on the kitchen table.

Marty looked up, held his fork expectantly in the air as if waiting for Dan to say something more, and then went ahead and took the bite. Through the chewing, Dan could still make out the syllables "Why not?"

"'Man pussy? I want your man pussy?' Where'd you come up with this?"

Marty slid the chair back across the linoleum and got up for another serving from the pot on the stove. "You're right. It's not like that. It's m…a…n   p…u…s…s…y." Marty stood for-ward on the balls of his feet as his legs and hips and groin traced the curves of each consonant and vowel.

"You'll get it. All you have to do is sing what you really want." Marty smiled as he sat down again. "Say, speaking of what you really want, when are you gonna call that lawyer guy who got us the job?"

"He said he would call me right after New Year when he got back. I haven't heard from him yet."

"So, what are you waiting for? You want that m…a…n p…u…s…s…y."

"C'mon, Marty." Dan blushed.

Marty pushed the phone across the kitchen table and looked at Dan. "You want that m…a…n   p…u…s…s…y."

"I have his office number. I'll call him in the morning."

◥ ◥ ◥

"Mr. Baldwin's office…. Hi, Chance… yes, he's right here."

When Steve closed the door to his office, there were two associates waiting outside for him, a junior partner and two more associates waiting in an office down the hall, and a conference call in progress on the speakerphone on his desk. Steve pressed the mute button and picked up the other line. "Hi, Chance. Hey, I'm so sorry, I mean, I've been expecting to call you since I got back. It's been crazy here. How are you? How's the Marc Jackson job going? … Yes, I'd like to have dinner, but let's not do a restaurant, especially if we're going someplace where we'll be interrupted. I'll make a dinner for us at my place. How about Thursday night?… Great. It's 780 Park. My apartment's the one on the top floor… Yes, I know that's the penthouse… Right. It sounds worse than it really is. I'll see you at eight. Bye."

◥ ◥ ◥

There was a framed photograph on the table next to the couch. Dan was trying to make polite conversation. "Is that you and your dad?"

"No," Steve said with an ironic smile, "he was my first lover when I came to New York, about seventeen years ago. He helped me come out."

"I guess that was a dumb question. It's just that he looks a lot older than you."

"Well, I'm not sure what you mean by a lot older. He was about ten years older than me. That's one of the few pictures I have of the two of us. When it was taken in 1982, he had AIDS, which has a way of making people look older than they are."

"What happened to him?"

"He… ah…" Steve paused and then as he finished the sentence, his voice trailed off. "He died. He died twelve years ago."

"I'm sorry. I didn't mean to pry."

"You're not prying. Victor was a wonderful man. He taught philosophy at NYU. When I met him in 1978, I had just finished law school and come to New York to work for the firm. We had a sexual relationship for only a few months. He helped me get over a man I was in love with when I was at Duke. Then we managed to stay friends."

"What about the picture of the other guy? I think I recognize him."

"That's Chad. You probably saw him on TV or in a newspaper, chained to the gates of a pharmaceutical company. He was what you'd call an AIDS activist."

"Were you and he… ah… "

"Lovers? Yes. And I'll save you from asking. He's dead, too. He died of AIDS a year ago. And, oh, by the way," Steve said, as he poured Dan a glass of wine, "here's the answer to the next question. I'm negative."

Dan could feel his face turning red. "I wasn't going to ask you that." He took the wine and gulped enough to clear his throat.

"Well," said Steve, as he sat down, "You were thinking it. It's OK, Chance. I've lost count of how many of my friends died of AIDS. You were eight years old when the epidemic started. I'm sure it wasn't something you paid attention to until you got here. It wasn't something I had to think about at all in college. Back then, I thought losing my first love was worse than dying."

"Yeah," said Dan, "now I do know what you mean. It must have been great, though, I mean, having someone like that when you were in college."

"We were inseparable from the start of our freshman year. We planned to spend the rest of our lives together."

"Wow," said Dan, "I didn't think gay relationships were that open back then. What did your friends think?"

"Are you kidding?" said Steve. "No one knew, not even our closest friends."

"*God,*" Dan thought to himself, "*I wonder what my father would have said if he knew?*"

"Why don't you bring your drink with you," said Steve. "We can talk while I finish making dinner."

There was a cooking island with a bar that separated the kitchen from the dining room. Dan studied the way Steve moved, the way he gestured as he spoke. "*I wonder what he's like,*" Dan thought. "*His ass isn't so bad, either.*"

Steve had his back to Dan, stirring the sauce, recounting the story as if over the years he had been able to make sense of everything but the ending. "We both went out with women. I dated lots of different girls. He had a steady relationship with a girl I knew before they knew each other."

Steve put the salmon on the broiler pan and opened the oven. "But, you know, nothing I'd ever had, or could imagine for that matter, was like the way I felt about him. He took my breath away." Steve looked at Dan… "Fuck!" Steve shouted. He pulled his hand out of the oven and reached for an ice cube in the freezer.

"Are you all right?" Dan asked.

"Damn it! I'm always doing that," said Steve as he rubbed the ice cube on his fingers. I can't seem to cook and carry on a conversation without burning myself. I'm OK, really. I guess I never got all the gay genes, you know the one that let's us do two or three things at once." Steve managed a smile. "Anyway, where was I? Just before graduation, he said he was going to marry his girlfriend. He said she was pregnant, but that wasn't the only reason he was marrying her. He said he loved her. I hear he's still married, so at least I know he didn't leave me because he couldn't make a commitment. Our relationship was over in one conversation. It was the worst day of my life."

"What was his name?"

"I shouldn't say. He's well known now, a very successful guy. I guess I think he's entitled to some privacy. So, tell me about your friend."

"My story's a little different. I grew up with the guy I told you about. We didn't promise to stay together like you and your friend. In fact, all through school, I never said a word to him about how I felt. We never had sex. I was totally fucked up when I got here and it came out. All he could say was "Dan, I know you're not gay.""

"Oh." Steve paused. He was thinking of what to say next. "So that's your real name, Dan."

The atmosphere of the moment was broken. Dan didn't look up.

"Dan… Gardner," said Steve. "Right?"

Dan was staring deep into his wineglass. "No, well, not exactly. I mean Dan is my first name."

"Fine," said Steve, "let's leave it like that for now. Maybe in a month or so you can tell me your middle name. We'll work up to it. I want you to be relaxed here."

Dan finally looked up. "Thanks. My middle name is Saul."

Steve smiled. "Two down, one to go. Now let's see, where were we? You were interrogating me and we've covered everything about my committed relationships. Is there anything else?"

"I wasn't thinking of it as an interrogation."

"I'm just teasing, really. Is there anything else you'd like to know?"

"Hmm, oh, I don't know. What was it like before college? What was your family like?"

"Well, I was born in Charlotte, in 1950. You do the math. My family has been in the textiles business for over a hundred years. I grew up, I guess I'd say, as a happy, well-adjusted kid. My parents were fantastic. They still are. I haven't been back there in twenty years, but we see each other on holidays. Sometimes we go to my sister's in London or to my folk's place in Palm Beach."

"When did you come out to them?"

"Right after I got out of the marines and I was in law school. We've always been honest and supportive of each other. I think they knew even before I told them. We didn't talk about it much. It simply became a fact of our lives."

"Why did you go to Vietnam?"

"Because I didn't care about my life. I didn't go there to die, but I didn't care if that happened. But, it was too late. The war was over by the time I got there. So I had to come home."

"You're not serious, are you?"

"Well, sort of serious. I really didn't care, although I didn't acknowledge it to myself at the time and, I should add, the war really was over. I helped with the evacuation from the embassy. By the way, is there a checklist of questions you're working from?" Steve laughed. "If your modeling career doesn't hit, you've got a great future as a pollster."

"My roommate says I ask too many questions."

"What do you do with all the answers?"

"That's how I get to know people."

"Uh-huh," Steve said. He was trying to pay attention to the conversation and measure the ingredients for the sauce at the same time. "Did you ever read *The Teachings of Don Juan?*

"By Castaneda?"

"Remember what Don Juan says about his past?"

"Um… That he decided he wouldn't have one."

"Right. Because whatever people think they know about someone's past is used to interpret the present… Maybe sometimes that's valid, but I think it's also a way to avoid dealing with the here and now on its own terms. Do you see what I mean?"

"I think so, but it seems to me that it's easier, you know, when you know about someone's past."

"Here," said Steve, "put these on the table." Steve kept talking as Dan set the placemats, cutlery, and napkins. "Maybe that's just what you're used to. We all hold on to our own past, even when we'd like to let go of it. Why should it be any different when we're dealing with other people? We're wired to be afraid of change."

Steve was pouring the sauce over the salmon and arranging the asparagus and rice on the plates. "Letting go of the past means stepping into, you know, pure potential. That's scary." Steve handed Dan the plates. "Here, carry these over and I'll open another bottle of wine. Given the choice between the unknown and grief, we choose grief."

Dan lifted the glass that Steve put in front of him. "Here's to stepping into pure potential."

Steve smiled and raised his glass. "To pure potential."

They talked and ate, without any of the interruptions that had so awkwardly punctuated their first three meetings. They were at ease with their mutual attraction. They kept on talking, even after they were done eating.

"Take your port glass," said Steve. "We'll go sit in my office. It has a great view of the city."

When they got to the doorway, Steve stopped Dan. "Hold on just a second. I've got to pick up some of this stuff."

Dan watched as Steve gathered several files lying on and around the couch and coffee table. "These documents are confidential. I'm working on a hostile takeover defense." He piled it all on a shelf behind his desk. "OK, the coast is clear." Dan came in and settled at the end of the couch, took his shoes off, and put his feet up on the table.

They talked for a while longer, but the food and the wine and the hour were beginning to catch up with them.

"You know," said Steve, "didn't you say you're going to meet Arthur Gould tomorrow at eight?"

"Yeah."

"His office is on Third and Fifty-ninth. If you don't want to go all the way to the East Village tonight and back here in the morning, you're welcome to stay with me. I could drop you at Arthur's on my way to work."

"Ah… yeah, sure. That would save me two cab rides. I'll get more sleep. But… ah… if it's OK with you, before we turn in, I'd like to take a shower."

"Who says you're going to get any sleep tonight?" Steve smiled and laughed nervously as he put his glass down on the table. He looked at Dan. He couldn't believe he had said that, but he could tell that Dan wasn't embarrassed.

Steve stood up and went over to where Dan was sitting. Then Dan stood up. The moment had arrived. They had each hoped for it, even prepared for it, but all the rehearsing that went on in their minds was nothing like the real thing. They were skin diving in some dark unexplored lagoon. There was the rush and confusion of conflicting sensations. *"I've waited so long for this." "I've been here before." "I want it all now." "I have to go slowly."* They stood there, kissing, and then Steve came up for air. "Didn't you say something about a shower? Want some company?"

All five showerheads were running, full blast, giving the bathroom the look and feel of a steam room.

Dan was standing under a stream of water. The overwhelming sense of happiness was unbearable. He had to open his eyes. He reached for the soap. "Hey, I'll wash yours if you wash mine." They both laughed.

Dan had only recently let go of his sexual inhibitions. Now he was letting go of himself. There were moments when Dan and Steve tore at each other's flesh like animals, and other times they stopped and held each other while an indescribable energy passed between them that both scared and excited them.

When they got out of the shower, Dan saw what looked like a flood on the bathroom floor. "Hey, look at this place. We've got to mop this up."

Steve was toweling off. "Don't worry about it. What doesn't dry, the maid will take care of tomorrow."

Dan emptied the rack of towels and laid them on the floor.

"Great," said Steve, "now that's taken care of. What were you planning on drying yourself with?"

Dan looked up sheepishly. "Oh."

"Don't worry, I'll be right back."

Steve went out through the bedroom, living room, and kitchen and found a stack of towels in the laundry room. As he was carrying them back to the bathroom, he passed the pictures of Victor and Chad. *"I hope you guys are getting a laugh out of this."*

"Where did you go for the towels," Dan asked, "Chinatown?" He had already mopped up the water.

"Now everything's neat," said Steve. "You know, you remind

me of someone else I knew who had to have things in order."

"What was it you said," Dan asked, holding the pile of towels, "something about letting go of the past?"

"Touché!" Steve smiled. "Well, anyway, you're pretty good at that. Maybe I'll hire you as my houseboy."

"Yeah," said Dan as he put the wet towels in the laundry bag, "you'd like that, wouldn't you?" Then he dried himself with a fresh towel.

They stopped, stared at each other, standing nude in the bathroom. It started all over again, the kissing, the touching. In bed, they kissed, sometimes softly, sometimes small hard bites. There was body lotion on the dresser. "Just lay still for a while," Dan whispered in Steve's ear as he massaged the lotion into his muscles. Dan was breathing easily, taking his time, finding his way. He rubbed the oil on his own chest, sliding up and down on Steve's back, ass, and legs.

When he turned Steve over, he was almost inebriated from the massage. He was already used to seeing hard muscled bodies, but the feeling he had when he looked at Steve was different. He felt at peace. There were times when their bodies touched that they felt as if they were one person. When they were finally exhausted, they collapsed in each other's arms. They fell asleep where they lay.

Steve woke up to the sound of his alarm at 5:30. He disentangled himself from Dan, went to the bathroom, and filled the tub. He came back into the bedroom and started quietly kissing Dan until he was awake. "Let's take a bath. It's six, I have to leave at seven-thirty." They got into the oversized bathtub. Steve rubbed the soap on Dan's shoulders.

Dan had his eyes closed, laying back in Steve's arms, his head rolling slightly with the pressure of Steve's hands on his neck muscles. "I've never felt this way. My father used to tell me, if it seems too good to be true it usually is. I never thought I would feel like this unless it was with Michael."

"Well, I guess I'm supposed to take that as a compliment, being a reasonably acceptable facsimile of someone else."

Dan sat up in the tub and turned around. He looked like he

was about to say something, but Steve stopped him. "Maybe I was a little too sarcastic. Let's just enjoy the silence for a minute."

They lay there for a while, neither of them speaking, then Steve noticed the clock on the counter. "It's time to come back to the cruel world. You get dressed. I'll make breakfast."

Dan found a disposable razor in the cabinet. He noticed a brush and a porcelain container of shaving cream, something he hadn't seen since the last time he saw his father using one. He lathered his face and remembered seeing the limo drive away from his apartment in the East Village. *"I wonder when I'll see him again. What will I tell him, that I'm happy, that I'm in love with someone? He would never get this."*

By the time Dan got to the kitchen, Steve already had the oatmeal and fruit salad, coffee and orange juice, on the table.

"You cleaned up rather well. You look like you're ready to get photographed. Remember, Arthur's only your lawyer."

"I used one of your disposable razors with your shaving brush. My dad has one of those."

"Oh, so now the truth comes out. I knew I couldn't keep it from you forever. I'm not twenty-three after all. I'm an older man. Eat your breakfast and I'll go put on my age-appropriate blue pin-striped suit and wing tipped shoes, and you can help me catch a cab." They both laughed.

The cab let Dan out on the corner of Park at Fifty-ninth. The traffic was stopped and Steve watched Dan walk toward Third Avenue. The silhouette against the morning sun was unmistakable. *"Don't go there,"* Steve said to himself. *"That was someone else, a long time ago."*

BOND

"This is what I'm talking about, here, in the classifieds. 'Female model wanted for up-scale fashion house, legitimate agency, no nudity.' This is such bullshit."

Michael was stretched out on the couch in their apartment in Tribeca, trying to read the Business section of the Sunday *New York Times*. He turned the page without missing a line in the story he was reading. "Angela, things take time, and besides, you need to be prepared when someone legit does notice you."

"What more do I need to do? I've got over a hundred photos in my book. I've been everywhere and all they say is I'm too exotic. I read in these stupid magazines about how ethnic is in, and the Latina community is booming. But when you look up on the agents' walls, all you see is blond white girls. Maybe I should start bleaching my skin."

"Maybe you should update your book, get some classier photos taken of yourself. Have you got the Sports section?"

"What are you trying to say, that I look like a whore? A few months ago, you thought these photographs were beautiful."

Michael looked up from the paper. "That was before you started bitching about the other models' books. So, now that you mention it, I realize that you probably need to get a real photographer like Chris Makos, not some Argentinean ex-boyfriend wannabe photographer. Angela, I'm trying to give you some constructive criticisms and—"

"Oh my God," Angela gasped. "Look! Here's an article about Dan and that strange roommate of his doing a show at the Palladium. You never told me Dan was a singer. I swear to God, I'm gonna bleach my skin and get a penis implant and then I'll land a modeling contract and have a record deal too."

Michael was rifling through the papers on the floor. "Don't

you think that's a bit harsh and very weird?"

"No, Michael. Here, look at this."

He held the page she tore out of the magazine like she had handed him something infectious. There was Marty, standing nude in a pair of pink high-heel pumps, showing his muscled back with a crucifix chain going down the center of his spine, right to the crack of his ass. Dan was dressed as an altar boy, coiled around the pink pumps, and underneath were the words "'Man Pussy,' a new single release by Blurred Gender." Michael put it down, but he needed to see it again to believe his eyes. He picked it up, stared at it for a moment, then crumpled the page into a ball and threw it away. "This is sick. I'm not going to see some gay freak show that Dan got mixed up with."

She grabbed the ad as if Michael had thrown away the winning Powerball ticket. "We have to get invited to this show. It's at the Palladium." She was smoothing the page on the table. "Look how much publicity it's getting. Everyone's going to be there." She picked up the phone. "I'm calling Dan. We've got to be on the list this Friday night. What's his number? C'mon, give it to me."

"I haven't spoken with Dan in months. Besides, I won't be back from the sales conference in Palm Beach until late Friday." He held the paper over his head, like a shield against an invading reality.

Angela reached under the drawstring in his sweatpants. "C'mon, sweetie, these shows always start late. Why are you being so selfish? What about my career? You have a job. It's me that's still a waitress." She could see she wasn't getting anywhere. She pulled the paper away and held the phone over Michael's head. "Last chance. What's the number?"

"Give me the damned phone. I'll call him, but I can't make any promises."

"Give me a break. Dan would do anything for you. He's in love with you. Remember?"

Michael rolled his eyes and dialed the number. He got the answering machine with Dan's voice. "Hi, you've reached 212-564-6141. If you'd like to leave a message for Marty, push 1; for

Chance, push 2; for Dan, push 3; or Mary, push 4."

"Oh, great," said Michael, as the recording was finishing. "How many fucking roommates does he have?" When he heard the beep, he went into his "Hey, buddy," voice. "Hey, Dan. This is Michael. Sorry I haven't been in touch, but I've been real busy at the firm. Anyway, I was just hanging here with Angela at the apartment and she noticed you're doing a show at the Palladium on Friday night. Call me back and let me know how Angela and I can get tickets."

She interrupted urgently. "Michael, the guest list, it's the guest list we have to be on. Anyone can buy a ticket, I... we..."

Michael hung up the phone. "Dan will put us on the guest list. Remember, he loves me. He'll do anything for me. Now, let me finish the paper."

◪ ◪ ◪

The Palladium was packed. Most people knew Marty's act as Mary and only a few knew Dan at all, but nobody knew what to make of "MAN PUSSY."

Dan was pacing backstage. "Marty, I'm nervous as hell. It's one thing in rehearsal and the recording studio. Did you see all those people?"

"Don't worry. I always start out with this nervous energy, like butterflies in my stomach, then you see the lights, the audience, you start feeling larger than life. Let's go. It's show time."

The band members took their positions. The white light followed Dan as he walked across the stage and sat down in the confession box. He was sweating profusely, but that only added to the effect.

Dan began. "Forgive me, Father, for I have sinned."

Marty's voice came from the confession box. "Yes."

"Forgive me, Father, for I have sinned."

Marty's voice answered with the music, pulsing, rhythmic. "Your secret's safe, your secret's safe."

Then Dan, "I'm wanting. I'm denying. I'm needing. I'm fighting."

Marty stepped out of the confession box. Bleached blond short hair, long eye lashes, dark makeup, black latex gloves, a crucifix in hand, and a long red robe. He sang into Dan's ear. It sounded like a whisper. "Your secret's safe, they know you're straight. Your secret's safe, they know you're straight."

Marty started to take off Dan's white lace surplus and black cotton cassock. The lighting accentuated the contrast between Dan's white skin and his red latex gloves and black pumps. Two dancers entered the stage dressed as nuns, standing in point shoes, pushing a bed on wheels toward Dan.

There was a break in the music. Dan started screaming the words, "Father, Father, Oh God in heaven, forgive me my sins."

Marty pushed the cross in front of Dan's face and forced him onto the bed, while the nuns tied his feet and hands. Marty pulled out a small bottle of Holy Water and sprinkled it on the bed, while Dan was convulsing, straining against the satin cords.

Marty sang in a haunting voice, pointing to the audience, "Stop your lies and manipulations. Let this boy's soul be free to feel the urge deep down inside. Stop tormenting him with denial and guilt. I command you. Set him free!"

The nuns tore at Dan's flesh, singing in unison, "Set him free! Set him free!"

Dan was singing, screaming, "I'm wanting. I'm denying. I'm needing. I'm fighting." He broke loose and stood in front of the bed. At first he looked as if he didn't know where to run and then he stopped, looked at the audience, and began singing calmly, seductively. "Now I understand. Now I understand."

Slowly, Marty slipped out of his robe and embraced Dan as they undulated like flames, mixing the sweat of their bodies, both moving in unison to a slow erotic rhythm.

The lights changed to a mixture of orange, red. The nuns, dancing wildly, throwing off their habits, singing, "Amen! Amen! Free at last! Free at last!" and exited the stage.

Dan started singing again:

I'm wanting
I'm needing
I'm talking
I'm saying

Marty joined in:

Man Pussy
I need your man pussy

Marty went solo, pointing at Dan as he walked across the stage:

Your secret's safe.
They know you're straight
Your secret's safe.
They know you're straight.

The beat of the music quickened as Dan and Marty sang together:

We're talking Man Pussy
Not woman
It's man
Not woman
It's man
Man to man

Standing near the stage, Michael was getting sick. "I knew he was gay," Michael shouted at Angela, "but not a circus act!"

"You're so uptight," said Angela. "This show is incredible. Besides, a lot of celebrities are here. Don't fuck this up for me."

"Angela," screamed Michael, over the music, "they don't even know you exist! They're too busy watching the *freak* show!" He headed for the men's room. The walls were spinning. He splashed water on his face. As he heard the audience clapping, he thought, *Thank God, the show's over.* When he returned, he grabbed Angela by the arm. "Come on. Let's go. This shit is getting to me."

"What are you talking about?" Angela said as she pulled her arm away. "We have to go back stage to see Dan and Marty. Plus there are a lot of casting agents here."

"Angela, I'm ready. Let's go."

His words were futile. She was already headed backstage with one of the passes Michael got from Dan. She ran up to Marty and planted a big kiss on him, just as a cameraman took the picture. "Hi, Marty, you are so incredible, you're going to be a star, a big star." Angela was as unsubtle as the flash of the halogen light.

"Who the hell are you?" Marty asked.

Her eyes were scanning the room. "I'm Angela, my boyfriend is Dan's best friend. I've heard so much about you and your show and the modeling. You're just so incredible."

Marty was about to tell Angela to go latch onto someone else, but Michael's shouting carried across the room. "Dan, I don't care if you are gay, but my God, this is just some sacrilegious bullshit. Are you on drugs? Is all your money going up your nose? You shouldn't be prostituting yourself like some piece of white trash. Think about how your parents are going to feel when they see you in all those stupid celebrity papers."

Dan was having a hard time holding his tongue while Michael lectured him, but as soon as the subject of his parents came up, he stuck his finger in Michael's sternum to punctuate each shouted sentence. "Why should you wonder about what my parents would think? You sound just like Jack O'Brien. I don't need any fucking lecture about prostitution from a bucket-shop stockbroker who's hustling loser stocks to widows and orphans. So why don't you take your up-tight ass out of my face and take your star-fucking cunt girlfriend with you?"

Michael shoved Dan up against the backstage door, "Listen, faggot, I'd beat the shit out of you if it wasn't for the fact that I—"

Dan tackled Michael, strangling him. The room went silent accept for the sound Michael made, gasping for air, and the noise of whirring motor drives on the cameras and then the sound of Angela screaming "Stop it! Stop! Michael!"

Marty moved in and grabbed Dan. "Bwana, what the fuck is up with you? We don't need bad press over some childhood bullshit."

"Mike, Mike, baby, are you OK?" Angela's script for the evening hadn't included this encounter. She experienced a momentary flash of awareness. She felt alone in the room as she clung to Michael.

"I'm OK," he said hoarsely as he got up. "Let's get the fuck out of here."

It was too late. The press loved the cockfight. The cameramen and reporters were chasing Michael and Angela. "Hey, was that you and your boyfriend fighting? Is Chance Gardner sleeping with your girlfriend?" Michael didn't say a word. He knocked two of the photographers on the ground, camera equipment flying everywhere. He grabbed Angela and pulled her out through the stage door, down the alley, and into a waiting taxi.

"Michael," she asked, as he opened the door of the taxi, "what about our limo?"

"Fuck the limo," he said. "We made our dramatic exit, wouldn't you say?"

On the way back to Tribeca, Angela was fuming. "Why are you so angry? It was just a show!"

"Angela, I mean it, shut up! Don't talk about this with me, ever!"

At the Palladium, Steve found Marty after the worst was over. "What was all that about?"

"Steve, I really don't know, but I don't need this shit going on."

"The security guard told me Dan got in a fight. Who was he fighting with?"

"Michael, his buddy from North Carolina. That's all I know."

Steve went into the dressing room, where he found Dan, sitting at a table with a three-way mirror. "Dan, are you OK?"

Dan kept staring straight ahead. "Of course I'm OK. I'm

always OK. Why don't you start telling me I look like some stupid faggot, some wannabe performer? I'm sure I've embarrassed you. Maybe you should leave before I ruin your career."

Steve took a chair and sat on it backward, hunched over it with his arms leaning on the back as if he were talking to Dan across a fence or a wall or some great distance. "What are you talking about? I thought the show was great. Who was that guy you were fighting with?"

Dan drew a wet cloth across the makeup on his face. It only made a smudge. He was staring at his reflection. "He said I was a prostitute… Maybe I am." He cocked his head sideways to get a slightly different view. "What do you think?"

Steve, the lawyer, leaned his chest against the back of the chair. "*Objection, Your Honor. Counsel is being illogical. We move to strike that statement from the record.*" "Oh, for Christ's sake, Dan, what are you talking about? What do you know about being a prostitute?"

Staring blankly into space, hurtling through space, the space between himself and the mirror, the space between himself and the straight back chair with the lawyer sitting up straight, Dan found something to get a hold of, something else floating in the void, looking for an attachment. It was his own anger, but at least it could be projected outward. "Fuck you! Fuck you! That's what I know about being a prostitute! Get the fuck out of here!"

◥ ◥ ◥

It was two o'clock on a Friday, the middle of February. It hadn't stopped snowing all day. LaGuardia was closed. FDR Drive was a parking lot. Everyone was going home early. Beverly Rosmore came in to check on her boss one more time before she left.

"Any messages?" Steve asked as he stared out the window.

"No, he hasn't called."

"What do you mean?" Steve turned around, but he was looking down at the papers on his desk, avoiding eye contact.

"Don't worry, you're not so transparent with everyone." She picked up a few files off the credenza behind his desk. She put her hand on his shoulder and whispered in his ear. "And it's not just because I've known you for seventeen years either." She pushed on the back of the chair and Steve turned to face her. "He isn't going to call you. He's twenty-three. He's immature. He's screwed up. Now, go home. Take a hot bath. Have a good time at Joe's fortieth wedding anniversary party."

"Is that still on?" Steve asked, grateful that Beverly had given him a chance to change the subject.

"I talked to his daughter-in-law this morning. She said they have to go ahead, even with the storm, because Joe and Rita are leaving for Aruba in the morning. She said she still thinks they have no idea that it's a party for them... Listen, it kills me to see you in such a hopeless relationship. Promise me you'll go out tonight and have a good time."

Steve smiled. "I love you too, Beverly. Bye."

She sighed as she went back to her desk, got her coat, and walked toward the elevators. He sat still for a while, looking out the window, watching the snowfall. Then he picked up his phone book and started turning the pages. He knew Dan's number by heart, but stopped at the page with the last names beginning with G. Dan Gardner 564-6141. He yawned. He thought. He tapped his teeth together a few times. Then he put the book down and picked up his phone.

◼ ◼ ◼

"That's the fourth time you've been in there in the last hour. Call him."

"No." Dan closed the refrigerator door and sat down at the kitchen table.

"You're starting to get on my nerves." Marty was slicing the ginger root with an aggravated chop. "Call him."

"No."

"Why?"

"Because I don't want to."

"That's a lie and you know it."

"OK, so maybe I *do* want to call him, but why *should* I?"

"Isn't wanting to enough?"

"He should be calling me."

"All this should-and-shouldn't stuff is such bullshit."

"Well, what other word should I use?"

"See, there you go again."

"Oh, Marty, stop tormenting me."

"Stop tormenting yourself."

Dan got up from the chair. "I think I'm gonna work out. C'mon, let's go."

"I've got to pick up a costume at Butch's. Can you hold yourself together for another hour?"

"Yeah," said Dan as the phone rang. "What if this is for you?"

◪ ◪ ◪

The apartment on Bond Street was dark. Luke had been asleep since he got home in the morning, around ten. He was still a little groggy from his all-night outing. He had started Thursday night around eleven with some friends at the Bowery Bar and then went to Jackie 60. He was trying to get over a cold, otherwise he would have gone home with a boy who showed up around five in the morning, saying he just got into the city on a bus from some place in Illinois called Normal.

He would have let the answering machine handle the call, but he had to get up anyway, to go to the bathroom. "Hello."

"Hi, Luke, it's Steve."

"Steve? Oh... Steve... Hey, baby, how are you? I've missed you. What's going on?"

"Not a lot... ah... I was thinking I'd come by to see you."

"Yeah... sure... I was just going to get dressed. Maybe I

should stay in bed, eh?"

"No… no, you can get dressed. I just want to talk. I have to go to a surprise party for a friend of mine and his wife at the Roma Club in Little Italy. I was going to work out at Crunch. I thought maybe you'd like to get some exercise with me."

"Oh, God," Luke moaned as he squinted. "I don't know about the exercise, but, yeah, sure, come on over."

When he hung up the phone, Steve Baldwin was not in control of himself. Or at least it would have been accurate to say that the cool, mature, rational Steve Baldwin wasn't in control. It had been a week since he left Dan, hysterical, in the dressing room at the Palladium. *He'll call. Give it time. He'll call,* Steve kept telling himself. But he didn't. The pressure was getting unbearable. He put on his coat, grabbed his gym bag and his briefcase, and walked two blocks to the subway at Fifty-first and Lexington.

"Hi," Luke said as he opened the door, wearing a pair of old cotton sweatpants and a baggy sweatshirt. "What took you so long? You look terrible."

"Huh." Steve smiled as he leaned forward to kiss Luke. "How nice of you to notice. I figured there was no point in trying to get a cab, so I took the 6 train. I was treated to a half-hour of standing like a steer in a packed cattle car with no air while we were stuck at Twenty-eighth Street. Once we got moving again, it took another half hour to get to Astor Place."

They walked into the dimly lit and cluttered living room.

Steve sighed as he took off his coat. "Gee, I see you haven't changed a thing since the last time I was here."

"Poor malisch," said Luke. He took Steve's coat. "You're a mess. Why don't you take a shower and I'll put on some coffee?"

Steve paused for a moment. He looked at Luke. "Ah… Yeah, that's a good idea… I'd like some coffee."

The hot shower rinsed the sweat off Steve's skin and relieved some of the tension. He didn't bother to clear the water from his eyes when he heard the shower curtain being pulled back. He felt Luke begin to knead the muscles in his neck and shoulders.

When they were in bed, as they had been many times

before, neither mistook their physical proximity for intimacy. When they first met, several years ago, Steve just wanted to fuck. Luke needed the money. It was a fair exchange. But their trade became more complicated as they grew attached to each other. Then in November, Steve stopped calling.

"I have to go," Steve said, as he was getting dressed quickly. "There's a dinner I promised I'd go to." Then he looked at Luke. "Do you want to get in a work out. I don't have to be there until eight o'clock."

❚ ❚ ❚

"So then what happened?" Marty was in the chair, needle in hand, squinting at the hem he was trying to fix.

"He asked me if I wanted to go to dinner with him…" Dan was pulling the loose threads out of the arm of the sofa as his voice trailed off.

"Uh-huh." Marty looked up. "If you want to do the twenty questions thing, I'm not in the mood. Are you gonna tell me what happened or not?"

"He showed up at the gym right after you left with this trick and goes way over in the corner to do legs like I'm supposed to pretend I didn't know he was there."

"You said that already."

"Marty, can I tell the fucking story *my* way?"

"OK." Marty put the costume down. "Go ahead, I'm all ears, but please stop tearing the stuffing out of the couch."

Dan sat up. "I don't know what's up with him. It's like he totally has his act together. He's so cool, but I dunno. I mean he wants to spend all our free time together, but then he says, you know, that all men are dogs and that it's OK for us to have casual sex when we're not together."

"So?"

"That's not what I want, Marty. That's not what I want…"

◰ ◰ ◰

"Oh, Steven, you are such a Gemini, always looking for your soul mate, your lost twin," Victor had said. The admonition from his former lover was as clear in Steve's ears as it had been when it was spoken. Now from the framed picture on the end table, his mentor's smile interrupted the conversation he was having with himself.

It was midnight. He didn't want to go to bed, so he stretched out on the couch in the living room. Too drowsy to read, too anxious to sleep, he let himself drift on an indulgence, fragments of memory brought into the present to keep himself company.

"So what do you want, Steven? What do you really want?"

"I don't know. I guess I want to be happy, but I don't know what that means to me anymore."

"Try this." The blue eyes carried the advice across the years, a gift again as simple as it was profound. "Begin with fantasy."

"Oh, Victor." He adjusted the pillows on the couch behind him to try to get comfortable. "I'm too old for fantasy."

"If you believe that, why did you go to his gym?" The deep voice was the sound of the boom being lowered. "You *knew* he would be there."

Steve put his head back, looked up at the ceiling, and sighed. "Yeah, I guess I did."

"And the deep squats with three hundred and fifteen pounds, that was to impress Luke, right?"

His back was stiff and his legs were already feeling sore. "You're right. I guess that was overdoing it… I don't know, Victor. He has this amazing ability to draw me in and yet he cut me off after we had that stupid argument at the show. It's like he just closed a door."

"So, he's a Scorpio. They can do that. Baby, there's got to be some price for the passion. But he said 'Yes' to the dinner, right?"

Steve frowned like he was trying to sort it all out.

"Will you stop with the mental masturbation? He went to the anniversary party because he *wanted* to go. I can't stand listening to someone with their head up their ass complaining about how dark it is. He wanted to go and he wants to be in a relationship with you."

"OK. OK. But why... why does he want to be with *m e*?"

"Because you're beautiful, Steven. Didn't I always tell you that? Now it's your turn to believe it. It's your turn."

◼ ◼ ◼

There were hundreds of balloons dotting the twenty-foot ceiling, pink ones and blue ones to celebrate the marriage of the girl to the boy forty years earlier. Tied to the balloons, pink and blue ribbons wafted gently to the tables set up around a parquet dance floor. Observing from the edge of the room, leaning back on his chair, Dan watched Steve make his way from the bar, stopping to exchange pleasantries.

"*Marty, he is so hot. I mean, like in a suit, he is the sexiest man I have ever seen.*"

"Here." Steve offered the glass of champagne. "Sorry that took so long. He took off his coat and sat next to Dan at the empty table. Their shoulders were touching as they surveyed the scene. "Thanks for coming. Now that I've made an appearance, we can leave in a little while."

Dan took a sip. "I'm fine. We can stay as long as you want. I don't suppose we can dance, though, huh? I mean, you know, with the kids around."

Steve laughed. "Not at all. If you want to do the Hully Gully, I say let's go for it."

"*God, Marty he is so cool. It's like there's nothing he's afraid of.*"

They looked at the couple at the head of the table, greeting friends, receiving congratulations. Forty years married, three boys and a girl, five grandchildren, a house in Scarsdale and a condo in West Palm.

Just the thought of almost too much happiness and Dan needed another gulp of champagne to wash down his anxiety. "So, who was the trick at Crunch?"

"Did that bother you?"

"Nope. Just curious."

"Why did you lie to him?"

"I dunno. I thought maybe I shouldn't bring it up."

"There you go again with that should-and-shouldn't shit."

Steve put his arm around Dan's shoulder. "I'm sorry about what happened at the show. I really don't know what I said that upset you so much, but whatever it was, I'm sorry... Hey, I'm over here." Steve continued after Dan turned to look at him. "Please don't shut me out. I would like to go out with you. I mean I would *really* like to go out with you. I just need some help to avoid the minefields."

"Can you believe it? He asked me to make a list of the things that make me feel safe and the things that make me feel upset. I mean, c'mon! Sometimes he's like a robot looking for an instruction manual."

◣ ◣ ◣

"Besides the amazing sex, what is it about him? Why are you making yourself a mess?"

"He's the most amazing person I've ever met, Victor. I can't tell you why, but he is."

"He's a dreamer, Steven. He looked at that couple tonight at the head table and he said, 'That's what I want.'"

"Yeah, and of course I didn't tell him about Joe banging his secretary for two years while Rita was growing a mustache. All he sees is the dream."

"Well, then, now we know why you're in love with him."

"Oh, please, Victor. I'm not in love."

"Where is he?"

"I dropped him off after the party. He has to be up to get ready for a shoot in five hours. We said we would think about where we go from here."

"Take a cue from the boy. He knows you're beautiful, Steven. So now it's your turn. Let go… and begin with fantasy."

PART III

*I desire love beyond all thought and reason
I desire love for more than just a season.*

Ultra Naté

ECHO

They spent every available moment together. They knew they were addicted to each other. And yet, they kept their separate apartments, separate jobs, separate circles of friends, all as a way of not fully experiencing the intensity of their relationship. Perhaps they understood, instinctively, that nothing so intimate could be maintained without discomfort, that love, which craves love, also fears abandonment. So arises the conflict of attraction and avoidance.

There were grand gestures to make up for arguments over small hurts: dinner in Bermuda, a show in London, a hotel suite full of flowers. When they were apart, they kept in touch by e-mails and voice mails and Beverly's mastery of two overbooked calendars. Their separations were like the gaps between the notes of a complex musical score.

Subj: Sorry about the party
Date: 5/26/96 0800 GMT
From: SBaldwin@sasma.com
To: DSOxl@aol.com

Dear Dan,

I'm sorry. I thought the party would be a fun break from the city and you said you'd never been to the Hamptons before. I knew you were upset when you dropped me at Kennedy, but there wasn't time to talk about it. Please don't worry about the Trophy Boy comment. Barry was drunk. And besides, it's not so bad to be a trophy. It could be worse—you could be a wannabe movie mogul and look like *him*. Anyway, we won't go there again. It's Sunday morning here so it was a quick ride from Heathrow. I tried calling you at the apartment. I guess you must still be out... having fun, I hope. Call me whenever if you feel like it. You have the number at the Savoy and my office. Beverly knows how to reach me at any of my appointments. I miss you already.

S

Subj: Happy Birthday!!!!!
Date: 6/17/96 1700 GMT
From: DSOxl@aol.com
To: SBaldwin@sasma.com

Hey, babe. I just realized it was your birthday this month. Was it last week or the week before? Happy birthday. Naples was fun and I got a Brioni suit for you. Went to see Pompeii. It was so cool. I'm back on Wednesday, but I just talked to Beverly and she said you're in Washington. Am I ever gonna see you again? I just jerked off and I am still sooooo horny. (Are you sure no one at the office can read your e-mail?) Gotta run. cya. xo

Subj: 4th July
Date: 6/25/96 0500 EDST
From: SBaldwin@sasma.com
To: DSOxl@aol.com

Dear Dan,

It was great to finally see you last weekend but we both have to slow down a little. When did you say the season is over? I'm stuck here through the end of the week. I would take the shuttle back and forth, but we've been working late every night. I have an idea. Let's go to

Provincetown for the 4th of July weekend. A friend of mine has a house there and we could stay in the guest apartment. It's private and I swear I don't know anyone else there besides Roy. I'll get out of work early on Wednesday and we'll come back Sunday. You can get your flight to London from Boston. Can we do dinner this Friday? I'll eat you for dessert.

S

◣ ◣ ◣

"Hi, Beverly, it's Dan."

"Oh, Dan, I'm so glad you called. He's just gone over to the bank. There was some big problem with the deal he's been working on."

"Beverly, it's Thursday. We were supposed to leave yesterday."

"Oh, I know, it's terrible. I've never seen him this bad before. He asked me to get a table at Balthazar for nine o'clock and he promises not to be late. Try not to be too mad at him, Dan."

◣ ◣ ◣

It was Friday afternoon when they finally left New York, like two refugees, fleeing with only carry-on duffel bags, clinging to the unexpressed expectation that a long weekend might make a difference in their unresolved lives. They were packed with the masses on the four o'clock shuttle from LaGuardia. Dan tried to pass the time reading the in flight magazine. He was checking out the people on the flight when the man across the aisle noticed his picture in *GQ*. Their eyes met. He winced and looked down. He couldn't wait to get off the plane.

They said nothing on the short flight from Boston across Cape Cod Bay. Steve sat behind him in the cramped cabin of the nine-passenger plane. In the dunes at the edge of the shore, there was a single airstrip and a hangar made of rusting corrugated metal. Dan stepped off the plane and onto the tarmac like a man who was most of all happy to be someplace where he could pretend that no one recognized him.

It was a short cab ride from the airport through the dunes and a forest of beech trees to the West End of town where they were left at a house on the bay. There was a note tacked to the gate.

Hi, Steve,

Make yourself at home in the apartment downstairs. After you get settled, we're at a cocktail benefit that my neighbor is hosting for the Fine Arts Work Center. It's four houses on the right as you head into town.

Roy

Steve didn't speak until they got inside. "We don't have to go."

"I know," Dan replied as he threw his bag on the chair. "But, we're settled now, right? We can at least go over there and say hello."

◼ ◼ ◼

Dan made his way through the crowd. He approached the man standing at the edge of the deck and extended his hand. "Dr. McGovern?" There was a brief pause as the man tried to figure out who Dan was. "I'm Dan Gardner. I met your wife at the bar. She pointed you out to me." There was an air of expectancy in Dan's greeting.

"I'm pleased to meet you, Dan." McGovern used the napkin

he was holding to wipe nothing from his mouth. He needed another pause to think of something to say. He scanned the crowd, hoping that he might be rescued.

Dan's face was lit up like he'd met a movie star instead of a UCLA neuroscientist. "I read your book on serotonin when I was at Duke."

"Oh," said McGovern, realizing it was safe to take another sip of his drink. He had a place to start the conversation. "So, you're a psychologist now?"

"Oh, no." Dan flashed his "aw shucks" smile. "I'm, ah… I'm working as a model, but I did a minor in psychology…"

Steve realized how much he liked to watch Dan. He could see McGovern's curiously amused face and the backside of Dan. They were off in a corner, at a distance where they could be observed without making it obvious. Steve saw McGovern being gradually taken in, nonplussed at first to find anyone at the party interested in the chemistry of behavior, then delighted to be the subject of such enthusiasm.

There were a few other guests at the party, some in polite conversation, some daydreaming, their eyes occasionally, furtively looking over at the way Dan gestured to make a point, the power in his arms and shoulders, the way he shifted his weight from one leg to another. Some would have called it seduction, the peacock preening his feathers even as he engaged in the most intellectual of conversations. But observing Dan had become one of Steve's favorite avocations, and he understood, as no one else did, that the power of Dan's attraction was precisely that it was not seductive. Dan was at his most compelling when everything about him was visible, at the surface of perception.

"No, no, no." Dan was absorbed in the conversation. A few gin and tonics for a twenty-three-year old with a resting pulse of forty-eight and he had no problem pressing his point with one of the world's leading authorities on the subject. "I mean, I get what you're saying about testosterone being elevated, so that makes the guy horny, but I, well, I don't mean to offend you or anything, but let's say a guy goes to a bar and his testosterone is off the charts. Dan lowered his voice and leaned forward, "And he's there to get l…a…i…d."

"You're not offending me," McGovern responded matter-of-factly. He ran the largest primate lab in the world. He was used to reading nonverbal cues. So he couldn't help but notice the way Dan raised his eyebrows and lowered his bottom lip to bare the incisors behind it when he practically whispered the word "laid." McGovern took another slow deliberate sip of his drink. "Go on."

"OK, so he goes to the bar and if it's just testosterone, then he'd hit on anything that moves. It would be that quick and simple."

"Well." McGovern laughed. "Sometimes it is that simple, but usually not. You're forgetting that what you're talking about is a nonspecific feeling of lust. You know, the ship's coming into port and the sailor starts thinking, how did you say it, that he's got to get… laid?"

Dan smiled. "Yeah, right."

"So, the sailor's in town," McGovern continued, "but he doesn't know anyone. There's a whole other set of hormones like dopamine and norepinephrine that come into play. That's when he sees his intended across the room and suddenly, no one else will do. That's attraction, and, as I'm sure you've experienced yourself, it can be very, very specific."

"Yeah, but how do you explain why that attraction drops off after, you know, as soon as…"

McGovern looked back. "He gets his rocks off?"

Dan laughed. "Well, yeah. I'm sorry if this is getting gross. I only came over here to say hello."

"It's quite all right," McGovern continued, "this is the most interesting conversation I've had all weekend. The last part you're missing is the transition from attraction to attachment. The quick wham-bam-thank-you-ma'am follows from elevated levels of testosterone, and then to attraction that is coincident with the other neurotransmitters. But there's this other thing going on which I guess I saw anecdotally for the first time when I was at medical school and doing a stint at Boston City Hospital. The girls who used to sell their services by the hour would come there for their shots. Now, in their case, and for their clients, the attraction was definitely for a quick-quick humpy-humpy, finish-it-up-and-get-out-of-there-activity, yes?"

Dan was delighted with the physical demonstration, and anyone else watching would be wondering what the hip gyrations were supposed to mean in the conversation between the married professor and the wide-eyed student. Steve figured it was just too interesting not to join them.

"So," McGovern was noticing his wife waving at him from across the deck, "it's when you do things like kissing and cuddling that you involve oxytocin, which is associated with attachment. That's why, in anonymous sex, whether it is for money or otherwise, you don't see this kind of attachment-related activity."

Steve put one hand on Dan's shoulder and extended the other to McGovern. "Sounds like you guys are having quite a conversation. I'm Steve Baldwin."

"Hello, Steve. I'm Martin McGovern. Yes, we have been. But I'm afraid I need to move on to a much less interesting dinner party. It's been an unexpected pleasure meeting you, Dan. You'll have to keep me posted on your field research, eh?"

"What field research?" Steve asked after McGovern left.

"Oh," Dan replied, "we were talking about neurotransmitters."

◪ ◪ ◪

It was the low muffled blare of the foghorn that he heard when he first woke up. Lying on his back, his legs and arms intertwined with Dan's, Steve could see the mist condensed on the windows and the screens and even on the walls of the bedroom, cold and wet and penetrating everything porous except the space under the blankets where they kept each other warm. It was early. Dan was sound asleep.

After the cocktail party, they had ordered a pizza and lay in bed watching *Blade Runner*. He was relieved that even Dan occasionally had the kind of sex that was more like just another act of getting ready for bed than the screaming all-nighter they had come to Provincetown for. They were both so tired.

His "problem" crept into Steve's consciousness, as it usually did in the first moments of waking. It lay heavy on him and left a film, a reminder of his all too private conflict. He wondered when it was that most of what he remembered about Jack had gone. All that was left was the recollection of touch, the intoxicating aftertaste of almost too much love, and then the searing pain of separation. He noticed the sound of the foghorn again and wondered what there might be this time to warn him not to go off course.

◪ ◪ ◪

By ten o'clock the fog had burned off and left a cloudless blue sky. In the open Jeep he borrowed from their host, Steve was driving toward the National Seashore at Race Point. "Roy told me his houseguest, Paul, is an actor. Did you get a chance to talk to him about your plans?"

"Not really. I just talked to him on the deck for a while. We kinda figured out who we knew in New York. I didn't want to ask too many questions, you know? I didn't know what his deal is with Roy."

"I should have told you," Steve said as he turned off Route 6. "According to Roy they're not lovers. They met at a party. I guess you'd say he's become Paul's patron. But there's no *quid pro quo*, if you know what I mean."

"No *quid pro quo* ?" Dan asked.

"I meant no sex," Steve replied. "There's never anything for nothing. I guess you could call it an easy trade for both of them. Acting classes and airfare are small change to Roy. Paul's twenty-eight and good looking. They show up at parties together. It's only a slight variation on most marriages."

They were driving through the beech forest. The branches

made a canopy that crossed over their heads. The wind in the leaves alternated flashes of broken light and dark on the road. As they came out of the forest, Dan noticed up ahead a line of cars and what looked like a full parking lot, the kind of crowd you'd expect at the beach on the Fourth of July weekend. "*Oh my God,*" he thought, "*are we ever gonna be alone?*"

Steve made a sudden right turn and headed down a sand road. He stopped where a locked chain was strung between two steel posts.

"What are you doing?" Dan asked. "This is a fire road."

Steve pulled out a key from his pocket and smiled. "It's a surprise." He got out and unlocked the chain. In another minute, they were driving into a vast horizon of sand dunes.

Dan was speechless.

"Thirty years ago when they turned this place into a National Park there were still about twenty cottages out here. They're called dune shacks. They've been preserved, mostly by private owners, but there are a few that are rented. I got us one for the day."

Dan's crestfallen look that had been so plain as they approached the beach was now an ear-to-ear grin. They drove south along a sand track through low-lying brush. The shack was set back off the crest of a dune, which looked over a stretch of unspoiled and empty beach.

"This is so beautiful," Dan said as the Jeep came to a stop. "How did you get this place?"

When Steve shut the engine off there was no sound except of the wind in the grass and the waves in the distance. "We made a donation to the trust that manages the shack," Steve said as he lifted the cooler out of the Jeep. "C'mon, grab those towels."

There was a small open space at the edge of where the dune dropped off like a low cliff. The grass there had given way to the wind, which carved a dish of sand about eight feet wide. They lay naked on a blanket.

"This is what I wanted," Dan said as he applied the sunscreen to Steve's shoulders, "just the two of us." He craned his neck and looked around. When he was sure the coast was clear, he leaned forward and whispered in Steve's ear, "Can we do it out here?"

"Is there ever anything else on your mind?" Steve grinned. "We're not likely to see a park ranger, but it's still a felony if one sees us... We can go inside if you want."

Dan slid over Steve's well-oiled body. "I'll just say I was applying the sunscreen."

"Hmm. I don't think I'm likely to get a burn where you'd want to put the sunscreen. Let's wait a while and we'll go inside for lunch."

The breeze off the ocean cooled them and carried the sounds of the waves. They saw a hawk circling overhead. Dan lay on his stomach, reading a book. Steve drifted in and out of sleep. Occasionally he opened one eye and glanced over, noticing the way the breeze rearranged the patterns of Dan's hair, even the light fuzz on the nape of his neck. To distract himself, he reached in the bag for the *New York Times* but he skipped from one article to another as he was trying to get settled in the moment. There was an article in the Business section, which he put back in the bag, and he turned to the Science section. "*This isn't working.*" He turned to Dan, who seemed absorbed in his book. "What are you reading?"

"It's a Virginia Woolf book, *To the Lighthouse.*"

"Really? That's been on my list of 'Gee, I'd like to read that someday' books, but I don't know when I'm going to get around to it. It's about a family tragedy, right?"

"Yeah, in the first part it introduces everybody. The father is a professor who talks to himself. He's not close to his kids. The mother is, like, trying to hold everything together. She's like the peacemaker. Anyway, so they all want to go to the lighthouse, except for the father who doesn't want to go because he's saying that there's a storm coming. That's how it begins."

"And the second part?"

"Well, in the second part, it's the summer and Mrs. Ramsey is dead and they're still trying to get to the lighthouse. That's where I am now... So, why are you interested in Virginia Woolf?"

"A girl I knew in college was a fan of hers and I had this idea that I would someday go back and read it. I just never got around to it. How 'bout you? It's not your usual pulp fiction."

"I know. It was one of my mother's favorites, which I've been meaning to get to for a while. She reads a lot... I guess she reminds me of Mrs. Ramsey."

"Maybe I'll get to meet her someday."

There was an awkward pause before Dan said, "Yeah, sure." He looked over to the opened *New York Times*. "What are you reading?"

"Hmm?" Steve looked back at the paper. "Oh, it's an article about a high tech phone that can detect the changes in someone's voice when they're telling a lie."

"C'mon."

"Seriously. It's expensive, but I guess it works on the same principle as a polygraph. It says here that first you establish a person's voice pattern for truthful responses—like you ask him to spell his last name—and you use that to measure the rest of what he says."

Steve continued skimming the article.

Dan put his book to the side and his head down on the blanket. "I know what you're thinking."

"No you don't."

"Yes I do."

"OK, go ahead, tell me."

"You're thinking that you couldn't use that phone on me because you don't know my real last name."

Steve put the paper down. "As a matter fact, I could ask you to spell the name you've made up, assuming you agree to spell that correctly, but no, that wasn't what I was thinking. I suppose, though, by your answer, that I could guess what's on your mind."

"Yeah, I know," Dan responded dejectedly, "I do think about it sometimes, but it's just such a mess, and I like what we have and... I'm sorry..."

"Don't be sorry on my account. I've told you I'm curious, but we've been over this before. First of all, your past isn't that important to me. I like what we have too. But what I care about is right now. Second, I want you to have time to work this out, and us being lovers doesn't mean you have to do it with me looking over your shoulder."

Steve sat up. He couldn't say what he wanted to say lying prone on the ground. "I think people are entitled to privacy. Just because we've been inside each other, you know, physically, doesn't mean that we have to share every thought." He reached into the beach bag for the phone. "Suppose we were talking on the phone and I could look at this and it would tell me if you're lying or telling the truth. Forget about how it works. OK? People aren't meant to live that way. You know how we have our saying, 'No lies in this bed,' that's important, but we can't pretend that we tell each other everything. You know how some people say they talk about everything? Well, that's not true. They don't."

"I want to tell you. I'm just afraid of dragging you into everything."

"*Tell him you love him,*" Steve said to himself. "*Go ahead.*" He was looking at Dan, looking straight into his eyes. "*Say it now.*" He wanted to say it even though he knew what it felt like. Love felt like pain. He looked down. "Tell me when you're ready." The ringing cell phone was a welcome relief.

"Hello."

"Steven, I have to talk to you."

"Richard?"

"Where are you?"

"What's going on?"

"You have to get to a land line right away."

"Richard, I'm lying in a sand dune in the middle of nowhere."

"You're not going to believe this. One of my guys in the Investment Management area knows Carl Herrington, right?"

"Am I supposed to know who that is?"

"On the fucking board at NCBT."

"Oh, yeah. I remember. So what?"

"So, they're at a dinner in Washington for... for... oh, I

don't remember but who cares… so they're talking, you know, off the record, about the deal. My guy's saying what a shame it is that O'Brien won't let the merger go through with Moore as CEO, yadda yadda yadda, for just a year in a transition, yadda yadda yadda."

"This can wait 'til Monday morning."

"No! So, Herrington goes berserk. He says O'Brien never put that proposal in front of the board and he gets on this tear about what a megalomaniac O'Brien is."

"It's Saturday morning. I haven't had a day off in six months."

"Listen to me! Herrington tells my guy we should make our pitch to their big shareholders and maybe they can put pressure on Blake Reynolds. Two days later he meets my guy in New York with their shareholder list."

"Have you been doing coke again? What the fuck difference does that make other than knowing that—" Steve stopped himself and lowered his voice just before he said Jack's name, "he might have a problem with his board?"

"If you'd give me a fucking minute to finish, I'll tell you why. The fucking list isn't just the DTC sheets with all the stuff in street name. It's reams of their internal tracking data with detailed trading activity."

"Richard, depending on how he got that stuff it may be theft. If he used the mail to send it—"

"Stop. Herrington got it from O'Brien's secretary. She used to be Herrington's secretary before O'Brien fired him. I've already talked to your guy Bernstein yesterday afternoon. He says it's messy, but war is messy."

"What are you doing calling Marty Bernstein about this?"

"I tried to get to you yesterday, but your cell phone wasn't on and I figured you were fucking Boy Wonder. Steven, you've got to get to a landline. What I have to tell you is huge."

"And it can't wait twenty-four hours?"

"No."

◨ ◨ ◨

The deck over the guest apartment extended out toward the water for about fifteen feet and cast a long shadow in the afternoon when the sun was behind the house. In the cool dark bedroom, Dan lay on his back with his arms folded behind his head, naked, just out of the shower, staring at the ceiling, listening to the faint shrill sounds of children playing on the beach a few houses away.

He looked at the clock radio—two o'clock. Steve said he'd be back by four. It wasn't the two hours he was anxious about. Once Steve killed a whole day waiting for him to get back from a shoot that was supposed to be over in the morning. No problem when he finally got back. After the quick explanation there was just a smile, a "How are you?" and hot sex. It wasn't the two hours. It was his life. Steve was so intense about his stuff. Dan didn't feel that way about anything. He wanted to. He wanted it all to make sense, to have something, to have someone. To him, Steve was *the* someone.

He was waiting, waiting for the world to reveal itself, as if there would be some flash and he would say, "Oh, of course, now I understand." There was no sudden insight, no recognizable pattern to his thoughts and memories. He suddenly remembered an appointment he had forgotten with a trainer and made a mental note to call the gym when he got back. He thought of a book he got from his mother as a present when he graduated from St. Alban's, *Oh, the Places You'll Go* by Dr. Seuss. Then his memory was shifted further back to when he was a boy and the time he told everyone he was "Sam I am" and he "would not eat green eggs and ham." There was a page in the Seuss book he got for graduation where the character winds up in the "Waiting Place."

> Waiting perhaps, for their Uncle Jake
> Or a pot to boil or a better break
> Or a string of pearls or a pair of pants

Or a wig with curls or another Chance
Everyone is just waiting

It's such an awful business—waiting—feeling like you're
missing something. Was there a piece missing that would
appear when he was older? *"How can Steve be so cool?"* He
just wanted to figure it out. The day had started so well with
the surprise at the dune shack and then came their conversation, and *"The fucking phone rang. Oh, God, I should just tell
him and get it over with."* And the modeling, he was tired of
that already. *"I want to be an actor."* He looked at the clock
radio again—two-ten. Waiting made him anxious. He was
pulling absentmindedly on his dick.

He heard the sound of Paul walking on the deck above him.
He got out of bed, put on a pair of shorts and socks and gym
shoes. At the top of the spiral staircase, he found Paul at the
table on the deck. In the shadow of an umbrella, he was taking a
hit from a joint.

"Hey," Dan said as he approached hesitantly.

"Hey, Dan. What's up?" Paul extended his hand with the
joint in it.

Dan reached out his hand. It was a reflex reaction. When
their fingers touched, for a fraction of a second a pulse of energy passed between them, though neither of them meant to
allow the other to notice. Dan pressed the joint to his lips and
inhaled slowly. He squinted through the smoke and saw Paul
looking at him.

"Where's Steve?" It sounded like a question and a suggestion.

Dan looked out at the bay as he exhaled. "He went into
town for a fax. There's supposed to be a call at three. He said
he'd be home by four."

Paul had a face made for screen acting, displaying what
seemed like an infinite combination of subtle changes to his head
position or the angle of his eyebrows, or the way he smiled that
would speak without saying a word. He was taller than Dan,
about six foot two, with a big frame of a body, but he was more

inviting than intimidating. He had brown eyes and brows that looked like they had been brushed on, a nose that was just large enough to be masculine, and a smile that belied a trace of sadness.

They talked in short clipped sentences. Through the haze of his mental torpor, Dan recognized someone who, like him, was struggling to establish himself but was just a few years ahead in the effort. *"If I weren't so stoned,"* he thought, *"we could have a great conversation."* They covered acting and modeling and living in NY.

"Roy has been helping me with classes at Atlantic," Paul said, "and the money for a coach. I'm going to L.A. in the fall."

"God!" said Dan, squinting as he put the roach in the ashtray, "that was really good shit. I'm fuckin' wiped out."

"Yeah," said Paul, "let's get some sun."

There were towels already draped over the two air mattresses on the deck next to the table. Dan flopped on one of them, not even having enough energy to take off his shoes. Paul came out of the house with a full glass of water. His eyes closed, Dan could hear the ice cubes in the glass as Paul set it down on the deck, the sound of a T-shirt and shorts coming off, and a body sitting down on the air mattress. There was the plastic "click" of the top of a sunscreen dispenser opening and the smooth sound of a palm rubbing lotion onto skin.

"Oh, shit," Dan thought, *"what am I doing here?"* He shifted his weight on the air mattress. *"I'm stoned out of my fuckin' mind and—"* "Shit!" Dan exclaimed. His pupils were dilated in his wide-opened eyes as he bolted upright.

"What's wrong?" Paul asked laconically.

"I can't get a sunburn. I have a shoot next week in London."

Out of the corner of his eye, Paul watched Dan apply thick globs of lotion to his chest. The multicolored Popsicle-shaped bottle added to the childlike awkwardness in which Dan handled the lotion as it dripped from his hand onto the towel.

When Dan had dropped the bottle for the third time, Paul couldn't help but ask, "Do you usually have such a hard time with sunscreen?"

"Huh?" Dan looked up sheepishly. "Kinda looks that way,

doesn't it. I hate this stuff. I get paranoid about missing a spot. And… I am kinda stoned." Then came the million-dollar smile.

Paul smiled back. "I see. Would you care for some help?"

"Um, yeah, I guess I would." Dan closed his eyes as he lay on his stomach. The warm smell of the coconut oil and the hypnotic circling of Paul's hands on his back relaxed him gradually, almost to sleep, until he felt the tug of Paul unlacing the cross-trainers on his feet.

Paul worked Dan's feet with the sunscreen while he lay with his eyes closed. The massage continued as Paul began to work his way back up Dan's legs to his shorts. "Didn't you say you were worried about tan lines? Even with the sunscreen you'll get a tan line with these on." He tugged lightly on the waistband and continued working his way up Dan's back.

Paul leaned forward onto the air mattress, which took their combined weight first with a loud "pop" and then the sound of a long fart as the air flowed out and they came to rest on the deck. They were both laughing when Paul broke in, "I guess that's our signal to continue this massage inside."

"OK," Dan replied, as Paul pulled him up and led him into the house.

The shades were pulled down and the drapes were drawn. The room was dark. They felt their way around, allowing their eyes to adjust. Dan collapsed on the bed with his feet dangling over the edge, taking in the coolness of the comforter, a welcome contrast to the penetrating heat of the sun.

Paul stood at the bottom of the bed and began by rubbing lotion onto Dan's legs, alternating the pressure on his quads with an open palm and a closed fist. The pot, the cool dark room, the deep tissue massage, all combined to pull Dan away from the attachment to his free-floating anxiety about Steve. At times, the tips of Paul's fingers reached up Dan's shorts, suggestively close to where Dan would normally have demonstrated his excitement. But Paul withdrew each time the tension in Dan's body evidenced his apprehension.

Paul's large open hands worked their way down Dan's legs. Dan felt them working his right calf as he relaxed into a memory of lying against Steve on the beach that afternoon. He was lost in the thought when he noticed another sensation. Not a hand, it was soft and moist. Paul's forehead pressed against Dan's toes as he licked from the heel to the ball of Dan's foot. It was about as far away on Dan's body as Paul could get from his crotch, the place Dan had always perceived as the center of his sexuality, so far on the periphery, yet this was an intensely sexual experience. It felt odd. It felt innocent, but at the same time exotic and strangely forbidden. The mere flicking of Paul's tongue over the arch of Dan's foot sent a wave of pleasure up his leg and into his groin.

The feeling of Paul's tongue between each toe, the softness of his lips, the hard enamel of his teeth, the experience of feeling each toe, one slowly at a time in Paul's mouth—Dan was acutely aware of each of these. The sensation was not a flood, but the experience of many tiny individual drops. It was as if pleasure itself could be experienced as many smaller pleasures, like Russian dolls, each contained, one inside the other.

Dan became the observer and the observed of his own enjoyment. His eyes remained closed. He was floating on the stream of his thoughts, intensely aware of each discrete sensation, the coolness of the room, the warmth of Paul's skin. He noticed the tension in his muscles giving way to relaxation. His skin was so sensitive that each touch created a pulse that traveled the length of his body. He felt more and more like he was floating above the bed. When he noticed the feeling of hands traveling gradually up from his feet to his legs again, he anticipated Paul's intention and opened his eyes. He reached down and pulled Paul up on the bed. "Wow," he stretched and yawned as if woken from a dream, "that was incredible. You really are into feet, aren't you? Is this something you've just gotten into?"

"Oh, no, I was first attracted to a guy's feet when I was five years old."

"C'mon!"

"Seriously, I was in kindergarten, and there was this pretty cute kid, Robbie. One time we were walking in a stream in our bare feet. I remember really being fascinated by the sight of his feet."

"But were you sexually aroused by feet at that age? I mean, Christ, were you aroused by anything at that age?" Dan was still lying on his back, looking up at the ceiling, and trying to remember being five years old.

Paul was lying next to him, his head propped up with one hand, the other hand tracing patterns on Dan's chest. "No, I don't think so." He paused a moment to ponder the question and then continued. "No, it wasn't until I was playing around with a neighbor boy, Eric, when I was about twelve, that I realized I was sexually into feet. He let me take his socks off and we would play a game. He would try to get his foot on my face. I tried to put up a fight, but I loved the smell of his foot at my face or if I was lucky, the taste of his foot on my tongue."

"Wow."

"I used to be really embarrassed about it, but now I'm much more comfortable with myself."

"So what is it exactly that turns you on about feet?"

"Well, one thing is that feet are usually concealed so that when you see the naked foot, there is some kind of sexy fascination with it. And it partly has to do with submission. If you think about it, when subjects stood before kings, they prostrated themselves at the king's feet. So it's about being under the control of a more powerful man. When you lick his feet, you are completely submitting. I would never lick the feet of a guy I didn't think of as masculine."

"I guess I'm pretty butch, huh?"

"Well, you're a pretty sexy guy." Paul made small circles with his finger around Dan's left nipple.

They lay still for a few moments as Paul rested his head on Dan's chest.

"I wondered if I was so weird, you know, until I realized there are lots of guys who seemed to live and breathe for feet. When I first signed on to AOL and put 'feet' in a search engine, I was amazed at how many different Web sites there are about feet."

"What?"

"Yeah, that's how I found out about Foot Friends parties at this one club that is mainly an S&M and fetish place. Guys get together whose interests range from licking boots to smelling socks to licking bare feet. They serve alcohol so no jacking off is allowed. At the Foot Action parties, there's no alcohol but sex is OK."

"Hmm, maybe we should check out one of those parties sometime."

"Um… that would be fine, but I think we should stick to the Foot Friends party. You never know what you'd be stepping in with your bare feet at the other one."

"Yuck! Yeah, let's definitely not go to that one." Dan looked up at the clock on the bureau—3:00. "Hey, I gotta go. Steve's gonna be home any minute and I should get a shower."

"Wait, you said he'd be home at four. I'm not done." Paul held on with his arm wrapped around Dan's chest. "We still have some time."

◾ ◾ ◾

Steve bicycled into town to the Mail Spot, a little place on Commercial Street where Roy said he could get a fax and make a private phone call. He wished they had gone someplace inaccessible for the weekend. But there was no place he could go to get away from it all because so much of what he was upset about was inside him. The back room where the owner let him take the call was the antithesis of the corporate lawyer's power office. He had a headache.

"OK, I see what's on the fax, but by itself it's not conclusive. These trading companies are in the Channel Islands, the Bahamas, and Hong Kong. Rothman will say he doesn't control them. Even if you're right, that all these entities are his, and he somehow controls more than five percent of NCBT, there's still the whole conspiracy issue. This is not something you're gonna get O'Brien indicted for."

"Steven, don't you get it? We have what looks like a pattern of buying by these companies. They accumulate when the stock's under selling pressure and then they dribble it back to the market when the stock is strong. Looks like manipulation to me. But I don't give a fuck if it's true. What I do know is if we leak this to the press, we won't have to connect the dots for them. O'Brien will be dead."

"First of all, Richard, I do give a fuck if it's true. Second, if Herrington gave you this stuff and he hates O'Brien, why didn't he call it out to you?"

"He's a moron. He had no idea what he gave us. It took my guys two days to do the analysis."

"And if we're wrong and the whole thing gets traced back to us… it's just not right. Rothman's in London. Can't your traders there get a better handle on this?"

"If it gets out that we're even snooping around, Rothman will sell his position down and have time to cover his tracks. Steven, we can't give them time to react."

"Richard, step back a minute. The NCBT bid is stone cold dead. So we don't have to ruin anyone to save our client. Second, if we decide to go ahead with this, we can't be wrong. There are too many reputations at stake."

"Why the fuck do you care anything about O'Brien's reputation?"

"This doesn't have anything to do with my feelings about O'Brien or his reputation… Who else knows about this?"

"So far just you, me, Bernstein, and a couple of my analysts."

"OK, give me some time to think about it. I understand why you called me but we can wait one day. Let's meet at your place Monday morning at ten."

◼ ◼ ◼

It was almost five when Steve got back. He found Dan in the beach-level apartment. "Geez, how come you're not up on the deck with Paul? It's so beautiful up there." No answer. He put his folders back in his briefcase and snapped the locks. "So, how was your afternoon?"

Dan was naked, kneeling at the foot of the bed, rifling through his duffel bag. "OK."

"Did you get a chance to talk to Paul about acting classes?"

"Um... yeah..." There were only three shirts and two pairs of jeans in the bag, but Dan kept rifling through it like he was looking for a way out instead of something to wear. "Where did you say we're going to dinner?"

Steve sat on the bed. "The Dancing Lobster. The owner used to be the chef at Harry's in New York. I haven't seen him in ten years. Roy says his place is really good... Come here and lie down."

Dan gave up pretending to be looking through his bag and stretched out on the bed next to Steve. He put his head on Steve's chest and his arm was wrapped around Steve's waist.

"I'm sorry I had to go into town for that call. I couldn't take it on the cell phone and I needed to get a fax. I promise, no more interruptions... Are you OK?"

Dan held on tighter. "Yeah, sure. I'm fine... I missed you."

They rolled over with Dan on his back. Steve ran his finger from the hollow in Dan's neck slowly down his chest and stomach to the tuft of pubic hair. In the time it would take for Steve's finger to slowly travel that distance, there usually would be a perfectly erect welcome at the end of the line. Dan looked away, not a dramatic body movement, just his eyes were turned toward the scene of the bay through the window.

The loud ringing of the phone on the nightstand interrupted them. It was Roy, suggesting that they bike into town for Tea Dance and then Steve and Dan could go to dinner from there.

Dan got up off the bed. "Yeah, that's a great idea. Let's go."

◪ ◪ ◪

Tea Dance was an afternoon cocktail party on the poolside deck of a hotel called the Boat Slip. Dan and Steve got separated from their host and his houseguest as they mingled with the crowd and greeted people they knew from the City. There was a fair assortment of eye candy to distract them as they stood on the edges of the crowd and sipped their drinks.

Dan exchanged a few furtive glances with Paul in the crowd. "Did your call go OK?" he asked Steve. They both had something else on their minds but the question helped to make up for the uncomfortable silence.

"Yeah, it went fine." Steve turned to Dan. "We could head into town if you want to take some time to get to the restaurant."

They started on their bicycles from the Boat Slip, but gave up after a few blocks. Commercial Street was crowded with pedestrians. It was like nothing Dan had ever seen. Not that he hadn't seen grandparents pushing baby carriages or tattooed rough trade in leather chaps with bare asses, but he'd never seen them in the same place before. There were kids on skateboards and what looked like an outing from a nursing home (complete with oxygen bottles) in threes and fours on the benches in front of Town Hall. He could tell the decidedly straight couples from the curious undecideds by the way the former held on tightly to each other as they made their way against the crowds.

It was as if Noah himself had come back to life and put the word out on the Internet: "Come to Provincetown, a pair of every kind, color, and variety, straights, bisexuals, sexually disinterested, and multisexuals, cross-gendereds, cross-dressers." There were Harley bikers walking indifferently by star-imitating drag queens. Dan stopped and talked to Bette Davis. He tried to imagine what she looked like as a man. It reminded him of the first time he met Marty. There was another pair named Ginger Vitas and Pearline. Ginger had a bone through her nose and a smile on her face as if he had finally discovered herself.

Pearline was a foot taller and a least a hundred pounds heavier with a trace of a five o'clock shadow. She looked like she was ready to sing at La Scala.

There were T-shirt shops, one called the Cotton Gallery, and art galleries and head shops. There were Norman Rockwell seaside restaurants with names like the Lobster Pot and Stormy Harbors with Formica tabletops, the kind where you expect Mr. and Mrs. Backbone-of-America to be sipping coffee and talking about how family values have gone to the dogs.

As they got through the center of town, the crowds thinned out. There were galleries clustered in the East End, but it was too early for the gallery crowd. Everyone was either at or getting ready for dinner. The Dancing Lobster looked like it had been blown over and reconstructed a few times from pieces of shipwrecks, the perfect location for two New Yorkers who felt more like flotsam and jetsam than a power lawyer and his high-fashion-model lover.

After stopping by the kitchen to see the owner, they were shown to a window table with a postcard view of the water—sea gulls trailing fishing boats into the harbor. The low-lying sun lit the curved outline of Long Point and the lighthouse at the very tip of Cape Cod, a painter's perspective of land's end at dusk. The laughter from a party at the bar, conversations from tables of tourists and weekenders, the clang of dishes being cleared all combined into background noise, a din that made it possible to have the most intimate conversation in a restaurant full of people.

They had their elbows on the table, facing each other. Dan couldn't take in the view without looking at Steve, so he read the menu intensely as if he were memorizing it for a test after dinner.

"Do you want to talk about what happened with Paul this afternoon?" Steve asked like he was checking on whether Dan wanted the oysters or the shrimp for an appetizer.

"Nothing happened."

"I'm not mad at you. I just asked if you wanted to talk about it."

"I swear, nothing happened. Well, we were stoned and... you know... I was sort of bummed about this morning. I mean, it wasn't what I was expecting. I wanted to have some time for us. I like hanging out with you, but not when you're on the phone and working on something you can't talk about."

Steve looked confused. "Is this your way of deflecting my question about what happened with Paul or are you blaming the whole thing on me?"

"Steve, nothing happened. Well, I mean..."

Steve looked across the table expectantly. "Remember, we said 'No lies in this bed.'"

"I swear nothing happened..." Dan took a bite of food and started chewing. "We didn't have sex, but..." He swallowed and looked up. "But he licked my feet."

"What!" Steve laughed.

"Wait!" Dan put his fork down and held up both his hands.

Steve inhaled, sat back in his chair, stared across the distance, and smiled softly. "I can't wait to hear this."

"He's a cool guy and he was putting sunscreen on me and that turned into sort of a massage and then... well, like I said, he licked my feet for a little while. I was really surprised. It felt incredible. And, I mean we could have had sex, but we didn't. That's not what I want. I told you what I want..." Dan looked across the table intently. "I want 'the dream.'"

Steve furrowed his brow, as if he were trying to squeeze forty-six years of experience into a single articulated thought. "OK, this is not such a good example, because obviously I would not have wanted to come back from my call and found you guys fucking around, but you know how I feel about experiencing the world. You just said it felt incredible. You didn't say it, but you *wanted* to experience it. I don't want our relationship to be limiting that way. I'm just trying to say that there isn't that much difference to me between the desire and the action. I've seen too many people get twisted up inside over bottled up desires."

What is there to say when it's all been said? They had not professed their love, though it was like a spring welling up inside both of them. They were both so sure of their hearts and so sure of their positions. What is there to say between two neighboring solitudes that can bring them together?

Steve took a few more bites of food and put his fork down. He could see Dan was waiting. "When Victor was getting really sick, it was in the summer of '86. I used to take him to the Big Cup on Sunday mornings. He loved to people watch and I loved to listen to his commentary. So anyway, one morning, we were sitting there, he was simultaneously doing the *Times* crossword puzzle and reading the magazine. I noticed this guy come in by himself... There's never been a particular type for me, like you and your Latino muscle boys. But I had this incredible rush come over me and I thought, *"Oh my God, look at those eyes."*

"Did you get the butterflies in your stomach?"

"Oh yeah, the big monarch kind."

They both laughed.

Steve noticed there were no lines in Dan's skin when he furrowed his brow, no crow's feet at the corners of his eyes. "I think I was going through a phase. I was thirty-six and working like a dog and, you know, I guess I was discovering a higher level of physical insecurity than you feel when you're in your late twenties. Anyway, so Victor's having his coffee and it looks like he's pretty intensely into the Week in Review section and I thought maybe I should go over and say hello, but I couldn't let myself do it. I figured, 'Oh, Victor will feel bad and I want to do the right thing and I shouldn't go over there. I'm supposed to be here with him now.' So this guy and I kept on exchanging the look, but nothing that was supposed to be obvious."

"So, what happened?"

"He left. I followed him out with my eyes, but that was it. I took Victor home and I was hooking up his IV and out of the blue, he asked me, 'Why didn't you go over to talk to that guy?' So of course I said, 'What guy?' He got pretty annoyed. 'You know, Steven,' he said, 'from the time that he walked in there, you did neither what you wanted to nor what you thought you should do. You weren't with him and you certainly weren't with me. If you think you were playing out that little flirt alone in your mind, you were wrong. Next time, save us both the trouble and go try your luck out.'"

"Wow," said Dan, "you must have been embarrassed."

"I was, but Victor never criticized me about it again. I wish you could have known him. He was an extraordinary man."

"Did you ever see the guy again?"

Steve took the last sip of wine. "Well, the end of the story is that we went back to the Big Cup for the next few Sundays. Victor teased me about not seeing the guy there. I think I looked for him from the moment we got to Chelsea and…"

"And?"

Steve ran his fingers over the stem of the empty wineglass. "And… I didn't see him. Victor went into the hospital. I went back by myself for a few times on Sunday. But I never saw him again. You know, there are so many desires we don't act upon. Stuff we think we're hiding from everyone else. But the truth is that they're too busy dealing with their own stuff or maybe we're all afraid of admitting the truth. And then there's the whole conspiracy thing. 'I'll pretend not to notice your unspoken fantasies if you pretend not to notice mine.'"

The light of setting sun reflected off the sand at low tide and cast a glow on Dan's face. His expression was open; his eyes were intently focused. He drew the side of his tongue against the molars on the right side of his mouth. He nodded his head gently up and down, still not saying anything, but signaling the immanence of a spoken thought. "Yeah, I get it that you choose to be polite to your friend and that he said you were free to do what you wanted, but… Victor wasn't your lover at the time."

Steve was caught by the sudden insight as he looked back at Dan. "*My God*," he thought, "*you are really incredible.*" He spoke as if they were the only two people in the restaurant, as if they were the only two people in the world. "I choose to be with you… every day. There's no long-term contact, no ring on your finger, and there never will be anything like that for us. It's a daily awareness for me of how I want to live my life. We can talk about these things. We've already said 'No lies in this bed.' So let's make another promise. We'll share our fantasies, OK? And… um… I promise when we get home to lick your feet."

Dan laughed and nodded his head. "Deal. So now you have to tell me your fantasies."

"I have a modest fantasy for tonight." It was the truth, but not all of it. He was tired and more than a little sad to think of what fantasies he had let go off in the last twenty years. He looked up. "We came here to have a good time. We have tonight, so let's have a good time. OK?"

"Yeah, sure," Dan replied. He had received an invitation that he realized he was eager to accept. They had come to live in neighboring gardens, each behind impenetrable hedges. "Walk with me" was the invitation Dan received. He was peering cautiously through the door in the garden wall.

It was only ten-thirty when they left the restaurant so they waddled full-bellied along Commercial Street back toward the center of town. They looked in gallery windows. Once when they were peering inside at a show of new paintings, Steve took Dan's hand and held it. Dan didn't even bother to notice if anyone was looking. It felt good.

The crowds of pedestrians had thinned out. There were no baby carriages. But the late evening strollers were a mix of the more exotic variety with plain vanilla, a few pairs of men in chaps and the Chelsea uniform—501s and a white muscle shirt. Mostly they were rather ordinary vacationers in polo shirts and comfort fitting jeans. When they got to the center of town, there was an obvious stream of people headed for one of only two dance clubs, the Atlantic House—also known as the "A" House.

"What do you feel like doing?" Steve asked.

"I dunno. We could go home if you want to."

Steve had his answer. "C'mon, we'll check it out. It closes at one anyway."

"This place looks like a bag lady dressed up as a drag queen," Steve shouted into Dan's ear over the music inside.

The strobes and laser lights hanging from the ceiling looked all too out of place in what was once a quaint eighteenth-century tavern. The wooden columns holding up the low ceiling and the warped floorboards added a measure of hazard to the dancing in the middle of the club. In other respects, it was like any other gay party scene—a few self-absorbed shirtless muscle boys showing off in the center of the room. Most of the rest of the crowd was busy trying not to be noticed looking around for that night's trick.

It was only eleven, but the town was crowded for the Fourth of July weekend and at that hour there weren't really many other places to go. Out of curiosity, they had ducked into a place called the Vault. It was a bar in a small dark room in the basement of an inn, full of middle-aged guys in leather with big bellies and more than a little too much hair. "I don't think you'd like it here," Steve said as he moved Dan back toward the door.

They sipped gin and tonics as they wandered around. There was a large garden area out back with two other bars and a little more room to breath and talk. It was warm outside, but there was the scent of a breeze coming up off the water at high tide. The air felt like it had been taken out to sea and washed and sent back clean. Dan was staring off into the middle distance, taking in the view of the crowd, a mostly ordinary collection of human shapes covered by a few standardized uniforms, and yet it all seemed new to him. He had the "Wow, did you see that?" look, familiar to Steve as a reflection of what was once his own view of the world.

Since the conference call that afternoon, he had been returning off and on to his dilemma. "*What am I going to do?*" he asked himself as he exhaled. "*I should just let him sink with his stupid fucking bank.*" But he couldn't. "*I have to think of something to do.*" He was sipping nervously on his drink until there were only the ice cubes left to crunch on. "*I can find out if it's Rothman buying that stock, but what if Richard is right? If they realize we're looking and they cover their tracks…*"

Dan turned back to Steve and smiled. "What are you thinking?"

"*He's so innocent. He wouldn't understand any of this.*" Steve looked at him and smiled back. "I'm thinking if you want to dance we should probably get in there before the place gets way to crowded too move."

The floor was packed. They managed to get to the middle.

It was like leaping between moving obstacles in a haunted house. Dan was still carrying the drink he had been nursing. In a few minutes they were sweating, getting bumped from all sides. They were laughing at how ridiculous it all was.

"Can you believe people come here for vacation to do this?" Dan shouted over the music.

"They didn't come here to dance," Steve replied with a sly grin. "And since you and I already know who we're going home with, maybe we should do that."

Dan leaned forward and kissed Steve's shoulder. There was a sensation of cold as Steve realized there was an ice cube in Dan's mouth. He was tracing it with his tongue across Steve's neck, to the other shoulder. They passed the ice cube back and forth in their mouths as they kissed.

Steve stopped to breathe. "I guess that means yes."

◣ ◣ ◣

They rode their bikes back through the center of town, past the late night pizza place where the paper plates and crusts were the only evidence of the crowd that gathered after the bars had closed, past the boat yard beach where the last of the night's singles were cruising each other, not so choosy as they had been at the club, in fact now openly eager, past the darkened windows of the guest houses. Dan looked up once and saw Venus chasing the full moon and then glanced ahead at Steve, leaning forward over the handlebars of his bike, pedaling, almost racing back. Dan rode behind on the empty street that was wide enough for two cars.

They put the bikes outside the sliding-glass door on the deck that led to the beach. They were sweating from dancing at the club. They smelled of cigarettes and the bodies of strangers.

"Let's go for a swim," Steve said. With the same breath he pulled roughly at the button fly on Dan's jeans and started to peel them off.

Dan stepped out of his Nikes, stood out on the edge of the deck, and watched Steve getting undressed. The moon reflected off each wave that lapped against the pilings in front of the house. Down the steps and into the bay, Dan swam a few strokes underwater. He opened his eyes and saw the phosphorescent light in the wake of his arms propelling him forward. When he came up for air, he had lost sight of Steve. He stood in the water up to his chest and cleared his eyes. There was nothing but the sound of waves and his own labored breathing until he heard a rush of water behind him and felt the weight of a body against his back and shoulders, knocking him under again. They came up for air in each other's arms.

Out of the water and up the stairs, they fell on the bed together, pulling back the covers until they were lying on the sheets, flesh pressed against flesh, wet. The moonlight reflected off the water and cast a soft glow over their skin and the pale sheets. They were alone in their delirium, rolling over each other, nearly falling off the bed, an intentional loss of balance, not from any drugs, but from the overpowering urge to share the conscious experience of their solitary physical existence. They lost all self-consciousness of what noises they were making, what evidence teeth or nails might leave. There was nothing and no one else, no one, not even at the edges of their awareness.

They were reclaiming their territory, retaking possession of each other, not with gentle caresses and soft touches, but with rough, physical sex, yet it was making love. The taste of salt water mixed with sweat and semen. Legs and arms and torsos sliding over each other, with each rise in intensity, they were straining, driving themselves. The experience of being inside each other was the physical analog to their passion, an exquisite fusion of pain and pleasure. When they collapsed, they lay there, gasping for breath between kisses, hands holding sweat-soaked hair, faces touching, breathing the same air. In their experience of exhaustion, of being completely emptied, there was also the feeling of complete fulfillment.

◪ ◪ ◪

They lay there like two pieces of polished beach glass, resting
where the waves had gently set them down at the edge of the
bay. Steve heard the early morning breeze in the noise of a hal-
yard against a hollow aluminum mast, an agitated clanging
sound, like an alarm bell, like an intruder. Steve untangled himself from Dan. He rolled to the edge of the bed and lay on his
side. *"How am I going to do this?"* The edge of his front teeth
scraped over his bottom lip as if he were digging for an answer.
"There's no time to ask anyone else. I have to ask him."

Steve felt the movement in the bed, the sound of feet on the
carpet, the toilet seat being lifted and a stream of water on
water.

"Oh… my… God." Dan's low hung-over voice sounded like
it was being replayed at slow speed. "I have hickeys all over my
neck."

Steve turned over and saw Dan, his hair in a cowlick, standing, braced by the frame of the bathroom door.

"Look at me. I'm a mess." Dan stumbled back to bed,
crawled under the covers, and leaned on his elbow. He stared for
a minute into Steve's eyes. "But that was sooooo incredibly hot.
You are so incredibly hot." The look he was getting was not the
one Dan was expecting. "What's wrong?"

"I need to ask you to do something for me."

"Sure, whatever you want," Dan said nervously. "What's
wrong?"

"Where do I begin?" Steve was taking short shallow breaths.
"Dan, this deal I'm working on…the guy on the other side of
the transaction…" *"He's so beautiful. Why do I have to drag
him into this?"* Steve swallowed and looked up at the ceiling.
For an instant, all he could focus on was the sound of the hal-
yard… "There's someone I know. No, wait. Someone I *knew*,
years ago, and now his company might be involved in something… maybe with his knowledge, maybe not. And he could be

in trouble for it. I just need to know for sure."

"Steve, what are you talking about?"

"I want you to deliver a letter for me when you get to London."

"Huh?" Dan laughed. "Is that it? That's all you want me to do?"

"I'm asking you to do something that could be considered… that is—"

"I don't care what it is. You don't have to tell me what the fucking deal is." Dan took Steve's face in his hands and looked deeply into Steve's eyes. "All I care about is you." He leaned closer so that their noses were almost touching. "I'll do whatever it is and I don't want to know any more. All… I… care… about… is… you. I love you."

The last words came out as if from a spring deep inside the earth, bursting forth, pure and perfect relief for a man so dry with thirst that he hardly remembered the simple joy in the taste of fresh water. Steve drew Dan close and held on. He whispered in Dan's ear so Dan would not see the tears in his eyes, "I love you too, Dan. I love you too."

◼ ◼ ◼

The phone rang in the dark apartment, rang like the sound of a distant nuisance in Luke's head. At a chair in the back room of the Mail Spot, Steve was hunched over an IBM Selectric, typing and listening, counting the rings. *"C'mon. C'mon, pick up the goddamned phone."*

"Hello."

"Luke, it's Steve."

"Huh? What time is it?" Luke squinted at the clock. "Baby, why are you doing this to me?"

"Luke, this is urgent. Wake up and listen. I really need you to do something for me."

◪ ◪ ◪

Steve kept one eye on the door to the back room as he typed the letter and talked at the same time. "Remember, make sure you're calling from a line that has no connection to you. When you get him on the phone, the only thing you tell him is that a letter concerning his client will be delivered sometime in the morning and that he must take delivery of it personally. That's it."

"Poor malisch, you sound awful. Why are you asking me to do this?"

"I can't tell you the specifics, Luke."

"It's not for money. I know you don't need that. And you're too careful to get yourself in trouble. It must be for love."

"Um, it is, but I can't tell you any more."

"Ah, so you have left your beautiful boy, yes?"

"No, I'm still with him."

"Hmm…" Luke paused. "Then you are in love with two people. No wonder you are a mess."

HEAT

They were in a king-size bed. There was enough room to make love lying across it and not have feet or hands over the edges, but now they used the space between them as an open trash pile. Their contact lenses were out and they each wore glasses, reading through piles of his and her mail, stacked high on two matching nightstands. It was a Monday night ritual. The TV was on, no sound, just the picture of a baseball diamond and the progress of the game marked occasionally on the screen; no runs, no hits, no errors.

The patterns of a marriage develop slowly, like individual layers of lacquer on an oriental tea tray. It starts with the simplest, who sleeps on which side, and progresses with each year until even the act of getting ready to sleep becomes elaborate and ritually fixed. Either of them would have been hard pressed to remember when the mail opening routine started or how it developed. They tried putting wastebaskets on the floor on each side, but they were either sized right for the nightstands and too small for all the paper, or big enough for the job and looked awkward as furniture, and, either way, most of the paper wound up on the floor. So they took to piling discarded envelopes and throwaway stuff between them. And then, when they were through, it was one sweep of an arm to clear the mess into a wastebasket.

Carolyn opened her mail carefully and lay whatever she was finished with in a neat stack aligned on an eight and a half by eleven sheet of paper. Jack ripped envelopes open—"Who cares? They're not reusable"—and he worked them into little compressed wads. He liked the finality of crumpling what he was about to throw away. The sounds of her husband tearing through even this ordinary task used to bother Carolyn, but like so many other small irritations, it had long ago ceased to be worth complaining about.

It was a hot July night in Charlotte and the central air-conditioning was on. She wore a sleeveless pale cotton nightgown, he a plain crew-neck T-shirt, the clothing they always wore to bed and slipped off just before lights out. They were propped up by pillows and their mail opening custom, each in their own way trying to maintain the distractions of busy and purposeful lives.

"I promised Helen that I'd ask you about going on that Kenya safari in August."

He looked over his glasses, but only straight ahead. "Honey, you know we can't do that. I'm right in the middle of the New York Trust deal."

There was a brief silence and then the sound of Jack ripping open another envelope.

She had the brochure in her hand. "It looks beautiful, Sekenani Camp, right in the middle of the Serengeti. Helen says it's breathtaking. The Aldrichs are going, and the Zuckers. You get along with Alex and Bill. Helen said we'd go in their G-3. One stop in London. Maybe we could stay overnight and see a show. We haven't been away in almost a year... It's only six days."

Jack took his glasses off and looked over at his wife. It was the exasperated, exhausted, "Can't you see what I'm going through?" look. That was usually enough, but he reached across the crumpled papers between them and touched her arm. "Honey, I promise, as soon as this deal is over, we'll get away. You know I want to. OK?"

She looked at the brochure with pictures of lions lying at the foot of Mount Kilimanjaro for another few seconds, and then she put it down on the pile of discarded items without another word. The silence of the next few minutes said everything as they went back to the task of sorting through the mail.

There was an envelope on the nightstand she had already opened, heavy stock paper with a raised seal. When she opened it in the afternoon, in a hurry, she had almost thrown it away when she realized it was an invitation. They never attended university functions. Jack had repeatedly declined requests to be on the board of trustees. And she was so busy with her own commitments. She held the card and read it again.

> The president and trustees of Duke University request the pleasure of your company at a reception and dinner honoring the appointment of Steven Lee Baldwin as trustee of the university on Friday, the ninth of August, 1996, at 8:00 p.m. in the Grand Ballroom of the Excelsior Hotel.

It was as if he heard her thinking or felt something, some twinge of discomfort. "What's that?"

"Hmm? It's an invitation. We're invited to a dinner for Steven Baldwin. He's been made a trustee of the university." She extended her hand to give him the card.

He didn't take it. "Boy, now they're really reaching." He started to gather up the papers on the bed and put them in the trash.

"I think we should go." Carolyn said. "It's been so long since either of us have seen him. You know, it's the perfect setting to break the ice after all this time. I was thinking we could just briefly say hello after the dinner." Carolyn heard the answer in the silence. "I'm not making you go to Africa with me. The least you could do is agree to go to dinner here in Charlotte."

"I'll go to a dinner with you, sweetheart, but not for him."

"Jack, it's been twenty-three years. It's time to let go of whatever happened between the two of you. I really want to go… Jack, what are you doing?" She watched him clear off the rest of the stuff from the bed, shut off the TV, and reach for the light switch on the nightstand. "I know you're ignoring me, Jack."

He took off the T-shirt, threw the bolster on the floor near the bed, and slid under the covers. "C'mon, honey, let's get some sleep."

"Jack, he was your best friend and he was my friend too. We could just go to the dinner and say hello.

He reached over and put his hand on her thigh and squeezed it a little. "Carolyn, we're not going to the dinner. We've been through this before."

"Well, I want to go through it again. And stop squeezing my leg!" She got out of the bed and stood there in her nightgown. "I want to talk about this."

His eyes were clamped shut and his head was on the pillow. "I don't."

◼ ◼ ◼

There was the regular crowd of early arrivals at the gym in the basement of the Reynolds Tower, the guys who showed up a few minutes before six when the place opened. They were a self-selecting collection of what most people would call steady guys, the kind who get up regularly at five, make coffee, glance at the headlines while they're getting dressed. They never use the search button on the car radio because it's always tuned to the same station, the one where the news comes on right at five-thirty as they're driving into town.

As gyms in the basements of office towers went, Fitcorp was a big place, almost ten thousand square feet. In the mirrored weight room with the machines, three racks for dumbbells and a space for mats, you could hear the music from the aerobics class that started at six-thirty. Membership was expensive by Charlotte standards. The younger guys paid the big bucks because the gym was a place where you could make connections as much as it was a place to keep in shape. It was reassuring, the routine of it all, the sense of community, which, in Jack's mind, was everyone minding his own business.

This was a Tuesday so Jack was there to do his circuit of exercises on the Nautilus machines. Then abs. He wondered why the fuck he did ab exercises any more. He hadn't seen the outline of a stomach muscle in he couldn't remember how long. It's not that he wasn't in shape. Jack looked great for his age. But that didn't mean you could bounce nickels off his flexed pecs. It meant he still had all the hair on his head. The Just For Men kept it from being all gray. And his chest was still eight inches

wider than his thirty-four-inch waist. He went through the routine while he thought about everything except what he was
doing. Then it was time for the treadmill. He liked the treadmill
because he could watch CNBC and listen with the earphones
that the gym provided.

Between seven and seven-thirty, everyone headed for the
locker room. It wasn't like there was a bell or anything like that.
But they were all there at six so they could work out, shower,
and be at their desks by eight, maybe eight-thirty at the latest. In
the locker room, there were a half dozen sinks on each side of a
tiled drying area. Jack always took the one toward the back on
the left-hand side. Only a fool wouldn't have known that was his
sink. He put the shaving kit down on the counter with a towel
and headed for the showers for a quick rinse and then the sauna.

It was a squared-off horseshoe of a room with two levels of
redwood benches. Even naked, in a room where they all looked
more or less alike, there was a certain deference afforded to the
senior executives in this last routine before they went their separate ways. Jack said hello to a few of the guys he knew from the
bank, a few others he knew from the law firms and accounting
firms the bank did business with. But without any more than a
perfunctory greeting, he took his seat in the back on the upper
bench and closed his eyes.

There were conversations going on all around him, but he
kept his eyes closed and let the heat penetrate his body. He
thought about the way he had left that morning.

"Aren't you gonna say good-bye to me?"

"Good-bye, Jack."

"Oh, c'mon, honey."

"Good-bye, Jack."

It took a few minutes for the sweat to bead up on his skin.
Then it ran like streams. *"Maybe I should call him,"* he thought.
"Fuck, I can't call him. He's their fucking lawyer." He heard the
springs on the door to the sauna and then the thwack of it slamming shut, the creaking of the benches as someone took a seat
or someone else got up.

There were conversations in twos and threes about the

Braves or a deal or a three-hundred-yard drive out at Ballan-
tyne. Two guys in their twenties were on the lower bench in
front of him in their own world.

"So she's really lovin' it, like writhin' around and moanin.'"

He felt his heart beating, heard it in his ears as if he had a
stethoscope to his own chest. *"Maybe we should go to the dinner. I wonder what he looks like."*

"Yeah, Amanda's the same way. It's like playin' pinball with
your tongue."

He could hear his own breath. He kept his eyes closed and
let the heat drive the sweat out of him. He inhaled deeply and
sighed. *"I've got to do something with Carolyn. I wonder if we
could do that safari thing? I could probably keep in touch by
phone."*

"You're a fuckin' dog."

"Woof, woof."

Jack made a fist and discreetly flexed his bicep. He was
forty-six, turned forty-six in April. He'd been running at a sprint
since they made the offer for New York Trust last June. This
was all supposed to be over by now. He puffed his cheeks and
exhaled. *"I just want this to be over. I haven't seen my son since
Christmas and now my wife is mad at me over some loser lawyer
I haven't seen since college."* He had his head down. He opened
his eyes and looked at the lines of sweat running down his skin.
He looked at the folds of skin on his stomach, at the coarse gray
hair. He looked down at his dick.

"So, we're lyin' there and then," the narration continued in
a whisper, "she says, 'Why don't you ask Kyle to come in.'"

"C'mon!"

"No, I swear. So me and Kyle did her, for like, I dunno, two
hours. It was so hot."

Jack looked up. *"Jesus Christ, I gotta get out of here."* In the
shower, he stood and let the hot water run over him in a steady
pulsing stream long after the soap had been rinsed off. He took
his time drying off and got dressed slowly. He made a note in
the little pad he carried in his breast pocket. *"Call Carolyn. Get
satellite phone info."*

It was hot when he got outside. Hot and humid. He sat on a bench inside the air-conditioned lobby of the Reynolds Tower and listened to the fountain and the architectural waterfall. He had a pain in his stomach. He didn't want to go upstairs right away and he didn't know why.

He saw the expression on Fred Bonham's face as he was nearly running through the lobby toward him. He looked awful. As he got closer, it was worse.

"Buddy, I've been lookin' all over for you. We got problems."

They were alone, but they spoke in whispers as they rode up the elevator. Jack was looking down as he listened.

"The stock opened in London this morning under some pressure but nothin' real bad. About two hours ago, word got out that there were twenty million shares for sale."

Their eyes met.

"Twenty million shares?"

"Jack… the stock's at $50."

Jack looked straight ahead. "Oh my God."

"I just got off the phone with the specialists and they're sayin' they might have to delay the opening in New York."

Jack squinted as he listened. "Where's Blake?"

"I got the Citation goin' to Chatsworth for him."

"What does he know?"

"Nothin' except that I told him he ought to come out this mornin'. He's fine, Jack." Fred covered his mouth briefly as the elevator approached the top floor as if to keep the next sentence from coming out. "Jack, our guys on the floor are telling me there's a big seller in London. I think it has to be Rothman."

The elevator doors opened and Jack was already in motion, headed for his office. When he got inside, as he was taking off his jacket, he turned to Fred. "OK, we can't deal with that now. Get Walter Weckstein on the phone. Tell him—"

"He's already on his way."

"Good. Get Alan Schwartz up here. I want to know what we can do with the stock buyback program. Maybe we can do something with that. And call Ron Duby. Tell him to stand by for a conference call. And—"

Catherine McDonald appeared in the doorway. "Mr. O'Brien, there's a Mr. Bridges from the New York Stock exchange on the phone. He's says he needs to talk to you. He says it's important."

◪ ◪ ◪

It was supposed to be the end of a good week. His client was almost out of the woods—a hostile takeover attempt in shambles. They were close to a deal on some messy litigation, but he felt nauseous and he knew why.

"They want Bendell." Marty Bernstein looked across his desk at Steve Baldwin. He exhaled the smoke through his nose, the last puff of a filterless cigarette. When it started to burn his fingers, that's when he knew it was time to light another one.

Steve listened impassively, as if he were hearing a report on hog futures on the commodities exchange. "What about the fine?"

"We're sort of stuck on that one right now. Your guys are trying to keep the number down but the Justice Department guys are looking to out-do the SEC." Another drag on the cigarette. "Look, they're at three hundred million. They want it to be bigger than the GE fine, you know, the one for Kidder. I know you said Moore wouldn't go above two-fifty. So maybe the thing comes down at two seventy-five, but you gotta get your guy used to the fact that it's gonna be a huge number." Bernstein leaned back in his chair, pursed his lips, and exhaled as if he were writing the number in smoke in the air.

Steve noticed the stainless steel lighter with the *Semper fi*. They had not known each other in Vietnam and in fourteen years practicing law together, it only came up a handful of times. They talked about the memorial when it was dedicated in Washington, but only in brief clipped sentences. They both went to the funeral of a colleague who shot himself, a delayed casualty of the Tet Offensive. But otherwise, their common experience was merely something that was there, like so much else not talked about but always looming, a shadow that seemed to alter the visible light spectrum and their capacity to see the world.

Steve exhaled to expel his thoughts of the past out with his breath. "What if we agree to the fine? Can Mary Beth's office do without the criminal indictment?"

"Stevie, Lis… en… to… me." Bernstein punctuated each syllable with a short karate chop in the air and then he put the angular ax blade of his palm against his own forehead. "You're not getting this." He leaned forward in his chair. He put out the cigarette by crushing it into tobacco, paper and ash fragments in the lunch plate on his desk. "The crowd wants a head. They wanna do the whole thing with the handcuffs and the TV cameras. Yeah, the fine is important, and yeah, we're gonna agree on that. But there's no fuckin' way they're gonna settle this without blood. You're a smart guy, Stevie, so you gotta make it clear to Moore." He reached for the lighter and another cigarette and inhaled deeply before he continued. "The crowd wants a head and they're not goin' home unsatisfied. You got it?"

At this point, Steve was merely marking time in Bernstein's office. Of course he got it. He noticed the way his partner took another drag on the cigarette, pressed his lips on the thin paper and inhaled as if he were drawing life itself through the thinnest filter of a burning poison. This was just one of the more common addictions, afflictions, compulsions, distractions, whatever, that either got him and his partners through the day or kept them from getting through it more effectively.

He thought of the M&A partner, Lee Torrel, who was working on the New York Trust deal with him. The guy gave up booze twelve years ago, not a drop since, but he drank Diet Pepsi like a lab rat pressing on a dispensing bar. It had become a wholly unself-conscious addiction. The guy walked into all-day conference room meetings with a six-pack of two-liter containers in a carry bag and swigged the stuff warm from the bottle.

The deal they'd all made, the agreement that no one talked about, was that they each had their own thing, their own way of surviving or coping or just getting through the day. No one ever mentioned any of this except in the lightest teasing, because that might mean a serious conversation about his or her own stuff and that was way out of bounds to everyone.

There were guys who took long lunch breaks to eat pussy or suck dick in some studio apartment conveniently located on Second Avenue or Tenth Avenue, the outer boundaries of where their real lives were supposed to be lived. A quick half-hour, maybe even ten minutes, not even enough time to take their socks off, but just enough to satisfy a hard-wired oral craving.

Then there were the ones who Steve called the robots, the ones who so thoroughly obliterated all recognition of desire that they were left like napalm-scarred emotional landscapes, hard-won territory cleared of enemy thoughts, but unable to support what may have once been lush and fertile consciousness. They came from their Upper East Side townhouses or their Connecticut farmhouses. He thought of the journey Thoreau described from the "desperate country to the desperate city," the perfect phrase for their condition, a practiced resignation without hope.

Of course, there were the exceptions, the guys who seemed to have it all put together. For however many there were who had given up, or covered up, there were the few who had come through childhood and adolescence into adulthood and who could say they were happy. He counted himself among the lucky few. He had no delusions about the mass of men but he had a sense of himself that was fundamentally different from the world he observed. And though he had the real comfort to know himself as an exception, he let himself be sad to think of how different the world could be, how different he wished it were.

◼ ◼ ◼

The few stacks of papers on the desk were neat and ordered like nearly everything else in the room. It was a period writing table, built in the days when there wasn't so much need to keep things in or on a desk. Like the rest of the furniture in the apartment, it was purchased by a decorator with little consultation and no regard to cost. It looked perfect in the space that he never got used to calling a den (sounded too much like the name an elderly straight man would have used) or a library (another generational reference that didn't fit him) or a study (he didn't think he was serious enough any more to have a study). Steve called it his office, even though he hardly ever worked there, because that seemed like an acceptable name for a room where he kept a desk.

He was trying to pay attention to what he was reading, godawful boring motion papers that were going to be filed in the Delaware Chancery Court next week. He thought about Dan, about what they were going to do, about what he thought they should do. When he let himself take the time to think about it, he wondered what they were going to do, now that they had talked about their love. But it was all so impractical. It wasn't the "can you believe that" stares from strangers, the constant explanations to friends that he wasn't having a midlife crisis or chasing after his youth or anything else for that matter. Who could possibly figure out why his love relationship was any more objectionable than any other relationship between two men? It started out as illegal and then got unbearable when the age difference was added in. Who could figure it out and why the fuck did he care? He stopped and put his elbows on the desk, took off his glasses, rubbed his closed eyelids with the tips of his fingers. When he looked up, he saw the framed JFK quote on his desk:

> The great enemy of the truth is not the lie—deliberate, contrived and dishonest. But the myth—persistent, persuasive and unrealistic. Too often we hold fast to the clichés of our forbearers. We subject all facts to a prefabricated set of interpretations. We enjoy the comfort of opinions without the discomfort of thought.

He rubbed his eyelids again and thought again for a while. Of course he didn't give a fuck what people thought. This wasn't about that at all. He pushed the chair back and put his feet up on the desk. He looked around the perfect apartment. The phone rang. It was Richard Wein.

"I wasn't sure if I'd find you at home. You're such a party animal with your Boy Wonder these days. How come you're not out celebrating your victory?"

"Richard, please, would you get off the Boy Wonder kick, and do I need to remind you that the war's not over yet?"

"Steven, what's got into you? You should be in a great mood. Their offer is dead. We've got our guys, Solomon and Morgan, lined up to finance the counteroffer. This is huge. Just think of the cash and prizes."

"Yeah, well. it all sounds great, but there's still the litigation to settle."

"Oh, c'mon. Carlton told me he met with you yesterday. They'll pay the fine and throw Bendell to the lions. You'll have the settlement papered in time to announce our counter."

Steve took his feet down off the desk and sat forward in the chair. "Can you believe that? You know as well as I do that they were all in that derivatives stuff up to their eyeballs. I mean, there's a picture of Moore, Carrol, and Bendell on the inside cover of the annual report with half the chairman's letter talking about their trading profits. All of a sudden, Moore is acting like he's shocked to find out they were in the business."

"So, what's the part that I'm supposed to find hard to believe?"

Steven closed the folder on his desk and placed it neatly on the stack of New York Trust documents. He took the portable phone over to the couch, slipped off his shoes, and continued. "I guess I'd say from these guys I would have expected something different."

"What, honor among thieves?"

"You know what I mean, the objective reality here is that Moore and the board knew Bendell was involved in this stuff. They authorized it. They even crowed about it while he was making them all rich."

"Steven, I'm not concerned with objective reality. What I'm concerned with is that in this situation… What was it Bernstein told you, 'The crowd needs a head,' right? So, it sure as hell isn't going to be Moore's head. Carrol knows too much. They're going to give up Bendell like a prom dress because they have to. Is it distasteful? Sure it is. But look at it this way. Bendell will hire somebody like Steve Newman. He pays a big fine and gets a year, eighteen months tops at Farmington, which is not exactly Sing Sing. While he's there, he has his teeth fixed. He loses a few pounds and maybe he signs a book contract. And when he comes out maybe he only has fifty million in the bank, but seriously, am I supposed to feel sorry for the guy?"

Steve was looking up at the line of dentil molding in the ceiling, thinking of the Wall Street power brokers in their prison overalls waiting their turn to get their caps redone. "No, I guess I was thinking of Moore and the way he was so quick to give up Bendell. You should have been there. 'I couldn't believe it when I heard it,' he said. 'Of course we'll cooperate with the authorities. Such a tragedy. He was like a son to me.' It was enough to make you throw up."

There was a loud laugh that came through the receiver as Wein continued. "Now I know you've really flipped. Do you think that family pedigree and a Yale degree means those guys are any different than the rest of us? It's all a veneer, Steven, the Purple Labels, the Episcopal charities, the whole thing… Listen, you need to get out. Let's go to G Bar and see what's walking around."

Steve rubbed his face and yawned. He looked around at the books on the shelves and the paintings on the walls and realized that there wasn't a single picture of Dan anywhere. *"I have to get a picture of him."*

"Hey, are you there?"

"Yeah, I'm here. Thanks, but I'm going to pass."

"Well, it's not like you to be home on a Saturday night. I'd ask you if you're OK but I know better than to expect a straight answer."

Steve pulled the throw blanket over his legs and adjusted the pillow behind his head. "I'm fine, really. I'm just a little worn down. Have a good time, Richard. I'll talk to you Monday."

◼ ◼ ◼

He was tired, so tired when he finally got into the back seat of the car that he couldn't even think about being happy to be off the plane. His driver put his bags in the trunk and headed for Manhattan. The flight from Paris had been uneventful until they were over Nova Scotia. The pilot made the announcement about a minor mechanical problem and a landing somewhere before they reached New York. There was a rush of adrenaline and fear that finally drained away into exhaustion with the sound of the wheels on the runway in Boston. The anxiety was replaced by frayed nerves as the 747 planeload of passengers were herded through Customs to make a connecting flight, the air shuttle to LaGuardia, a cattle car with no distinctions between first class and no class. Then there were the passing thunderstorms so they sat on the runway in a poorly ventilated metal tube until the captain announced that New York was temporarily closed. Back in the terminal, they sat for hours waiting for news. "*Oh, God,*" he said to himself. "*I hate this shit.*"

He occasionally looked out the window of the car at the skyline of the city as they sped along the BQE. He put his head back on the seat and closed his eyes. They were burning from what felt like the flash of a thousand suns.

"Just like that… yeah, yeah… great… OK, hold it like that for a minute, perfect… now, turn your head to the left a little… fantastic, fantastic… just like that… Chance, these are great… you're so incredible… Gina, put a little more highlight on his eyelids… yeah, yeah… these are great, baby."

He was one tired motherfucker. London, Paris, Milan, back to Paris, then back to New York and who knows how much more until the ride was over. How many times can one person stand to be photographed, to be captured on film, to have the look they want, to be of the moment? He asked those questions only of himself, infrequently, and always followed by some form of physical distraction.

He knew he had what they all seemed to want: polished sophistication layered over a seemingly unstudied innocence. He played with it. He played with the photographers, the designers, he played with them all, played like he'd been at it since he was a child and now he was a twenty-three year old virtuoso. He played with a seemingly self-renewing nuclear fusion source of energy. He knew he had it. He was aware of every bone and muscle in his body, of every attachment and insertion, aware of movement, aware of the smallest seemingly insignificant changes in posture. But now he was slouched in the back seat of the car with his knees pressing against the passenger seat, collapsed in a heap of world-weariness.

It was midnight. He noted the time as the limo pulled away from his building on Avenue B at East Eighth Street. He followed it with his eyes for a moment to see if it would turn into a pumpkin. Marty wasn't home. The first light on in the apartment was the bulb in the refrigerator. He sat down in the near darkness with a plate of Marty's leftovers and pressed the button on the answering machine as if it might offer him some company while he ate.

> Hey, Chance, this is Arthur. I heard you're back today. Listen, we need to get together on Monday with Bob Pirraglia to discuss the terms of the Marc Jackson offer. They want to extend their exclusive for another six months, but I know you said something about time to take acting classes and maybe do some work in Hollywood. And they're bringing up Marty again and his show. I'm sure we can work that out with Bob, but we need to talk about it. OK? By the way, you looked great in the *Vanity Fair* spread. Call me Monday morning.

> Hi, Dear, it's Mom. I got the birthday card and my God the necklace is beautiful. Should I remind you that my birthday isn't until August? I guess I'd rather get something a lot early rather than a day late or not at all, but I don't know what it is about you and your father not being able to keep birthdays straight. Anyway, I was

thinking that what I'd really like for my birthday is to see you. It's been since Christmas and, you know, I see you in all the magazines and everyone's talking about you... and... sweetheart, I miss you. I know I said I didn't feel comfortable, you know, being secretive and seeing you when your father's not here, but if that's the only way we're going to get together, then, OK, I'll agree to do that. I've never kept anything from your father but—

He pressed the "Next Message" button, not so much because he couldn't take any more, but it was such a relief to know that he didn't have to.

Hey, there, I checked with Air France and they said your flight was diverted to Boston and then I heard LaGuardia was closed. I've been working on documents here for the day. I'm gonna close my eyes for a while. Call me when you get in. I love you, Dan.

He wondered as he pressed the "Erase" button why there was so much he couldn't erase. He remembered seeing a rerun episode of *Star Trek*. Spock did some spooky Vulcan thing with his fingers on Kirk's skull and when Kirk went into a trance from that, Spock whispered into Kirk's ear, "Forget... forget," and Kirk woke up and had no recollection of a painful event. Dan rubbed the side of his head unself-consciously as he put the empty glass and plate in the sink.

He thought about calling Steve. He thought he should call. He loved Steve. He knew it even before he said it in Provincetown. He had a great feeling of being connected, the feeling that he wasn't on a stage or on a runway or a set with someone gawking or staring with this clingy sort of longing look. With Steve, he felt understood and never judged. Steve was great company, great conversation, and great sex. It was a fantastic feeling of being held close but not being held on to.

He threw his bags on the bed and turned on the computer on his desk. As it started to boot up, he got undressed, hung up clothes, walked by the phone a few times, threw a bag of things in the wash pile, opened some mail. He wanted to call, he wanted to get in a cab and go there, to get in bed and feel like there was a special place for him, a special someone. But then he remembered all their talks about being two independent people. *"I just want to go over there. Why should I feel bad about that?"*

Dan and sat for a while staring at the screen saver, a pattern of pinpoint stars which gave the effect of hurtling through space. He didn't want to talk about what was going on. He thought about going over to Steve's. He picked up the phone.

Steve was stretched out on the couch in his office with a stack of papers on the coffee table. At first he thought he was dreaming when he heard Dan's voice on the answering machine in the living room.

"Hey, babe, it's me. You must be asleep. I just got back and I was thinking of ..."

Steve fumbled with the receiver of the phone on the end table, "Hey... Dan... No, I'm not asleep. I've been working on some papers and I just closed my eyes for a while... How are you?"... Steve heard the anxiety in Dan's voice. It wasn't his style to pry and, besides, he knew better than to ask anyway. "Sounds like a grueling trip. You must be exhausted... Ah, gee, are you sure you want to go tonight?... But you just said you're tired... Well, yeah, if you want to go... Sure, OK, I guess we could do that and then come back here. I'll meet you there... No, you don't have to wait for me. Go ahead in and I'll meet you at the bar near the entrance. I'll see you in about a half hour."

Dan went into Marty's room and got a hit of Ecstasy and some gum. When he got to Roxy, the line was halfway down the block on Eighteenth Street, but Derek waived him in.

The bars at either end of the club and the space around the perimeter were raised a few feet higher than the floor so there was a kind of streaming going on as guys walked to get a drink or drifted on the current to see what was happening. They were cruising, trying to look like they had someplace in mind to go or at least not look like they were standing in any one place too long. The music made real conversation impossible. The lights were bright enough to see, but they were low enough to make it hard to see clearly. This was a place of the never-rising sun. The strobes, the pulsing stage lights, the lasers all offered flashes of mostly blank stares. The light played off glistening sweat and gave the effect of a swarming sea of bone and flesh, a nearly indistinguishable mass of shirt-less bodies in the center of the floor.

Dan recognized Sean, one of the guys dancing on the far end of the bar. Sean had preceded him by only a few years in New York with aspirations to completely change modern chore-ography. They met at the Crunch gym on Lafayette Street, and worked out together occasionally, but hadn't seen each other since Dan got the Marc Jackson job. There was a middle-aged guy trying to get Sean to bend down so he could put a dollar in the G-string, but Sean was oblivious to it all. Dan remembered once listening with a sense of tragic inevitability as Sean talked through tears about getting his "stuff together." Nothing ever worked out and now he was trying to make some extra money on weekends while he repeated a line about people with connec-tions who were coming through with funding for his new show.

Dan was brought out of his reflection by his friend Ruben who was serving drinks in a sailor suit, something to do with the theme party that night. "Hey, babe," Dan said as he reached across the bar for a kiss.

"Hello there, Mr. Fashion Plate. What brings you out all by yourself? Should I give you the keys to my place? Eh?"

"Oh, Ruben, it would never work for us. I could never han-dle you." Dan smiled the way he had learned to smile, with a distant affection for all the times he was casually cruised or bluntly propositioned. "Besides, I'm meeting my boyfriend. Babe, could you get me a gin and tonic?"

He took the free drink and another kiss and stood out of the stream of people. He watched the way guys lingered or danced or hovered around the edges of what was going on. They were mostly in threes and fours; a few guys were on their own. They came from cramped studios in Chelsea and the Village or from split-level houses on Long Island or in Jersey. A select few, the ones everyone was staring at, had the Look, like they expected to get what they came for. The rest would be leaving the way they arrived.

The drugs that most of them took, legal and otherwise, helped to heighten their sense of release and daring and numb their awareness of nearly everything else. The pattern was uniform and predictable. They had come out dressed for sex, thinking about sex. They stood around like they were waiting, but too obviously eagerly, to meet someone. They drank or smoked or snorted to reduce their inhibitions. The go-go boys on the bars, the glimpses of a few beautiful muscle boys groping on the floor or in dark corners of the club, represented both a promise and a cruel tease.

It was almost two o'clock in the morning and while most of the rest of New York was asleep, this collection of mostly young and otherwise average young men were playing their part in an inevitably disappointing drama. Maybe it was the fear of AIDS, or the regrettably acceptable substitution of sexual facsimiles, or the truth that most of them were too unhappy to excite themselves let alone anyone else. But somehow the images of sex had replaced sex. The bathhouse casual and anonymous encounters that had driven the epidemic had been replaced by visual and psychopharmacological stimulation. This was a world apart from the generation that had preceded Dan. He remembered the time he was at dinner with Steve and a few of his friends and they all laughed when Dan asked what one of them meant by a "glory hole."

It had been a year since he walked through the doors of the Sound Factory with Marty. Then he stood in awe at what he thought was what he wanted—complete freedom, the antidote to free him from his past, his memory of growing up, and the agony of his love for Michael. Now he looked out at the crowd. Freedom had won them nothing more than the discovery that they were all alone. And the scene before him seemed more like a collective denial of this reality than anything like the reverie it was supposed to represent.

He felt a hand on his shoulder and then another one on his waist and lips on the back of his neck. Of course it was Steve.

Any of his friends would have known better than to do that and no one else would have dared. Dan turned and kissed him, relieved, as Dante once was to greet Virgil. Steve declined the offer of a drink from Ruben, but Dan took another one, something to sip on compulsively. There were those first few moments when they were face to face, the music blaring, a steady primal beat, hundreds of guys walking by them. They stood as close as if they were lying in bed.

"Well, you said you wanted to dance," Steve said as he motioned toward the floor. "Let's."

As they made their way among the schools of silver-lighted bodies, Steve took Dan's hand and went first into the crowd. There were bodies to maneuver around, bump into, to push without shoving. All the while, Steve's trailing right hand held Dan's lightly by the fingertips. *"Don't let go,"* Dan thought as they reached the middle and Steve turned around.

They danced apart from each other, in the space that they made in the crowd, face-to-face. It was like making love without touching, standing up, purposely unaware of everyone else around them. They smiled and looked into each other's eyes. For Dan, the rush of the Ecstasy and the alcohol intensified and then became indistinguishable from his attraction to Steve, the unspeakable urge to lose the boundaries of self in the arms of another human being.

"I wonder if it is *my turn?"* Steve asked himself. *"Can it really be happening?"* The form in front of him, such a breathtaking combination of erotic imagery and physical reality, had become almost too intense. *"Is there such a thing as the one? Is he the one?"*

The music was a seamless mix, an unbroken stream of sounds that washed away all thoughts of anything else but the moment. The pace changed, from the driving strobe punctuated beat to slow darkened motion, but it never stopped and neither did the movement, the swimming in the primal urge. They danced on. When their shirts were off and tucked into their back pockets, their bodies touched, their sweat mingled, their lips touched. In the cab, on the way home, speeding in the darkness up Park Avenue, Dan rested his head on Steve's lap. Steve ran his hand through Dan's hair, looked down at his sleeping lover, and sighed as he wondered why they had gone anywhere that night but straight to bed.

◩ ◩ ◩

The sun filtered through the narrow slats in the horizontal blinds and gave the effect of contrasting side-lit layers of suspended dust particles and layers of darkness. The light and shadows traced a striped pattern on the white linen sheets. The ceramic study on the glass writing table, a man in the style of Rodin's *Thinker*, watched impassively as the subjects on the bed shifted slightly in their deep sleep. Like the unglazed clay, the intertwined bodies were a work in progress.

When they got back to the apartment, just before dawn, they had barely enough energy to rinse off the smell of cigarettes and sweat in the shower and fall into bed. Now, four hours later, Dan lay draped across Steve, who was awake, his head propped up by his folded arms on the pillow. From seventeen floors above the street, the only Sunday morning sounds that could be heard in the apartment were the occasional passing siren and the distant whine of jet engines in takeoff from LaGuardia, evidence of the world outside in motion. But inside the apartment, the lighted motionless dust added to a feeling of suspended animation.

In the mirrored closet panels at the foot of the bed, Steve could see the reflection of the painting on the wall behind him. It was a large four-by-five-foot canvas in an ornately carved gilt frame. A stream running through a forest by David Peikon, it reminded him of his family's hunting lodge in the Appalachian foothills of North Carolina. He hadn't been there since before Dan was born. The scene, at the edge of late spring or beginning of summer, was highly charged, new leaves, a rush of winter runoff. Sometimes in the morning as he was drifting in and out of sleep, he would look at the painting and hear the stream, the water falling over the rocks, the wind in the trees. It was a long time ago.

He shifted slightly under the weight of Dan's head on his chest. Dan reached an arm across him, held on to his shoulder. With his right hand, Steve traced his fingers along the sculpted outline of the muscles in Dan's back.

"I can't believe you're awake," Dan moaned in a low voice with lips partly pressed against Steve's skin.

"I need to get up and go to work."

Dan picked his head up and with bloodshot eyes stared pleadingly. "Oh my God, you're like a robot. Don't you ever take a break?"

"Sure, I'm taking one now."

Dan looked up again. "No you're not. Your eyes are open. Go back to sleep."

"I'm looking at my paintings and I'm thinking about them. That's a break, isn't it? And by the way," Steve reached down and grabbed Dan's hard on, "I'm not the one who's a robot." Steve rolled on top of Dan and began thrusting his pelvis and moaning, "Oh, oh, oh."

"Stop! Stop!" Dan pleaded.

Steve laughed and lay on his back again with his hands behind his head.

Dan resumed his sidesaddle attachment. "OK, so you're awake and you're not going back to sleep. What are you thinking about your paintings?"

"Well," Steve continued analytically as he reached over to the nightstand for his watch. "I was looking at the one you can see in the mirror. I know where the scene is and I know the details but, you know, it began as a drawing, and sometimes I think of what the lines are underneath that started out one way and got changed as the artist painted."

"What is that, pentimento, right?"

"Yeah, the artist changed his mind. That's very good for someone who's still asleep."

"Do you think the weird one started as a drawing?"

"What weird one?"

"That one." Without opening his eyes, Dan lifted his arm and pointed behind him and to his right in the direction of the painting on the wall over the glass writing table.

"Oh, that one… gee… I don't know, but I don't think so. I bought that one from Philip Greenberg almost twenty years ago. He was an art teacher before he became an agent… hmmm… it's not representational, you know… or at least it's not supposed to be."

It was another oil on canvas, a moody work of earth colors, browns, raw sienna, and umbers, layered with turbulent brush-strokes. It was darkest at the edges, with angular lines, and lightest at the center. The lighter tones were washes, where the artist had thinned the pigment with oil. Titanium white gave the impression of fire, faint streaks of blue that looked like low intensity gas flames. Once Steve thought he saw the outline of a body in the center of the painting.

"I guess you could say it's a little weird… The guy who painted it was Richard Schiff. I don't know much about him except that he studied at Cooper Union, that his first show was a big hit. Let's see, Philip bought this one from his second show, which didn't go so well and then he killed himself."

"You're kidding."

"No, I'm not really."

"I definitely need to go back to sleep." Dan rolled over and lay with his mouth open and his eyes closed.

"I see a forest in that painting too, but a different kind of forest. If I'm just lying here and looking at that one I think of Dante's *Inferno*, you know, 'In the middle of our walk of life, I found myself in a dark wood, in such a way that the straight path was lost…'"

Dan wet his lips with his tongue and continued. "'So cruel and hard and treacherous was that place that to think of it even now renews my fear.'"

"Yes," said Steve, "of course. I forgot you knew that one." He turned on his side and propped his head up in his hand with his elbow on the pillow. "Dan… I've been thinking."

Dan kept his eyes closed and spoke as he yawned and stretched. "Ya… I know, and I do *not* know how you do it sometimes."

"I'm thinking I might like to give the dream another chance. I mean give it another chance with you."

Dan turned his head and opened his eyes. He was awake. "Um…" He wet his lips again. He smiled, but it was a hesitant smile. "Really?"

Steve reached his hand behind Dan's neck and whispered. "I love you and I am also *in* love with you. That's a big dream."

"So… what are we gonna do? I mean with being independent and spending time alone and all that stuff."

They drew close together. "Well… Someone told me that Scorpios have a secret place where they keep their heart, you know, to protect themselves, but that what they really want is for someone to discover them. I want you to understand how I feel and I want to understand you. I want to look for you, to discover you." He smiled. "Like the time I discovered you at the basketball game, all alone in a crowd."

Dan leaned forward to kiss Steve. "I want to be found. I love you too."

CATALYST

They finally bought an air conditioner. Clothing and mechanical cooling were the only material concessions to their sudden six-figure incomes. In one of the three dormered windows in the mansard roof, the unit strained to deliver the cold air past the kitchen, where they were sitting, and down the hall to the bedrooms.

"I'm not mad."

"Yes you are."

"Fuck you."

"See, you're mad."

"I said get the fuck out of here."

"Marty, first of all, this is my apartment too. Second of all, I was the one who stood up for you. I was the one who said that you should be able to do whatever you want with your show. And I was the one who said I wouldn't do the extension if they didn't use you. Remember?"

"And now you're sayin' different."

"No, no, that's not what I'm saying. I'm just saying they're offering a one-year extension on a big money contract and all they're asking for is to tone the act down a little... a little, Marty. Are you telling me that every flashing pussy and dick in that show is sacred? You couldn't change a thing? Not one thing?"

"They'll team you up with someone else."

"I don't want to be teamed up with anyone else. I'm just talking about compromising, you know. Give in a little. Marty, you've been doing that show for almost ten years. It's like... I'm saying, Think about it. That's all. And you know I'll hang with you no matter what you decide."

"What are you talkin' about, 'I'll hang with you'? You're not in the show anymore."

"Yeah, I know. We talked about that. The show never was

me. But this gig is about us and I'm not going to stay with it unless you do."

Marty had his back to Dan, pounding the chicken breasts with the tenderizer, draping them in flour, placing them in the pan. Dan was opening his mail. Nothing mattered to them in that moment other than coping with the drama in their own worlds. They paid no attention to the TV droning on in the background.

> Today, Federal Marshals made two dramatic raids on Wall Street. They entered the headquarters of New York Trust Company at 100 Wall Street and arrested Patrick Bendell, the bank executive once credited and now blamed for the bank's high profile position in the murky world of derivatives trading.

The camera went to close-up on the blank stare of a middle-aged man in a pin-striped suit being led out of an office tower in handcuffs.

> Bendell is charged with multiple counts of violations of Federal securities regulations as well as mail fraud and racketeering. Executives at New York Trust had no comment except to say that they are cooperating fully with authorities.

Somewhere there was a lawyer frantically preparing motion papers, somewhere there was a wife crying on the phone. Somewhere children were being hurried out of town to stay with grandparents. Somewhere there was a bank chairman saddling his horse. But in the self-contained, mechanically cooled apartment, the two young men carried on with their own tasks at hand, frying chicken and opening envelopes. Neither of them would have said they were paying attention to the drama being reported on the television and yet somewhere in the recesses of Dan's consciousness, there was some processing of even the background noise, something that said, "*Look up.*"

> Just a few doors up the street, Federal agents also raided the headquarters of D. L. Baird, a notorious penny-

stock operation that has been the subject of publicity and controversy for several years. They arrested several of the top officers of the company who had no comment at their arraignment in U.S. District Court. Authorities have charged the officers with multiple counts of interstate commerce fraud, racketeering, and securities violations.

There was just a brief flash, a view of Michael and four other men being led, stone-faced, out of the building. From a distance, it seemed a comical procession, the line of them shackled together, like they were holding hands the way schoolchildren do when they're out for a walk at recess.

"Oh my God." Dan looked over and could see that Marty, too, must have caught out of the corner of his eye the beginning of the news segment. "I think I'm gonna throw up."

Marty reached for the waste bucket under the sink as if Dan had asked for a Kleenex. "Here, don't throw up on the table."

"I can't believe it." He looked at Marty without taking the bucket. "My father told him it was a scam operation."

Marty sat down at the chair in front of Dan, deftly sliding the bucket under the table. "So why are you all shocked? I told you the guy's an asshole. Considering the way he acted at the show, why do you even care?"

"He's my brother."

"He's not your brother."

"I have to help him."

"No you don't."

"Oh my God. I should have called him. I knew he was going to get in trouble."

"There's nothin' you coulda done and there's nothin you can do now. His ass was never worth your trouble and it sure ain't worth it now."

"Marty, you don't understand."

"What's to understand, Dan? Besides, what can you do anyway?"

"I could ask my family to help him. My mother would want

to know."

"Dan, the guy needs a lawyer, not a tin of fucking home baked muffins. Ask your boyfriend to help him… if you really want to do something for him."

Dan's mind was racing, playing out the two scenarios, thinking of which was worse—involving his family or involving Steve.

◣ ◣ ◣

Carolyn contemplated the nature of spirits. Maybe they were a grown-up's version of the make-believe characters invented as her playmates when she was a girl. Real or not, she sensed their presence in her life and they were important to her. They took form as places and things, in the breezes at the beach, in the flowers of her garden, in paintings and photographs — tangible associations with the intangible. In the worst of times, they came to her aid the way her imaginary playmates once did. Now, alone in the bedroom of the suite at the Pierre, and thinking of the crisis of Michael's arrest, she summoned her spirits.

Whenever she thought about it, which wasn't often, she was pretty sure that she didn't believe in God. At least, she didn't believe in the Judeo-Christian God of Abraham and Isaac. *"Only a man could invent a God who would ask a father to kill his son."* Man created God in his image and what a great likeness it seemed. The inclusion of women in modern church structure was window dressing. Somehow women clergy didn't do it for her, but it wasn't like she had anything else in mind as an alternative. "Maybe they need to start over again," she once admitted to Carla. "The Old Testament is full of guys killing each other, and the New Testament, I mean, does anyone take that stuff from St. Paul seriously anymore?" She became more a-religious than irreligious. Drifting away from the ceremonial aspects of worship, she developed an awareness of her own spirituality. The busy-ness of her life left her little time. But in quiet moments of meditation and in the first moments of awakening, she tried to see what was real beyond what she could see with her eyes.

Lying quietly in bed, covered by the white linen sheets, drifting in the space between sleep and dreaming, she heard Jack's voice in the sitting room. She felt the strength of his words formed in the sureness of his conviction. There were other voices on the speakerphone, but they made crackling sounds in the air like dry twigs breaking underfoot. She wanted to call him back to bed, but the clock on the bureau reminded her of the conference call he had arranged from the plane on their way to New York.

Waking slowly, she was watched by three spirits framed on the walls. Two of them were by Gustav Klimt, the other by Egon Schiele, bought at auction in a rare moment when Carolyn used the Reynolds fortune to indulge her own sense of wanting to own anything. The pale, flawless, porcelain skin of the woman in the first Klimt painting was covered with decorative patterns and swirls, eyes closed, laying mostly covered, but the outlines and curves of her body belied a shimmering sexuality beneath the garments. The Schiele painting made the perfect visual contrast, its female subject awkwardly straining on the canvas, eyes open wide as if in shock to suddenly see the vulgarity of the world. The lines were angular and unrealistic and yet evoked a sense of structured confinement.

Carolyn lay on her stomach, her arms up around the pillow, her head to one side. Listening to her husband on the phone, she noticed the rhythm of her own breathing. She was thinking of the sound of the waves she could hear from their bedroom at the beach. The conversation was carried into the bedroom as if by a morning breeze, from somewhere far away. Jack had been angry when he first heard the news, but he responded instinctively to protect her, to relieve her distress. Now he sounded as if he were Michael's staunchest defender.

In her sideward glance, she saw the two paintings on the far wall with no irreconcilable conflict. They were only two images of the same reality. The third spirit, her favorite, on the wall at the foot of the bed, was a study of Klimt's, *The Kiss*, an early drawing of the later famous painting. She liked it best as a signal of her own point of view. The female subject was in the embrace of a man, both of them covered in cloaks of Byzantine gold and silver. In a two dimensional setting that negated both space and time, they lived for the moment in their own world. They were kneeling in a field of flowers that ended as if at a cliff, evidencing one of Klimt's recurring themes that life is more potent in the vicinity of danger, a constant tension between ecstasy and the fear of falling.

"Jack," said the voice on the speakerphone, "I've already spent an hour on this with Joe Silva. He was with Rudy for six years and he knows Mary Beth's people really well. I'm telling you, Jack, the kid is radioactive. What little we've been able to find out, they've got him and his pals on scamming something like sixty million out of mostly widows and orphans. They're gunnin' for him to grow old in jail."

Jack was sitting on the edge of the couch, in his underwear, his elbows on his knees, chin resting in his folded hands. He was listening, but he was also thinking of what he was going to do. Out of the corner of his eye, he saw Carolyn emerge from the bedroom in a sleeveless satin nightgown and sit in the chair across the room. He rubbed his face and his closed eyes with the open palms of his hands. "I hear what you're saying, but you're leaving out the only important point to me and that is that he's like a son to my wife and me. We can't let him go without the best defense... Maybe there's something there that your guy and the Feds don't know yet."

"Jack, they've got him on tape."

"Henry, I said I heard you and I did, and I still want you to try to get him bail... Of course we'll cover his legal bills."

"I'm not worried about getting paid, for Christ's sake. I'm worried about you standing up in front of a magistrate on Monday, swearing for the kid's agreement not to leave the goddamned country and posting what might be a million-dollar bail. Jack, we're in the middle of a ten-billion-dollar takeover fight, and if the press connects you to Baird they're gonna have a field day! Please, listen to me on this one."

From across the room, Jack could see Carolyn's eyes were closed, but the pain on her face was in the hint of a grimace. "All right, Henry, hold on, I really am listening to you." Under his breath he murmured as he thought, *"What the fuck am I gonna do now?"*... "OK, didn't you say there was a chance that they might cut a deal with him if he testifies against the principals?"

"Yeah, but we're talking maybe he's middle aged when he gets out instead of old. Look, I haven't heard the tapes, but from what Mary Beth's people are telling Joe, your boy is not a bit player. He's a ring leader."

"Henry, my son will be here in a few hours. Get him an appointment out at Rykers and we'll tell him that he's got to get Michael to testify. OK? We'll take this one step at a time."

When the call was over, they sat across the room from each other. He watched as the curtains billowed out from the window and enveloped her in lace and sunlight. She saw him sitting on the couch, staring off into the middle distance, straining to keep his thoughts and the world organized.

"Sweetheart, I'm doing everything I can, but this sounds really bad. Michael's probably going to jail."

"I heard."

"I can't fix this one."

"You're doing what you can. Why don't you come back to bed? We can order room service. Dan won't be here for another four hours."

He was propped up by the pillows. She lay on her side with her head on his chest and her arm wrapped around him. She could hear his heart beating.

It began with a kiss, then many kisses, like petals of a many-petalled flower, laying back and yielding nectar, intoxicating kisses. The flower that succumbs to the songbird is also ruled by desire. Her eyes were closed. His hand reached behind her head as if the pillow might give way and they might fall into a void.

He lay on top of her. The coarseness of his chest hair caught the smooth skin of her breasts, raising the nipples to points, an overload of sensation, drowning awareness of any world other than the space between the sheets.

His kisses traveled down her body as if drawn into a vortex. His hand caressed her thighs, spreading her legs, arching her back. Her only thought was of yielding. She could feel her racing pulse as he pressed his forehead against her abdomen, evidence of a human body in an otherwise delirious experience.

She was joyously unconscious of a thousand other thoughts and distractions. She felt bodiless—peeled back by his tongue, his lips, his hands, even the skin on his face—released into space, free floating above and yet riveted by the sheer physicality of making love. She writhed, she danced lying on the bed, with her spirits and her lover. She lived for the briefest moment in the touch of what felt like many hands.

Each wave of pleasure traveled the length of her body and then back again until her only awareness was of the connection between his tongue and her skin. The spirits looked on, mute witnesses as she cried out and fell again, back to earth, enveloped in the sheets and held in his embrace.

◾ ◾ ◾

"It really looked like what you would imagine a prison to look like."

"Dan, I know what a prison looks like."

"So I was thinking, Oh my God, I've got to get him out of here. You know, it's just so weird."

"Like I said—"

"Then I met with this guy from the U.S. Attorney's Office and he starts telling me all this stuff that Mike did and how he won't cooperate with them."

"Lemme guess, you were shocked, right?"

"Well, yeah, I was. It just sounded so unbelievable but... then... he played some of the tapes... and it was Mike's voice... but I kept thinking, How could he do that stuff? Then this other guy came in and they showed me this agreement they wanted him to sign and... I didn't read it or anything... All I kept hearing was how they would reduce his jail time."

"So?"

"C'mon. Mike in jail?"

"Sounds like he's finally found a place to belong."

"Marty, please. Anyway, so they say that his lawyer is coming later and he doesn't have to sign anything now, but I'm supposed to talk to him about it and I'm like, 'I don't know what the fuck is going on, and you want me to convince him to do what you want?' So they say, 'Just convince him that he's in a lot of trouble and the best thing for him to do is to cooperate."

"Then what?"

"They bring me into this room, just a room, like a big box, with a table and two chairs and a window with bars on it. They leave and I'm walking around, like pacing, and I start to think again how horrible it is and how there must be a way to get him out of there. Finally the door opens and he comes in. He's in overalls and he comes over. He's smiling and he hugs me."

"Hey, Dan. What's up?" he says.

"I'm saying to myself, what do you mean, what's up? You're in fucking jail, Mike! That's what's up. But, you know, I'm trying to be cool, so we sit down and we're talking and he asks about my family and Marc Jackson and it's like we met at fucking LaGuardia or something and he's about to catch a plane to Miami and I'm on my way to L.A. So finally I had to, like, bring the conversation into the real world."

"Mike, we're in a jail and you're in a lot of trouble. The guys that I just met with told me that if you cooperate they would reduce your jail sentence."

"Why are we in a private room? How did you get in here to see me?"

"What difference does it make?"

"I want to know."

"Ah, I'm not sure of the details. I called my parents yesterday morning. They flew up last night and we met this afternoon. My father told me—"

"So it was your father. I figured."

"Mike, get a grip. What difference does it make?"

"You know why he's doing this? I'll tell you why. Because he fucked my mother, that's why."

"What are you talking about?"

"Wake up, Dan. Come out of that dream world you're in."

"Mike, I don't want to get in another fight with you."

"I saw him. I did. I saw him with my own eyes. I was only a little kid but I saw it. Both of them on the bed. His bare fuckin' ass in the air. He was—"

"Shut up! Shut up! That could never happen... It must be like... I dunno... one of those weird made-up memory things—"

"Ask your mother. She knows. Ask her."

"Shut up! You're crazy. This is crazy. I don't even know what I'm doing here. My family could get in a lot of trouble for trying to help you and all you want to do is trash my father."

"I just want you to open your eyes."

"Maybe my eyes *are* open, Mike. Maybe my father was right. You don't want my help. You don't want anyone's help."

"So, you left. That's great," Marty said.

"Well, I did, but not right away. It was weird."

"You keep saying that."

"Well, it *was* weird. I mean the whole thing was. But at the end, you know, when I told him I was leaving, it was like he went into this trance. He was staring down into the table. Then he looked up."

"You're all I have left," he said. "Please don't go."

"And his face, it was different. It was like when we were in school. He got up from the chair and he came across the room to the window where I was standing."

"Don't say it."

"He kissed me."

Marty was shaking his head.

"No, I mean he *really* kissed me, like the way I always wanted him to. And I was thinking, Oh my God! It wasn't like that time when we were drunk and I wasn't sure, you know, did he really mean it?"

"So?"

"But it wasn't like I thought it would feel. It was something

I wanted my whole life but then, when it happened, it was like kissing a stranger on Ecstasy. You know what I mean? It was hot and it felt good but then as soon as it happened... I was thinking, What if he got out of jail... would I? ... I just felt bad."

"He would have done anything to keep you from leaving."

"Marty, I felt really bad."

"So, what happened this morning?"

"I met my parents at the court. We sat toward the front, but there were a bunch of reporters there so it wasn't like we had much of a chance to talk. First the judge came in and the lawyers said a bunch of things. Then they brought Mike in and he sat with the lawyers at this table in front of us. We couldn't talk to him, but he turned around and... I guess he smiled at us."

"Yeah, the killer smile."

"Then Mike's lawyer stood up and said that he had agreed to cooperate with the U.S. Attorney's office. He said something about a 'proffer' that my father would swear for Mike's honesty and integrity and that he was putting up the bail money. Can you believe it was a million dollars?"

"You came here broke and he got a million dollars. Sometime you'll have to explain that to me."

"My mother held my hand for a lot of the hearing. My father just sat there like he was a statue. So the judge said Mike could go, but they had to take him back to meet with his lawyers and the government guys. The lawyers told my father he probably wouldn't be out until later today. When they were taking him out of the courtroom he looked back at us and smiled again. He kind of looked at me and I could tell he was saying, 'I'll call you.'"

"And that was it."

"The reporters followed us out of the court so we didn't say anything until we got in the car. I rode with my parents to LaGuardia."

"Your dad came through, huh?"

"Yeah, he did... He looked really tired. We got to the general aviation terminal and when he took his coat off I realized how much weight he's lost. They were sort of in a rush because there was something going on with the bank... There's always something going on with the bank... He hugged me and... he said he was sorry that we got all screwed up. He asked if we could start again."

"What are you gonna do?"

"I don't know, Marty, what is there to start over again? All we've ever had is a relationship where he's either in control or trying to be in control. I mean, I appreciate what he did for Mike. I didn't realize how serious it was for him until today. But there's no place for us to go back to that ever felt good to me."

"He didn't do what he did for Mike."

"OK, maybe he didn't do it for Mike. He probably did it because my mother asked him to."

Marty sighed. "It's your thing, bwana."

◼ ◼ ◼

When hope fades, it leaves a trace of what was once hope, a sometimes cruel reminder. Hope isn't binary. It doesn't go from on to off. It runs out in gradual measures until at some point there isn't enough anymore to say "There is hope," but there is still something.

It had been two weeks since the hearing. No call from Michael. He had the number on his speed dial. Now he was sitting at the kitchen table. There was an envelope with the stamp Marty had given him, a pad of paper with lines of words, strings of words, fragments of his feelings that spilled out on the page. The phone was cradled on his neck. He let it ring, ten, twenty, maybe fifty times. He lost count, staring down at his inability to simply say, "This is me."

Ten o'clock. He had to be at Bob Pirraglia's office by eleven to sign the new contract. His flight to L.A. from Newark left at one. "*I'll start on it again in the park. I just need some air.*" He put the pad of paper in his backpack, grabbed the duffel bag, and headed out.

Sitting on his bench, he was about a half a block closer to

the L train than he had been at the kitchen table, but no closer to knowing how to put his feelings into a letter. He noticed the rap dancer with his boom box practicing his routine for no one else. In the corner of the park there was a circuit training area. A shirtless guy with a Walkman was doing pull-ups.

In the grass in front of the bench was a squirrel standing up on its hind legs, checking him out. He took a piece of the peanut butter Promax bar he was eating and tossed it in the squirrel's direction. It landed a few feet in front of him, but he didn't go for it. Dan understood his reticence.

"Hey, Meester." She was practically standing in front of him before he noticed her.

"Meester, I do a reading for you. Fi dollars."

"Huh?" He looked up.

"Psychic reading. Fi dollars." She sat down next to him.

"Oh." Dan gave her the "aw shucks" look. "No, thank you. I'm trying to write a letter and I only have a few minutes."

"You have fi dollars. I give you a good reading." Slight build, gray hair, Slavic, she could have been Russian or Ukrainian, Slovenian, not that it made any difference to him. "Gimme your hand." She reached out hers and beckoned him.

"I don't have much time," he replied as he extended his hand cautiously.

"I see a long life. You live a long life."

"Right, isn't that what they always say."

"You have a gooood strong heart, a gooood heart." She had his right hand, facing up, in her two hands, her thumbs pressing each side of his palm like she was opening it up, exposing the lines. "But there is an energy in your life that you must understand."

Dan noticed the squirrel, still eyeing the piece of the Promax bar.

"A turtle, I see a turtle by a lake. You know about the turtle and the scorpion, yes?"

"Um… I don't… but I don't think I have time."

She was working the skin on the palm of his hand as if there were something in there that she was trying to force out, like a splinter. They were looking right at each other. He noticed she had a cataract in her right eye.

"The turtle, he lives by the edge of a beautiful lake. One day a scorpion comes to where the turtle lives. The turtle, he is safe in his shell, but the scorpion knows that he is lonely, yes?"

Dan looked down.

"The scorpion saays, 'Give me a ride on your back and I will show you a place on the other side of the lake where you will be happy.' The turtle is afraid but he thinks of the scorpion's promise and he knows the scorpion cannot swim."

The wrinkles in the skin of her face looked like the patterns of waves a rock makes when it splashes in the water.

"So the turtle gives the scorpion a ride on his back and they are crossing the lake. But then he feels this terrible pain." She squeezed his hand. "And he knows that he will soon be paralyzed. He saays to the scorpion, 'Why did you do that? Now we will both drown.' And the scorpion, he saays, 'Because I am a scorpion, and scorpions sting.'"

Dan pulled his hand lightly.

She held on and stared into his eyes. "You have someone with *veery* strong energy in your life, *veery* strong energy, but you do not understand it."

"*How could she know about him?*"

"You must understand this energy or you will both suffer. I can help you. I have special crystals."

Dan noticed that the squirrel was gone. A pigeon swooped down to take his offering.

"Two hundred dollars. Thees are *veery* special crystals."

Dan pulled his hand away. He was suddenly alert, but disoriented, as if he had been jarred awake. "Lady, I don't want any crystals." He reached in his pocket. "Here's your five dollars."

She put her hand on his leg. "One hundred dollars. I do it for you, one hundred dollars."

Dan grabbed his backpack and duffel bag and hurried away. "Meester!"

When he got to the corner of Tenth Street and Avenue A, there was a mailbox. He sat down on a bench, pulled the pad out of his backpack, and wrote. He didn't have time to think of what he had wanted to say to Michael. He dropped the letter in the mailbox like the castaway who trusts his message in a bottle to the sea. He wanted to be discovered.

Dear Mom and Dad,

I have been meaning to say thank you for what you did for Mike. I called this morning a few times but I didn't want to leave a message on the machine and now I am heading out of town for a week. I haven't heard from Mike since he was released. I guess he is busy with the lawyers. I realized when we were at the hearing that it has been almost eight months since we were together at Christmas and I feel really bad about that. My life is not what you thought it would be or what you wanted it to be. I was never cut out for business but I am finding my own way here. I have a roommate who is my best friend and I have fallen in love with someone who has made me very happy. I would like you to meet them and for you to find out about the person I am becoming. I will ask them to come to the beach with me the weekend after Labor Day if it is OK with you. I got an e-mail from Julie this week and she said you would all be there. Dad asked if we could start over again. I don't want to go back to anything but I will try to understand and love you the way you are now. I just want the same from you.

Love,

Dan

Michael had arranged for it from the time he first knew he might need it; traveled with his grandfather to Barcelona, where his mother had been born, to get it. It was a maroon leather passport with a gold embossed seal of the Kingdom of Spain, issued to Miguel Antonio Henrique, now a passenger en route from JFK to Buenos Aires. In the first-class cabin of the 747, he reclined the aisle seat and sipped a Glenlivet on the rocks.

At the window seat next to him, Angela had her headphones on, listening to music, oblivious to everything except the facts that concerned her at the moment, all the clothes she had left behind in New York and where she would go to get new ones when they landed. Michael didn't tell her that by using her account for an intermediate transfer of the money from the Caymans to Paraguay, he had made her an accessory to his crimes and a felon herself. In the end he figured that it wouldn't have mattered and besides, there was so much else to stay focused on.

He knew that the Feds would find the Cayman accounts, eventually. Once they realized he was gone, they'd look harder. With a warrant and some work, they'd trace the money to Montevideo. So he and Angela would be there the day after landing in Buenos Aires and convert everything in the accounts to bearer instruments. Then, back to Argentina, where they'd find a place to disappear. The statute of limitations in the U.S. was ten years. *"Who knows?"* he thought. *"Maybe by then I won't want to go back."* There was so much to plan, so much to figure out, the currency transactions, so many calculations to do in his head.

He reached for the portfolio in his carry on bag to put away the passport. In the side pocket, there was the picture of him and Dan, the one from his desk at the office. He was sorry, but only for the way things had worked out. The thought of staying, as he promised he would, never crossed his mind once. The potential consequences to Jack were even a collateral benefit. "Aren't you going to leave Dan a note?" Angela asked as they were packing. "No... He'll be OK... I'll send him something later." That was it. Twenty years together. "Like two peas in a pod," their mothers used to say. But all of that never affected Michael's core instinct for his own survival.

He closed his eyes. *"What will Dan say? What will he do?"* They were passing thoughts, serious thoughts in the moment, but without any self-reproach. He never confused consciousness for conscience. His musings about the outcome of his actions floated to the surface like bubbles that arise from rotting objects in the dark depths of a lake. They briefly have form, but only as they rise in the water. At the surface, in an instant, they are dispersed in the air and are carried away. Gone.

Michael understood it all. He looked at the picture and knew that they would never see each other again. He wanted to care, but he cared more about surviving. He had done what he had to do. The catalyst plays an essential role in a reaction, but it leaves in essentially the same state in which it entered. It does not assume responsibility for the reconfiguration of elements it has touched. Michael closed his eyes again, and fell asleep.

◣ ◣ ◣

They had finished a simple lunch of black bean soup and homemade bread.

There was a dog-eared copy of D'Aulaires' illustrated *Book of Greek Myths* on the table in front of Julie. It was the one that Carolyn read to her when she was a little girl. In her head she heard the refrain of the song she was trying to write.

I have a choice
I want my voice

The lyrics flowed from her memory of the Nymph named Echo who delayed an angry Hera while Zeus escaped. Hera punished Echo by taking away the gift of forming her own words. From then on, she could only repeat the words of others.

Carolyn was copying a soup recipe. "So you don't have to

use the fresh ginger but I think it works really well and the boys will be impressed."

"Oh, Mom, they're impressed I'm going to make anything."

"Juanita can get you the corn bread at the market or I'll make a pan of it for you. Are you sure the boys have everything else you need?"

"Yup," Julie replied as she took the index card and put it inside the book with her scribbled lyrics. They had been talking since they rode back from the Yoga class together. She was waiting for Carolyn to bring up the dinner, but now it was nearly time to go and she couldn't wait anymore. "You haven't told me what happened last night."

Carolyn looked away and sighed. "Oh, Julie, I didn't... I saw him... but I didn't talk to him."

"What happened?"

"Well, I skipped the cocktail party like I planned and I sat at a table in the back of the room. He was sitting up at the head table."

"And you said you were going to say hi to him after the dinner."

"I don't think I want to talk about this."

"Mom! This is *sooooo* pathetic. You went all the way into town to see someone you haven't seen in a hundred years and you chickened out at the last minute?"

"It hasn't been a hundred years and I didn't... chicken out."

"Who cares how many years? Tell me why you didn't talk to him."

"I guess I just figured, what's the point? I mean, I love your father. Look at what he did for Michael, against the advice of his lawyers and even against his own judgment."

"Mom, c'mon, you spent four hours yesterday getting ready. You can't tell me you didn't want to talk to the guy. And leave Dad out of this. It's not like you were going there for sex."

"Oh, God, Julie," Carolyn blurted out as she reached for Julie's plate to clear the table. "First of all, no, I wasn't going out there for sex, and why do you have to add a layer of obnoxiousness to this conversation? Second, I did want to talk to him, but when the dinner was over all I could think of is that your father, for reasons I don't understand, has some lingering hostility toward Steven. So what is the point of choosing to satisfy some vague curiosity and risking getting your father upset during a particularly difficult time?"

"You wanted to talk to him. That's the point. And it's the only point that counts."

"Julie, you're wrong. I wish you could see that understanding the other person's needs and wants is part of a relationship"

"Oh, yeah, right. Like he understands yours."

◼ ◼ ◼

"So, how was the weekend in Charlotte?" Richard Wein was rummaging through the bags on the table in Steve Baldwin's office, looking for fortune cookies.

"It was OK," Steve replied as he tried to focus on the document he was reading.

"'Your past will become your future.'"

"Huh?" Steve looked up.

"It's your fortune cookie, 'Your past will become your future.' So, really, what's it like to be around all those tasty little undergraduates? Are you breaking through the 'under-twenty-one' barrier now?"

"Don't be pathetic." Steve was making notes in the margin of the document. He looked up briefly and smirked and then looked down again. "Besides, we don't spend any time with the students." He was shuffling through the papers on his desk, looking for a notepad. "Speaking of the past though, there was something weird at the dinner Friday night... I was sitting at the head table and I would have sworn I saw a girl I went out with in college."

"What's so weird about that?"

"Well, I was looking out at the crowd and I thought I saw her. I would have sworn she recognized me too. Then this guy next to me at the head table started droning on about some-thing. I turned to him for just a minute. When I looked back, she was gone."

"I still don't get what was weird."

Steve looked down at the document in front of him. He was trying to find the next thing to say. "I swear I'm gonna go blind if I read this one more time. Talk about magnum *opus*."

"Yeah... Steven, this is so huge. I would have given it a zero chance a few months ago. Remember when I told you last year that we were out of a client?"

"It's still a long shot. The Reynolds Trust has a blocking vote. But there's not a base we haven't covered." Steve put the pages in order and a binder clip at the top left. "By the way, I was talking to your guy Frank Gascon this afternoon. You know, he did a great job on the filing. We hardly touched his draft. Anyway, I said something to him about him missing his calling, that he should have been a lawyer."

Richard was picking out the last of the cashews from the Chinese food they'd had delivered for dinner at ten. "Yeah, and..."

"It may have been my imagination, but I got the impression that there was something about my comment that bothered him."

Richard wiped his fingers with several paper napkins. "Well, there's nobody here but us and General Gao's Chicken, so I'll tell you something that you're not gonna repeat, right?"

"Sure."

"The truth is he always wanted to be a lawyer. He got a scholarship to Cornell and he figured he'd come back to the City, get a law degree, do the law clerk thing, you know, be the first Puerto Rican Supreme Court Judge, right?"

"So what happened?"

"Freshman year, he's eighteen. After a party, he winds up in bed with his roommate who just happens to be a guy. They're both stoned out of their minds. They have sex. The roommate wakes up the next morning and flips out, goes to the police, and has Frank arrested for rape."

"Oh my God."

"Judge has him spend a night in jail. He has to call his family; they disown him, of course. He gets thrown out of school. After six months' probation with counseling during which the guy shrink comes on to him, they let him back into Cornell and the charges are dropped. But he doesn't want to have to explain the expulsion on his application, so… sayonara to law school."

"And this was when, late eighties?"

"Yeah, we hired him as a trading clerk after they let him back into Cornell and he graduated. He got an MBA nights at NYU and applied for a transfer to Investment Banking. Obviously he's not interested in the story being broadcast, but he told me when he interviewed for the transfer." Richard took a swig from a can of Coke. "I hired him on the spot."

"God, there's no end of incredible stories." Steve looked across the room at the picture of Dan on the shelf… "Speaking of incredible stories, I'm going with Dan to meet his family."

"You're kidding me."

"No, we're going right after Labor Day."

"Steven, first of all, as I recall, you don't even know this kid's real name. Second of all, don't you think it would be easier for him to first tell his family that he's gay and then get them over the fact that his lover has more in common with Dad than Junior?"

"Oh, Richard, c'mon, let's go."

"If you think I'm gonna let you off the hook because it's two o'clock in the morning… you're right, but you c'mon. Steven, you gotta deal with this stuff. He's already gonna have a hard enough time with the gay thing. You just add the whole—"

"Don't say it. Don't even think about going there. I'm doing this his way because he asked me and I love him. I'm not here to tell him how he should or shouldn't come out to his family. Let's go."

"*Love* him! Steven, you hardly even *know* him! And as far as meeting his family is concerned, isn't he supposed to get the benefit of having a lover who happens to be a lot older? You're supposed to know better."

"Richard, I have my jacket on and I'm going home. If you're not leaving with me—"

"OK, let's go."

They didn't speak on the ride down the elevator. Separate cars were waiting for them at the curb. When they got outside, the humid air hung like a sweaty towel over the city.

"I'm sorry," Richard said to Steve as he kept walking. "Hey, stop."

Steve turned around.

"I'm sorry. I'm not trying to rub your nose in it. I just can't believe from what you've told me that it isn't gonna be a big problem. I swear I wonder how you manage to be so street savvy and naïve at the same time…" No response. "Do it your way or his way or whatever. I'll be here when you get back."

Steve looked down. "I'll think about what you said, but I want him to make his own choices. I do love him, Richard. I'm only just realizing how much. As for his family, his father won't be the first bigot I've ever met and, you know," he continued as he pulled on the handle of the passenger door, "I don't expect him to be thrilled about it at first. But if he's anything like Dan, maybe there's hope for him."

"G'night, handsome," said Richard as he leaned over to kiss Steve good-bye. "Sweet dreams."

HALF-LIFE

Jack was sitting forward in his chair, his elbows on the table in front of him, his hands clasped, as if there was nothing else to hold on to. He was staring ahead but not at Blake, who was sitting at the other end of the table. On his left, Fred Bonham and Bill Hunter were silent and looking down, waiting for their boss to begin speaking, to say something that would let them know he had figured out what to do and how they were going to get out of the mess they were in.

He turned to the white-maned lawyer on his right. "What is it you always say, Walter? 'It's never as good as it seems and it's never as bad as it seems.' Right?"

The answer came back in the look. The words only added a blow upon the bruise. "Jack... I'm thinking right now that this may be worse than it seems."

The *Wall Street Journal* and the *New York Times* were in the middle of the table. They had all read the front-page right column article in the *Journal*.

Collapse of Eagle Financial Embarrasses Underwriters and Angers Investors.

Memphis—The news last Friday of the Chapter 11 filing of the once high-flying auto loan finance company, Eagle Financial, is sending shock waves that are being felt from New York to Charlotte and in all quarters where institutional money is invested. Barely six months ago, the IPO for Eagle, which was underwritten by North Carolina Bank & Trust Company, was supposed to be a shining example of how commercial banks are entering the once exclusive domain of large investment banking underwriters. It may be years before the mess is sorted out but it appears that some big-name institutions and lenders will lose hundreds of millions of dollars. Everyone is pointing fingers at Charlotte based

NCBT, which has had no comment since the surprise bankruptcy filing last week. There are confirmed reports that the Justice Department, the SEC, and several States Attorneys General are investigating.

"I'll resign, Jack. I'll take the responsibility for this." Bill Hunter spoke as he was staring down at the table.

"No way, Bill. We all got caught with our pants down on this one. We'll all ride this out." Jack turned to Fred. "We need to pull off something that'll give the guys at Harbor and Pilgrim a reason not to bail out of the stock. Have you got something you can put in the third quarter, you know, something that'll make us beat the Street's earning targets?"

Fred winced. "Boss, the cupboard is empty. We pulled out everything we had in reserves in '96. We'll be lucky if we meet last year's numbers on an operating basis … But… I'm gonna have to take a big hit to cover this Eagle thing." The words came out like they were vomited on the table. "We're probably gonna report a net loss for the third quarter."

As Fred went painstakingly through the five divisions and how each one had been overextended to hit the prior year's record that Jack had pushed for, Blake and Walter Weckstein glanced across the table at each other and then at the article on the front page of the Business section of the *New York Times.*

> *Key Stockbroker in Investment Scam Flees Country*
> NEW YORK—Federal authorities announced today that Michael Hendricks, the top broker in the now defunct D. L. Baird, is believed to have fled the country.

Weckstein pulled back the French cuff from his shirt and took a sidelong glance at his tank watch. He had been waiting for Blake to bring up the subject of the article in the *Times.* They had discussed it before the meeting. But now he had to get to another appointment.

"Jack, we need to spend a few minutes on this *New York Times* article before I go. This thing with the broker where you vouched for him and put up the bail." Weckstein reached across the table for the paper. "For now this is coming off as a local story." He opened the Business section and pointed to the column on page nine where the story was continued. "But see here where it says 'Hendricks was freed on one million dollars bail posted by Jack O'Brien, chief executive officer, blah, blah, blah.' Weckstein's voice trailed off. "Jack, this story is fresh meat. Unless they catch this kid right away and it becomes a nonstory, it's going to fester. And when it does," he put the paper down on the table like it was infectious, "they're going to hang you with it."

◪ ◪ ◪

This was supposed to be a wrap-up meeting. Twenty minutes with the client to get the go-ahead on the counter-offer. Gear up the troops. Win or loose, send a big bill. But there was something bothering him. "This isn't going to work." He said it under his breath like he wanted to test the sound of it. "This isn't going to work," he said a second time, louder.

Carlton Moore looked across his desk at Steve and then at Wein, who was at least as surprised. "Steven, what do you mean, this isn't going to work?"

He cleared his throat. "I apologize to both of you, but it just occurred to me and there isn't a delicate way to put it."

Moore took his bifocals off, folded them, and rested them on the desk. "Is there anything else you'd like to share with us?"

Wein was staring at his colleague.

Steve began slowly. "If this were just about the numbers, this plan would be a winner, but these things are never just about the numbers. I know we've covered this already, but here's the scenario I see playing out. You make the stock-for-stock offer. And, yes, there'll be institutional pressure to take it because their stock is in the toilet. But Blake Reynolds isn't going to sell out his son-in-law because of some short-term pressure. So, O'Brien buys time. Six months from now, they're out of the woods on this Eagle Financial thing, their stock has recovered. Meantime, you've spent a few million on fees to me and Richard, your management is distracted, and you throw in the towel."

Moore was paying close attention to Steve so he didn't notice the look on Wein's face, the shock of a boy at an outdoor party whose cake has just been decorated by a passing bird.

"I know we dismissed the idea early in the process, but let me bring it up again. The idea of a cash offer is a smarter move. Hypothetically it has less of a chance but there are two big reasons to try it. First: the shareholder pressure will be exponentially higher if it's a cash offer. Second: it will have a quicker outcome. You have less of a chance of getting bogged down. And… I should add… I looked again at the analysis that Richard's people did on the business units." He was flipping through the pages of the memorandum they had been looking at. "They're so distinct… really separate businesses. We've already done the valuation work just to come up with the stock offer."

The furrowed brow was the sign that Moore was thinking about the option. "So, we'd keep the one division we really want and sell the rest."

Steve glanced over at Richard. *"Don't worry, I'm baking another cake."* He turned back to Moore. "Right, we'd need a week to line up the buyers for the stuff you'd sell. They'd be offers subject to due diligence, but they'd be credible. As for the cash you'd need for the custody business, Richard could get you that pretty quickly. Right, Richard?"

"Um… yeah… right." Wein was recovering by virtue of the size of the deal he saw Steve putting in the oven. It was decorated with big green dollar signs. "Of course, we'd handle the sale of the other divisions and we'd raise you the cash… It would be a lot more work, but, yeah, we could do that."

They were out at the curb before they were alone and Wein had recovered enough to speak. "What the fuck was that all about, and since when did you become an investment banker?"

"I'm sorry. I just knew the stock deal wouldn't work and there wasn't time to ask for a recess. C'mon, Richard, you'll make way more money on the break-up."

"Yeah, I figured that. I mean, it's never been done with a bank before, but they're not a typical bank."

"Hey, listen," said Steve as he stuck his arm out to flag a cab. "I've got fifteen minutes to get to the Upper West Side. Your guys should start on the potential buyers list. We gotta move on this fast if it's gonna work."

In the cab, speeding up the West Side Highway, Steve leaned back in the seat with both windows down and let the warm air stream over his face. He closed his eyes and concentrated on the logistics of his plan, the breakup of NCBT. He was distracted by the incongruous memory of a nursery rhyme. "Jack and Jill went up the hill to fetch a pail of water. Jack fell down and broke his crown." The image that kept recurring to him was of shattered worlds. "*I wonder what will happen to her.*"

◼ ◼ ◼

Even before recorded history, from the first days when man set about to rearrange the order of his surroundings, there have been gardens. And in every era, every culture, gardens have been a collaboration of man's will and nature's authority. The gardener can choose to combine the blues of delphinium with the yellows of marguerites, but they must be planted in rich soil and they only bloom in June, not May or September, no matter how hard the gardener might wish or work otherwise. Thus a successful gardener finds the Zen balance between his own purposefulness and utter surrender to the design of nature, a way of finding direction without struggle.

In the early morning, the very first light, the gardens had the air of potential, as if anything was possible. The landscape architect who laid out the plans for the grounds at Chatsworth had included both English and French gardens. But in the late nineteenth century, a Chinese garden had been added. In the Chinese design for contentment, which is the basis of Chinese philosophy, every individual possesses a garden. The Chinese feel that unless a man has a garden, he scarcely grasps the reason for existence.

Carolyn sat on a glider under an arbor, a mug of coffee on the armrest, a book in her lap. She heard the sound of shoes on the gravel behind her. The crunching sound grew louder with each step. "My God, Julie," she said as she turned around, "what are you doing up so early?"

"Hi, Mom." Julie gave her a kiss and sat down on the glider. "It's not like I'm never up in the morning."

"Yes, I know, but you're more often going to bed at this hour."

They sat in silence and watched the day brighten. The light through the morning glory leaves cast a translucent glow under the arbor.

"I used to think it was horrible for you to grow up here," Julie remarked as she started to push the glider back and forth with the tips of her feet. "Being by yourself most of the time, I mean it's beautiful, but it must have been lonely."

"I suppose I was alone, but I never felt alone. I can remember going barefoot through these gardens when I was a girl. I had the run of the stables. The carpenter made me twenty-four stick horses and I gave them all names." Carolyn took a sip from her mug of coffee. "If I had an imaginary party, I made a hand-written invitation for each of them. I terrorized the neighbors' children when they came to visit by making them memorize the names of all my stick horses."

"Oh, Mom, it's hard to imagine you as a terror."

"Well, maybe that's too strong a word. I loved the gardens the best. This is where I learned the names of all the flowers. When I was a little girl, there was an old man who had been here since before your great-grandfather's time. He taught me how to pat a bee."

"Mom," Julie looked with a kind but firm disbelief.

Carolyn pointed at a spot near a fountain, the intersection of two walkways. "It was right over there… His skin was so wrinkled. He looked a little like one of those small show dogs with the folds of skin. He walked with a cane, really slowly."

"You didn't get stung?"

"No. He told me the bee was happy on the flower and wouldn't mind. I watched him do it." Carolyn held out her hand. "Just the tip of your forefinger. I was never afraid of insects after that."

"Mom, why are you here? I mean, you haven't been home for two weeks. And I mean, it's your birthday next week. What's wrong?"

"Oh, for a few reasons, I guess. It's quieter here than in Charlotte. All the things in the papers about the bank, and your father… and Michael."

"Did you have a fight with Dad?"

No response.

"Mom, you don't have to make everything nice for me… Why are you smiling?"

"I was noticing a picture this morning of your grandmother, and I couldn't figure out why it looked so familiar. I just realized how much you look like her… You're leaving, aren't you, Julie?"

"Mom, I'm getting stale here. It's not like I'm leaving you."

"It's OK, sweetheart. Really. I want you to go if that's what you need to do. I think your father and I held on to Dan too tightly. I've wanted to tell him that, but of course, now he's so determined to stay away."

"It's not your fault, Mom. It's Dad who he's mad at."

"I'm not buying that anymore. When he comes after Labor Day, I'm going to tell him it was my fault too for letting it happen."

"Yeah, what's going on with that? I got a weird e-mail from him. He said he's coming with his lover and his roommate."

"I didn't get much more from him. I told your father and he said he'd be at the beach that weekend. So I guess we're all meeting there."

"What do you think he meant by his 'lover'?"

"Oh, Julie. I don't know what he meant—lover, boyfriend, girlfriend. Your brother's world is so unconnected to ours now. I just left a message saying your father and I would be there. I told him I loved him. What else is there to say?"

■ ■ ■

The flight from Charlotte the night before had been eerily quiet. Jack, Blake, Fred, and Ron Duby, the outside director whom the board had agreed should go with them, made the two-hour flight with a minimum amount of small talk and nothing said about the deal. They had agreed before leaving Charlotte that the meeting at NYT on Monday would be a courtesy call, to politely listen to the offer, to say no, and then to formally withdraw their own offer. "Let's get this over with," said Blake, "and get back to minding our own business."

Jack got up early and wanted some exercise. He didn't like the gym on Fifty-ninth Street as much as the club in Charlotte. It reminded him of everything he didn't like about New York. There was too much of everything and everything was crowded together. Dozens of treadmills, two rows in front of a mirrored wall, another row of stair climbers, and a row of stationary bikes. At seven-thirty in the morning, it was like the FDR or the BQE, all the motors were running, but no one was going anywhere. There was what the brochure called a gym at the hotel, but Jack went to the New York Sports Club because they had the same model treadmill as the club at home and there were TVs so he could watch the news while he worked out. *Who could run for so long and not have something else to pay attention to?*

He picked a treadmill off to the side, the end of the second row where he had a good view of the TV tuned into CNBC. He put on the headset and plugged in the numbers. It was all part of the routine. The display lights went on and the conveyer started moving, slowly at first and then up to speed. He set it to run six miles in forty-two minutes. *Pretty quick for a guy who just turned forty-six.*

In the reflection of the mirrored walls, he could see all the other machines and the people on them, men and women, a variety of ages and shapes, all so close together, yet all in their own worlds. He was mostly looking up at the TV.

This is Daybreak with Deborah Marcussi and Peter Webber.

Jack could hear the audio broadcast on his headphones but he was following the dialog in the closed captions at the bottom of the screen.

Marcussi: Good morning, everyone. This is Deborah Marcussi. Topping our news this morning, there are unconfirmed reports that New York Trust will make an eye-popping six-billion-dollar cash offer for North Carolina Bank & Trust Company. This would be a record cash offer for any bank and one of the largest cash transactions in U.S. merger history. Our sources tell us that the offer will be financed largely by the breakup and sale of all but one of NCBT's business units. We'll have more on this story later in the broadcast.

"*That's impossible,*" Jack said to himself as he reflexively tore the headphones off. "*How the fuck can they do that?*" But he didn't stop running. "*I can't believe the shit they put on TV as news.*"

He put the headphones down on the console and watched as they fell to the floor. "*Fuck the TV. I just want this to be over.*" He started counting the strides in each inhale and then the number of strides in each exhale. But then he lost track, or lost interest, and took to noticing the way the LED display showed the number of calories burned or the minutes elapsed.

"*How could they come up with that much cash? It must be some whacko deal with a thousand contingencies.*" He was just passing the first mile mark. "*Five more to go. I don't feel like doing this. Maybe I should get off and call Blake.*" He went on for another minute, thinking about everything and nothing. "*For Christ's sake, don't get rattled. Just finish what you started, get a shower, get dressed, then call Blake.*"

He was feeling clammy, like it was humid in the gym, which

he thought was weird because the gym was cool when he came in. There was a guy on the treadmill next to him, walking and reading a magazine. Jack noticed the article the guy was reading in *GQ*. They were so close he could see the large type in the article and the display on the treadmill—five miles an hour. *"That's a twelve-minute mile,"* he calculated, *"but he's pulling on the handrails. Someone should tell these goddamned people that's how the machines get broken."*

The guy was nearing the end of his workout. Jack could see the display counting down the remaining time, three minutes, two minutes, one minute. When he was done, he walked away, leaving the magazine on the console and his sweat dripping down the handrail. *"Somebody should tell that guy to get some manners, wipe down the goddamned machine when he's done."*

Two miles done. *"God, I feel like shit. I gotta get some aspirin for this headache. Maybe I should stop."*

He noticed the back cover of the magazine after he had actually seen it, the way vision takes in an entire horizon of images and then somewhere in the recesses of consciousness, details of the picture get processed. He looked over at the magazine. The back cover was a full-page ad for a cologne, the unmistakable shape of a young man's smooth-skinned torso leaning against a reflecting wall of some polished silver metal. The face looked directly into the camera. It was Dan.

"Jesus Christ! Now I gotta spend," he looked down at the LED display, *"I gotta spend the next twenty-five minutes looking at a picture of my son parading his half-naked body for who knows how much money. Why do I have to see this now?"* He pulled his shirt up to wipe his face and noticed as he pressed it against his forehead that his right hand was numb. *"Three more miles to go."*

He thought for a second about balancing on the edges of the treadmill, reaching across, and turning the magazine over. *"Don't be ridiculous. Someone would see me and I'd look like a fool. I don't have to look at it."* He turned his attention back to the closed captions and the business news in progress.

Marcussi: We're talking to Judy Mencher, partner of DDJ, and a longtime follower of financial institution stocks. Judy, tell us what your take is on the rumors of an all-cash offer for NCBT. Mencher: Normally you'd have to dismiss such a rumor as unthinkable, but given how distinct NCBT's business lines are, their lack of any retail branch network, a breakup would not be as hard as you might first think. And then take into account the remarkable reversal of fortunes of these two banks in the last few months—I mean, just look at the shifts in their relative stock prices—I'd say it's not out of the question.

"She doesn't know shit." He couldn't see out of his right eye so he pulled his shirt up again to clear the sweat from it. He glanced down and tried to make out the large printed warning under the electronic display.

IF YOU ARE IN PAIN, STOP RUNNING

He looked over again at the magazine. It was a blur. He squinted at the caption, *Take me*, and then his vision blurred again. He could hear his heart beating in his ears, louder than the sound of all the machines around him.

"I gotta get off this thing." He looked ahead, to get himself oriented, and reached for the side rails to steady himself as he planted a foot squarely on the conveyer. He was already unconscious as he was thrown backward against the wall behind him.

◪ ◪ ◪

"You need to read the forms, initial at the bottom of each one, and sign the last page, acknowledging that you're being released —AMA—against medical advice."

"I've done that."

"Mr. O'Brien, you haven't read the forms and you're not listening to me. If I can't determine that you're making a competent decision, I'm required to keep you here for twenty-four hours' psychiatric evaluation as a potential danger to yourself."

Jack turned from the mirror where he was adjusting his tie

and glared. "You can't do that."

It was nine o'clock. The doctor was supposed to be in surgery and he had two other emergency consults to see. He looked down and gave away his bluff. "It would be an extreme measure... Please sit down. If you're determined to leave, this will only take a few minutes."

Jack sat in one of the two chairs in the room, standard hospital furniture. The doctor sat in the other, clipboard and forms on his lap.

"We haven't taken all the tests that we should. We did an ultrasound when you came into the emergency room this morning. You have moderate carotid stenosis, which means that the artery leading to your brain is partially blocked. What probably happened this morning is that you had a TIA, a transient ischemic attack. A piece of the blockage broke free and traveled to your brain. It's what you'd call a mini-stroke. The brain recovers and you feel better. If we could get you to stay for the MRI at ten we could make a better determination of any damage."

"I feel fine now... and I need to go."

"The effects of these incidences, if they're small to begin with, usually last only a few hours. That's why you feel better now, though I did notice you had some trouble with your tie, but that will probably be gone in the next eighteen to twenty-four hours."

Jack was looking at his watch.

"Mr. O'Brien, you were lucky today. You got a wake-up call. When you were admitted this morning, your blood pressure was 220 over 115. That's *severe* hypertension. You're not only at risk for the kind of cerebral event you had at the gym; if you don't address this right away it will either cripple or kill you... soon."

"I'll take care of it when I get home."

"Right, we're forwarding the records to your doctor at University Hospital. In the meantime, I'm giving you these medications, which you must start taking now. The Diuril will make you pee, but it will bring down your blood pressure. The Lopressor will gently dilate your arteries. The Cardizem is a calcium channel blocker, which will..."

"Thank you, Doctor." Jack interrupted him. He took the medicines and got up. "I've got to run." He put the three bottles in his coat pocket and extended his arm again, but there was no feeling in it when he shook the doctor's hand.

◪ ◪ ◪

They were flying south, ahead of the front. Reclined in the rear starboard seat, Jack had a view of the towering thunderclouds in the distance. Rising sixty thousand feet, almost into space, the clouds took form as water, an apparently single mass, but in fact an uncountable number of discrete drops, suspended briefly before being released to the earth again. He was drifting in and out of sleep. He had finally taken the medicine, whatever it was, that the doctor had given him before he got on the plane. Now he felt exhausted, aware, but in a dreamy state.

A dream, or perhaps it was a memory that came back to him each time he closed he eyes and drifted back to sleep. The image was of waves at the shore, of holding Dan in the water when he was a little boy, maybe nine or ten years old.

"*Here comes a big one, Dad. A really HUGE one!*" Dan was shouting as he looked over Jack's shoulder."

Jack could see the excited look as he held Dan up with arms extended. Then he felt the wave lift him from him from behind, going over his head.

"*That one was the biggest one, Dad.*"

They floated in the water, Jack holding his son on a glorious summer day, the ocean yielding an occasional roller for Dan's pure excitement.

Suddenly Dan's face looked as if an urgently perplexing thought had occurred to him. "*Dad, what happens to the wave when it gets to the beach? Where does it go?*"

Jack smiled at the miracle of unconditional love he was holding. "*Dan, it doesn't go anywhere. It just becomes part of the ocean again.*" He was reminded of his question last night,

"Where does the fire go when you blow out the candle?" Dan was on a "Where does it go?" jag.

"Oh." Dan squinted, looking up a gull circling overhead. Again, the urgently perplexed look. *"Dad, do you think there could be people living on Saturn?"*

Jack chuckled, but only in awe at the breath of Dan's curiosity. *"Kiddo, I guess I really hadn't thought of it. What do you think?"*

"Well, you know how it's made of gas." He held his hands out and opened his eyes wide as if he was about to reveal an amazing insight. *"Well, I was thinking that maybe the people live on the inside and we just can't see them."*

After another wave had rolled in and Jack held Dan over his head, he cleared the water from his eyes. *"I think somebody probably already checked into that, but, you know... when we get back to the house, we'll look it up, OK?"*

"OK... Hey, Dad..."

Jack looked back, right into Dan's eyes, ready for another question.

"I love you, Dad. You're the best Dad in the whole universe."

Jack opened his eyes and looked out at the storm clouds again.

A wave rises from the ocean, sharing the nature of all water and yet it takes on a new name—wave. What occurred to him in his delirium was a wave as it rose taking on an awareness of itself. *"I am a big wave. I am the biggest wave. I am force, energy in motion. I am a tower."* And yet as the wave approaches the shore, driven inexorably, there is the realization, *"When I reach the shore, my time will be over."* He tried to put the thought out of his mind, but the question came back to him.

"Dad, what happens to the wave when it gets to the beach?"

He shifted uncomfortably in his seat, closed his eyes again, and made himself think about how he was going to get out of the mess he was in.

What happens to the wave when it reaches the shore? It returns to its element. It becomes water.

◪ ◪ ◪

From the front of the plane, Blake could see Jack sleeping. He was sitting at the table with Fred Bonham and Ron Duby. "At least he's finally getting some rest."

Fred shook his head as he turned back to Blake. "He looks awful. It's gonna be some work to get us all recovered from this one."

The cabin lights were on, but dimly. The clouds to the west obscured the setting sun.

Blake was still looking at Jack even as he continued talking. "We're going to accept the offer." He didn't stop to notice the two shocked faces. "You're right, Fred. It would take years. I know what it took when we did it in the eighties. We were all younger then. From what I can see now, we wouldn't get through it again in one piece." Blake finally turned to Fred and Ron, to give them some reassurance in his steady look. "Let's get home and get some rest. I'll talk to Jack privately in the morning and then we'll make it official at the end of the day."

◪ ◪ ◪

The lights were flashing at the Atlantic Theatre Company on 20th Street in Chelsea. The crowd was making their way to their seats

He was supposed to have had time to reflect and prepare. But frantically jumping from the subway to a cab and finally running on foot, and still being twenty-five minutes late, did not leave much time for either. Paul tried to block out the sounds of the other actors' vocal warm-ups and distracting banter. He was left with the sound of the many voices in his head pulling him in and out of concentration and focus. He couldn't wait to be out of this place and away from these talentless people and their hackneyed dreams of stardom, which seemed as tenuous as their grasp on reality. As he sat in front of the mirror he looked at them and began to summarily dismiss them, "Bad hair, crooked teeth, she has a face made for the stage."

The stage was merely a necessary evil — the basic training for the film career he longed for and knew he was made for. He applied his makeup in the mirror and thought of the hours he spent watching his mother do exactly the same thing while he posed and preened behind her. He looked into his own eyes. "You're going to be a star." He blew himself a kiss, turned out the lights over the mirror, and headed downstairs to take his place backstage.

�£ �£ �£

Marty was on the corner when Dan came out of the station on Twenty-third Street.

"Sorry I'm late. C'mon, we can still make it by eight."

They walked up a block and then started speed walking on Twenty-second.

"I don't get it. You say this guy killed his father and then married his mother, right?"

Dan was checking his pocket to make sure he had the tickets. "Well, the thing is, he doesn't *know* it's his father when he kills him and he doesn't *know* it's his mother when he marries her. That's the incredible part."

"Only a white guy would think of a story like this."

"C'mon, Marty. *Oedipus* is a classic."

They were breathing heavily when they arrived a few minutes late for the curtain up. They sat in the lobby, the rear of a converted church that housed the theater.

"OK, I'll give you the beginning. They'll let us in at the next scene break."

◪ ◪ ◪

Paul took the stage and waited for the lights to go up. In the darkness he could hear the rustling of programs, old ladies unwrapping their butterscotch or peppermint candies, and the giggles from friends not aware of proper theater etiquette and the respect one should have for an artist at work. He looked across the stage and studied the strips of glow tape marking out the boundaries of the stage like an airstrip warning to prevent an actor from the disaster of crashing and burning in the darkness. He took a deep breath and felt the butterflies in his stomach flutter up and escape through his mouth. The ones left inside frantically beat their wings against his stomach. It was his moment to take the stage, capture the audience, and set the momentum for the rest of the players. He was Oedipus after all, the King of Thebes. The lights came up, freezing him in time, eyes on him, looking for answers, some waiting for cues, others still looking at their programs. The seconds before his first words stretched on in dead silence. The program named him as the king, but in that brief eternity, he was naked, a fraud. The audience could see through him, read his mind, and condemn him for the worst sin of all—being ordinary. He stepped forward, into the light, as if in a dream.

◪ ◪ ◪

From the comfort of an overstuffed chair at the Big Cup, Marty sipped on a cappuccino and sounded as confused as Dan was captivated. "I don't get it, why didn't he just hang out and be king?" He looked around at all the Chelsea boys in the coffee shop and reminded himself to never go west of Broadway again unless it was for a paid performance.

"Don't you get it? That's just it," said Dan, eyes wide.

Remembering the scene in detail, he was desperate to ignite some excitement about the play. "He's totally committed to find out the truth. It's so cool the way Paul had everyone with him. That's what I want. I want to be able to do that." Dan sat back, the echoes of the play drowning out the conversations around them.

> Even if I be proved born from nothing,
> Let me find that out the truth.
> Oh, I am a child of chance, a lucky child!
> My fealty to that family makes me move
> True to myself my family I shall prove.

"OK, whatever you say." Marty took the last sip from the Styrofoam cup. "Let's get out of here. These queens are getting on my nerves."

Walking back to the East Village, Dan was still charged by the performance. "I'm sick of modeling. I'm gonna be an actor. That's what I wanted to be all along. I'm gonna go out to L.A. as soon as this thing with Mark Jackson is up."

"Uh-huh," Marty extended his arm to keep Dan from walking into the traffic on Fifth Avenue. "What are you going to do about Steve?"

"He says he wants me to do it. He says we can like have a place here and there, but I dunno…"

They walked a few blocks without speaking, crossed the southbound lane on Park Avenue and were standing on the island, waiting for the northbound light.

"OK, are you gonna tell me or do I have to do the twenty questions routine?"

"C'mon, Marty." Dan stepped back onto the concrete curb, a stage to deliver the answer to his audience of one. "We live in the same city and I don't see him enough. I mean, I totally love him, but I want someone who wants the dream, you know, like waking up next to me every morning." The light changed and yet they stayed, Dan continuing his soliloquy. "You know, he says let's just keep going and things will work, but what if they don't work. I mean," Dan raised his hands, pleading now to some unseen gods in the Flatiron Building, "my whole life has been…" He looked up at the sky… "Stuff happens to me and I just have to figure out what to do next. It's like, always someone else's agenda." He put his hands down, palms open. They had missed the light. "I want to have some control, Marty, like the way Paul was on the stage. I want to be the one that people are watching, not just floating along waiting to see what comes up next. I know he loves me, but I want something to be about *me* instead of fitting into somebody else's plan." He looked around, realizing they had stood through two lights. He felt enough discomfort to change the subject. "I'm definitely going to be an actor. Paul was so great at the end of that play."

"You mean when he blinds himself? And you think *my* stuff is weird?"

"Well, he struggled so hard to find the truth and then it was too much for him, Marty… the truth was too much."

They crossed the street and walked slowly while Dan revisited the scene in his head.

> I am deserted, dark. Ah!
> A nightmare mist has fallen adamantine black for me—
> Abomination closing. Cry, cry, Oh cry again!
> Those needled pains are pointed echoes of my sinning.
> Oh yes I pierced my eyes—my useless eyes—why not?
> When all that's sweet has parted from my vision.
> Nothing left to see, to love, nothing to enjoy,
> I should be free from parricide;
> Not pointed out as wedded to the one who weaned me.
> Now I'm god-abandoned
> What kind of eyes should I need to gaze upon my father's face
> In Hades Halls, or unhappy mother's?
> I cast away?—most cursed I the Prince of princes here in Thebes
> Now self-damned and self-appointed pariah
> The refuse heap of heaven on display as son of Laius.
> By all the gods, then, hide me somewhere far and soon

or kill me.

Drown me in the seas, away from your vision. Come!
Take the broken man. Don't shrink from touch.
My load is mine, don't fear. No other man could bear so
much.

◨ ◨ ◨

The LED of the alarm clock on the nightstand read 3:00 a.m.
when she noticed that Jack was not in bed. She put a bathrobe
over her nightgown and went downstairs. The lights were off in
the house, but she noticed the unfamiliar smell of cigarette
smoke coming from the library.

"My God," she said as she reached to turn on a floor lamp,
"Jack, what are you doing in here? What are you drinking? And
what, in heaven's name, are you doing with a cigarette?" She
took a seat in the other club chair in front of the dark fireplace.

Jack was staring into the empty hearth. The color of his skin
was as pale as the ashes falling to the floor by the chair. "I could-
n't sleep. I felt like having a drink."

"Jack, you look terrible."

He looked over at her as he lifted the glass to his lips. When
he had taken a sip and put it back down on the table, he took a
drag from the cigarette and put it out in the ashtray. "Did you
come all the way down here to cheer me up?"

"What are you talking about? I came down here because I
didn't know where you were."

"Well," he said as he picked the drink up again, "now you've
found me."

"Jack, you really don't look well."

"You said that already. Are you rubbing it in?"

"I think you should see a doctor."

"I'll have plenty of time to see a doctor, soon enough. I'll be
unemployed. Rich, but unemployed."

"What about the prescriptions in your shaving bag... the

Cardizem and the other two drugs? I asked Dr. Guille about them."

"What were you doing in my shaving bag?"

"I've... I've been worried about you. We haven't talked. I wanted to leave you a note that you'd find at the gym. Sort of a surprise, I guess. It was just a little note from me. I wanted you to know I love you."

"Let me get this straight, you saw the pills and I didn't get the note. Huh? I can't get arrested these days."

"I was frightened, I didn't know what they were for. I didn't want you to think I was snooping."

"But you got over that and called the doctor."

"Jack! I found the pills by accident. They're for severe high blood pressure. You're twisting this all around as if I've done something wrong. Don't you understand? I'm worried. There's something terribly wrong and I want you to talk to me about it."

"The bank is gone, Carolyn. They're going to buy it and break it up. It's going to disappear from the face of the earth as if it never existed."

"I don't care about the bank."

"I do, Carolyn. It was my life."

◥ ◥ ◥

The voice came from behind the high-back swivel chair turned to face the window and the view up Park Avenue.

"Yeah, that's right. We heard this afternoon. Blake Reynolds called Carlton Moore." Josh Angel was sitting at his desk, beaming, demonstrating that man alone among the hunter species gloats over its fallen prey. He turned and looked up in time to see Steve Baldwin walking into his spacious corner office. "OK, Henry, we'll give you another running start on the next one. I gotta go." As he hung up the phone, Josh flashed a big smile. "Well, if it isn't Stevie Wonder. Hey, kid!" He bounded out from behind his desk with the enthusiasm of a patrician greeting a favored general on return from a stunning victory. Steve got a bear hug and a slap on the back. "We did it again, eh? Didn't I tell you we would? Didn't I?"

Steve smiled. "Yeah, Josh. You were right. You're always right…" He leaned away from Josh's embrace. "I need to talk to you. Have you got a minute?"

"For you?" Josh answered. "Anything. Here, come sit on the couch."

They put their feet up on the coffee table. In the glow of it all, Josh was content to sit for a while in his English club chair with his hands behind his head. From his vantage point at the end of the couch, Steve could see Josh's wall of photographs, letters, and awards, smiling pictures of his wife, children, and grandchildren, accolades from CEOs, awards from charities.

"So, what's up, Stevie?"

Steve looked back at Josh. He frowned, pursed his lips, flared his nostrils and exhaled through his nose. He was looking for someplace other than the obvious place to start the conversation.

"What's wrong?"

"I'm… I'm leaving the firm." That came out too timid, he decided, so he started over again in a deeper, firmer voice. "Josh, I've decided to leave the firm."

Josh put his feet down on the floor, to steady himself and to mark the change in mood.

"You're not telling me you're leaving to go somewhere else… Are you?"

Steve sighed in relief as he answered. "No, no, that's not it at all. Josh, I'm getting out of the business."

"Whada ya nuts? Kid, you're at the top of your game… You need a rest. That's what you need."

Steve had just turned forty-six, one of the most prominent corporate lawyers in the country, a grown man, even four inch es taller than his mentor. He chuckled as he put his elbow on the back of the couch and cradled his head in the palm of his hand. His head was tilted sideways as if to get a different angle of the situation. "You're right, Josh. I do need a rest. I'm leaving New

York too. I'm going to L.A."

Josh seemed relieved as if he had heard something that made sense. "Oh. Oh, if that's it, well, you could take a few months off and set up in our office out there. You can still handle deals." He was talking himself into feeing better. "What've we got, a hundred lawyers there?"

Steve rolled his head off the palm of his hand and looked up at the ceiling. "I'm talking about a long rest and I'm not going out there to practice law." He looked straight at Josh when he finished the sentence. "I want to have a life with Dan."

"Dan who?" Josh asked as his secretary came in with papers for him to sign.

"My lover," Steve answered, "the guy I've introduced to you every time he comes in to pick me up."

"Sylvia, close my door." Josh sat up in his chair and began again in a whisper, "You mean the kid?"

"He's not a kid and Sylvia doesn't have to close your door. Sylvia, you can leave the door open." Steve sighed again. "I want to really have a life, Josh… And I've found someone I want to share it with."

Josh got up and walked to the window. "What are you, forty-four?"

"Forty-six."

"You're at the top of your game."

"I won't forget how to practice law if I change my mind." Steve got up and stood next to Josh. "I have to go." He extended his hand.

Josh looked down at Steve's hand and frowned. "C'mere," and he gave Steve another bear hug. "OK, kid, I've seen some crazy things in my day, but I gotta tell ya, you're a piece of work."

They stood facing each other.

"I'll see you on Friday," Josh continued. "We got champagne over at Carlton's office."

Steve turned reticent again, like the sixth-former who was telling his headmaster that he wouldn't be at evening mass. "I won't be there. I'm going to North Carolina with Dan. I'm leaving Friday morning."

There was a look of shock and disbelief.

"You can take the bows for both of us."

Josh's look was unchanged.

"Josh, he's taking me home to meet his family. It's a gay thing. Do you want me to explain it to you?"

"Oh, no..." Josh held up his hand. "No, you don't have to do that, Stevie... You do what you gotta do. I'll call you on the cell phone when we get the word. OK?"

"Sure, Josh. Bye."

◤ ◤ ◤

"Hold on to that end. Hold it steady." Jack peered across the workbench at Dan. He lined up the bit with the hole in the hinge and took another look at his son. *"Have you got it?"*

"Yeah, Dad... Hey, Dad, can I do it?"

Jack's look gave way from hesitation to pride. *"Ah... sure, sport. Let me put some blocks under that end."* Jack adjusted the door of the cabinet they were making so it lay level while they screwed in the hinges. He put Dan's left hand over the top of the drill and his right hand on the trigger. *"Just let the drill do the work and keep the drill bit flat on the head of the screw."*

Three screws in each of six hinges and the doors were set.

"Wow, Dad, this is so cool. And it looks just like the one Papa made with you."

"Hey... hey!" Marty said it loud enough the second time to bring Dan out of his reminiscence. "Are you OK?"

Dan wiped his eye, sniffled, and sat up against the pillows at the head of the bed. "Yeah, I'm fine."

"What's that, a scrapbook? Oh, c'mon, lemme see." Marty came in and sat on the edge of the bed. "So this is Dad and Junior, huh? How long ago?"

"I was twelve. That's a picture of us with the trophy case we made... It was the last thing we ever made together." Dan sighed as he looked away.

"Wassup? What are you worryin' about now?"

Dan closed the scrapbook and put it on the nightstand. "I was just wondering how we got… like so hostile with each other. When I was really little we used to do all kinds of stuff together. And then… I dunno. When I was in junior high school it was like… everything changed. He just didn't have any time for me anymore."

"Bwana, you ain't gonna solve that riddle this weekend."

"Yeah, I know. I was just thinking about it, that's all… I love him, Marty. I still love him. I want to tell him that."

"Well, maybe layin' the fact that you're gay on him and your lover is a guy his age… I mean, I think you're gonna have a hard enough time explaining Steve to him… So have you figured that one out?"

"Well, I was thinking about that. You know, we haven't really decided what to do about me going to L.A. But I've always been waiting for the perfect moment to explain stuff and I've decided that I'm not going to do that anymore. I'm just going to say, "Hey, this is where I am right now in my life. It's not all neat and tidy with a bow on it, but it's me.""

"Hmmm, that's impressive. Maybe you finally figured out which end is up… Anyway, try to get some sleep, OK?"

EVENT HORIZON

"We land in Charlotte at eleven. The commuter flight to Wilmington gets in at one. Beverly says she got us an upgraded car. We should be at the beach by two."

"Are you nervous?" Steve interrupted Dan's recitation of their itinerary with the question they had both been avoiding.

Dan looked back like he was peering cautiously from behind a wall. "Yeah, I am... Aren't you?"

Steve laughed and shook his head slightly. "You really *are* incredible. Do you *always* have to deflect a question away from yourself?" Then he nodded. "But, just for the record, I'm nervous too. So that makes us a pair."

The waiter came to refill their coffee cups at the small cafe table perched on the corner of Ninth Street and Avenue B. Steve turned his cup over. "No thanks. I'm wired enough."

They had pulled two chairs so close to the corner of the table that their knees were touching. Their elbows were on the table. They were leaning forward, holding hands, looking into each other's eyes. With the breakfast plates cleared away, there was nothing to distract them except the parade of New Yorkers hurrying along to their morning appointments. What can you say when it seems like there is nothing more to say? They took turns looking around and then back at each other.

Without letting go of Dan's hand, Steve checked his watch. "The car should be here by now. I arranged for Marty to get picked up at seven." He noticed in the pulse on Dan's skin that his heart was racing. "Hey, are you sure you want to go through with this now?"

"Huh?" Dan's voice trailed off as his eyes fixed on a young man, a little older than him, dressed in A&F gear, standing on the corner, like he was looking for something, a bus, a friend. Dan leaned over and whispered, "Don't look right away, but on the corner, there's this guy who is totally checking you out."

Steve frowned.

"Seriously," Dan continued. "He's totally staring at you."

With a slight turn of his head, Steve caught the gaze of his admirer, like more than a few he had seen before. He looked back at Dan and sighed. "OK, we'll pretend not to notice that you ignored my question. Yeah, he's very cute. So what?"

"He looks like your type. Could you do him? I mean, it would just be sex, right?" It was a taunt, a gratuitous hurt that came from a place where fear lived deep inside him. Dan had no idea how hard he was trying not to think about where they were headed for the weekend.

Steve looked back across the table, but not from behind any wall. He was still holding Dan's hand, holding something fragile, something intensely beautiful. He answered as if he had stepped from a dark wood into a meadow to discover a perfect flower. "Yeah, maybe I could do him, but he would be a snack… I've lost my taste for snacks… I love you, Dan… You are my life." He had the contented look of someone who had made a suddenly peaceful discovery. "You are my life."

Dan heard the words and knew what understanding sounds like when it is spoken. He knew the "one song" the universe makes when, in an instant, a soul breaks free of doubt and longing. "*You are my life… You are my life…*" He heard the echo in his head. He blinked to clear a single tear from his eye and to see in the smile of the man in front of him, the fulfillment of his dream. "You are my heart," he answered.

Steve nodded his head slightly and smiled, as if to acknowledge the song. "You are my soul."

A gentle fall breeze lifted the tablecloth slightly. Dan slid the glass of water to hold down the tablecloth without taking his eyes off Steve. "You are my breath."

"You are my life," Steve said as he leaned forward to kiss Dan. Their lips touched. They had to rest their foreheads against each other when they closed their eyes to keep from falling over. When they opened their eyes, their faces were only a few inches apart. "I've quit my job, Dan. I sold my apartment yesterday. I'm coming to L.A. with you."

"What? You quit your job?" Dan was beginning to realize what was happening.

"I guess I figured I would tell you after we left the beach, that you had enough to worry about, but... I don't know why. It just came out. I love you, Dan. I was sure I would never feel this way about anyone. The truth is, I lived my whole life and I had no idea what love is until now."

Dan reached his hand behind Steve's shoulder and drew their foreheads together again. "You are my dream."

"HEY! HEY! Guys, enough with makin' out! We gotta go or we're gonna miss the flight!" Marty's voice boomed from the sedan car pulling up at the sidewalk. He was leaning out the window and waving his hand as he shouted, "C'mon, let's go!"

◣ ◣ ◣

They flipped coins for the seating arrangements. Steve wound up in the middle seat. Marty got the aisle. Dan sat looking out the window. It was only a two-hour flight from New York to Charlotte. There was a look of approval mixed with a touch of jealousy as the flight attendant served them drinks and noticed Steve holding Dan's hand.

There was nothing in Steve's experience to compare to what Dan was about to do. "It wasn't at all like this for me," he said as they were leaving. "I was a little nervous, but my parents and I had a different relationship. Anyway that really doesn't matter. I'm here for you, whatever you need." He looked at Dan staring out at the sky and the ocean. "Hey, are you OK?"

"Yeah, I'm fine." He forced a smile and then looked back out the window. His father had been right about Michael. *"I can't believe I ever loved him."* He played out the scene in his head. *"Dad, I'm so sorry. I was such a fool. And oh, by the way, I'm gay and my lover is a guy you knew in college."* But the discord faded, as he heard, over and over again, the echo of their song,

"*You are my life.*" He knew he could get through anything. There was a place on the shore along the road to his house where he had chosen to tell Steve his name, his story, and everything else that had been unspoken between them. He felt at peace, as if nothing was impossible. He felt brave, even brave enough to face his family. Whatever the result of the next twenty-four hours, he would leave them all and begin his life with the man who had transformed his dream to reality. "*You are my dream.*" He heard their song again. With his seat reclined and his head on Steve's shoulder, he closed his eyes and wondered how even heaven could possibly be better.

◼ ◼ ◼

The room had the mood of a wake. Thirteen directors gathered in the boardroom of the North Carolina Bank & Trust Company. The meeting was a formality, the outcome a *fait accompli*. All of the outside directors had been briefed the night before in off-line conversations. And now, at the appointed hour for the service, the lawyers from Carter, Squire & Monroe were like skillfully caring and yet professionally detached undertakers.

Blake sat at the head of the table with Jack, an observer at his own funeral, on his right. Carl Herrington was on the opposite side of the table next to D'Arcy Commerford and Pamela Briggs. The "gang of three" could hardly restrain their glee at the outcome of their efforts. In the takeover on which they were about to vote, the sisters would be cashed out of their beneficial interests in the Trust in an amount that Herrington had calculated to be in excess of three hundred million dollars each. As for Herrington, his stock and options would be worth a mere five million, but his revenge on Blake and Jack was more than enough to make up for a decade of stored hatred.

Blake began, his voice low, but resolute. "We're all here so I'll begin." He turned to Henry Bradford, the CS&M partner.

"You are here today," Bradford's intonation sounded like the "dearly beloved" speech, "to vote on the proposed cash purchase of all the capital stock of North Carolina Bank & Trust Company by the New York Trust Company. I am here to advise the board of its obligations under Delaware law and also to act as the secretary of the meeting. Before we officially begin the meeting, I would just like to remind you that this has been a very heavily litigated corporate action. There may yet be further shareholder actions, so as a policy, we generally advise directors to refrain from taking notes or making statements during the meeting that might later be used in the discovery phase of a lawsuit."

"Well then, I want to say something right here." Elliot Packard's voice came from the other end of the table. "I was never in favor of this goddamned idea to take over a New York bank and neither was most of the board. We got talked into it and now we're the scourge of the entire city."

"Elliot," Blake interrupted.

"Blake!" Elliot shot back, "you're either gonna hear what I have to say now or you're gonna hear it on the record. Me and the rest of the board got sold a bill of goods by your hotshot son-in-law on this deal. I said I was opposed to it then and now look at what we've got. Blake, they're gonna lay off five thousand people, five thousand, in this town that we all live in, for Christ's sake. I just want to know if Mr. Big Shot here," Elliot raised his hand and pointed to the end of the table at Jack, "has anything to say for himself now that we're taking a hundred years of sacred tradition and selling it for forty pieces of silver."

Heads turned as if on pivots from one end of the table and followed the pointed finger to where Jack was sitting.

Jack's eyes took in the whole room. He saw Fred Bonham staring blankly ahead. He turned to Blake: there was no reproach, but there was no comfort. In that Jack understood that he was a beaten man, totally alone. He turned back to the directors and cleared his throat, but still when he spoke he began hoarsely. "No." He cleared his throat again. "I don't have anything to say." Then he looked down and folded his hands on his lap.

It was all over in less than an hour. As expected, the board voted to accept the New York Trust offer and when they were done voting, they left without saying a word to the man who had made them all rich. The final price tag on NCBT was $6.8 billion—a windfall for the shareholders, but a humiliating defeat for Jack O'Brien.

Blake sat in silence and then spoke as if with an afterthought. "I'm afraid there's one more bit of business we have to conduct. We have to call Carlton Moore."

Moore received the call graciously but added to Jack's humiliation when he asked him to consider staying on in some capacity with the combined bank. Jack couldn't tell if it was a gesture that Moore knew he would decline or if he was delusional enough to think that Jack might agree to be part of the eradication of the company he had built—the defeated general watching the slaughter of his own troops. "Carlton, I appreciate the offer, but no, I have some family business to attend to. I'll be resigning as soon as the purchase takes effect."

Blake looked across the desk and was struck by the irony of it all. "When I handed you the keys to this place, my family's interest in the bank was worth six million dollars. Now, even after the payout to my sisters, it's over hundred times that." Blake nodded his head. "Almost a billion dollars. And yet you come out the devil. All of the men who said you had betrayed them today walked out of here richer than their wildest dreams. I'm reminded of the T. S. Eliot line my daughter used to quote to me when she was in college: 'Neither fear nor courage saves us. Unspeakable acts are fathered by our heroisms; virtues are forced upon us by our impudent crimes.'"

Jack's skin was the color of ash. He was forty-six years old but could have been taken for a man at least a decade older. He spoke with total resignation. "Well, we know what unspeakable acts happened here. I guess I'm about to find out what virtues are going to be forced on me, eh? I'm on my way to meet my son's lover. I guess that's what they call a girlfriend these days."

"Try to get some rest, Jack. I know this has been awful for you. You look like I did when I came back in '45. Remember, that was real war. This was just about money, no matter what anyone says. And Charlotte's not going to dry up and blow away because this bank got bought."

Jack walked across the office and looked out at the view from the forty-ninth floor of the Reynolds Tower. He once surveyed the scene like it was his domain. Now he contemplated living in exile. "I'm going to take some time off, Blake. I think I'm gonna go up to New York and spend time with my son." He walked back to Blake's desk. "I'll try to, you know what they say, hang out with him for a while, get to know him. Maybe Carolyn and I can get a bigger place up there. I can work on him and her, two things at once, maybe three. I'll get my batteries recharged." Jack bit down on his lower lip, something to distract him from a realization. "You know I was just waiting for this deal to be over and then I was going to do all that stuff anyway. Now I don't have anything to keep me waiting." He tried to smile at the irony of it all, then the thought of what had happened that morning washed over him. He looked down and shook his head. "This bank was my life. I feel like shit. It'll do me good to see my family again."

◼ ◼ ◼

The captain's voice came over the intercom in the small turbo prop plane. "Sorry for the bumpy ride, folks. I'm afraid it's gonna get a lot worse as we get toward Wilmington. There's a pretty severe storm coming up from the South so please keep your seat belts fastened low and tight. We'll have you on the ground in about forty-five minutes."

Dan and at Steve exchanged unconvincing "Don't worry, we'll be fine" looks at each other. Marty had been quiet since they left New York. He sensed, he knew, they were heading into something that would be much worse than an atmospheric disturbance.

"Why don't you tell him before we leave."
"I want to tell him at the beach."

"What, so it's too late for him to run away?"

◪ ◪ ◪

The car was buffeted by high winds as they sped along the state highway. Dan occasionally pointed out landmarks to Steve, who feigned the interest of a first-time tourist. The radio reported that the storm would intensify throughout the afternoon.

"Shit, I hope the rain holds off or we'll have to talk at the diner in town." Dan saw the thick heavy-looking clouds rolling in as he was driving, racing to where he would reveal his past to his intended future.

Steve alternated between staring out the window at the approaching front, pondering his hollow victory over Jack O'Brien, and looking over at Dan, wishing there was something he could do to take away the pain.

Marty observed the silence of the driver and his passenger from the back seat as he changed CDs on his Discman. *"This is so fucked up. I can't believe I agreed to do this gig."*

The cell phone rang in Steve's pocket. He checked the caller ID. It was Josh. "Hey, I was expecting your call. How'd it go?... What's that?... Josh, you're breaking up... I can't hear you." The call came in again with the same results. "Dan, is there a place where we could pull over for just a minute? Maybe I can get a better signal out of the car."

Dan was staring straight ahead, gripping the steering wheel. "Sure, there's a vista just up ahead at that rise. I was gonna stop there anyway."

From the promontory where Dan pulled over, they could see for miles up and down the shore. There were already huge waves crashing on the empty beach.

Steve was dialing as they walked. As his call was going through, they stopped and sat on a picnic table. Steve pressed the receiver to his ear and turned his back to the wind as he shouted into the mic. "That's great, Josh... Yeah, it's a total win.

You called it perfectly as usual…. Listen, I'm standing outside in a hurricane, so I'll call you later, OK?… Yeah, congratulations to you too." He turned to Dan as he put the phone in his pocket.

Dan swallowed hard. "There's something I want to talk to you about." He pointed to a shelter at the edge of the vista. "Let's go sit up there."

It was a lookout, painted plywood on three sides, with a shingled roof on top. They sat inside on a bench, out of the wind, and took in the view of the waves, rolling up and then crashing—relentless, stored energy released as destructive force.

Steve had his elbows on his knees, his hands clasped together. "Wow, look at that. I hope your parents' house is ready for this." He looked down at his feet.

"What's wrong?" Dan asked. It was such a habit for him to deflect his own pain, that he wasn't even aware of it.

Steve lifted his hands to his head, ran his fingers through his hair, and exhaled as if he were preparing for an enormous relief of pressure. "Dan, you know how we always say, 'No lies in this bed.' Well, we said some secrets were OK, right? I always told you that it was OK for your name to be a secret and that I had a few secrets too. I mean, some of them were about my work, like I couldn't talk about confidential stuff." Steve's hands were still clasped together but now his elbows were pressed against his stomach. "I've had a personal secret too. It was related to the takeover project so it became confidential, but now the work part of the secret is over. Dan, the man who I told you about, the one I loved in college, he was the president of the bank my client has taken over. His name is Jack O'Brien. I'm just sitting here realizing what all this means. I'm sorry to be bringing this up when you have such a big event with your family."

It was a small lookout. If the winds had been any stronger, if the nails holding everything together had been fewer, it might have already blown over. It was the coincidence of the measured force of nature and man's design that kept them sheltered from the storm. But the look of horror on Dan's face evidenced total devastation.

Dan was rocking back and forth as if he was comforting himself, yet he was unaware of the movement. "My name is Dan O'Brien. He's my father, Steve… Jack O'Brien is my father. And he's coming here today to meet you."

Even between the closest human beings, infinite distance continues to exist. In love's embrace, in the sharing of touch and taste and breath, there is a purposeful forgetting of that truth. In an instant, in a single revelation, Dan and Steve, sitting so close their bodies were touching, awoke to see the vast space between them. Time in the present was frozen as they each raced back to reassemble the past in broken sentences and anguish. Steve had his arm around Dan who was doubled over in pain, rocking back and forth, sobbing.

"My mother just said that you knew my dad, that you guys had a fight in college, and that she hadn't seen you in twenty years. I only called you because I was desperate for work."

It was as if the bindings had been torn from the books of their lives and all the pages were scattered on the beach. They were wandering in shock, picking up shreds and fragments. *"How far back does this go? Where does this fit?"*

"Oh my God. Oh my God," Dan moaned. A few hours ago he had been soaring. Now he was falling, shot from the sky and hoping that there might be some relief when he hit the ground. "Steve, what are we going to do? I can't believe this is happening. What are we going to do?" Then a fragment, a realization, floated by as if blown in by the wind. "My father was gay. I mean… you were lovers. Julie says he knew how I felt about Michael. He made me feel so bad. Oh my God, what am I going to say to him?"

They were perched on the edge of the bench, holding each other. There was no order to Dan's outbursts. "Marty was right. I should have told you before we left New York. He said I was telling you here so it would be too late for you to run away." Dan looked across at Steve. "Are you going to run away?"

In the moment of groundlessness, Steve found his balance in the awareness of someone whom he loved and who needed his love. "Hey, you are my life. Remember? I'm not going to run away, but look, there's something really basic we have to decide here. We have to decide what to do about today. This is not the meeting you were planning."

"I don't want to tell them alone."

"Then I'll stay here with you."

"But I don't want to tell them today."

"Dan, this won't be easier tomorrow or the next day."

"Oh, God. I know you're right. But I feel like I just want to get it over with and get the hell out of here."

"Well, you decide about the timing. If you want to go through with this now, I'll be here with you. But you don't have to worry about getting the hell out of here. There's no way we'll be sleeping in your father's house tonight."

They ran back to the car through the light rain and sat in the front seat, each turned around to deliver the story to Marty. "Unfuckingbelieveable," was the first and the second thing he said, "Unfuckingbelieveable. And now we're gonna go do *what*?"

◪ ◪ ◪

The town was a bustling village in the summer season. But on the weekend after Labor Day, in the middle of a storm, it was practically deserted. Dan went into the pharmacy to get some antihistamine for his sinuses. Steve went into the general store to see if there were any more reports about the storm.

Carolyn was driving the car the way she had for been driving for twenty years, in apparent control of a motor vehicle but unnaturally cautious of bumping into something with it. She was "at two" with all things mechanical. She was nervous. It took her a few tries to pull into the parking space, so Julie got a second look at the black guy sitting in the back seat of the car to their right. He looked strangely out of place and that was what drew her attention and her interest.

"I'm just going to get the candles and some fuel for the hurricane lanterns." She looked at herself for a second in the rearview mirror and spoke as if she had just noticed something. "Isn't it strange that I don't think to buy emergency stuff until a storm is coming. Can you think of anything else we need?"

Julie was looking to her right at Marty, who was lost in the music of his Discman. "No, I'm just gonna go check out the pharmacy. I'll meet you back here in a few minutes."

They were within a few feet of each other and yet totally unaware of each other's presence. Dan was in the back of the pharmacy waiting for his prescription to be filled. Julie was in the front checking out the nail polish colors.

Carolyn walked purposefully into the general store and practically right into Steve. She had the exaggerated comic book look of someone who has been completely preoccupied and suddenly has her attention shifted to someone she has not seen but been thinking about for more than twenty-five years. Steve had been preparing himself to meet her, but his mind had been on what he was going to say at the house later, not now in an aisle of the store.

"Steven… Steven Baldwin?" She was stunned and trying to regain her composure.

"Hello, Carolyn." Steve extended his hand. It gave her something to hold on to.

Not letting go of Steve's hand, Carolyn began to steady herself by filling the awkward silence with small talk. "Oh, it's so great to see you. Has it really been twenty-five years? I suppose you've heard we're expecting a storm." Finally, there was nothing left to do or say except to ask the one question that she instinctively feared and Steve desperately wished he didn't have to answer. "What brings you to Cape Fear?"

He was locked in a look that transported him back in time. He realized it had been her at the dinner in Charlotte. His heart was racing. His mouth was dry. He understood the devastation of the only answer he could give. "I've come here with Dan."

Carolyn turned her head slightly, as if struck by a blow. "My son?" she asked hoarsely.

There was no turning back. Steve was still holding her hand. "Yes."

"The number, of course, I gave Dan the number," Carolyn remembered. But the "of course" didn't quite take her any-where. Her arm was stiff. She noticed her legs were beginning to feel weak. *"Oh, his roommate."* She was trying to assemble it all in her mind. *"This is so strange. Why wouldn't Dan have said they were living together?"* She swallowed the lump in her throat. "We've been expecting to meet Dan's roommate… and his lover… Isn't it amazing after all these years to meet you like this?"

Steve eyes were riveted on Carolyn. "I'm not Dan's room-mate."

She blinked several times. Her head was spinning.

"Carolyn, there's a bench over here." Steve was already guiding her back to the bench near the window. "You should sit down for a moment." She sat down and he sat down next to her. He still had her hand. "I only found out a few minutes ago. We have lot to talk about."

In the pharmacy next door, Julie was trying to time her mother's errand, absentmindedly browsing at the cosmetics counter. The clerk, one of her summer friends, came behind the counter and asked if she could help with anything.

"No, I'm just waiting for my mother. She said she just need-ed candles, but she's always finding more stuff to get whenever she goes shopping. Oh, guess what, my brother's coming home to introduce his lover to us. I think he might be gay."

The clerk looked back with astonishment. "Oh my God. I can't believe it."

"Julie!" Dan shouted from across the store.

Julie wheeled around. "Dan! Hey, it's really you." They hugged and she kissed him. "This is so cool. I'm so happy for you. So where is he? Where's the lover boy?"

The embarrassment was involuntary. His face was red. But then he just let it out, momentarily forgetting the enormity of what he was about to unleash on his parents. "He's in the gener-al store."

"Oh," Julie replied matter-of-factly, "Mom's over there to get some candles. Have you heard about the big storm coming?

Wouldn't it be a riot if they bumped into each other and they don't even realize who each other is... Dan? Hey, where are you going?"

Dan burst through the front door of the pharmacy, almost hard enough to shatter the glass, and around the corner as if he could prevent the happening of what he had come so far to do himself.

He found his mother in a state of shock, with Steve sitting next to her, still holding her hand. He stopped short as he approached them. The looks told him that the news was not going to be delivered as he had planned.

Carolyn stood up and Steve with her. "Hello, Dan." She was taking shallow breaths. "I was just talking to Steve. He told me—"

"Mom," Dan interrupted. His chest was heaving from having sprinted around the corner and realizing that the moment had finally arrived. "It's not his fault. I mean it's not anybody's fault. Um... He didn't know. I didn't know. I mean we just found out a few minutes ago." He was searching her face, looking for some sign of reassurance.

With her right hand holding Steve's, she reached with her left and touched Dan's shoulder. "I think we've all had quite a shock. I think we should go home. We can talk there in private."

She didn't say a word on the drive home. She had her arms extended as she drove, both hands on the top of the steering wheel, looking ahead as if it was too frightening to look around.

"Mom, this is incredible! This is totally incredible... Mom, why won't you answer me?"

"Julie, you sound as if the more shocking things are, the better. You haven't asked me a question and to tell you the truth I don't think I could answer anything right now. We need to get home and decide what to do."

◧ ◧ ◧

They were in the kitchen, just the two of them. Everyone else had retreated to their rooms to deal with the shock. There was at least some purpose in preparing a meal and they recognized quickly in each other the disposition to speak openly about what they saw going on.

"Dan said you were really cool. It must have been amazing to realize that some of this was going to happen."

Marty was layering the lasagna noodles into a pan. He shook his head. "Babe, I knew it was gonna be a mess, but I had no freakin' idea it was gonna be this bad. I mean, you couldn't make this shit up if you tried."

Julie laughed. "Steve is really cute. I can't wait until my father gets here."

Marty finished pouring the sauce and put the lasagna in the oven. "Yeah, well, there's no way out so I guess I'm gonna stay for the fireworks, but then I'm makin' tracks home… OK, this needs forty-five minutes."

"C'mon," Julie said, "we can go up to my room for a while, and can give everyone else a chance to talk about the mess."

◩ ◩ ◩

Steve helped Carolyn light a fire in her study. She watched the movements of his arms, noticed the details of his hands, the curve of his back as he bent over the hearth. She watched him, imagining all the points in a connect-the-dots picture that had begun when they were children and been interrupted before they could have imagined the enormity of the intervening years. She gave him a tour of her life since college in the pictures on the mantel and on the wall. He followed her from frame to frame as they had once followed each other. She touched his shoulder as she handed him a picture of him and Jack receiving gold medals at the NCAAs.

He smiled sadly as he handed it back to her. "Shall we sit

down?"

"My friend, Carla, the one I showed you over there," Carolyn gestured to the picture on her desk, "she used to insist that everyone knows everything, that the truth is always there right in front of us. It's just that we decide what we're going to pay attention to." She looked across the couch at him, across time as if there had been no time. He had been her first love. She felt the ache as if it had been there all along. "I guess that means I knew. I knew about Jack."

"Are you sure?" Steve asked. "I mean, it's one thing to say you knew about me and Jack, but if you're saying Jack was gay, I don't know for sure if he was. It's not always so cut and dried, Carolyn. Not everyone is only gay or straight or one way or the other through their entire life."

"I knew," she said in her own private reproach without explaining or responding to Steve's point. "It was probably obvious to everyone but me."

Steve leaned forward and put his hand on Carolyn's knee. "Sometimes we take an argument to the extreme to show it doesn't always work."

She stared back at him.

"Carolyn, if everyone knows everything, and it's just denial that screens out what we can't or don't want to handle, then I knew Dan was your and Jack's son."

No response.

"And you knew I was gay when you gave Dan my number. You knew he was gay."

The silence was broken by a voice at the bottom of the stairs, "Mom… Steve…" They looked at each other for an instant long enough to know that, at the very least, they knew so much more than they would ever wish to admit.

"Dinner is ready," Dan said as he entered the study. "How are you guys doing?"

◤ ◤ ◤

To calculate literally means to count, to take into account all the factors in a situation or the events in a time line or to count precisely all the numbers in an equation. A correct calculation is admired, but to be calculating is a pejorative description. Carolyn had always been described as the opposite of calculating. She had missed so much. Whether by the bliss of innocence or the power of denial, she had largely seen what she wanted to see. Now she was struggling with her eyes wide open. She had asked for some time by herself to call Jack. She promised to join the assembly for dinner in a few minutes. "I want to call him before he leaves and suggest that he come in the morning."

There was just too much to see, too many events rushing back with sudden import. To make even the basic calculation, to figure out how to survive, she had to decide, she had to make a conscious decision what to cut off and what little she could focus on. She calculated briefly. Then she decided and picked up the phone on her desk.

◪ ◪ ◪

There was a place set at the head of the table for Carolyn. When she joined them, she made the third point in a triangle with Dan on her left and Steve on her right. Marty and Julie sat across from each other, next to Steve and Dan.

She began speaking even as she was getting adjusted in her seat and looking down to place the napkin in her lap. "Well, I have some news. I talked to your father…" She reported the news, belying none of her anxiety until she had to answer questions. "Yes, Julie, I told him Dan did not bring his girlfriend, but no we didn't get into the particulars. He insisted on flying out here tonight. He says the storm is now supposed to be mostly heavy rains and a surge tide."

Dan could imagine the force of the impact of his father's arrival. And yet it seemed as if the explosion had already taken place many years ago and he was getting a view of the rubble on the other side of a very long time line. He felt himself perched on the edge of a black hole, peering into dark unfathomable space. A black hole forms after a very massive star explodes and gravity crushes its remains out of existence. Because the gravity of the black hole is so strong, it has a boundary beyond which matter falling onto the hole can never escape. This boundary is called its "event horizon," which—compared to the enormous distances in space—is tiny.

Steve and Carolyn were practiced at making polite conversation when they were uncomfortable. With some success, they filled the silent gaps by directing questions to Marty and Julie. Dan was listening to the way Steve and his mother talked to each other, the way they looked at each other. They had been friends since childhood, but they hadn't spoken for as long as he had been alive. So much of their conversation was about past events. In a few hours his father would be there. And time would flow backward again into the past. He was just beginning to see the enormity of what had been drawn into a darkness, a blind spot in his universe that had been obscured by his vision, his dream. He looked at Steve. The past, for both of them, had been, by mutual consent, unexamined. It was as if a veil had been lifted, a veil that once covered everything but his enjoyment of the present and his expectations of the future. He thought of gravity, of his father's impending arrival and the velocity of an object as it approaches the event horizon. He peered into the black hole and wondered how he would keep from being pulled inside.

◼ ◼ ◼

They had made a simple dessert of ice cream and coffee. The ice cream sat mostly uneaten. The candles dripped wax on the tablecloth. They had managed so far not to talk about the arrival they were dreading. It was ten o'clock.

"Carolyn, I hope you understand we'll be leaving after Jack arrives. There may be some time when we'll all want to plan to be together, but I'm sure it's not a good idea for us to stay tonight. I hope you'll be OK," he added with an air of expectant but anxious hope.

She looked to her right at Steve as he was talking, but then to her left at Dan and Julie when she replied. She was ready to say what she had been thinking about since the dinner began. "There's no need to worry about me… I'll be leaving too."

Dan expressed the shock of someone who was witnessing an escape from the most intense gravity. He lowered his head and swallowed. "Mom?"

She looked right back at him. "We all have our own lives to lead." Without looking away, she folded her napkin, placed it carefully on the table, and stood up. "I'll call the flight center and find out what time your father is expected."

There was only the sound of the rain on the skylights when she left the room. Dan looked to his left at Julie and then at Steve. The candles flickered when he exhaled through his pursed lips. "I guess we really shook things up."

"Oh, Dan." Julie was reaching for the silverware across the table. "This isn't *all* about you. Mom's got her own stuff to deal with."

Marty got up and began helping Julie clear the plates into the kitchen. Dan and Steve were left staring at each other.

"We did shake things up," Steve said, "but not just for your family. "We won't leave the same way we came here… We can't."

Before Dan could respond, Carolyn appeared and took her seat at the table with a look of relief. "I just spoke to the flight center. Jack went there, but he couldn't convince them to take off. So, he's coming in the morning."

◪ ◪ ◪

She had them all settled. It was the hardest when it came to Dan and Steve, but she managed it. "Dan, there are fresh sheets on your bed. You'll need to get towels for you and Steve in the linen closet." She kissed them good night and watched them close the door.

There were a few things she wanted to take to Chatsworth, some pictures on her desk, a few books. Her bags were packed and in the car when she sat down in front of the fire in the great room. The wind rattled the storm shutters over the big windows on the ground floor. The rain on the shutters made a metallic rapid-fire sound like tiny marbles being poured into a tin can. She watched the fire and thought about her life. There was a lot to think about. She had just turned forty-six. It didn't seem old, but it felt like a long time. She was intently watching the dance of the flames, letting random thoughts dance across her consciousness. If a fire is made up of many individual flames, where do the flames go when the fire goes out?

◤ ◤ ◤

Will—the power and force of will—is attributed mostly to sentient beings. But sometimes things are described as if they have intention. Storms turn viciously. Heat waves punish relentlessly. But these are phenomena in discrete events in time. Some inanimate things are constant in their will. Water has will. It wants to be everywhere. It wants to get "in" everywhere. It flows on and even through the earth. It rises in towering clouds. It settles in dark fetid pools. It wants to be everywhere. Man contends with water's will by building dams or draining swamps. He builds channels and walls and pumps and seals, but water wants be in everything. Water wants to be everywhere.

In the sealed enclosure of the car, Jack was speeding east as the wind drove the water west in horizontal sheets. The sound of the wipers on the windshield, the steady beat, was like the sound of his heart beating in his ears. He was alone in the car. He was totally alone.

"Jack, I think you should come in the morning."

Exhausted, he could barely keep his focus on the road.

"Yes, you heard me correctly. His lover is a man. And, please, let's spare each other the shocked response... No, I don't want to discuss it now. I have some other things I want to talk to you about, but I think we should all get a fresh start in the morning."

He was staring ahead into the darkness, barely able to see the road in front of him, even at thirty-five miles an hour. As the car reached the exit on 74 to go back to the house, his arms were frozen in place. *"Oh my God. What am I gonna do?"* He couldn't go to the empty house in Charlotte. He couldn't spend the night alone. It was eight o'clock. He checked his speed, figured time for delays, calculated that he could be at the beach by midnight. *"I've got to get home."* By sheer force of will, he drove east into the storm.

◼ ◼ ◼

He could not sleep so he lay on his back and listened to the storm, the wind and the rain beating on the windows. It was as his life was being washed away. With each successive conversation since their world was exploded that afternoon, Steve had noticed Dan withdrawing. Nothing specific was said about what this would all mean. They had hardly said a word when they got into bed. When they kissed good night and Steve heard the words "I love you," it sounded like they had come from a place far away. There was no time now, everything was happening so fast, and he wondered how or if time could ever make a difference. Dan had become part of all the elements in his life. Just by being there, he made the walls stand up. He had even become the air that Steve breathed, so unnoticed and yet so elementary, so necessary. And now, all form was falling down. All the elements were dissolving in the rain. He was looking for some shelter from the storm that was raging inside.

The rain, flowing in sheets on the windows, lit from below by the lights outside the house, made irregular chaotic patterns on the ceiling. He lay still in the bed, taking hold of his breath, noticing the rise and fall of his chest. *"You are my life."* He heard himself repeating those words. He had finally let go and let himself believe in the dream. Then it came over him, in a sudden and yet profound understanding. This was a dream that had come back to him, like a nightmare. Time is supposed to flow from the past into the present and the future. But now the river was flowing backward, drawing him into a vortex. He felt himself drowning in memories. *"You are my life."* He had said those words once before. He lay on his side and propped his head up with the pillow. There was only a patch of skin on Dan's shoulder that was not covered by the blanket.

"Are you awake?" The question came from the body turned away from him.

"Yeah," Steve said as he reached over to touch Dan's shoulder.

Dan turned to lie on his back and adjusted himself to lie close to Steve; their faces were almost touching. "I can't sleep either. What are you thinking?"

Steve placed his hand lightly on Dan's chest and felt his heart beating. "I'm realizing this is the first time we've been alone since this morning. There's so much to say and we're being really quiet. To tell you the truth, I'm really wondering what *you're* thinking. I try hard not to ask you that question. I'm afraid to ask, but now I really want to know."

Dan looked up at the ceiling, as if suspecting that in his eyes there was a way to see into what was on his mind. "I dunno." He took a deep breath and exhaled slowly. "I still don't know what I'm gonna say to my father in the morning." He looked back at Steve. He looked deeply. "I guess I've been thinking a lot of things."

"Like what?" Steve took his hand away from Dan's chest to adjust the sheets, but then he let it lay by his side.

Looking back up at the patterns on the ceiling helped Dan

to find the safety of distance in his reply. "Well, I guess I was wondering about the letter I took to London. The way you explained it at the beach, you asked me to do it so you could keep from ruining my dad. I mean, I know you guys were together a long time ago, before I was born, but, I was wondering... like how you felt about him when you asked me to take that letter. Were you using me to save him because you still loved him?"

"I'm sorry about the letter. Of course I would never have asked you to take it if I had known. But, you know, there are so many things that would have been different if we had known what we know now. But... as for your question, well, yes, I still loved him, but not like a lover, not the way I love you. And it really wasn't until this morning, really, that I understood how much I love you. Try to understand, Dan, that today he's not the man I fell in love with. We were together for almost four years. But that was decades ago. Nothing I can say to you tonight or tomorrow is going to make this all better. I'm in shock. We're *all* in shock. Your mother is holding up incredibly. And you have to deal with your father on your issues and also with him and your mother splitting up. Let's just get up early tomorrow morning, break the news to your father when he gets here, and then go home and deal with getting to L.A."

Dan nodded his head. There was no way they could speak about the flood of thoughts. They were both barely keeping from drowning. "OK, yeah, let's try to get some sleep and we'll talk about stuff when we get out of here tomorrow."

They kissed. Dan turned on his side and lay against Steve, who wrapped his arm over Dan's shoulders.

"I love you, Dan." Steve said it as much for reassurance as to reassure.

"I love you, too, Steve."

Without another word, they lay there until they fell asleep.

SATORI

The clock on the microwave oven read 1:00 am as Jack walked through the kitchen. He put his keys down on the counter and felt the release of tension. He was home, with his family. He walked through the great room and found Carolyn asleep on the couch. She was so beautiful, sleeping peacefully. He didn't want to wake her, but he wanted her to come up to bed with him. He sat down quietly on the couch.

She opened her eyes. "Jack… What are you doing here? What time is it?"

"Hi, sweetheart." He put his hand on her shoulder. "It's one o'clock. Let's go to bed. We can talk in the morning.'

Carolyn began to prop herself up, moving behind him so she could sit up on the couch. She put her face in her hands and rubbed her eyes with her open palms. "How did you get here? I thought the airport was closed."

"I drove. I knew you were upset when we talked. I got here as soon as I could so you wouldn't be alone."

Carolyn turned to look at him, her head still supported in her hands, elbows on her knees. Her hair fell loosely down on her shoulders. She had an overwhelming feeling of being maneuvered into position and an intense reaction to begin instead with her own agenda. She got up and moved to the chair at the end of the couch, looking directly across at Jack.

"What's wrong?" he asked.

She was staring at him intently, trying to think of what she should do or say now, but not calculating. She was ready to say whatever was on her mind. There was so much on her mind. "I know about Carla." It just came out. Not loudly, it didn't even sound like an accusation. It came out like she was matter-of-factly validating in speech something that she had kept for so long a secret.

"What?" He had been driving for five hours, exhausted when he started out and now too tired to be shocked at the apparent incongruity of her statement. "Honey, what are you talking about?"

"I know."

He was squinting, wincing like an old injury had just recurred, when he looked back at her. "What do you want me to say?"

"I'm not sure really... I just wanted to let you know that I know about it."

Jack leaned forward, his hands clasped together. "Sweetheart, that was twenty years ago. I was sorry but I couldn't undo it. What did you want me to do? I mean..." He was struggling, not just to find some sense in this topic at this time, but also to put a lid on it, to put it back in the deeply buried past. "What could I have said? Once it was over, I was so embarrassed. Carla seemed OK with putting it behind us. Then you and she became such close friends. I didn't want to say anything that would ruin your relationship with her."

"Do you mean to tell me that you let me go on being friends with a woman who had sex with my husband? You lied to me so it wouldn't upset me?" Carolyn considered the possibility of driving to Chatsworth that evening. She realized how much she wanted to be out of there. There was a scream building up inside of her.

"Well, I wouldn't put it like that—"

She cut him off. "No, I don't suppose you would put it like that." She had had enough, but he broke in again.

"How did you know?"

"Carla told me herself. Actually she told me about a year after it happened." Carolyn was ready to move on to the next subject. "I know about you and Steven Baldwin. I know that—"

Again he interrupted, "Carolyn, what is this all about?" He was reeling, knocked down, and he was pleading with her for a chance to get his balance.

She was busy taking in possibilities that were unthinkable only a few hours ago. "Did you marry me because you felt sorry for me?"

"Oh my God, please tell me what the hell is going on. I married you because I loved you." He saw only the look of accusation on her face. "Yes, Steve and I were—" He swallowed hard. "We were together... but I made my choice. I would never have done anything differently."

"And you didn't tell me even decades later, when I pressed you to talk to him again. Was that to spare me too?"

"No... No..." Jack was shaking his head. "Carolyn, I love you. Why are you doing this to me?"

"What if I hadn't been pregnant? I was going to London. You were going to Boston with Steven. We wouldn't be married now, would we?"

There was no answer. His head hung from his shoulder, limp. When he finally spoke, he kept his head down. "It was half a lifetime ago. I've never regretted the choice I made. Never." When he looked up, she could see he was crying. "I love you."

"I love you too, Jack. But I've realized that there is so much we've kept from each other. I don't know what it means when you say you love me." Remorse, she was awash in remorse. Old hurts, old wounds, she was experiencing them all over again. She wanted to go and sit next to him, but she was frozen in the chair. There was still more on her agenda.

"I've decided that we need to be separated for a while. I'm not blaming you for what happened. I'm just as responsible as you are. But I'm angry. I'm hurt. I need some time to heal. Maybe there's something left to save our marriage. If there is, we have to rebuild it on being honest with ourselves and with each other."

Jack's body shivered. "What do you mean—*separated?* I married you because I loved you. I made one mistake, which you're ready to crucify me for hiding even though you tell me you've known about it all along..." He was waving his hand slowly to clear the fog in front of his eyes. "Carolyn... Please don't do this to me... Please don't leave me."

"I'm not doing this *to* you. I'm doing this for *me*. I know we're not going to come to a sudden understanding of each other in one conversation. I need some time by myself without you trying to manage the answers for me." She leaned forward, but that was as close as she dared. "Jack, my bags are in the car. I was going to drive to Chatsworth tomorrow morning. But I think I'm going to stay the night at the cottage."

Nothing ever comes out of someone that is not already inside. If we are willing to pay attention, we discover ourselves —we are revealed to ourselves—in the events and circumstances of our lives. It was finally sinking in to him. She was leaving him. He couldn't talk her out of it. He couldn't control what was happening. He began to find something to hold on to in the anger that was welling up inside of him, anger that was there all along in a store of consciousness. The doors to the storeroom had been loosed. He was becoming unhinged.

"Did you just wake up?" he glared at her. "Did you just figure out that life isn't always a pretty picture? And now what are you doing? You're running away. Let's forget for the moment the fact that you're walking out on me. What about Dan? You told me a few hours ago that he's here with his goddamned boyfriend. And he's upstairs." Jack was pointing behind him and then he pointed back at Carolyn. "He's upstairs and what are you doing, huh? You're running out on him."

"Maybe I have just woken up," she glared back. "But you need to wake up, too. Dan isn't a boy anymore. He's twenty-three years old. Did you really think you were going to rush back here and *save* him? You knew he was gay. You could see the way he felt about Michael. But you were so busy trying to keep your own past buried. Well, I have news for you, Jack. He doesn't want your help now. He has all the help he needs and wants from his lover." She took one last look at him before she delivered the blow. It had the taste of revenge as the words left her mouth. "His lover is Steven Baldwin."

Jack shook his head. His face was red. "*What?* That's impossible. How... How could they have even met?"

"I gave Steven's number to Dan when he left here last summer." She sat up in the chair. "I wanted Dan to call him."

"Carolyn, how could you do such a thing?"

She stood up. "How could *I*? How could *I* do such a thing? How could *you* abandon your own son? I *begged* you to help him!" She was screaming at him. Her body was shaking. "Do you remember saying he needed some time on the mean streets? I gave him the number because I wanted him to have someone to turn to." She stopped and noticed that Jack's face was flushed. It made her slow down. "I'm leaving, Jack. I'm leaving you because I can't live like this anymore. I'm leaving because I want to live with the truth, whatever it is. When the truth doesn't fit into your world, you're either strong enough to change it, or strong enough to ignore it. Well, not even you are strong enough to change this truth."

"How could this have happened?"

" Maybe we should wake them up now," she said as she picked up her purse from the table. "You can hear it all for yourself. I'm not staying here tonight with you."

He couldn't accept what he was hearing. His mind was racing. In what was only seconds of silence, he was searching for an explanation. He looked up. "Steve Baldwin hates me, Carolyn. Don't you understand? He hates me for leaving him. He's carried that grudge for twenty-five years. He was the one pushing the buttons on the New York Trust deal. He destroyed what I spent my life building and now you tell me he's fucking my son. You tell me you're leaving and I'm supposed to deal with it. It's you who can't handle it. This isn't neat and tidy. I think I finally get it. You're leaving and you expect me clean up this mess!"

Carolyn was frozen in place. She was staring past him.

"Is that what I am to you—a mess?" Dan's voice, an even mix of anger and sadness, turned Jack around slowly to face his son, and standing behind him, Steve Baldwin.

Dan started slowly and carefully, as if he had rehearsed his speech several times that evening. "For twenty-two years I was the perfect son and now I'm a fucking mess. Is it because I'm gay? No, that can't be it. We all know now how experienced you are on that subject. You just chose not to tell me about that when I needed you so much. So it must be because of what you said earlier. Steve Baldwin is fucking my son. *MY* son! Sounds just like Steve Baldwin smashed *my* car. Steve Baldwin burned down *my* house. I'm not your possession. I was never your possession…" Dan's voice trailed off as he stared across the room at his father.

Steve stepped forward with his hands open. "Jack, there is so much more here than any of us realized this morning. We've had a day to sort through things. You've only had a few minutes. Why don't you sit down and listen to Dan. Listen to what he has to say."

Dan came around in front of the chair where Carolyn had just been. Steve stood behind him. Jack sat down on the couch again. Dan sat down in the chair. They were so intently staring at each other, that none of them noticed that Carolyn had left the room.

"Dad," Dan began. He was gripping the chair. "I left here because I was suffocating. I literally couldn't breathe. I wanted you to understand, and I hated you because you didn't. I took Steve's number because Mom kept trying to give it to me. She only told me he was a lawyer and that you were his best friend in college. She said she had a crush on him in college, but that she hadn't seen him since then because you and he had a fight that she never found out about."

"When I got to New York, things didn't work out for me living with Michael. I was desperate. I changed my name and tried to put a show together with Marty so I could get money to eat. I was hungry, Dad, and I still wouldn't call you for help. What was I going to say, 'I made a mistake, please take me back.' I tried to get something at a firm on my own, but when that didn't work out, I got desparate. That's how low I was at when I called Steve. I just wanted to get a job. After things started happening for us I didn't want to tell him my real name because my life was finally working and I just didn't want to get caught up in whatever it was that you two fought over."

"Steve never told me anything about the bank until this morning. I was sick when I heard it was you, Dad. I was sick. And then I told him my real name and he was blown away. Then we drove into town and Mom was there and she was blown away too. So we've all been sitting around here wondering what we're going to tell you. And now all I can think of to tell you is that I'm not a fucking mess. The only thing messed up in my life right now is you."

Dan stopped for a moment to keep from crying. "Dad… *please…*"

The pain was drawn in the lines on Jack's face. He had become a force of nature, a hurricane searching for landfall, someplace on which to spend his fury. He was staring at Steve. "You're my age, you're old enough to be his father. Wasn't the bank enough? Wasn't that enough revenge? And now what do you expect me to do, just sit here and accept all this? Do you? I know somehow you got to Rothman. I know it. I know you got the stockholder information. I don't know how, but I'm going to find out. You may regret the day I left you, but I swear you'll soon wish you had never met me at all!"

Jack rose to his feet. Dan got up, but Steve was already coming in front of the chair.

Before Steve could respond, Dan broke in. "You haven't heard anything I've said. All you can think of is that stupid fucking bank! I was the one who took the letter to London! Don't you understand? Steve did it so you wouldn't get in trouble. Dad, please! *Please*, listen to me."

Jack's fury finally had its landfall. "I *knew* it! It *was* you!"

Steve kept Dan from stepping forward with his outstretched right arm. When he looked over his shoulder at Dan, he couldn't see Jack's fist make the sudden impact with the left side of his face. He fell backward into Dan's arms.

No one noticed the sound of Julie screaming until Marty had had Jack on the floor.

Jack's shock at being tackled in his own house, by a man he had never seen before, momentarily deflected his rage. His face was pressed to the carpet. "Who the fuck are you?"

Marty's adrenaline was running. "Look, motherfucker, this may be your house, but that is my roommate and that is his man. You ain't makin' no moves on either of them 'less you want to mess with me, and I'm too motherfuckin' bad fo' your old ass to be messin' with. You hear what I'm sayin?"

There was blood coming from Steve's mouth and nose, spilling out onto his face, onto Dan's shirt. He was struggling to upright himself, to regain his balance.

Marty let go of Jack to help Dan with Steve. As soon as Jack was free, he was headed for the kitchen. Now there was only one thing on his mind—to get to the cottage, to find Carolyn. Stopping only to take his keys, he bounded down the stairs on the deck, got in his car, and sped south along the shore road.

Julie had left the great room in search of her mother. When she returned, she was breathless. "Mom's gone. Her car is gone."

There was blood everywhere. It flowed out of Steve's nose and mouth. Julie came from the kitchen with ice wrapped in a towel. He was finally able to sit up. Marty and Dan helped him into the chair.

"Oh my God." Dan was crying. "Steve, I'm so sorry."

Steve was slowly regaining consciousness. There is simplicity in the world of survival, in the riveted attention one gives to basic elements of existence. He was trying to pay attention to his breath. "*Breathe, you're alive*," he told himself. He pressed the ice-filled towel against the side of his face and turned to Dan. "I'm OK. Where's your father?"

"His car is gone," Julie answered. "Mom's car is gone. He must have followed her into town. He had this crazy look on his face as he ran out."

◼ ◼ ◼

Survival, holding on to his family, first he had to find Carolyn. He was reduced to near-blind madness. The road ended at a point where the ocean had broken through the dunes in a hurricane in the fifties, creating a tidal marsh. At the end of the road was the house where Carolyn was headed. It was a short drive and she couldn't go any further from there, yet he was speeding, desperate to overtake her. In the view from flashes of lightning, he was struck by the foolishness of Carolyn's intent to spend the night at the cottage. From the surge tide and the water rising in the marsh, the little house would soon be an island.

Jack turned into the driveway and noticed that his right hand was numb when he put the car in park. He shook the hand, briefly distracted at the thought of hitting Steve Baldwin. He looked in front of him at the dark house. *"She's in there with no goddamned power and no water. At least she had the sense to put the car in the garage."* In the few steps it took to get from the car to the stairs, his white shirt and suit pants were soaked through.

"Carolyn! Carolyn!" He shouted as he banged his fist on the door. "Carolyn!"

He circled the house, trying each window and the door at the front, coming back to the kitchen door, shaking it, accustomed to the expectation that locked doors would yield and let him in. He broke one of the small panes and reached through, finally opening the door.

"Carolyn!" He was shouting madly in the dark house, checking each room as if she might have been hiding from him. Walking back into the large living room at the front of the house, he could see over the dunes to the waves crashing on the shore. The realization finally washed over him. She had gone the other way, into town. When everything else had fallen away, when all his resistance was gone, he finally succumbed to the aching fear that he was totally alone. His knees were weak. He sat down in a chair. He had raced all the way to the end of the road and found no one.

He cried, a casualty in his own battle for control over the ultimately uncontrollable—life. He wailed, with his head in his hands, tearing at his hair, teeth clenched, eyes closed, to emphasize the darkness. He rocked himself, back and forth on the edge of the chair, contracting his body with pain, sometimes letting a scream punctuate the sobbing. But there was a point when he opened his eyes. The pain would return, but in life as in nature, the experience is defined by its contrast. He opened his eyes and put his hands down. For a moment, he was transported back in time, looking around at the little house he had restored and made into a sanctuary. Everything in it had some special meaning to him, the furniture, the mementos, everything told a story of the past where he had shaped a world according to his dream of happiness.

He raised his right hand to wipe the water dripping from his hair into his eyes when he saw the blood. It was a long cut from his wrist almost to his elbow. He hadn't felt it when he had put his hand through the windowpane. He touched his forearm. It was numb. Brought out of his dreaming recollections, he struggled to his feet. There was nothing for him there. He had to get to town. She might be delayed at the bridge. He started calculating how fast he would have to drive to catch her.

He tripped running down the stairs to the car. When he reached out to catch himself, he couldn't get a grip. His hand glanced off the railing and he fell the last few steps into the sand at the bottom of the steps. Finally in the car, he backed slowly along the driveway to the road, which was already covered with a few inches of water. Urged on by how fast the water was rising and how much distance he needed to cover before his car was swamped, he was also aware of the need to take care not to drive off the road, which he could no longer see. He drove by instinct in the space between dunes on his right and the sandy shoulder on the left.

He opened his door to check on the water level, a brief look, because he was having trouble seeing through the windshield. Driving slowly forward, staring at the water rushing under the car, he didn't see that the waves had broken through the dunes just up ahead. Finally looking up and realizing that he was heading into open water, he struggled to put the car in reverse. He gunned the accelerator with the car still in drive and ran straight into a slab of uplifted pavement. He was leaning forward, not wearing his seat belt, when the airbag was triggered. Thrown back against the seat, knocked out by the impact and by his own exhaustion, he slumped forward over the deflated airbag, unconscious.

◼ ◼ ◼

"Slow down!" Steve was holding the ice compress to the side of his face, bracing himself with his other hand every time the car made a sharp turn. "If we go off the road, you can forget about catching up to them."

Dan knew every rise and fall, every bend in the road into town. "It's OK. We'll be there in a few minutes. They would have to go over the bridge. We'll go there first." He glanced in the rearview mirror at Julie, her eyes wide. She was holding on to Marty.

The town was deserted as they sped down Main Street. Dan was straining to look ahead and steer around the debris that had been blown into the road as they drove past the lighted General Store.

"Stop! Stop! It's Mom's car!" Julie screamed as she banged on Dan's seat. "It's parked in front of the store."

The car hydroplaned as Dan hit the brakes and turned the wheel. Sliding sideways and spinning, it was already turned around by the time it came to a stop. Dan floored the accelerator and then hit the brakes as the car screeched to a halt in front of the store. He was pulling on the door handle even as the car was stopping.

"Mom, are you OK?" he was already shouting to her as he came through the door.

Carolyn saw Steve, Julie, and Marty behind Dan. She took Dan's arm. "I'm so sorry. I don't know what came over me. I *had* to get out of the house. I was driving into town before I came to my senses. I was just going to drive back."

"Where's Dad?" Dan's face was undiluted panic. "He went tearing out of the house right behind you."

"I don't know…" Her hand was shaking, making ripples in the coffee cup. "The cottage. He must have thought I was going there."

Now there were two cars speeding along the shore road, the Saab with Steve driving Carolyn, following the tail lights of the rental car with Dan, Marty, and Julie. Dan passed the house at the top of hill and raced downward into the darkness lit dimly by the headlights of his car.

◧ ◧ ◧

Jack was shivering when he woke up. The driver side door was open. He heard the sound of water rushing into the car, the sound of the rain on the windshield. Inside the mostly enclosed space, there was shelter. But for the cold penetrating his body, he had an eerie complacency about staying put and waiting out the storm.

It was an effort to swing his legs out of the car. He wondered how long he had been lying awkwardly as he noticed that his right leg had fallen asleep. He stood up holding on to the roof with his left hand. His right hand was still numb so he draped his right arm over the door. He tried leaning on the right leg, waiting for pins and needles, a sign that he was getting feeling back, but there was no feeling. The best he could do was keep the right leg stiff. Without bending the knee, he could swing it forward from the hip and use it like a cane. *"C'mon, just one foot in front of the other. Just get to the other side and then figure out what to do next."* He was looking across the flow of ocean coming in through the gap in the dunes, over what had been the road and into the marsh.

"You can do this." He stared intently ahead at the open water. His teeth were chattering and he was shivering. *"At least I don't have to get Carolyn across this."* He managed to laugh to himself as he looked down, trying to figure out how deep the water was in front of him.

Limping, dragging the right leg behind on each step, he edged forward. He was having trouble concentrating. It was ten or fifteen feet of slow progress when he put his left leg out and stepped into nothing but the surge tide that had made a channel across the road. The current carried Jack, at first under water, flailing, desperately trying to get some air. Gasping for breath as he broke the surface intermittently, he twirled like a corkscrew several times before finally getting some coordination with one arm and one leg.

Finally, on his back, using his left arm to keep his head above water, it occurred to him that he might drown, but the thought washed away with his intense will to survive. He got his bearings, realizing that the current would still carry him toward the marsh; he made an angled course to get to higher ground.

He was exhausted when his body became limp briefly and went under again. The water in his eyes and nostrils shocked him back into the struggle to live. Then, suddenly, he felt the sandy bottom with his left foot. *"Keep going."* He stayed on his back, until he could feel the sand with his left arm and then he rolled over.

The euphoria of surviving a near death experience came over him. *"I made it!"* He was kneeling in the water, propped up with his left arm. He looked up to get his bearings. His contacts had fallen out. Everything was a blur. He felt drowsy. He noticed he wasn't shivering anymore. In fact, he felt warm, even comfortable. Pushing back on his left arm, bracing himself with his left leg, he managed to get his right leg under him and, in small movements, to stand up. Without being anxious about the depth, he moved forward slowly in water that was gradually getting deeper again.

He felt himself reviving, bathed in a warm feeling that seemed more emotional than the physical heat from exertion. His right arm was still limp, but his right leg felt well enough to walk on. *"I'm gonna be OK. I made it."* He noticed that he couldn't hear the storm anymore. He couldn't hear anything. In the distance he saw a light. It was diffused, he assumed, by the blur of the salt in his eyes. It was gradually growing brighter. *"Everything is going to be OK."* He heard his own voice as if it were coming from outside his body.

The light was coming toward him, growing brighter. He felt

his body completely recovered. He raised his right arm to shield the glare. Looking ahead, he continued to walk toward the light.

◾ ◾ ◾

The scene in front of Dan was like something Noah might have witnessed. The road was a receding strip of land between the dunes and the flooded tidal marsh. "Oh, fuck!" he shouted and banged his open hand on the steering wheel as he got closer. "We're not going to be able to get to the cottage! Look!" He pointed to where the storm surge had risen over the beach and washed away the road.

The roof of the Mercedes appeared like a marker buoy where the road had once been. It was all that there was above water. As they sped to the edge of the flood, Dan's eyes followed the flow pattern from the car toward the marsh. A patch of white, a white shirt on a body, a body floating like a stick in the stream. Dan was already opening the door as he jammed the car to a stop.

The water was only up to his knees when he reached Jack's body, floating face down. Dan was behind Jack with his arms around his chest, dragging him backward, when Marty came and took Jack's feet. They carried him to the edge of the water and laid him down near the car.

◾ ◾ ◾

To the seagulls circling overhead, the different manifestations of sound and water were unimportant. The wail of the wind and the flow of the ocean were indistinguishable from the cries and tears of the assembled circle around Jack's body. The gulls had only come to see what fragments of life the storm had delivered up. Marty stood over Julie. Julie was holding Carolyn. Carolyn was holding Jack's hand. Steve and Dan took turns administering CPR, Dan calling Jack's name as if calling might somehow guide him back across the river.

"Dad! Dad!" Dan was pumping Jack's chest. "Dad!" There was no admonition, just the repeated calling of his name to punctuate the CPR.

It had stopped raining. The storm had spent itself. No one kept track of how long their efforts went on, but they were exhausted and Jack was dead. It was about five in the morning, no sunlight, but the softer color blue of the sky to the east signaled the new day. Dan kneeled over Jack's body, crying. Steve leaned over to embrace Dan. The scene was of five survivors of the storm gathered around its one casualty.

They laid Jack's body across the back seat of the rental car, his head in Carolyn's lap. Steve turned for a moment in the driver's seat and saw her wiping Jack's face with her handkerchief, her tears mingling with the salt water. Dan was shivering, his mouth open, his eyes blank. Marty drove Carolyn's car with Julie. The first rays of sun broke over the horizon as the procession wended its way back up the hill to the house.

EPILOGUE

There was a dull pounding ache that radiated from the side of his face. Watching from the deck, Steve saw the ambulance arrive to take Jack's body to the plane waiting in Wilmington. He knew somehow that he needed to stand off at a distance to let Dan be with Carolyn and Julie. They had agreed on all the arrangements. Dan would drive with his mother and sister in Carolyn's car to the waiting jet in Wilmington. Marty and Steve would take the rental car and a commuter flight back to Charlotte. In the span of twenty-four hours, he had become an outsider in Dan's life. He had never felt so alone. He watched Dan follow the stretcher with Jack's body being wheeled out of the house. When the doors were closed and the paramedics went to the front of the ambulance, Dan leaned for a moment against the window. He put his open palm against the glass. Then he turned and walked to where Steve was standing.

Dan raised his hand to touch Steve's face. "That looks awful."

Steve reached instinctively to take Dan's hand and protect himself. "It's OK, but please don't touch it." He took Dan in his arms.

Dan pressed his face against Steve's shirt. "I don't know what to say. I don't... I don't have any feelings right now... My father is dead. I watched him drown." He was looking off at the distance, toward the surf. "There were so many times in the last year that I wanted to tell him to go to hell. Today I came to tell him that I love him... but it was too late. I waited too long." Dan stopped for a moment so he could keep from crying. "And... about us... I don't know what to say."

Steve extended his arms with his hands on Dan's shoulders so they could see each other. He could barely keep his focus on the pain Dan was experiencing. There was so much of his own pain that had hollowed him out and left him like an empty shell. When he spoke, his voice was carried up from the bottom of a very deep, dry well. "This wasn't just about you or what you did. We were all part of this... But we can't deal with that right now. You have your family to tend to. As far as us is concerned... I'm not going back to New York. There's nothing for me there now. He inhaled deeply and exhaled as he continued, "I guess we'll see what's next for us."

"I'm sorry. I'm so sorry..."

Steve needed to end the conversation. He realized he couldn't hold on much longer. "Dan, do you know why they say God made the world round?"

Dan was searching for the answer in Steve's eyes. He shook his head. "I don't know."

Steve leaned forward and pressed his forehead against Dan's, the way he had only a day earlier, to keep from falling over. "So we couldn't see too far down the road."

THE END

Gene Naro's education and career have moved between the worlds of classic Greek and Roman literature and finance. He developed an interest in the plays of Sophocles, the most successful writer of ancient Greece and most studied in modern drama.

His academic training includes a BA from Dartmouth College and an MA from Cambridge University where he was Reynolds Scholar. After working in banking and corporate finance he decided to pursue his lifelong curiosity regarding the historical mystery of Sophocles' "lost plays." Sophocles was reported to have written over one hundred full-length plays in a career that spanned fifty years and yet only seven have survived intact to the modern era. *Unspoken* was inspired by Oedipus and asks the question, "What could be worse than killing your father and sleeping with your mother?"

Gene currently divides his time between New York City and Provincetown Massachusetts.

gene@genenaro.com